RAVEN'S EYE

ADAM GOWANS

SCRIVENER BOOKS

Editorial work and production management by Eschler Editing.

Cover art by Brandon Dorman.

Additional cover design by Jason Robinson at Atlas Graphics.

Interior print design and layout by Joy Johnson at Prolific Ink LLC.

eBook design and layout by Joy Johnson at Prolific Ink LLC.

Published by Scrivener Books

First Edition: July 2018

Printed in the United States of America

10 9 8 7 6 5 4 3 2

ISBN 978-1-949165-01-2

AUTHOR'S NOTE

This novel takes place in a country *similar* to South Korea and is not an accurate depiction of its history, language, and culture.

DIRECTORY OF KOREAN
PRONUNCIATION

A (ㅏ): "Ah"

Ae (ㅐ): "A" like *apple* or *sang*

Ai (아이): "I" like *nine*

E (ㅔ): "Eh," like *editor*

Eo (ㅓ): "Uh" like *umbrella* and *young*

Eu (ㅡ): This is like the sound a person makes when punched in the stomach. It sounds like a mix between "eh" and "uh."

I/Yi (ㅣ): Ee

O (ㅗ): Oh

U/oo/Woo (ㅜ): As in *food*. The *w* in *woo* is silent.

Ui (의): Combine "Eu" and "I" really fast.

Ye (ㅖ): As in *yeti*

Yo (ㅛ): As in *yo-yo*

Bb (ㅃ): An aspirated *b*

Dd (ㄸ): An aspirated *d*

Jj (ㅉ): An aspirated *j*

Ss (ㅆ): An aspirated *s*

L/R (ㄹ): Generally a mix of the two letters. Some

Korean words do have a discernible *l* or *r* sound and are reflected in the novel.

OTHER LANGUAGES

Burgos: Bor-yoz
De la Mare: deh lah mar
Ivan: Ee-vahn
Kisasszony Vajda: Keh-shush-szo-ny Vie-dah
Mijares: Me-hahr-ez
Vanya: Vahn-yah
Vires: Veers

"The shortest moments cause the greatest change."

— THE OBSERVANT

L isa made her way through the palace hallways with her head down but her eyes as straight ahead as possible, just as any musuri was supposed to do. When she stepped out of the elevator into the royal children's wing, she hoped she wouldn't run into the princess again. They had enough run-ins that Lisa didn't want to repeat them, and she was more concerned than ever that she might lose her temper, considering the princess had just dishonorably dismissed her favorite nain, or personal assistant, for donating half her wages to support those in need of welfare in Vires, a land of witches.

Due to the splashes of color on her hanbok, the Balhaen traditional clothing, her faint reflection in the glass enclosing the garden caught her eye as she walked by. Navy blue colored the trim on the apron and the sash that bound it to her long skirt, or chima—also the same color as the trim and sash.

Lisa refocused on her duties and stopped at a tapestry to run her finger down its left side, allowing it to pop forward and slide to the right to reveal a storage closet filled with cleaning supplies and a cart. Lisa took the cart laden with cleaners, fresh rags, and dusters, then closed the door. She walked a little farther and stopped at a wooden sliding door beautifully carved with cranes flying low near water. She knelt beside it and knocked.

"Eorin Wangja-Mama," she called to the prince in a humble tone using Hasoseoche, the palace speech. "May I enter?"

Lisa listened for a few moments, but no response came from within. She slid the door open a crack. She couldn't see the prince in the large living room. Lisa opened the door the rest of the way, stood, and wheeled in her cart. The room was a mess. Toys—mostly action figures, vehicles, and large toy stations from several popular children's programs —clothes, and blankets were strewn around the floor or, in the blankets' case, hung to form a fort.

"Wangja-Mama, are you not here?" she said with a playful lilt now that she was in the safety of his room.

Silence answered her.

Lisa picked the clothes up off the floor and tossed them into three different woven baskets in the corner of the room: one for shirts, one for pants, and one for everything else. As she worked, she whistled a merry tune, one with lots of notes so she sounded like a cartoon bird as it flew, just as the prince liked her to, because she didn't believe for a single moment that she was alone in the room. She approached the fort—taking care of where she stepped, moving toys around with her toes so she didn't smash them—to gather a suspiciously large pile of discarded shirts. When she bent down, a hand shot out of the fort and snatched her wrist. Lisa laughed in response.

"You almost scared me that time, Eorin Wangja-Mama."

A childish giggle she recognized as the prince's came from the fort.

"Come out, Wangja-Mama."

The finely dressed thirteen-year-old boy—though his clothes had wrinkles—crawled out of the fort. His short, neatly trimmed black hair stood up in odd places. His chocolate-brown eyes shone brightly against his dark, caramel-cream skin. The childlike demeanor surrounding him testified to his being mentally young.

"I really didn't scare you?" His voice came out breathy and childish as he spoke to her in Hapsyoche, the speech of the wangsil, or royal family, reserved for palace servants and among themselves.

She smiled. "Almost, Eorin Wangja-Mama, almost."

He smiled in return, showing perfectly straight teeth. "Can I help again?"

"Can I stop you from helping, Wangja-Mama?" Even as Lisa spoke, he grabbed a rag and bottle from the cart. She added in a whisper, "I'm going to get in trouble again."

He started dusting the top of his giant wardrobe. Lisa shook her head and resumed gathering the dirty clothes.

They worked well together, never getting in each other's way, and spoke of his favorite shows—which mostly consisted of him giving a perfect rundown of every episode that aired after the last time she cleaned his room. They were now in his adjoining bathroom scrubbing the large tub when the princess's voice, full of indignity, interrupted them.

"Geum Su, what are you doing?" she asked her much younger brother in Hapsyoche.

They spun to face a young woman about four years older than Lisa who bore a strong resemblance to the prince. She wore a richly dyed red chima that went up to just under her breasts, paired with a jeogori—a long-sleeved upper garment dyed a much lighter red and embroidered with a floral design. Guilt filled both Lisa's and Su's expressions, though Lisa's was for show, while exasperation was dominant on the princess's face.

"I was just helping, noona," Su said, addressing his sister in Haeche, the lowest form of speech in the Balhaen language.

The princess sighed. "Su, you know you're not supposed to."

"But I like helping Lisa! She plays with me when she finishes early."

"Wangja-Mama, please," Lisa whispered with a worried glance toward his sister. "You are not helping me with Gongju-Mama."

"Su, I came because you're late to Hwang Seonsaeng's lesson," the princess said, referring to one of Su's teachers. "Make yourself more presentable, and go to your lesson."

Su nodded begrudgingly and left the bathroom. The princess entered and closed the door, letting all her frustration show in her expression.

Lisa, with her right hand covering her left and resting at her navel, bowed from her waist. "Gongju-Mama."

"How many times does this make?" The princess addressed her in Haeyoche, the second lowest speech form, letting Lisa know how angry she was.

Lisa kept her head bowed, though her irritation and the urge to be uncivil raced through her veins. Still, she managed to keep her tone humble, though her thoughts had turned to Rosalina, the dismissed nain from Burgos. "Five times, Gongju-Mama."

"What will help you remember that Wangja does not help musuri clean?"

"I do remember, Gongju-Mama. It is just Wangja, he . . . he does not listen when I tell him not to help."

"I'm going to Hwang Seonsaeng now, noona!" Su's voice drifted in.

"Have a good lesson, Su," the princess called back in a lighter tone, though her expression remained hardened and fixed on Lisa.

They listened to him run out of the room and the door slide closed. The princess let out the breath she held.

"That is no excuse." Her tone was stern again.

Lisa's feelings burst a little. "Then what would you like me to say, Gongju-Mama?" Her own tone was sharp, and she looked the princess in the eye, making her step back in shock.

"Excuse—"

"I cannot control your bro—" Lisa started to say in Common before switching back to Hasoseoche. "—dongsaeng. It is not my responsibility either. I can only remind him of what is proper and decline his help, but he does what he wants. So what do you want me to do, Gongju-Mama?"

The princess composed herself before she spoke. "You are to do your job and leave my dongsaeng out of it. I shall speak to Irene Bomo Sang-Goong about rearranging your schedule so you have no contact with Wangja. Do you understand?"

Lisa bowed. "I understand, Gongju-Mama."

When the princess left, Lisa returned to scrubbing the tub, her movements filled with more vigor. She hated that she needed to work for such a family—one whose great-grandfather conquered her homelands and the other northern kingdoms a hundred years ago, one who now made life increasingly difficult for her people in Vires to survive, and one who would dismiss a loyal servant for donating money to support Lisa's people.

I rene walked through the halls of the lower palace, fuming, but it was only noticeable in her eyes. Still, it was enough to keep the other servants, mostly nain and musuri, out of her way. She entered the kitchen and paused, scanning the room. Her eyes stopped when she saw the back of Lisa's light-brown hair in its tidy, cushion-like bun. Irene made her way through the spaces left between the kitchen hands and whichever station they worked at. Lisa wiped her hands on the apron that covered her robin's-egg-blue jeogori and half of her navy-blue chima before turning to face Irene, her light-brown-honey-colored eyes shining brightly through her epicanthic eyelids.

"Bomo Sang-Goong-Nim." Lisa bowed, addressing her in Hapsyoche and with her position once she saw Irene's expression.

"You talked back to the gongju?" Irene asked her in Common, letting Lisa know just how frustrated she really was with her.

"I merely reminded her of my duties," Lisa replied in the same language.

"You even looked her in the eye!" she whispered vehemently as the other workers started to pay closer attention to them.

"It happens when people talk." Lisa's tone sounded innocent.

Irene took in a slow, deep, ragged breath, clenched her fists, then let them slowly relax. Lisa waited patiently. "I gave you this job despite knowing your temperament and feelings toward the wangsil, so I can only blame myself." She closed her eyes and took another deep breath. "Why couldn't you have gotten more of your father's personality?"

Lisa cracked a smile, and Irene knew she had lost to the girl. "Because my mother couldn't temper me of the personality I inherited from her like her grandmother did to her."

"If only your mother had lived, bless her." Irene sighed and clapped her hands together once in respect for the dead. "But now is not the time. You will need to apologize to the gongju as soon as possible. Do you understand? I don't want you to end up like Rosalina."

"Yes, ma'am."

Irene sighed in relief, knowing that Lisa would make more of an effort. "Good." She glanced down at the table behind Lisa. "What are you making?"

"Dessert."

Irene couldn't help but feel excited. "Are you making Placlova?" Lisa cracked a smile again, and Irene couldn't help but smile as well. "You wicked thing. You want us all fat?"

"I wouldn't dream of it," Lisa teased.

Irene laughed. "You siren. How do you know how to get out of trouble so well?"

Lisa shrugged. "I just can."

"One of these days that luck of yours will run out."

"I don't doubt that." Lisa grew serious. "I know it's only a matter of when."

Irene nodded, knowing Lisa's words were probably true. "Remember to apologize soon."

"I will." Lisa turned back to her table and picked up a rolling pin.

The elevator door opened, and Lisa stepped out the door of the servants' access to the royal children's wing. She turned left, away from the wangja's room, and quickly had to turn right. She walked passed the crown prince's suite door, resisting the urge to spit on it, and had to turn right again after a minute's walk.

"Why did you change her schedule?" Su's agitated voice filled the hallway.

There was a muffled response from his sister.

"I don't care! She's my chingu!" Unbidden, Lisa's lips twitched when she heard him call her his friend. Su was the only one of his family she could tolerate.

The gongju's voice became slightly irritated.

"Why does that matter? I like her! She's the only person who will play with me even though she's *busy*!"

The door slid open with a bang, and Su ran the opposite direction from where Lisa stood, not seeing her. One of his nain bustled out to close the door, glanced at Lisa, and then followed Su. Lisa made her way to the door and knelt beside it.

"Gongju-Mama, it is Lisa," she announced in a humble tone.

"You may enter," Ha-Na said.

Lisa slid open the door and entered the spacious living room. Traditional paintings adorned the walls at evenly spaced intervals, and a tapestry hung on the opposite wall. The gongju sat at a loom weaving a tapestry. Though Ha-Na wasn't looking, Lisa bowed to her.

"I came to apologize—"

"Is your apology sincere?"

"Y—" she stopped and quickly reconsidered her response. "No, not really—at least not for the words, but for the tone."

"Well, at least you are honest." The gongju put down the needle and folded her hands in her lap after she turned to face Lisa. "You have a lot of pride, don't you? Perhaps you are from a prominent gajok wherever you are from?"

Lisa did not let her discomfort show as the gongju referred to her family. "I chose to work here, though."

"Yes, you did, though I think you were hoping for responsibilities that would put you less in my gajok's path."

"I . . . will not deny that."

"But Su likes you."

Lisa couldn't stop herself from grinning slightly.

"You know he is challenged," the gongju said, showing some pain for her brother, "but it's for that reason that he is a good judge of character." She sighed. "I'm only trying to do what I think is best for him."

"I know, Gongju-Mama," Lisa said in a softer tone.

The gongju went back to her tapestry. "I will talk to Irene Bomo Sang-Goong about your schedule. Please don't make me regret leaving it unchanged."

Lisa bowed. "Thank you, Gongju-Mama."

She turned to leave, but Ha-Na's voice stopped her. "I hear you are the reason for the meals' improvement."

Lisa turned back around, a little surprised and confused at the casual turn of conversation. "It cannot be that much of an improvement, Gongju-Mama."

"My gajok and the officials say differently."

"Thank you for the compliment, Gongju-Mama," Lisa said sincerely.

"You may go."

"Yes, Gongju-Mama." She bowed again.

She began to turn but stopped as she realized that the princess had just tried to be friendly with her, which made her think of Rosalina and how close the woman used to be to the gongju. Rosalina had reignited the camaraderie she and Lisa had shared in the nain institute, two of the few Northern Territory citizens in the school, and since Rosalina was a higher noble, she knew Lisa's true identity. She always spoke highly of the gongju to Lisa whenever they shared a meal together, almost allowing her to respect the gongju, to think that if she had the chance to confess her secret to the gongju, she just might accept her. A desire to be subtly mean made her turn back.

"Growing up as gongju must not be easy, especially since you are the only woman in your gajok. It is not likely you have ever had the chance to have a chingu who could be as close as a sister"—she said the last word in Common, then corrected herself in Hasoseoche—"jamae. It is probably impossible for you, even with other girls born into nobility, especially those who choose to become nain." She paused as she saw the gongju's hands stop working. "You are a good person too, Gongju-Mama. I can tell by how much Eorin

Wangja loves you and tries to get more of your attention."
She bowed. "I will take my leave now, Gongju-Mama."

As she slid the door shut behind her, she saw the gongju
put the needle down again with a trembling hand.

A bright light kept blinking in Lisa's room, interrupting her sleep. She turned on her left side and pressed a button on her nightstand. The screen brightened, the time moving to the bottom right corner as a message came into view. Lisa groaned as she read:

> You have been assigned morning nain duties to the gongju. She wakes at 0830 every morning and eats breakfast at 0835. You must be in her apartment at 0825 to ready her table and be on call if she needs anything.
>
> This assignment is temporary until we find a formal replacement. You will have a 20,000-merit increase for each day you act as her nain.
>
> Have a nice day.
>
> — IRENE, BOMO SANG-GOONG

"I'm a musuri," she yelled into her pillow. "I don't want to act like a nain!"

She looked at the clock again—0630, 04/13—and screamed into her pillow before getting out of bed. She showered quickly and put on the undergarments of the hanbok before stepping into the chima and shrugging into the jeogori, which she wrapped around her and belted tightly so it wouldn't slip out of place. Then she put the apron on over it all and fashioned her hair back into the tidy, cushion-like bun. She glanced at the mirror to make sure her appearance was acceptable, then left her room, quickly exiting the servants' lodge and heading toward the large, modernized, traditional-style pagoda palace. The path was a five-minute walk to the kitchen, and once she was in, she ate a breakfast of oatmeal and toast, hurrying to the gongju's cook after giving the washers her dishes.

"You're slightly late," the woman said, sounding a little peeved.

"I'll get it done in time," she answered in the same tone.

The cook handed her a large tray, and she bustled away. When she entered the suite, she found she had one minute before the gongju woke. She set the tray on the breakfast table and made her way to the bedroom door. At precisely 0830, she knocked lightly to announce her presence.

"Come in."

Lisa entered the dark room and set the lights to a low glow. She opened a wardrobe and retrieved a silk robe before going to the gongju's bedside. Lisa held the robe open wide as the gongju stood, then helped her into the garment, tying the sash comfortably around her waist.

"You are not the new nain."

"Ne, Gongju-Mama, I am only filling in until a new

replacement is obtained," Lisa said. She bowed. "Please be patient with me until then."

"Is breakfast ready?"

"Yes, Gongju-Mama."

Lisa opened the door for her, then hurried to help her sit at the breakfast table, where the dishes were uncovered and waiting for her to begin her meal. The gongju ate quietly, and Lisa stood two steps away from the table. A nain announced her presence, and the gongju called her in. Lisa bowed and left her post, going to the bathroom to begin preparing the bath. She and the attending nain helped the gongju remove her clothing before she stepped into the tub. The nain dismissed Lisa with a glance, so she gathered the nightgown and robe as she left the bathroom, closing the door behind her.

She widened her eyes and let out a quiet sigh of relief.

Lisa put the nightclothes in a hamper, then began clearing away the breakfast dishes. She wiped her hands on the clean towel that came with the tray and opened a few wardrobes, choosing a jeogori, chima, and daeng-gi—a pony-tail ribbon that denoted the gongju's status. Lisa also prepped the undergarments behind the dressing partition. A second nain entered the room as she closed the wardrobes, and Lisa bowed before taking up the tray and leaving the apartment to hurry to her regular duties.

Noona?" Su looked up from the toy truck he had just crashed into the action figure he had given Ha-Na to play with.

"Yes?"

"How much longer is Lisa going to be doing nain duties?"

Ha-Na set the toy down as she straightened up from the floor. "I'm not sure. Why do you ask?"

"She doesn't have much time to play with me anymore since she keeps helping you more and more." His breathy voice was harder to hear because of his sadness.

"I'm sorry, Su," she said sincerely.

"Why don't you take one of my nain so Lisa can be mine?" He brightened.

Ha-Na took a moment to muse on her next words. "Lisa can't be a nain; she hasn't taken the test, nor has she the qualifications. That's why she's only a musuri."

"She passed the test. She just chose to be a musuri."

Ha-Na blinked and leaned back in surprise. "What?"

"Lisa is qualified to be a nain. Just ask her imo, Irene Bomo Sang-Goong. She'll tell you."

"Irene's her imo?" Ha-Na couldn't hide her surprise. She had seen none of this information in Lisa's file. She narrowed her eyes in suspicion. "How do you know this?"

"Because I ask questions about people I like." Su stood and walked over to a toy set. "I know you like Lisa too, but I call dibs."

Ha-Na laughed as a spark of hope bloomed inside her. "You brat."

L isa hit the button on her nightstand again to stop the insistent blinking. The screen brightened again, the time moving to the right corner and another message blooming in front of her eyes.

She stared in amazement:

You have been promoted to the gongju and eorin wangja's nain. You will trade between them, alternating between mornings and afternoons, starting with the gongju this morning and the eorin wangja this afternoon.

Your salary has increased appropriately to 2.5 million merits per month.

Have a nice day.

— IRENE, BOMO SANG-GOONG

Lisa got out of her bed and opened her closet, feeling dumbstruck and even a little sick. Inside hung several navy-blue chima, jade colored jeogori, and the undergarments of the nain—the attendants to the royal family and trainees to become sang-goong, more specialized servants, like her aunt Irene, whose sole task it was to manage the royal children. She walked to her nightstand in a trance, picked up the phone, and punched in Irene's number.

"No," she said vehemently when the phone was answered on the other end.

"You have to." Irene sounded apologetic.

"I quit."

"You can't. The gongju and eorin wangja specifically requested you."

"How can they request me if they don't know I'm qualified?" she said, frantic, knowing that if she became a nain she would have to stay at the palace unless she retired or the wangsil dismissed her.

Irene was quiet on the other end, and Lisa's insides twisted as she realized what might have happened.

"Aunt Irene?" Her voice was cold.

"The eorin wangja told the gongju you were qualified, and she asked me if it was true."

Lisa heaved a sigh at the confirmation.

"You know about the eorin wangja by now, I'm sure."

"How could I not notice?" Lisa was on the verge of tears. "The only way out is to be fired or wait to retire."

"I know, sweetie," Irene said, obviously sympathetic to her plight.

She sighed again. "I should have bombed that test on purpose."

"It's too late to change it. Why didn't you? I thought that was your plan all along."

"It's hard to explain," Lisa answered.

She heard a faint, impatient tapping on the other end, but Lisa didn't give in to her aunt. She didn't want to give her any satisfaction at the moment.

"You should go to the groomers. You know that nain have to keep up their appearance more so than musuri," Irene finally said.

She looked at the clock—0243; 05/01. Her self-loathing for not failing the nain test changed. "I hate you."

"I love you too, honey. Gods only know why even the gongju requested you as a nain."

Lisa hung up, put on her civilian clothes, and headed to the groomers' section of the servants' lodge. They were unsurprised to see her enter, but they looked a little peeved.

"You couldn't try to make our job a little easier?" a man asked in Common, taking in her tangled hair.

"Let me wallow in my own misery, if you please," she said as she approached.

A woman tsked. "You tried so hard not to become a nain."

"Not hard enough, apparently," she muttered.

The woman patted a reclining chair that would allow Lisa's hair to fall into a basin. "Let's get you ready, Nain-Nim."

Lisa gave her an irritated look for using the title before she sat down and promptly fell asleep as they trimmed her hair; exfoliated and moisturized her face, hands, arms, and feet; worked on her nails; and performed a little hair removal on her eyebrows, hands, arms, and legs. They woke her to move her to a massage table, where she fell asleep again as they worked her muscles and lotioned her body. At six, she drank a large glass of water, and they ushered her into a bathroom with a large tub before they thoroughly cleaned, exfoliated, moisturized, and groomed her once again. They would not allow her to leave until she relieved herself twice and ate breakfast.

"We're finished, Nain-Nim." The groomers bowed. "Please remember to return every two weeks."

She bowed back. "Thank you for your hard work."

Lisa left and returned to her room. The closet doors still hung open, showing off her dreaded new clothes. She looked at the clock—0753. The clothes seemed to find their own way onto her body, and her fingers moved of their own accord to form four parts in her hair before fashioning it into a saeng-meori ponytail with a red negadak daeng-gi dangling at the end. She checked herself in the full-length mirror and looked at the time—0824. She sighed as she left her room, but she slowly grew determined to use her position to get some justice for Rosalina.

Ha-Na sat with two other nain standing behind her and Lisa in front of her. She had her arms folded as displeasure and disappointment coursed through her. "Well?"

"I have nothing to say, Gongju-Mama." Lisa kept her expression bland.

"What do you mean nothing?" Ha-Na scowled. "You are constantly late and barely polite. You treat Su better, for which I'm grateful, but it doesn't excuse your attitude these past five days. Now explain why."

Lisa did not speak, but she glanced up at the other nain, clearly giving Ha-Na the hint to dismiss them.

"Leave us," she commanded the others. The two girls bowed and left. "Start talking."

"I never wanted to be a nain. Being a musuri was plenty for me."

"Why would you want to be a musuri?" Ha-Na's tone came out patronizing instead of curious like she wanted.

"Because I could leave after earning enough money for

college," Lisa snapped in Haeyoche. "I'd rather work out in the world than be a palace servant for the rest of my life."

Ha-Na leaned back in shock at the expression of resentment that overcame Lisa. "But if you became a sang-goong—"

"A servant is still a servant, no matter what title you give them." Ha-Na's shock turned to bewilderment, but Lisa kept talking. "Unless I am honorably dismissed, fired, or retired, my chance for earning a higher education is now over. I had plans, Gongju."

Ha-Na's posture fell with guilt as the weight of Lisa's words hit her. By making Lisa a nain, a possible bride to the wangsil, Ha-Na had tied her to the palace. "I didn't know."

"You didn't bother to find out." A tear fell onto Ha-Na's cheek, but Lisa paid it little heed. "Why did you want me to be a nain so much that you would completely disregard my choices?"

"I—" Ha-Na pinched the bridge of her nose to stop the tears. "I wanted a chingu beside me."

Lisa flinched. "What?" She drastically softened her tone.

"I wanted a chingu, not a servant," Ha-Na said, feeling helpless. Her thoughts turned to Rosalina, but she quickly pushed them away.

She and Lisa couldn't look at each other, their silence hanging over them like a heavy curtain. Lisa moved her mouth, but no sound came. Ha-Na turned her gaze to the floor, her demeanor radiating defeat.

"Gongju . . ." Lisa's voice was almost at a normal volume. Using Hasoseoche again, she said in a harder tone, "Gongju-Mama, I am not one you would seek to be chingu with."

Ha-Na looked up at her in confusion. "Why?"

"I am not one whom you, your abeoji the wang, or your nam-dongsaeng the wangseja would find appropriate."

She let out a snort of laughter. "If it's because you're from the northern territories, don't worry since you're not from Vires or helping the witches like Rosalina." Pain shot through Ha-Na's heart at mentioning her former favorite nain.

"Gongju-Mama . . ." Lisa's expression turned even more serious.

Ha-Na's smile faltered even more. Lisa was from Slovka, one of the five northern kingdoms her jeungjobu had conquered—along with the Western Empire—nearly one hundred years ago, a matriarchy and ally of Vires, the homeland of the witches. However, she realized a little too late, nobody knew who Lisa's abeoji was. "Are you not Lisa, Illegitimate Princess of Slovka, Daughter of Sonya, Deceased Former Second Grand Illegitimate Princess of Slovka?" she said the titles in Common.

"I am, but I have another name and title as well." Lisa sounded ominous.

Ha-Na was mystified by this unknown information, but Lisa didn't speak. "What is it?"

Lisa drew in a deep breath. "Vasilisa Aleksandrsdöttir, Sitting Princess of Vires."

Ha-Na felt her face pale, and her breath stilled. Aleksandrsdöttir, or "Aleksandr's daughter," in Common—his ddal. "How—"

"The North keeps its secrets well. My eomeoni turned down her arranged marriage at the altar and chose my abeoji instead. They lived in separate houses, keeping the pretense of close chingu. This was easy since the matriarchy rarely attends events with their consorts or adeul. I, of course, being unable to inherit the title of Grand Illegitimate Princess of Slovka, was of no great importance to the public, so when my eomeoni passed away, I quietly slipped into my abeoji's house without the notice of your gajok."

They were quiet for a couple of minutes as Ha-Na let Lisa's words sink in. Lisa's abeoji was Aleksandr, Prince of Vires, a strong witch, and Ha-Neul and her abeoji hated witches.

"It explains so much."

"What does?" Lisa looked a little lost.

"Your titles," Ha-Na answered. She met Lisa's gaze. "I understand your behavior so much better now."

"Well . . ." Lisa squared her shoulders again and looked more determined. "I know the consequences of what I have revealed, and so I will take my punishment just as Rosalina did."

"Stop." Ha-Na said in a berating tone, her anger and resentment bubbling up at Lisa's mention of Rosalina. "I am not Abeoji or Ha-Neul." She kept the eye contact between them, not backing down at Lisa's cold stare, though she felt hurt that Lisa would think she supported the laws her abeoji enacted that limited the jobs witches could work, which absolutely forbade them from the palace. But then she realized that Lisa did not know her very well. The nain Ha-Na wanted as a chingu didn't know that Ha-Na didn't share the hatred for witches. "Rosalina was kicked out after Ha-Neul and my abeoji learned about Rosalina's donations to Vires."

Lisa's eyes narrowed in suspicion. "What do you mean?"

"I am not stupid as to how my nain use their money, Lisa. I knew how Rosalina donated money to various Vires charities. I knew about it for two years. I can think for myself." She sighed and shook her head. "If you wish to be dismissed, I will provide an appropriate reason that will not dishonor your record."

Lisa was astonished. "What?"

"I would like you to stay, Lisa, if you can trust me."

"What about—"

"Do not worry about Ha-Neul or my abeoji. They won't find out your full identity from me." She smiled. "If Su finds out, I'm sure he will keep quiet. He was fond of Rosalina as well."

Lisa bowed to show her gratitude, though her expression was conflicted. "Thank you."

"So you'll stay?" Ha-Na knew her hope shone through her expression and tone.

Lisa hesitated, then breathed out quickly and smiled. "Yes. For now."

"Really?" She couldn't keep the hope out of her voice even if she tried.

"Yes, Gongju-Mama."

Ha-Na stood and took Lisa's hands. "It's Ha-Na when we're alone."

S u, Ha-Na, and Lisa were out in the gardens having a picnic. They sat on a blanket under the shade of an ancient oak, leisurely sampling the food Lisa had prepared. Occasionally Su ran off after some bug he had not yet captured to put into his new terrarium when he got back to his room. Just as he went off for the fifth time, Irene appeared from behind a long row of bushes, walking purposefully toward them. He slowed and watched. Irene's expression was calm, but when Lisa looked her imo in the eye, she grew uneasy.

"Gongju-Mama." Irene bowed.

"Bomo Sang-Goong-Nim." Ha-Na bowed her head.

"I have received news from Wangseja-Mama," Irene said. Ha-Na perked up, and Su ran over to them. "He returns late tonight. He wishes to be received by you at your earliest convenience."

"How late will he be?" Ha-Na's eyes were bright with excitement.

"I believe it will be close to midnight, perhaps later."

"That's way too late," Su said. He now stood next to

Irene, fingering the sleeve of her jeogori. "Noona goes to bed at ten thirty."

Ha-Na smiled at him before glancing at Lisa. "I must, of course, have some sort of greeting for him when he arrives. I will have my nain welcome him home tonight, and I will receive him after dressing tomorrow."

"Of course, Gongju-Mama." Irene gave a small bow. "Which of your nain shall lead your welcoming proxies?"

"It would be discourteous of me to have no one but my closest nain lead," Ha-Na said.

The air slightly tensed as Irene's eyes flicked to Lisa's face for the briefest moment.

"Very well, Gongju-Mama. I shall gather six other nain so a proper greeting is carried out."

"Thank you, Irene Bomo Sang-Goong-Nim."

Irene bowed and quickly left. Lisa returned to the food, though her interest seemed to be elsewhere. She didn't notice Su's and Ha-Na's worried expressions aimed at her. Wariness also flickered behind Ha-Na's eyes.

"Will you be okay?" she asked.

Lisa looked up from the food and caught their expressions. She laughed uncomfortably. "Like you said, it would be discourteous for you to have anyone else lead your proxies."

"I wish he wasn't coming so late, otherwise I would receive him."

Lisa gave her a reassuring smile. "I know. You will be busy tomorrow even without the added event of receiving Wangseja."

"I'm sorry that it will draw his attention to you sooner."

Su sat down again and pulled a large helping of salad from a container as Ha-Na speared a piece of ddeok on the end of her chopstick and started nibbling at it.

"He may look into your details to make sure you're not like Rosalina," Ha-Na went on.

"Hyeong won't find anything incriminating with the light investigation he will conduct in meeting you," Su said to Lisa with his mouth full. "Besides, hyeong would do a heavier investigation if you didn't lead the greeting and found out later that we are so close to you."

Ha-Na drew back a little as he spoke, looking at him incredulously, and Lisa shot a quick warning glance at him that Ha-Na didn't catch.

Su looked up at the trunk of the tree and let out a delighted squeal, allowing food to fly from his mouth. "A beetle!" He sprang up and ran toward the tree.

Behind him, Su heard Ha-Na say, "What was that?"

"I don't know," Lisa answered.

L isa stood at the head of the six other nain lined up in two rows behind her. And just behind the wang's own receiving proxy delegation, twelve nain lined up in two rows behind three men. The leader of the men was a tall, youthful man with bright-ginger hair. The dark suit he wore made his pale skin seem paler. It also marked him as the wang's personal adviser, a chamsagwan —most likely Ryu Chamsagwan's newly hired successor. He turned to speak briefly with a much older man, and Lisa quickly noted that the young man did not have the epican-thic eyes the natives of the Southern Continent all shared. He was a rarity among the nation—if not the whole continent.

A bell chimed half past midnight. She sighed and quickly stifled the yawn it turned into. The young man put a hand to his left ear for a few moments.

"Wangseja has arrived," he said. His voice betrayed his true youthfulness.

Lisa turned to the nain behind her to her right. "Hyeon-

Jeong, the wang's chamsagwan—he can't be older than twenty, can he?"

The nain shook her head. "He's—"

The main entrance opened, and a delegation slightly larger than the wang's proxy entered the palace. Lisa and the nain behind her caught sight of Ha-Neul, the crown prince of Balhae, dressed in one of his customary fitted suits. The nain shifted awkwardly, as if they wanted to check to make sure that everything was in place, but not Lisa. She studied him like a warrior studied an opponent—taking in as much information as possible.

Ha-Neul's black hair was long—the sides and back nearly brushing his shoulders and covering his ears, but it was stylish and neatly trimmed. His eyebrows grew neatly straight across his brow and were wide, making his eyes appear slightly smaller than they actually were at an unobservant glance. Unlike Ha-Na's and Su's eyes, his eyes were more lidded, giving him a sterner—but more mature—appearance. His face was of average southern Balhaen width, but there was no childlike roundness to it—the facial bones were nicely crafted but not sharp. His nose, like Ha-Na's and Su's, was more defined as well. His head sat neatly on a longish neck that accentuated his jawline and shoulder width. The wangseja, though obviously toned by the way the suit teased his form, could not be muscular. He stood straight, four inches taller than Lisa. She noticed that his hands were large, with big palms and long, sturdy fingers, though his feet were a bit small for his height. In short, he was crafted of mediocre features that came together to form a person with slightly better-than-average looks.

The wang's proxy delegation took a few steps toward the wangseja's delegation and bowed.

"Wangseja-Mama," said the young foreigner, "on behalf

of your abeoji, the wang, we welcome you home. The wang regrets that he cannot be here in person tonight as business will make him rise earlier than usual tomorrow."

"Thank you." Ha-Neul's voice was deep, soothing. "You are new. What's your name?"

"Evan, sir." Evan bowed his head.

"I thank you again, Evan," Ha-Neul said. "I will visit Abeoji at his earliest convenience."

"Of course, sir. I will inform Irene Bomo Sang-Goong of the best time."

They bowed to each other, the other two advisers and all twelve nain bowing at the same time. The three advisers walked down the middle of the nain, the women having left space for the men to do so, and once the men were behind them, they turned and followed them, walking past Lisa and her delegation, who stood off to the side.

Lisa and the nain behind her moved toward the wangseja as he moved forward, Lisa's stomach starting to roil as they drew closer. When he caught sight of her, he stopped, his eyes narrowing even more, taking her in. She remained calm and expressionless on the outside, though she wanted to throw up at his obvious checking her out. She kept control, though—it wouldn't do well for her to let on to her hatred for him. She and the other nain bowed.

"Welcome, Wangseja-Mama. We are here on behalf of your noona, the gongju. She sends her sincerest apologies for not being able to receive you tonight and is looking forward to receiving you in the morning."

Ha-Neul didn't speak. After a few moments of silence, Lisa ventured to look up into his chocolate-brown eyes. Their eyes locked, and she had to fight harder to conceal the revulsion of being so close to the man who'd oppressed her people and had Rosalina fired for helping them. It became more difficult as his eyes left hers to take in her body once more before meeting her eyes again.

"Thank you." His teeth were slightly off-center, but not so terribly that it detracted from his features. "You are new as well. What is your name?"

Lisa forced a smile. Though it was, in fact, a very crooked smirk, it was the best she could do at the moment. She bowed to him. "Forgive me, Wangseja-Mama, but I do not believe I am of much importance to be taken of such notice by the wangsil. Again, we welcome you home."

She and the other nain bowed again. She walked through the middle of them, and they turned and followed her once she was behind them, leaving the wangseja standing in shocked silence.

10

Ha-Na came out of from behind her dressing partition wearing a soft-pink chima and light-green, floral-patterned jeogori. She just barely sat down to have her hair braided in a gwimit meori ponytail when a nain announced the older of her nam-dongsaeng. She called for the nain to let Ha-Neul enter as her feelings went into turmoil. She was angry with him for dismissing Rosalina and feared what would happen should he find out about Lisa's full identity, but she also missed him a great deal. The door slid open to reveal Ha-Neul wearing a black, three-piece suit with a deep-crimson tie.

"Ha-Neul." She smiled, her feelings of joy at seeing him again winning out. Her nain stepped back after tying a dark-red jebiburi-daeng-gi with gold lotus blossoms guembak at the end of her ponytail, and they hugged. She held him at arm's length. "You look wonderful." She folded her hands lightly at her waist.

He smiled in return. "And you're just as beautiful as always, noona."

Her smile grew warmer, though she waved away the comment. "Have you seen Abeoji?"

He nodded. "I just came from his apartment."

"We have so much business to attend to today for the upcoming military review. Woo Su-Han Daejang still hasn't informed us of his schedule, so things are quite hectic with the planning."

"Yes, I've been told, but I may be able to help lift some of the burden."

"That would be very welcome. Come, sit." She took her seat again, and Ha-Neul sat down next to her. "What time did you arrive?"

"A little past twelve thirty."

"Was the journey stressful? You've never been on such a long tour before. Su and I missed you so much the past four months."

"It was tolerable. Being so busy helped the time pass, but I did miss you both as well." Ha-Neul cleared his throat. "By the way, noona, who is the new nain—the pretty Slovkan one with the honey-brown eyes?"

A moment of panic surged through Ha-Na, but she hoped she had concealed it from Ha-Neul well enough. It helped that she realized Ha-Neul seemed a little too interested in Lisa in a good way. "You mean Lisa, who led my delegation?"

"So that is her name."

She felt confused. "Did you not ask her last night? I thought you would."

"I did, but—"

"Gongju-Mama, it is Lisa," came Lisa's voice. "I have brought Eorin Wangja as well."

"Please enter," Ha-Na called, wondering what had happened the previous night.

The door slid open, and Su barreled through, then jumped into Ha-Neul's outstretched arms as he came to a stand.

"Welcome home, hyeong!" Su said as Ha-Na laughed.

"Thanks, you little terror." Ha-Neul was smiling brightly.

"Did you bring me anything?"

Ha-Neul laughed along with Ha-Na. "Of course, but I'll give it to you later."

"Assa!"

Ha-Na watched as Ha-Neul looked toward the doorway, where Lisa stood next to the wall. Lisa observed them with a careful, blank expression until he looked in her direction. Ha-Na noticed that the air around Lisa seemed to tense, giving her natural beauty a sharp severity. Lisa held out her hand as she looked down to Su, the tension lessening, allowing softness to pour in.

"Eorin Wangja-Mama, we must go to your lesson now. Jang Seonsaeng will be waiting."

Su hugged Ha-Neul's waist tighter before letting go. "I'll see you later, hyeong!"

"Take care and be good."

As soon as Su took Lisa's hand, her whole countenance changed as she focused entirely on the boy. The severity was gone, replaced by warmth and gentleness as a smile lit her face and eyes. The door slid shut behind them.

"She doesn't like me, does she?" Ha-Neul sounded perplexed.

An uncomfortable giggle burst from Ha-Na. "That's ridiculous."

He turned to her, but she began to intently check the work on her loom so he couldn't see through her lie. "Noona"—she stiffened at his voice—"I'm right, aren't I?"

She cleared her throat but didn't dare to look up at him. "Lisa is difficult at first, but once she gets to know you, she is such a good person. We've been close for the past month and a half. Trust me, she's so amiable."

"Gongju-Mama, it is Irene Bomo Sang-Goong."

Relief flooded Ha-Na because of the interruption, but she did her best to hide it from her dongsaeng. "You may enter."

Irene entered with two other nain, who bowed. "Please excuse the intrusion, but it is time to move to your first appointment."

"Of course. I am ready." Ha-Na stood.

Irene turned to Ha-Neul. "Wangseja-Mama, your schedule has been filled for today. Your chamsagwan will inform you of your duties."

"Thank you, Bomo Sang-Goong-Nim. By the way, you look in perfect health as always."

Irene smiled. "I see you have not changed, Wangseja-Mama."

"Bomo Sang-Goong-Nim," Ha-Na cut in with a sudden idea to help Lisa get to know Ha-Neul, "will Lisa be joining me again during lunch?"

"Yes, her duties have remained unchanged, Gongju-Mama."

"Very good." She turned to her dongsaeng. "I hope to see you during lunch. Lisa is a wonderful cook."

Ha-Neul looked intrigued. "You will if I can make it."

11

Ha-Neul entered the small dining room close to Ha-Na's public office. Ha-Na and Su already occupied two chairs while Lisa unpacked a large lunchbox filled with various traditional side dishes, four small containers of rice, and a large container of mixed fruit. They looked over at him as the door shut behind him, drawing smiles from Ha-Na and Su but a very controlled, blank glance from Lisa.

"Hello," Ha-Neul said.

Ha-Na smiled. "Come sit."

"Did you bring my present?" Su asked, looking excited.

Lisa merely bowed and muttered his title as his nammae continued to talk to him. He answered their questions about his tour while Lisa opened all the containers and placed utensils in front of all of them. Then she poured some herbal tea in their cups before she took her seat at the table. Ha-Na picked up her chopsticks and began eating, followed by the others. From his peripheral vision, Ha-Neul noticed Lisa ate quietly, not taking any interest in what he said.

"Did you go to Vires during your tour?" Su asked, breaking through Ha-Neul's observation of Lisa.

Everyone paused in their eating except Su. Lisa returned to her meal without any interest in the subject before Ha-Neul answered.

"Briefly, but I didn't meet with their so-called prince," he said. "I was quickly introduced to his adeul, Ivan Aleksandrsson, though."

"R-really?" Ha-Na quickly controlled the concern in her expression. "What was he like?"

"I didn't talk to him." He shrugged. "Why should I? He may not matter in the coming months."

A small cough escaped Lisa, but she quickly grabbed her tea and swallowed some, clearing her throat a little. Ha-Neul was about to ask if she was all right, but Ha-Na interrupted him.

"Why do you say that?" she asked.

He let his triumph show. "Abeoji is finalizing a draft of resolution that will not only more clearly define a noble and what kind of political power or symbology they will hold in Balhae, but what kind of people can retain a claim to nobility."

"So Abba is kicking out the Viresian prince from having any kind of power?" Su asked.

"That's right," he smiled. "You're such a smart boy, Su."

Su beamed and returned to his food.

"How did this come about?" Ha-Na asked.

He gave a short, derisive laugh. "Those creatures place too much importance in their champion 'prince,' and because he is technically considered nobility under our current law, they feel they are on equal footing as normal people and deserve the same rights and privileges. So I introduced the first draft after careful research into our own and other countries' nobility classifications. That research will be the springboard for introducing the bill to our nobles and governors once Abeoji finishes the draft and makes sure there are no technicalities that will allow any hope for the Viresian prince to be seen as a true noble."

"That's—"

Lisa put her chopsticks down hard enough to catch their attention. An innocent smile spread across her features at seeing their surprise. "Excuse me, I did not mean to make so much noise." Her eyes briefly met his, and his blood chilled for a moment. "While I have your attention, may I be excused for a minute to use the restroom?"

"Of course," Ha-Na said, a kind smile gracing her face.

Lisa bowed after standing and quickly made her way out of the room. Ha-Neul turned to his noona, who was carefully avoiding eye contact.

"I get the feeling I was wrong about her."

"What do you mean?" Ha-Na asked, forcing a tone of ignorance.

"I think she hates me." Some of his confusion came through his voice.

Su giggled. "That's because she does."

"Geum Su!" Ha-Na looked mortified as Ha-Neul looked back and forth between his nammae.

Su's eyes went wide in confusion. "What? She does hate him."

"Don't say anything else about it," Ha-Na said. "We can't know for certain what Lisa feels toward Ha-Neul."

Su picked at his rice, looking glum. "Fine."

Ha-Neul looked from Su to Ha-Na, sensing they were hiding something from him. "Noona, is there something I should know?"

"No." Ha-Na's tone was nearly normal, though touched with a trace of annoyance.

Lisa reentered the room and bowed to them, making Ha-Neul drop the issue. He watched her as she went back to her seat, keeping her eyes down or trained on the food closest to her. She picked up her chopsticks and resumed eating.

"The food is delicious," he said sincerely, trying to earn some points with the nain. "I'm glad I was able to come to lunch. Ha-Na said you were a wonderful cook, and she's right. Who taught you so well?"

Lisa politely dipped her head in his direction, but her tone was cool and distant as she said, "My abeoji taught me to cook all the traditional foods found within Balhae's original borders. I thank you for the compliment. I am glad that you, Wangseja-Mama, enjoy it."

Her demeanor effectively silenced him, though the topic of her abeoji made him curious. None of the Slovkan consorts were identified, especially Lisa's mother's. He turned away from her and resumed eating. When they had their fill, they picked at the fruit until Lisa reminded him and Ha-Na that their next appointments would be in twenty minutes. She quickly repacked the lunchbox and handed it to a newly arrived musuri. Ha-Na and Su took their leave from him until dinner, and Lisa bowed to him once more before following Ha-Na out, leaving the room feeling cold. Soon afterward, Irene entered the room and bowed to him.

"Irene Bomo Sang-Goong-Nim."

"Yes, Wangseja-Mama?" She seemed surprised at his serious tone.

"Will you get me the employment details of Ha-Na's,

Su's, and my own nain? I wish to review their records once more to see if the nain have been appropriately placed."

She shifted a little. The last time he had requested this information was when he had received a tip about Rosalina's donations. "Of course, Wangseja-Mama. I shall have the records on your desk before the evening meal. Now, if I may kindly remind you that your next appointment will take place in the throne chamber with your abeoji the wang."

"Certainly, Bomo Sang-Goong-Nim. It's truly wonderful that you are on top of everything." He gave her a roguish grin.

Irene rolled her eyes but was at ease again. "I must to help keep you in line."

"Ah! That hurts!" He put his hands over his heart.

"And yet you are over it by now, Wangseja-Mama."

"Who could ever stay angry with a beauty such as you?" he smiled at her again.

She seemed unaffected by his words. "Please, Wangseja-Mama, the throne chamber."

"Right. Well, I'm off!"

Irene bowed as he left the room, joining his chamsagwan and three nain just outside the door. He glanced quickly at Irene and noticed that she watched him with a mess of emotions swirling in her eyes.

12

H a-Neul stood at the corral, watching as Ha-Na ran a horse through a course of jumps. Several of her other nain stood by, watching alongside the stable master. Lisa stood a little apart from the other nain for a few minutes before breaking away to go into the stables. Intrigued that she would leave, Ha-Neul excused himself from his entourage, leaving his horse's reins in his chamsagwan's hand, to follow her. He watched as she bypassed all the docile horses and walked to a stall where a white-and-black-spotted mare tramped restlessly. As she approached the horse, it quieted and waited for her. She stroked the horse's nose a few times before encircling her hands about its neck and resting her cheek against its nose. Both let out a deep sigh.

"I thought she wasn't broken," he said.

The mare backed away, and Lisa bolted upright, turning to face him. Then the horse went back to irritably tramping around its stall, making him wish he hadn't interrupted the moment.

"Wangseja-Mama." She bowed. When she rose from

the bow, her eyes flitted around to his shoulders, his arms, and his chest, which stood out more prominently in his riding gear. A light heat started to bloom in his chest until she looked back up at his face, her expression hardening more than it ever had in the few times he had seen her in Ha-Na's or Su's company.

"So the mare is tame?" he asked to be conversational and to try to dispel the awkwardness.

"No, Wangseja-Mama. As you can see, she is not." Her voice was cooler than usual.

"But she let you touch her," he pointed out with interest.

Lisa's cool, focused look slipped and a wistful smile appeared. "We just understand each other." Her smile disappeared as the coolness returned. "Those who want their freedom will fight harder the more you try to control them." She turned to leave after a brief bow, but her words intrigued him even more, and he stopped her with his words.

"What do you mean exactly when you say 'want'?"

She looked back at him, then turned to face him. "I mean precisely what I said."

He suppressed a shudder when her demeanor worsened. "I wasn't entirely sure for the past couple of weeks, but now I'm convinced. You hate me," he searched her face, looking deep into her eyes.

Lisa laughed, but it held no warmth, no amusement. "Yes, it is difficult for me to conceal it when you are in front of me."

"Why?" His voice was a little soft, and his chest felt cold.

"Because you're a monster." Lisa spoke in Haeche.

He never believed he could see her countenance sour as

much as it did at that moment. She no longer hid the extent of her hate for him, and it terrified him. The degree of it went past loathing and abhorrence. She held him in complete execration.

"You call yourself human, yet you seek to totally dehumanize a group of people—no, not dehumanize them, but make them the lowest scum of the planet—untouchable, unworthy to converse with, something to be exterminated."

"That's not—"

"Really!" she laughed again. The stable was quiet. Fear hung thick in the air as fury radiated from her. "Where will you end your campaign against witches? When you have punished their supporters to the point they are too frightened to help? Once the witches have left their *homeland*? The one they have occupied far longer than your people occupied ancient Balhae? Please, tell me when it will end!"

His own anger surged, overcoming his fear of her hatred for him. "Those lands no longer belong to them."

"It belongs to them, and they to it. Your claim is infinitesimal compared to theirs."

"I am wangseja of the country!"

"You are wangseja only because the last dynasty set your gajok above theirs hundreds of years ago. You are one person—just like everyone else on Dunia—with the same potential for good or evil, and you choose evil disguised under the name of good."

"Why do you care so much? You are nothing but a nain who wants to be a musuri!"

"I know you've seen my file, and I don't care what you think of me because I know you will show no respect for me. Your view of what is human is skewed. All who live in the northern territories know it. You are a joke, Wangseja"— she spat his title with such venom he almost recoiled, even in the midst of his own fury—"among those people, and I will tell you this one thing." She paused for the briefest of moments, her presence dominating everything around him. "The more you fight against Vires—against those witches— the more the other territories and those sympathetic with witches will rise against you."

A sense of dread chilled his body. "You mean the northern Balhaens."

"Yes."

"And you are certain of this?" His anger simmered underneath the sheen of calm about the implication that the territory and the northern Balhaens in his employ might betray him.

"As certain as I stand in front of you."

The atmosphere between them seemed ready to explode. He felt contempt just looking at her, and her utter revulsion for him permeated everything.

"You do realize what you have just done?" He was now determined to root out any witch supporters around him.

"I do." She held herself in such a regal posture that Ha-Na would have appeared wilted beside her.

"Get out of my sight."

"Gladly."

Lisa left with a grace befitting the most impressive empress. Once she was out of sight, he collapsed against the stable wall, sweating and panting and clasping his racing heart. Never had he felt more impressed, or terrified, by another person.

Name: Lisa, Illegitimate Princess of Slovka
Birthdate: 2194/08/06

Age: 17
Family: Sonya, Former Second Grand Illegitimate
    Princess of Slovka (mother—deceased); Astrid,
    Grand Illegitimate Princess of Slovka (aunt);
    Irene, Former Third Grand Illegitimate
    Princess of Slovka, Bomo Sang-Goong (aunt);
    etc. Unknown Father.
Education: Slovka Royal Academy, Balhae Nain
    Institute
Political Works: N/A

Ha-Neul darkened his desk screen, a sigh of annoyance escaping him. He sat back in his chair and tapped his fingers on his chest as he considered his next move. He looked at the mantelpiece clock on his desk—0143—and sighed again. Lisa took up too much of his thoughts. His hand brushed his desktop, lighting it up and enlarging her picture. He stared at it—disbelief, contempt, confusion, disgust, and despair cycling through him. He tapped the desk and reread her file before violently pushing it to the far-left corner.

He stood and began loosening his robe, then glanced at the cast-off file. Shaking his head, he moved to his bed but then circled back to his desk and sat down again. He called up his messenger and tapped Irene's name, a blank communication coming up. He looked once more at Lisa's discarded file.

13

L isa sat in a small room reading from a library tablet when the door opened and Ha-Neul entered. He didn't close the door. She stood and bowed but didn't say anything—the atmosphere was already near the breaking point between them. His expression remained cool despite the contempt that shone in his eyes.

"If you are right about the north," he said, "I will need to take measures so that a revolution doesn't happen."

She narrowed her eyes in disdain. "Why are you telling me this?"

"Because you are probably the best in-palace source available to me."

Her disdain became incredulity. "So you want me to advise you?"

"Yes," he replied in the same tone.

"No." She sat down and picked up the tablet.

"Why are you saying no?"

"I will not help you find a way to further subjugate the north in the least violent way possible. Will you deny that you would block a revolution through vague laws that seem fair but would actually give you vast amounts of power over them if passed?"

He didn't say anything, which confirmed her suspicion.

The corner of her mouth twitched up. "I thought so."

"What will make you help me?" he asked after a moment.

"Figure it out if you cannot understand what I mean." Her anger started to rise again. The tablet beeped as a notification came through, and she turned it off before she stood and faced him. "Excuse me, Wangseja-Mama, I must go to Gongju."

She bowed and left the room, making sure there was plenty of space between them as she passed—she had no desire to make even the slightest physical contact with him. Once she was far enough away to where she may not have noticed, she heard a loud bang and glanced back long enough to notice Ha-Neul nursing his hand as the door swung away from him.

S u knocked on Ha-Neul's bedroom door.

"Who is it?" came his hyeong's voice

He slid the door open and poked his head in to see Ha-Neul sitting up in bed, holding his tablet. He could tell that his hyeong was troubled, though Ha-Neul tried to keep it hidden. The clock next to him read 07/02; 0238. "You're still awake, hyeong?"

Ha-Neul looked at him with concern. "Yeah, bud. What's wrong? You can't sleep?"

He shook his head.

"You want to sleep with me?"

Su hurried into the room and quickly snuggled up to him. Ha-Neul turned off the tablet and set it on the bedside table, activating its screen to dim the bedroom light so there was only a faint glow, the way Su told him he preferred it. Ha-Neul lay down and turned to him.

"Bad dream?"

Su nodded.

"About who? Eomeoni? Abeoji? Me or noona?"

Su kept shaking his head.

Ha-Neul was confused. "What was it about?"

Su didn't say anything because he knew his hyeong wouldn't be happy.

After a moment, Ha-Neul's posture fell. "Is it the nain Lisa?"

Hesitantly, he nodded.

"What happened to her in your dream?"

Su whispered softly.

"I can't hear you, bud."

"You fired her." Su barely made his voice audible.

Ha-Neul couldn't say anything, but Su could see that his emotions were in turmoil, that it was Lisa causing the bulk of his recent troubled feelings.

"Please don't fire her, hyeong," he yawned. "She's too nice for you to fire her. Who else will play with me if she can't?"

"You like her so much you're scared for her?" Ha-Neul's voice revealed his surprise.

Su nodded and snuggled in closer to his hyeong, closing his eyes. Ha-Neul kissed the top of his head and put an arm around him, holding him tight like he always did. Soon, Su was fast asleep, listening to his hyeong's strong heartbeat.

Ha-Na and Lisa sat playing a game of six-tiered chess. Lisa had taken more of Ha-Na's fifty pieces—sixteen of hers were gone compared to seven of Lisa's. Ha-Na moved a soldier from tier two of level two to tier two of level three. Lisa grinned and moved her queen to block the piece.

Ha-Na sighed. "Who taught you to play?"

"I would watch my abeoji and obba play when I was really young and practiced what I saw them do at school. My abeoji always won against Vanya—Ivan, but it kept getting more difficult for him every year. One day when I was twelve, I asked to play against him, my abeoji, and he agreed." Lisa captured one of Ha-Na's rooks. "He went easy on me until he realized I knew exactly what I was doing. It took him a few turns to change the game to his favor, but after that, we would play often, and I beat him when I was thirteen."

"So you are going easy on me right now."

Lisa shrugged. "Perhaps."

Ha-Na laughed. "Maybe I should be thankful."

"We have time to spare, and it's all for fun anyway," Lisa said with a smile.

"What are your abeoji and obba like? I don't hear a lot about them except for the occasional report."

Lisa's face brightened. "They're the best men I know, and I've met plenty of men. They have the people's best interest in everything they do and are humble. They listen to every concern and do anything possible to soothe the people's worries, though Vanya does have less patience and more of a temper than my abeoji."

"That's as nobles. What about as your gajok?"

"Much the same." Lisa captured Ha-Na's last bishop. "I lived with my eomeoni in Slovka until I was fourteen—when she died. Vanya spent summers with us because that's the height of the festivals, and I would go to Vires during winter after the last major festival of the year. So once I moved in permanently, it took a lot of adjustment, but they were patient, which helped."

"It took a long time for things to settle once my eomeoni died." Ha-Na closed a trap on one of Lisa's daejang. "Su was still very young and needed her. He wouldn't settle down unless one of us was trying to soothe him. Ha-Neul practically raised him since I took up many of Eomeoni's political responsibilities while Abeoji handled the rest."

"So that's why they're close," Lisa muttered.

She shook her head. "It's not just that."

"What else is it, Ha-Na?"

The door slid open, startling them, and Ha-Neul walked in. "You two are close enough that you let her call you by name, noona?"

Ha-Na paled when she saw how angry Ha-Neul was. Lisa stood and bowed to him.

"Leave us," he ordered Lisa.

Once the door slid shut behind Lisa, Ha-Na colored. "Yes, we're that close."

He looked incredulous. "Noona, did you know she's a witch supporter?"

"I did."

His face reddened. "And you kept her here?!"

"She hasn't done anything to get her fired like Rosalina, and you don't know her like I do." Her cheeks burned with shame. "Lisa is a lot like Irene, kind and loyal. Actually, I should say she's better than Irene is. Yes, she has a temper, and yes, she can be easily provoked if you hit the right buttons, but who isn't that way?"

"She's dangerous."

"Why? Why is she so dangerous?"

"Her views—"

"She considers your views dangerous too."

"But you don't."

"You've never asked me what my views are. You've always assumed they match yours." The words were out of her mouth before she thought them through.

"Don't they?" Ha-Neul was puzzled but obviously thought they did, making her upset.

"No." The word came out forceful, angry, and full of reproach. Ha-Neul looked like she'd just slapped him, but she knew she couldn't coddle him anymore. "When it comes to witches, you are a bigot, and it is the only part of you I'm ashamed of. I knew about Rosalina's donations long before you did and kept silent even to her because she was an amazing nain and generous person, just like how I know how kind and generous you can be. It actually surprises me just how much alike you, Rosalina, and Lisa are, yet your prejudices are aimed at each other." She paused, and her shoulders slumped as she studied his distraught expression.

She reached out to take his hands, but he backed away from her. "Ha-Neul."

"You're ashamed of me?"

She could see and hear how deeply she had hurt him.

"Not of you; of your attitude," she said gently.

"I've only done what I believe is right," he whispered.

"Because you won't let go of your fear of magic, and you won't forgive."

"Stop." His voice rose to normal. "Don't say anymore."

"Ha-Neul—please don't go!" She reached out as he walked away from her.

He opened the door and came face-to-face with Su and Lisa. Su was crying, and Lisa was crouched in front of him, doing her best to calm him.

When the door slammed open, Lisa looked up at him. "He heard everything."

Ha-Neul's posture hardened. "You are suspended, Nain. Effective immediately, you are confined to the servants' lodge and the kitchen during meal times until further notice."

Ha-Na's heart broke as Su burst into tears while Ha-Neul hurried away, avoiding eye contact with their dongsaeng.

The whispers followed Lisa everywhere she went in the servants' lodge and in the kitchen, so she stayed in her room as much as she could stand it. At the start of her suspension, Irene had come to her and asked what had happened. She said nothing. Irene told her if Ha-Neul had nothing concrete to use to fire her, she would soon be back to work. Five days later, she was still suspended, though she went to the groomers for her biweekly appointment.

"People have been talking," Marie said as she massaged Lisa's scalp.

"They always talk when I get in trouble."

"Yes, but it was never the wangseja you got in trouble with." Her voice had a suggestive lilt to it.

"I don't see why that makes a difference." Lisa did her best to ignore Marie's tone.

"That's because I don't think you've heard the rumors." The lilt grew thicker.

Lisa's humor darkened. "What rumors?"

"About how much he seems to notice you."

She let out a derisive laugh. "That's only because we hate each other."

"What!" Marie's shock sounded genuine.

"Why else would he suspend me? It's because he hates me and I've made it clear to him that I hate him."

"That's not something to say with such pride." Marie sounded scandalized.

"But Lisa has never cared much for such decorum," Ha-Na's voice said.

Both women jumped. Lisa stood, and they bowed. "Gongju-Mama."

"Please leave Lisa and me."

"Yes, Gongju-Mama." Marie bowed and nearly ran out of the private room.

"Did something happen?" Lisa asked, allowing herself to worry, knowing that Ha-Na wouldn't be there for a social visit.

Ha-Na nodded but didn't say anything, making Lisa's heart sink.

"What is it?"

Ha-Na seemed to gather her courage. "Su stopped talking."

"Wh—what?" Lisa knew how much of a punishment that would be to both Ha-Na and Ha-Neul. Su loved spending time with his siblings.

Ha-Na inhaled deeply, then let out a quick breath. "He begged Ha-Neul for a day to bring you back, but Ha-Neul refused—apologetically, sort of. Su gave up and stopped talking to him, which made Ha-Neul more upset, but then Su slowly stopped talking to everyone. Abeoji called him in to talk to him alone, but I can't make out from Abeoji if Su actually spoke to him."

Lisa grew warier as Ha-Na's expression became more serious. "There's more?"

Ha-Na nodded. "Ha-Neul has been investigating other northern servants to see if they share your sympathies. To question their loyalty—it's brought down the whole palace's morale, enough so that Abeoji will have to step in and end it."

"Are you saying I may be fired since I'm the source of the conflict?" Her panic rose.

Ha-Na nodded.

"Oh, Ha-Na, I am so sorry. If only I controlled myself better."

Ha-Na shook her head. "I don't blame you, so don't blame yourself. If it's anybody's fault, it's mine because I made you a nain."

"No, don't blame yourself either. Let's not even play that game."

Ha-Na nodded, looking despondent. She took several slow, deep breaths. "I've talked to Abeoji about the situation, about how we could fix it without you getting fired, and he came up with one solution." She stopped and colored.

Apprehension filled Lisa. "What is it?"

"You will be strictly Ha-Neul's nain, starting tomorrow." Ha-Na looked her in the eye. Lisa stood aghast. "This is by order of the wang."

L isa woke early, showered, and dressed before taking extra care to do her hair. She squeezed some lotion onto her palms and rubbed it onto her face before applying some light makeup. Looking at herself in the mirror, she saw only the weeks' worth of grooming she'd been forced to comply with under the palace's standard of beauty for its nain.

She moved away from the vanity and left her room, making her way out of the servants' lodge and to the kitchen, where she ate a decent breakfast. Once finished, she made her way through the palace to the royal children's wing. She stood in front of Ha-Neul's door, her head slightly bowed and her hands folded, as a musuri announced her. The door slid open, and her eyes rose to meet Ha-Neul's as he sat at his breakfast table.

"You're on time. I'm impressed." His expression was cool.

She bowed. "Wangseja-Mama." She then bowed to the adviser by his side as she stepped in.

"It's time to greet Abeoji," Ha-Neul said.

The adviser nodded, and they rose to their feet. She followed at a short distance to their left. As they reached the elevator lobby, she saw Su leaving his room, his face brightening when he saw her. She quickly put a finger to her lips and smiled, Su nodded, and she entered the elevator with the men. She hid her shaking hands by folding and lightly grasping them under the material of her jeogori, which came down to her waist. When the elevator opened, they stepped out onto a path that ran between twin gardens. At the end of the path was a sliding door carved with forest and mountain scenery. They paused in front of it.

"Wang-Mama, the wangseja, his chamsagwan, and nain are here," an older nain who sat off to the side of the door said.

"Enter," said a deep, gravelly voice.

The nain slid the door open, and they entered, bowing

to a middle-aged man dressed in a royal uniform who sat eating breakfast.

"Sit, Ha-Neul." The wang sipped at his tea.

Ha-Neul sat.

The wang was slightly taller than Ha-Neul as they both sat upright, had great posture, and was of a more solid build than his son. His head and eyes were slightly wider than his children's, but his face was more rounded, like Ha-Na's and Su's. All three of his children shared his defined nose. He kept his thick, wavy, black hair short and tamed with styling wax. Despite his generally handsome appearance, he looked tired and burdened, though it wasn't completely obvious with a light review. All of this he wrapped in a stern demeanor that made him seem irreproachable.

"Are there any concerns about your schedule?" he asked.

"No, Abeoji."

"I am glad. You have handled all your responsibilities quite well for the past few years."

"Thank you."

The wang glanced up at his son's companions, and his amber-brown eyes lingered on Lisa for a moment longer than was customary, making her feel uncomfortable under his scrutiny. "Just focus on your responsibilities."

"Of course, Abeoji." Ha-Neul looked a little anxious. "Abeoji . . . is it true there has been another protest in front of the Vires governor's office?"

"Yes, there was." The wang leaned back in his chair, showing little concern about what happened in Vires. "Do not worry about it. It will be dealt with according to the law we established." When Ha-Neul seemed satisfied, though Lisa secretly seethed that the people's right to protest was being denied again, the wang went back to his breakfast. "Is there anything else?"

"No, Abeoji."

"Good, but I have one concern of my own," he said. "I wish to speak to your nain privately if you do not mind."

They glanced at her, and she made herself look the epitome of calm, though she felt quite the opposite.

"As you wish, Abeoji. Then take care for today." Ha-Neul stood and bowed.

"I will."

Ha-Neul and the adviser left the room, leaving Lisa and the wang in an odd atmosphere. She kept her eyes on the floor.

"Please sit, Lisa."

Her head and eyes snapped to look at him a little warily at his manner of respect. He gestured to the chair Ha-Neul had just vacated. Cautiously, she lowered herself into the seat.

"I've heard a lot about you and have personally looked into your records," he said. "You're quite the character, if I may say so."

She cracked the grin she often reserved for her aunt when in trouble. "Irene Bomo Sang-Goong, I am sure, would not leave anything out of my personality reports, Wang-Mama."

The wang returned a tiny smile, but his eyes betrayed how amused he really was. "Yes, I daresay she takes those reports rather seriously. However, it is because of those reports and the recent . . . disruptions," he placed a little emphasis on the word, "between you and Ha-Neul that I feel I can give you a necessary suggestion." She looked up at him again, meeting his gaze that nearly matched his oldest son's. "Tell Ha-Neul what you know about Vires."

She blinked in surprise and sat back a little. "Excuse me?"

The wang smiled kindly. "Tell him," he put a careful emphasis on the next three words, "*what you know* about Vires." He gave her a pointed look she did not quite understand, almost as if he were sharing a secret with her.

His demeanor and the weight of his words bore heavy on her, so she could only nod.

"Good," he said with a slight smile. "You may go now."

Ha-Neul's schedule mostly took place in his public office. Lisa's greatest task was to serve refreshments to his guests and occasionally to him and his adviser. Other nain made appearances mostly in between appointments and barely gave her a glance. During a short break before the last appointment of the morning (a video conference), the adviser excused himself to use the restroom. Ha-Neul scanned some reports on a tablet while she sat in a chair next to the refreshment bar to his left.

She took in a deep breath to calm herself before she took the plunge of taking the wang's suggestion. "The witches of Vires can't *not* do magic."

Ha-Neul set the tablet down. From what she could see of his face, he looked mildly caught off guard. "Are you saying they *have* to use magic?"

"I'm saying it's ingrained in them, almost like breathing," she said. "Just like how anyone can stop breathing voluntarily—for a short time—they can stop using magic for a time, but eventually, just like breathing, it has to happen."

He turned to her. "So?"

"You are persecuting them for performing a function as

vital to them as breathing is to all living things. To not use the magic born within them is to cut their life short. They have thirty years at most—those who don't use their magic their whole lives." She kept eye contact with him, not backing down from his coolness.

He turned away from her as he said, "Then it's for the best."

She felt her expression harden as her anger toward him grew. "So, what, you'll ban witches from using their magic? And if they do, what's the punishment going to be—execution? You would already be giving them a death sentence."

"So what?" he said calmly. "Every living thing dies at some point."

She let out a short laugh. "It would be a deal breaker. You would have a revolution on your hands." Ha-Neul turned to her with a look of incredulity. "The northern territories know about the witches' connection to magic. They would revolt in the name of human rights, and other supporters would join them."

"You'd have to be human to be treated like one." His tone was cold.

"There are plenty of 'humans' who don't act like they are human, Wangseja-Mama. That's what capital punishment is for—punishing those who act inhumanely to their fellow humans."

He looked at her as if she were stupid. "You're grossly overexaggerating."

"I am, and so are you, Wangseja-Mama."

The adviser came back before Ha-Neul could think of a reply. The man got Ha-Neul's attention and began discussing the important points for the video conference, so Lisa didn't speak anymore; instead, she watched him, anger smoldering in her gaze. The adviser looked in her direction at one point but quickly refocused all of his attention on prepping Ha-Neul for the conference. Ha-Neul didn't give her a second look.

Just as they were finishing, a screen rose from the desk and turned on, dividing itself into four sections, with Ha-Neul in the bottom right, before a short countdown appeared. The adviser backed off so he would only appear in the corner of Ha-Neul's screen. The countdown disappeared, and the other three screens were filled with the images of two middle-aged men and a middle-aged woman, who bowed their heads.

"It is good to see you doing so well, Wangseja-Mama," the man in the top left corner croaked.

"Thank you, Chae Jang-Gwan-Nim." Ha-Neul gave the minister a polite grin. "You all look splendid as usual, especially you, Bak Jang-Gwan-Nim," he said to the woman in the top right corner.

She blushed. "I am deeply grateful, Wangseja-Mama."

"I know you have many concerns," Ha-Neul continued, his tone getting a little more serious but still very much polite and charming, "especially about the housing market in Joseon-do and its influence on the rest of the economy in the province. I have been in touch with the governor and the mayors and heard their concerns and suggestions on the matter. I believe you have also sent some of your assistants to survey the citizens, Seo Jang-Gwan-Nim. Have you received the results of those surveys?"

"Yes, I have," Minister Seo answered.

"Excellent. Will you send us those results so we can look at them together? I will send all of you the reports from the governor and mayors so we can compare what we've learned. I think we will be able to get to the root of the problem by doing so," he suggested.

Lisa's anger gradually changed to resentment as she continued to watch him talk with the ministers about the governors' and mayors' reports. He looked calm, despite the problems he faced getting the three ministers to work together, and he held off their anger with charm, patience, and an unfaltering realistic optimism. His whole countenance and demeanor gently but firmly called for their respect toward him and toward the other ministers, whom she quickly realized—from their occasional remarks to the others and their suggestions—would only barely tolerate working with each other because they were all aligned with different political factions.

As she kept watching, she soon began to discern what Ha-Neul actually thought of each minister. Minister Seo was an annoying—but earnest—twit who subtly made jabs at Minister Bak, who tried hard to do the best work possible —earning respectability—but had to deal with Minister Chae as well, a manipulative man who only seemed to care about doing the work so he could keep his position. Ha-Neul was an experienced negotiator and, she dared think, puppeteer, who was able to get the three to work together long enough that a major dispute never occurred and so that they would think more about the situation to help the people in the long run.

It was a part of Ha-Neul's character she would have ignored if she hadn't known he would use it against her people.

L isa couldn't keep from observing him as he worked the next day. She needed to learn everything she could about how he operated, so she discreetly observed him even as he read reports. The adviser only spoke with Ha-Neul when he needed to, and as she watched their interactions, she soon realized that the adviser didn't doubt Ha-Neul's competence, even when Ha-Neul wasn't looking at him. Once Ha-Neul finished his duties for the day, he dismissed her to eat dinner with the other servants and then to her room. She bowed and left.

She ate with other off-duty nain, some in their early thirties. They mostly talked amongst their own age group. She recognized some of them as her aunt's own nain and listened a little to their conversation. Since Irene was in charge of the royal children, her nain naturally knew some of the personal news about each one, and at meals, the ones who were able to gather did so to pass along any information they needed. During a lull in their conversation, Lisa got their attention.

"How is working for Wangseja, Nain-Nim?" one nain

asked using Haoche, the speech level below Hapsyoche, due to her being their junior.

"Nearly intolerable," she answered in Hapsyoche.

The women laughed.

"It's hard to believe a nain can find life here nearly intolerable," a second nain said.

A third nudged the second. "Ya . . . do you not realize that she is the one who caused all the uproar? She is bomo sang-goong's joka."

"Eomeo!" The fourth woman looked at her appraisingly. "She's the troublemaker?"

Lisa cracked a smile. "The trouble I cause is never serious."

The women laughed again, but only half amused.

"Never serious?" the first asked. "Ya, do you know how many people were scared of being fired because of whatever it was that you did?"

Her smile grew more radiant. "I was one of them."

"Why did you make so much trouble in the first place?" the third asked out of concern. "Do you not know that the only way to make Wangseja's disposition sour is to mention the witches?" the woman whispered.

"Ah, jinjja!" said the second. "He is always so sweet and genuine with everyone. I wonder what made him hate witches so much." The woman glanced over at her. "If you're really a witch sympathizer, take my advice: avoid the subject and look past his prejudice. I've known Wangseja since I started working here, and he is a good person—and very charming in a good-natured way."

"I'll keep that in mind." Lisa's respectful smile didn't quite reach her eyes. She bowed and left the table, knowing their polite silence would only last as long as she was within earshot.

She went back to her room and messaged her family, mulling over everything that had happened during the day, of which she said nothing to them. As far as her father and brother knew, she was still a nain and friend of Ha-Na and Su, so they wouldn't worry more about her working in the palace. After messaging them and before she went to bed, she picked up her palace tablet and researched everything she could remember Ha-Neul discussing.

In the morning, she met Ha-Neul once he had dressed and eaten. She sat at the refreshment bar to serve those who came, and while the guests—and sometimes Ha-Neul—snacked, she watched him while pretending to read on her tablet. After his third meeting, he motioned for her to stay while he and his adviser escorted a foreign diplomat out of the palace. She set aside her tablet and cleared away their dishes. She then sat down, picked up her tablet, and began reading the news from the diplomat's country.

"How is such knowledge so common in the northern territories but not in Balhae?"

She looked up from her tablet to see Ha-Neul towering over her, glaring at her as though he was accusing her of hiding information from the whole world. She turned the tablet off and set it on her lap. "No one else has cared to know, and with you and your abeoji's bigotry toward witches, why would anyone want to let any information slip that could possibly be used against them in some law?"

"So why are you telling me if you are their supporter?"

She sighed. "I am taking a risk."

"Why?" His tone was almost demanding.

She hesitated, searching her feelings and thinking about

the wang's demeanor as he'd made the request. "There are . . . reasons . . . I cannot fully explain."

"And you're not going to try, are you?"

"No."

"But you haven't told me everything you know about witches, have you? There's more to the whole it's-a-vital-function thing, isn't there?"

"Of course," she nodded.

Ha-Neul looked ready to explode, but he took a deep breath. "What else is there?"

"You and your abeoji are not the first to persecute witches. There are thousands of years' worth of witch persecution. Slovka has its own history, of course, but that was nearly four hundred years ago, and most bias, if not all, disappeared about ninety years ago."

"Around the time Jeungjobu conquered Vires."

She nodded. "The trust between the northern territories was cemented at that time. Vires fought long and hard with the other northern kingdoms. With their defeat, a lot of hope was lost, but they all knew they could rely on each other in any situation. So the witches entrusted the other kingdoms with what little secrets remained."

"What do you mean 'what secrets remained'?"

"A country cannot persecute a group without learning something about them, and sometimes secrets are exposed, especially with the secrets the witches hide."

"Like what?"

"When were Slovka's economic and environmental crises?"

Ha-Neul took some time to remember. "During their occupation of Vires. It was the catalyst for Slovka letting it go."

"And what were they doing during their occupation just before then?" she prompted.

"For—" He stopped, clearly unwilling to go on.

Lisa nearly cracked a smile in triumph. "Keep going."

"Forbidding magic." He watched her nod. "Are you saying the witches caused the crises?"

She sighed in exasperation to let him know she thought he was deliberately being slow. "What did I tell you two days ago about witches not using magic?"

"They die young."

"Yes, but it is not just them. Nature dies as well." She sighed again, suddenly tired. "Slovka poured money into exterminating witches, and as they did so, their land started to die as well. In reaction to the environment dying, they poured money into research to stop the decline. Soon the situation became desperate—"

"And they forgot about the witches," he finished for her.

"Yes, and once they did and the witches' numbers started to grow, their crises ended."

"But that's not proof," he countered.

She gave a short, derisive laugh. "Look at any country's history and its interaction with Vires if they occupied it. You will notice similar trends. Once can be a fluke, twice can be a coincidence, but a hundred times is proof beyond reasonable doubt."

Ha-Neul only spoke to her when he needed to for the rest of that day and all of the next, and when he did so in private, there was more disgust in his voice than usual. When she wasn't doing anything for him, the adviser, or serving guests, she would turn on her tablet to read news or opinion blogs on as many subjects as she knew Ha-Neul was working on, keeping an ear on anything she might learn from him. Sometimes she would watch him and the adviser sift through vast amounts of information on the palace network, catching glimpses of information that only they had.

Toward the end of the fifth day of her employment with him, he and his adviser were discussing the housing problem in Joseon Province. She noticed that they had some difficulty with finding the information they needed. She watched them struggle for half an hour.

"Who organized this mess?" Ha-Neul asked, clearly frustrated.

"I believe Minister Seo's assistant did."

"It's terrible," he muttered.

She leaned over to her right to get a better view of the screen they were looking at. She sighed impatiently and stood, the two men turning to her in irritation and mild surprise.

She nudged the adviser away. "May I, Wangseja-Mama?"

Without waiting for his answer, she tapped in a command and pulled every piece of information up in the app they used to store the information.

"What are you doing?" Ha-Neul's tone was accusatory.

"Helping you," she said as she scanned everything.

She pulled up the command screen for the app and started typing, copying, cutting, and pasting. Ha-Neul watched as the smaller screens behind her screen flickered and were rearranged, occasionally combining to compare information from various folders.

"The assistant," she said as she worked, "is probably a newly elected official and does not know how to work the app properly. I will be very much surprised if the assistant is not new because if they were not, the information could have been easily linked together from the very beginning. That is because only government officials and servants, many of whom have inherited their positions and so have been trained to use the palace network, use it. A new assistant would not have received that training, which would lead to this mess." She moved a line and exited the command screen. "Their bosses should have trained them properly after being elected, considering many of them do not have any expertise in tech."

She went back to her chair and sat down. Ha-Neul and the adviser went through all the information together to check it out before they turned to her.

"You did an excellent job, Nain-Nim," the adviser said.

Ha-Neul looked at her as if he were appraising her again but didn't say anything. She turned on her tablet and began reading.

"You have been paying attention to everything, haven't you?" he finally asked. "That is why you were able to do so well on this."

"I have also done my own research, Wangseja-Mama," she said a little patronizingly. "I had to make some guesses here and there to link the information since I do not know everything about the problem."

"Well, you guessed correctly," the adviser said, still going through the app. "Everything that needs to be viewed or compared simultaneously comes up easily."

She bowed her head. "Thank you, Chamsagwan-Nim."

Someone knocked on the door and opened it. They looked to see Su in the doorway.

"Su, what are you doing here?" Ha-Neul asked.

He glanced over at her and waved shyly. She grinned and waved back.

"Su."

"Sorry, hyeong, but it's been so long since I've played with Lisa."

"Su—"

"If I may, Wangseja-Mama?" she asked.

Ha-Neul barely turned to glance at her. "Fine."

Su smiled as she stood and quietly ushered him out, closing the door behind her.

"Lisa—"

"Shhhh," she pressed a finger to her lips. She glanced around before crouching in front of him. "Listen, Su, it's going to be a lot harder for me to come play with you. Wangseja won't let me leave the office until he has to. Do you understand?"

He nodded and shuffled his feet a little.

"I want to play with you. I hope you know that, right?"

He nodded again and started scuffing his foot against the floor.

"Is something wrong?"

"Is . . . is my hyeong treating you better? Is he still angry with you? I want you to be chingu."

She smiled sadly at his innocent hope of her and Ha-Neul being friends. "I don't think being chingu is possible, Su. Wangseja . . . he . . . he treats me decently while we're working, but I can't tell you if he's angry."

"But he likes you, so he shouldn't be."

She frowned. "I don't think he can like or respect someone who supports witches."

"Maybe he doesn't know he can yet."

She put her hands on his shoulders. "Trust me, it won't happen."

"You're just being stubborn!" Su shouted, making her lean back.

"Su, please—"

"No! You're both being stubborn, and I hate it!"

Ha-Neul opened the door, but Su was running away when he called to his younger brother. He looked down at her, but she didn't look at him as she stood, feeling exhausted.

"Come back in," he told her in a normal tone.

She looked at him, astonished.

"What?" he asked, eyeing her warily.

"You did not say it—" She shook her head.

"I didn't say it what?"

She hesitated, and when she spoke, her usual disdain for him was absent. "You did not say it with disgust."

He blinked, then looked down the hall where Su had run off. "I guess I'm just tired, just like you seem to be."

"Well," some of her disdain was back, "I guess we cannot be constantly battling."

"No, we can't." He stepped aside to let her pass. As she entered, he said, "You can play with Su after dinner today."

She stopped and turned to him. "Th-thank you, Wangseja-Mama."

18

Lisa accompanied the wangsil, along with several other nain and sang-goong, to a national jokgu tournament. They were in a large private box that accommodated everyone who sat at round banquet tables while watching the games. Ha-Neul, in an act of begrudging gratitude for Lisa's continued file organization over the past four days, allowed her to sit with Ha-Na, who wore a traditional dangui with a lotus geumbak under her breast and a seuran-chima with geumbak around her hem, since they were in public.

As long no one interrupted them, the two women chatted, admiring the skills of the female competitors as well as admiring the skills and bodies of their male counterparts as they kicked the ball over the court's low net. When others would join the women's table, they kept their comments about the men discreet, only making eye contact and occasionally nodding and fanning their faces. It irritated Ha-Neul, especially when Lisa smiled as she eyed particularly attractive players.

At one point, he sat with them as they were paying

particular attention to a men's match. Not caring what he overheard, they continued their conversation about a particular player.

"Jae also attended the Royal Academy," Ha-Na half whispered. "He was on an academic and athletic scholarship. Anyway, he caught *many* of the girls' attention, even the seonbae. Many girls would try to watch the jokgu practices or workouts just to get a good look at him."

"Were you one of them?" Lisa grinned.

Ha-Na blushed a little and cast a sly glance at Ha-Neul. "Of course. However, I had to try to do it more secretly. What do you think about him?"

"He certainly is a great player," Lisa said as Jae kicked the ball to earn a point for his team as it barely made it in the line before bouncing out, "and very good-looking."

Ha-Na looked a little flabbergasted while Ha-Neul's blood ran warmer. "Only very good-looking?"

"Okay, okay. He's definitely a high score." Lisa watched Jae as he turned briefly to look behind him at another teammate—and in their direction—and Ha-Neul suddenly felt a dislike for the man. "He—he kind of looks like . . ." She shook her head, her face a little flushed as Ha-Na waited for her to continue, as did Ha-Neul. "Never mind, but he is really handsome."

Ha-Neul narrowed his eyes at Jae, appraising him.

"Well, I think you will definitely like the fact that he's northern Balhaen."

Lisa laughed as Ha-Neul rolled his eyes. "Of course, I could tell just by looking at him."

Ha-Na sighed. "He is so lucky to be blessed with paler skin, and his hair has the natural rusty tint everybody likes."

"Hey," Lisa nudged her, "you are beautiful too."

Ha-Neul couldn't help but feel grateful for the compliment toward his noona.

Ha-Na smiled again. "Thank you." She looked back at Jae. "He really is great to look at."

"Yes, he is," Lisa said appreciatively.

Ha-Neul cleared his throat, almost in a disapproving way, and they both turned to find him watching the game with a slight frown on his face.

"What is wrong with you?" Ha-Na asked.

He felt a little shock burst through him when he realized what he had just done. "Nothing, noona."

He quickly glanced over at Lisa before turning his attention back to the game. They turned away from him and continued to admire Jae until the match was over, a victory for the player's team—which resulted in Lisa and Ha-Na clasping each other's hands and staring in awe as he and some other teammates whipped off their jerseys in celebration. A fit of giggles burst out of both of them, making Ha-Neul's blood even warmer as he listened, and they couldn't stop until the next two women's teams took the court. Ha-Na excused herself to sit with their abeoji and Su for a while when the match started.

Lisa barely seemed aware of Ha-Neul clearing his throat again as her eyes sought after Jae's team until he started talking. "The prince or princess of Vires is always the most powerful witch, correct?"

She turned to him. "Not exactly."

He became a little confused. "But Vires holds competitions every ten years to determine who will be the prince."

"Yes, they do," she nodded, "but competitions are not always won by strength alone."

"Strategy is important too," he consented.

"But it can only take you so far." She pointed toward the

game. "Strength, strategy, adaptability, and experience are all important. So is the talent to inspire a sense of safety."

"So the current prince may not be the strongest witch?"

"That is correct, but he is definitely the most skilled that we know of."

He was silent for a few moments. "What do you know about his gajok?"

Lisa hesitated for the briefest moment. "I know a bit."

His patience ran short. "Well?"

She sighed in slight annoyance. "No one outside his gajok knows 'the secret' to their continued success in the competition."

"Five hundred years is a long time for one family to hold the title."

"Yes, it is."

"What do you think of the past violence of the princes?"

"I think you cannot take it out of the context of the events that surrounded the violence."

"What do you mean?" He leaned toward her, happier now that he had her full attention.

She looked at him as though the answer were obvious. "A prince is the champion of the people, for the people. He serves the will and best interests of the people. If the people are not happy with the prince, they overthrow him and install a new prince."

"So if the people want war, the prince takes them to war."

"Not always. Sometimes the prince can persuade them it is not in their best interest."

"However, since the prince is chosen from among the people, he—or she—usually shares their views."

"Usually."

He smiled, feeling he'd won some ground. "Would you say the current prince reflects the views of his people?"

She did not look pleased. "That is too broad of a question and is very loaded to answer with one word, Wangseja-Mama, so I will answer it this way: his biggest concern is keeping Vires stable, and he will do what he must to ensure that. However, you and your abeoji are making it increasingly harder to do so."

"So he'll go to war."

Lisa shook her head and glared at him patronizingly. "That is a last resort for anyone with any sense."

When Ha-Na reclaimed her seat next to Lisa, Ha-Neul sat back and turned his gaze to the tournament. He didn't speak to her again, even though there were opportunities to do so, but occasionally they did catch one another carefully studying the other. At the end of the tournament, their tables were pushed back and his gajok lined up to receive the winners of the men's and women's league, the nain and sang-goong standing in two rows behind them. Jae's team entered the box, and when he approached Ha-Na, he glanced behind her and did a double-take when he saw Lisa. A slow smile formed on the man's lips, which made Ha-Neul suspicious.

"Excuse me, Gongju-Mama; may I address the nain behind you?" Jae looked pointedly at Lisa.

Ha-Neul and Ha-Na glanced at Lisa, who seemed perplexed, and Ha-Na nodded. Jae smiled, thanked her, and performed a Slovkan bow—a military attention with a sharp bow of the head.

"You've become quite the beauty, my yak-honja," Jae said. Ha-Neul blanched, wondering if Lisa had indeed been betrothed to Jae.

Lisa's eyes widened before she beamed as if she had heard an out-of-use inside joke. "Yi Jae-Woo! It is you."

Jae and Lisa laughed, and Ha-Neul watched with contempt as Jae scratched his head in embarrassment but with awe as he looked at her. "Is your offer still good?"

Lisa smiled kindly. "Four years isn't as big of an age gap as it was five years ago."

A hint of nausea surged in Ha-Neul's stomach.

Jae looked more hopeful. "But you'll be eighteen soon."

Her smile deepened, and a light blush colored her cheeks, which made Jae smile and caught Ha-Neul's attention even more. "Yes, I will."

Ha-Neul stuck out his hand to Jae as his blood coursed hotly under his skin. He needed to put a stop to such a sickening display. "Congratulations on your win."

A little flustered, Jae shook his hand and bowed. "Thank you, Wangseja-Mama."

After one last glance and smile at Lisa, Jae continued down the line to the wang.

"They really like each other, Yi Jae-Woo and Lisa, don't they?" Su said a little too loudly.

Everyone looked at Jae, who looked back at Lisa and blushed. She blushed as well and looked down. Ha-Na shushed Su while trying to stifle her laughter. Ha-Neul wasn't amused at all.

Ha-Neul sat at the table in Ha-Na's room doing some paperwork while she weaved and Su watched a video on a tablet, earphones in so he didn't distract them.

"Were you upset that Jae liked Lisa better?" He tried to

look as if the thought had just occurred to him.

Ha-Na laughed. "No, it doesn't upset me at all. Apparently he's Grand Illegitimate Princess Astrid's joka, so he went to the Slovka Royal Academy until he transferred to Balhae Royal Academy. Lisa knew he wanted to be a professional jokgu player, but she lost contact with him after he transferred and was afraid to express her interest in him to Astrid's gajok."

Su giggled. "She almost kissed him when she was twelve. Isn't that gross, hyeong?"

"That's—that's something." Ha-Neul cleared his throat. "It seems he liked her even when she was a preteen. No wonder he makes no scruples about his advances toward her now."

Ha-Na laughed again. "Does Lisa often act her age?" He started to answer, but she cut him off. "Please don't answer that. I don't trust you enough to say anything decent. Anyway, they want to get reacquainted before trying out a relationship—you know, to see if there is still interest."

"They?" He couldn't hide his confusion. "They barely spoke to each other yesterday."

"I let her go talk to him before he disappeared. They exchanged messaging accounts and talked most of the night."

He let out a contemptuous laugh. "That's just great. Our country's MVP for jokgu is interested in a witch supporter. He's probably one too."

Ha-Na let out an exasperated sigh and replied a little bitterly, "Well, if things work out for them, Lisa will be gone sooner. I'm sure that will appease you."

"How is that possible?" He couldn't contain his shock.

She gave him an incredulous look, which soon turned

pensive when she saw his expression. His panic must have shown through. "You've seen her records. She has the power to quit honorably if she so chooses, and she wants to so she can attend university."

He went back to his paperwork. "I forgot about that addendum."

"I'll miss her when she goes," Su said.

Ha-Neul couldn't help but silently agree.

19

L isa set a teacup and piece of carrot cake in front of the Vires governor. The Balhaen woman barely glanced at her as she moved about the office. Once she sat down and the governor had taken a sip of tea, Ha-Neul got straight to the point.

"I've heard rumors that the unrest with Vires may be more widespread and dangerous than I previously knew," he said. "What exactly is going on?"

"What you have heard may be true," the governor said, "but nothing serious is forming. We have been working to contain and settle the people, as have the other northern territories' governors. Of course, our progress is slow considering we are palace employees."

Ha-Neul's eyes widened a little in surprise. "Are you saying there's peace but it's not because of you?"

"I am, Wangseja-Mama."

"Please explain," he said with interest.

The woman took a sip of tea. "The native nobles have calmed their own people better than we could."

"You mean the Prince of Vires and the Illegitimate

Princesses?"

"Yes, along with the remaining nobles of the other territories."

Ha-Neul sat back in his chair and looked a little lost. "We have so little control?"

"To be honest, Wangseja-Mama, past governors have never needed to step into such . . . forays. The native nobles always encouraged following Balhaen rule."

Lisa coughed as she grinned at Ha-Neul to show her triumph that the nobles of the northern kingdoms did more to keep the peace than he had thought.

He nearly gave her a quick glance. "Tell me about the prince. What has he been doing?"

"As you know, he is extremely wealthy. He has been using his wealth to keep the witches out of debt and living on a survivable income. It is to the point where his eorini need to work to attend university if they are able to gain admittance."

A chill went down Lisa's spine as Ha-Neul put up a hand to stop the governor from talking. "Wait—wait, did you say eorini?"

Lisa glanced up at the governor, who now looked uncomfortable.

"The prince had only the sitting prince, or so I was told." His tone clearly let the governor know of his displeasure.

The woman shifted slightly in her chair. "No, Wangseja-Mama, there is one more that I have recently come to know about. There is a younger ddal who's managed to keep out of sight."

Ha-Neul began tapping the desk with a finger. "He has a ddal? How old is she, and is she considered powerful like her abeoji and obba?"

"I know she has finished high school, and as for her magical ability, I have not heard any reports about it."

His eyes showed his frustration. "Why do you know so little?"

"His gajok is notorious for producing mainly males—"

"This should make his having a ddal well-known."

"Of course, you are right, Wangseja-Mama, so we are unable to account for not having known much earlier."

"It makes me wonder what else he is concealing and who is helping him conceal it."

The governor began to look panicked. "Wangseja-Mama, may I suggest you do not start accusing him, or anyone else, of concealment? We are already spending a fortune making sure he is not planning a riot, has spies amongst us, or anything else of that nature, of which we have been unable to find anything. He is the most influential voice keeping the witches and their supporters calm."

He took a few moments to consider her words. "Very well. Thank you for your time."

"I will send you more reports tomorrow." The governor bowed. "Take care, Wangseja-Mama."

The woman left. Lisa stood and began gathering the dishes. Ha-Neul looked up at her, obviously suspicious.

"You knew about the sitting princess, didn't you?"

She stopped and stood straight. "I did."

He closed his eyes and took a slow deep breath. "Will . . . will you tell me about her?"

She looked at him curiously before speaking. "She had no desire to be taken into consideration as a candidate to become Princess of Vires, and her abeoji and obba accepted that. Her highest title will be Sitting Princess of Vires."

"You said she had no desire to be considered. Does that mean she's powerful?"

"Her gajok keeps her magical strength a secret."

"But it's believed that she's powerful," he pressed.

"There have been many debates on that subject."

He nodded, slumping in a clear signal of exhaustion.

"Will there be anything else, Wangseja-Mama?"

He looked up at her, wonder in his eyes.

She studied him, wondering what she had done to deserve that reaction. "Wangseja-Mama?"

"I'm sorry, no. Thank you, Lisa."

Her eyes widened as a slight warmth, then shock at the warmth, slightly rocked her.

"What is it?" he asked, surprised by her response.

She shook her head, dismissing the sensation, and started gathering the dishes again.

"Please tell me why you looked so shocked."

She stopped, folding her hands at her waist. "You said my name."

He let her collect the dishes and take them out.

"You called me Wangseja-Mama without hate," she heard him mutter as the door closed.

Ha-Neul sat reviewing some reports on his desk while Lisa sat in her corner reading a novel on her tablet. Occasionally, she looked up for a moment when he would sigh in irritation and start scanning other information. After several minutes of this behavior, he put the reports together and laid his hand on top of them. The desk highlighted them, and he swiped them toward her. Lisa's tablet beeped as it received the reports.

"Wangseja-Mama?" Her curiosity got the better of her.

"They're reports dealing with the problems of the

northern territories," he explained. "Since I know you can keep your mouth shut about what you see and hear in this office, and you have specific knowledge and experience in the northern territories that I don't, I'm hoping you will review these and tell me what you think."

She hesitated, studying him as her suspicions rose.

"I will carefully consider what you have to say on the subject," he added.

She looked down at her tablet and opened the files. Ha-Neul turned away from her after a couple of minutes and began working on a different set of reports. The reports he had given her dealt with recent demonstrations, rallies, and an occasional riot that had resulted in numerous arrests and trials. They were all associated with the treatment of witches, especially the newly approved laws that further limited their employment opportunities. Lisa almost audibly sighed her own displeasure but checked herself.

"What kind of advice do you want me to give you?" she asked.

He thought for a moment and shrugged. "I'm not sure. Whatever you think is important."

She laughed, half amused. "What I have to say may upset you."

"I'm always prepared for that whenever you open your mouth."

She hesitated when she noticed he seemed a little too resigned to that fact.

"The laws should have never been made in the first place; however, I know that they will not be repealed any time soon." She scanned a different report. "Another thing that should end is the arrests of the peaceful demonstrators. There should be no reason for them to go to jail for doing something peacefully and within the bounds of reasonable law."

"They could be witches waiting to—"

"Wangseja-Mama, if the witches were going to attack at such demonstrations, they would have done so," she said. "From what I have read and seen and from my own experience, no magic has ever been performed in any demonstration, rally, or riot, so your fears are unjustified."

"So you think I should let them carry on and only arrest the rioters?"

"I do," she nodded. "At most, the people will be able to voice their concerns or displeasure publicly, which will go a long way to relieve pent up stress and anger for a time."

Ha-Neul thought about it for a moment. "I understand what you're saying." He turned away from her, highlighted another stack of reports, and sent them to her. "Read those in fifteen minutes and give me your opinion. I'm meeting with the Jeoncheon-do governor in an hour."

"As you command, Wangseja-Mama."

She opened the files and began to read.

L isa entered Ha-Neul's room just as he finished putting on his suit jacket. She bowed to him, turned on her tablet, and swiped a folder on her tablet over to his. He picked up his tablet and opened the folder.

"What is this?" he asked.

"My summary of the reports and my opinions on the matter," she said. "I thought it best to write my opinions first so you can get them in full without interruptions for arguments about points that will be explained. After you have read my summaries, if you still wish to discuss them, we may do so. I believe that will keep our arguments to a minimum."

He laughed. "You don't enjoy our arguments?"

She gave him a polite smile. "I think we can be more productive this way after the past five days of mostly arguing over reports."

"Very well, if that's how you feel, even though I've found them quite stimulating." He turned off his tablet. "What about the reports I sent you last night?"

"I have not had the chance to finish them," she said. "I will finish them soon, though."

"Good," he smiled, sending a buzz down her spine, "that's good."

"Wangseja-Mama," the adviser said, and she jumped since she hadn't noticed he was there, "the wang will be waiting for us."

Ha-Neul turned to him. "Yes, of course, we should go immediately."

She read as they walked. As they turned to the elevators, she noticed Su poke his head out of his room and gave him a small wave. He smiled playfully and waved back before she disappeared from his sight. She turned her tablet off as they approached the wang's suite. Much like the few times after her first visit there, the wang briefly discussed business and questioned whether Ha-Neul was doing okay. At the end of the meeting, they all bowed to him.

"Lisa, stay behind for a few moments," the wang said. "I wish to speak with you."

She bowed again. "As you wish, Wang-Mama."

Ha-Neul looked curiously at them but left without a

word. The wang motioned for her to sit across from him, and she took the seat, suddenly nervous.

"I wanted to see how you were doing with the task I assigned you," he said.

"We have talked a few times about Vires," she said.

The wang nodded to show his pleasure with her response.

She took a breath to gather her courage. "Please excuse me for saying this, but I do not understand why you would tell me to do this, or—for that matter—why I am even doing it. To do so is against my resolve to give Wangseja, or yourself, any information that may negatively impact Vires, its allies, and its supporters—like Rosalina."

The wang laughed. "Yes, I'm sure you've thought a lot about what you are doing, and I'm surprised as well that you took my suggestion." He became more serious, almost somber. "I'm just trying to put this country on the best path"—his last two words stirred a deep emotion within her that she could not quite identify—"and I need to use you to do that."

Her anger flared at his last phrase. "If you are using me to—"

He held up a hand. "I think you will see very soon the fruits of what you have done."

"I get the feeling I may not like what I will see," she said.

The wang smiled, looking a little disappointed. "You will see soon enough, I think. Anyway, know that we will speak privately again. You may leave now." He picked up his own tablet from the breakfast table and turned it on.

She stood and bowed to him. Once she was out of his suite, she shot a quick glance at the closed door before heading to Ha-Neul's office. Ha-Neul looked up when she entered and became a little wary when he saw her expression. The adviser excused himself to run an errand before the other nain came to receive their first assignments.

"Is there something wrong?" he asked.

"Have you been using the information I have given you to fight the witches?"

Ha-Neul's guard went up. "What makes you say that? Did Abeoji say something?"

"The only thing you need to say is the answer I've asked for," she spat in Haeche.

"No, I haven't. Are you happy now?" he spat back in Haeche.

She regarded him cautiously. "Do you promise?"

"I give my word that I've done nothing with what you've told me about Vires."

She was both relieved and disappointed by his answer. "Very well, Wangseja-Mama. I apologize for my manners." She bowed, using Hasoseoche again.

Ha-Neul deflated a little at her sincerity. "What was this about anyway?"

She attempted a smile. "It is nothing. Please forget it."

He studied her for a moment. "You may go spend time with Su or Ha-Na if you wish. You look like you need to relax before you spend the day here. Take a couple of hours to do what you want."

She was stunned but grateful. "Are you sure, Wangseja-Mama?"

"Yes," he nodded, "but I need you to finish reading those reports by this afternoon."

"I understand, Wangseja-Mama." She bowed.

Ha-Neul grinned. "Just go, Lisa."

She bowed again. "Thank you, Wangseja-Mama."

She left the office, made her way to the first floor, exited the west-facing doors, and went to the stables. The wild mare was still tramping around her stall when she reached it. The horse made its way over to her and nudged her, so she wrapped her arms around the horse's neck and rested her cheek against the animal.

"I haven't heard Lisa complain much about you for a week and a half now," Ha-Na said. "Nor have I heard you complain about her. Are you finally getting along?"

Su looked expectantly at Ha-Neul.

"No, not really," he said. "Perhaps we're just too tired to keep arguing."

Ha-Na grinned. "Perhaps that's a good sign, or maybe she will come back so refreshed from her day off tomorrow that you will both have the energy to attack each other once more."

He looked up at her in surprise. "She has a day off tomorrow?"

Ha-Na sighed and closed her eyes in exasperation.

"It's her birthday tomorrow," Su said. "Nire sixth, the first day of fall." He began to hum softly, then sang, "Fall, fall, happy fall. Time for new love."

Ha-Na let out a snort of laughter.

"What's so funny?" Ha-Neul asked.

She shook her head, a smile on her face. "Lisa and I

were talking yesterday about her plans for her birthday, and Su overheard us."

"What is it about her plans that has him singing that?"

"Lisa's meeting Jae tomorrow," Su said. "They have a date."

The door to their dining room opened as Ha-Neul's heart rate increased and Lisa came in followed by two musuri carrying their dinner.

"Lisa, come sit by me." Su patted an empty seat between him and Ha-Neul.

She smiled at Su and took the seat as the musuri left after setting out the dishes.

"Are you excited about your date tomorrow?" Su asked as Ha-Na began eating.

Ha-Neul quickly followed to hide his discomfort, grabbing food with his chopsticks and stuffing it into his mouth.

"Uh—ha!" The mix of expressions caused by her embarrassment was endearing, but then she blushed, which slightly soured the taste of Ha-Neul's food. "Yes, I am."

"You would think he'd be busy getting ready for the Tri-Country Tournament instead of going out on a date," he mumbled around his mouthful of food.

"He received permission," Lisa said. "It is his first time asking for personal time."

He stuffed more food into his mouth to keep him from talking.

"What're you going to do tomorrow?" Su asked eagerly and with his mouth slightly full.

Lisa smiled bashfully. "He's going to take me to the outer part of the city for a quiet breakfast. After that, we're going to the Museum of Balhaen Fashion History to see the design classes they offer there."

Ha-Neul let out a snort of laughter. "Really? He's taking you there?"

Ha-Na glared at him, but Lisa barely gave him a glance.

"He remembered I want to study fashion design at university." There was a touch of coldness in Lisa's voice. "He thought I would like to go if I have not already."

He stuffed more food in his mouth, feeling chastised.

"What about after the classes?" Ha-Na asked. "You didn't tell me that since Su interrupted us at that point."

"We'll do lunch at the park before hiking the low trail of Uirim-san. Then we'll do dinner in the city and go to a movie," she said.

"That's it?" Ha-Neul asked.

Lisa stopped eating and took a breath before she answered him. "The main purpose of a first date is to establish the foundation for a possible relationship, Wangseja-Mama, and to have fun. We chose activities we both enjoy. Do you have a problem with that?"

He just shook his head, feeling chastised again, and resumed eating.

"Well, I'm sure you will have a good day tomorrow," Ha-Na said.

"Thanks, Ha-Na," Lisa said with a grateful smile.

That night, Ha-Neul entered his apartment in a foul mood. He paced around for a while before going into his personal office. The desk lit up at his touch and he opened a website. Soon Yi Jae-Woo's photo popped up in front of him. He read all of the information he could find about the man and then searched for any recent news articles. One article, dated an hour before, caught his eye, and a thrill coursed through him.

21

L isa boarded the shuttle bus that would take her away from the palace grounds and to the city. A few musuri and other male servants were already on the bus. She took an empty seat by the window and leaned her head against the cool glass. The sun still hadn't risen, and it would be an hour's ride out and around the palace walls from the servants' access. From the main road, the ride would take another half hour. She was dozing before the bus started.

Someone nudged her awake when the bus stopped at the terminal. She grabbed her shoulder bag and hurried off the bus then exited the terminal, only stopping once she reached the busy city street. As she was getting her bearings, she noticed someone stop behind her.

"Got any plans?"

She whipped around and gasped. A young man with the sides of his shoulder length hair pulled back into a hair band stood in front of her. His ears were uncovered, revealing multiple piercings and a small bar running diagonally through the top of his left ear. He wore a tight black sleeveless shirt that emphasized just how toned he was and dark jeans to match, with a silver-studded belt. His hairstyle and his clothes gave his features a sharper, more masculine look, but she finally recognized him.

"Wa—Wangseja-Mama?"

He nodded before he leaned forward and said more quietly and in Haeyoche. "It'd be best if you called me Ha-Neul while we're out."

"Why are you here?" she asked, switching to Haeyoche as well.

"I heard Jae was in emergency surgery, so I thought your plans would be ruined."

"I had other plans before making some with Jae-Woo."

He leaned away from her, seeming a little uneasy. "Oh, well, I could still show you around."

"That's not necessary."

"Come on," there was a little desperation in his voice, "I have a free day today, and so do you. We're both here, so why not? I'll treat you. Think of it as a birthday present."

She looked at him warily.

"If I go back now, I'll be very bored." He put on his best puppy-dog face, which wasn't very good. "Please?"

She groaned. "Fine."

He brightened. "Assa. Did you have breakfast, or are you hungry?"

"I'm hungry."

"There's a great café in the arts district—about a ten-minute metro ride." He gestured to a pavilion with steps leading down below the sidewalk.

She stared at him in disbelief. "You take the metro and don't get recognized?"

"Would you have recognized me if I hadn't talked to you?"

She shrugged. "Fine, let's go."

Ha-Neul walked beside her as they headed down, and he paid for her day pass. They got on the train and sat down.

"I know that your gajok can't claim the Slovkan throne, but I don't exactly understand why. They're of the female line."

Lisa glanced at him, wondering why he was being so conversational. "It was to lessen the repercussions of extra-marital affairs. If an illegitimate ddal couldn't inherit the throne, there would be fewer power struggles."

"And that worked?"

"Obviously. Even though I'm not illegitimate, and neither are the rest of my living relatives, 'illegitimate' is still attached to our titles so the people know we have no claim to the throne. It's why your jeungjobu allowed my jeungjomo and her yeo-dongsaeng to live during the Expansion."

The train slowed to a stop, and they got off, their conversation about their great-grandparents having been cut off. Ha-Neul led the way with confidence and took her up to street level. They walked for five minutes among booths full of paintings, drawings, mosaics, handmade jewelry, and pressed-flower arrangements. He took her up a side path where the buildings quickly gave way to quaint stores with beautiful gardens. Among them was the café. As they ate, Ha-Neul noticed the chain around her neck.

"What's on your necklace?"

She smiled mischievously as she put her fork down and pulled on the chain. A glass orb filled with a liquid and another, darker orb inside hung at the end. "It's a raven's eye."

Ha-Neul looked a little revolted.

She laughed. "I know that expression, but it's petrified."

"Why do you have it?"

"Naturally, ravens are intelligent birds, and because of that, there's a lot of mythology surrounding them. They're protectors, observers, tricksters, and are associated with gods of prophecy or gods who have omniscience, like the Balhaen Samjogo, the all-powerful three-legged crow, or raven. Many ancient cultures regarded ravens as a sign of good luck."

"So why do you have the eye?"

"The eye is the gateway to the soul. You can see people's emotions and personalities through their eyes. The eye, for many creatures, is the ultimate observation tool. The raven's eye also contains all of that."

"So it's a good-luck charm."

"Basically." She put the necklace back in her shirt. "My abeoji gave it to me on my eighth birthday."

"What's your abeoji like?"

Lisa sneaked a grin at him since he didn't know who her father was. "He's the best man I know. I will consider myself lucky if I can marry someone half as good as he is."

"Okay," he tapped his fork against his plate a couple of times, looking a little put out, "so what do you want to do today?"

"I was thinking the zoo, lunch, a movie, an amusement park, dinner, shopping, and then the fireworks show."

He nodded, though he looked skeptical. "I'll pay for the food, and then we can go."

She watched him go up to the counter, confusion and interest playing within her about what he meant to accomplish by spending the day with her. When he turned back toward her, she picked up her bag and met him at the door. They made their way back to the metro, and after a couple of transfers, they came out in front of the zoo. Ha-Neul paid for their admission and they went in. She took them to all the outdoor exhibits first and then to a bird show, followed by an aquatic show, before heading to the indoor exhibits.

"You know, Balhae City Zoo has Dunia's largest indoor jungle, desert, aquarium, and butterfly garden," he told her.

"I know," she rolled her eyes. "That's why I wanted to come."

In the aquarium, they watched the shark exhibit. At one point, the zookeepers fed the sharks bleeding fish, causing them to go into a feeding frenzy for the visitors. Ha-Neul watched her reaction, but she was calm.

"Some people protest the feeding frenzy show," he said as the sharks finished eating.

"But it's a part of nature," she replied, "and the sharks are already calm."

They were silent for a few more moments, and an idea clicked about why he might hate magic. She turned to him. "Do you hate magic for how violent it can be? If so, have you not seen what it can create?"

"And what does it create?" he asked derisively as he turned to face her.

She sighed. "Many witches believe magic is the remaining power the gods used to create life, and in return, new life creates more magic. Nature and magic feed each other, and at the height of their work together, they inspire wonder and love. With wonder, the imagination is stimulated, and with love, nature and magic come together in perfect harmony. Love balances the chaos and destruction that is so natural to all life. So, in a way, all humans are capable of using magic. It's just that witches have a better talent for using it. Most witches share the belief that all humans have magic, that it is the love and wonder in humans that creates even more magic. That is why they are upset when they're treated like monsters."

He didn't respond to her words but turned back to stare at the sharks. After a few minutes of silence, she moved on to the next exhibit, knowing he wouldn't respond, but Ha-Neul stayed at the shark exhibit for a short time before following her.

Her curiosity about his life got the better of her during lunch, so she asked, "Will you tell me something about you that I don't know?"

Ha-Neul chewed on his food for a long time. Just when she was about to give up on him, he swallowed.

"On my eighth birthday, two witches from Vires came to the palace," he said, making her look up as her heart started racing. She wondered if she would finally hear the history she had been dying to hear for so long. "I was like Eomeoni—I loved magic, was fascinated by it. One of the men was the prince, Aleksandr, and the other was his hyeong." Lisa swallowed her food. He was talking about her uncle, who'd died in prison. "While Abeoji talked to the prince, his hyeong was showing my noona and me some magic—simple transformation spells—while Eomeoni supervised us. At one point, he was transforming a flower blossom between our hands. When we pulled apart, it was a viper. It bit Eomeoni and me before anyone had time to react. Eomeoni grabbed it before it could get noona, but it caused the viper to bite her again."

Horror and sadness filled her. "That's how your eomeoni died."

Ha-Neul nodded, looking bitter. "Yes, but upon Abeoji's insistence, it was kept quiet that witches were involved. Abeoji had the prince's hyeong thrown in prison, while Aleksandr was free to leave as long as he kept his silence.

Abeoji said it was to help keep the peace, especially since Eomeoni had always liked witches."

"But that was only one witch." Her tone was soft.

Ha-Neul remained silent as his anger simmered. They finished their meal in silence, then left.

"How often have you been out like this?" she asked when they were on the metro and he seemed calmer.

"I started when I was thirteen. I would meet up with school chingu, and we made other chingu while we were out, so I kept coming out as much as I could to meet them," he said without looking at her.

"Is that when you got all your piercings?" She touched one and quickly withdrew her hand when he flinched.

"Yeah," he said softly, then smiled and chuckled. "Abeoji and noona make me keep my hair long so they're hidden. It's to keep appearances," he said with some irritation.

She grinned back at him. "I wonder how this hasn't leaked out."

Ha-Neul said in mock disbelief, "Our wrath is hard to deal with, obviously," he rolled his eyes.

She couldn't help but laugh. The metro stopped, and he led her to a transfer. At the ticket office of a movie theater, she paused and turned to him. "Pick one."

"What?" he said, a little astonished.

"Pick one. You've done everything I've wanted to do so far, so pick one."

"But it's your birthday, and I crashed it."

"That's why you're paying for everything and doing what I want. I want you to pick the movie, Geum Ha-Neul."

He nodded dumbly, went up to the cashier without her, and paid for two tickets.

She looked at the title on her ticket. "Why this one?"

"I figured you'd want to see it," he mumbled.

She rolled her eyes and punched him on the shoulder. "You totally missed the point of picking the movie."

"Do you want popcorn?" He rubbed the spot where she'd hit him.

She sighed, a slight smile on her face. "Yes, please."

She came out of the movie crying.

"Why are you crying?" he nudged her playfully. "It ended well!"

"Shut up! I heard you sniffle and saw you wipe your eyes before the lights came on."

Ha-Neul cleared his throat, looking forward. "Amusement park is next?"

She let out a short laugh, thinking he looked a bit adorable. "Yes."

Lisa dragged him to all the rides she soon realized he was frightened of and laughed the whole time they rode them. Then she gave him his choice of rides. When he suggested they get dinner, she made him buy amusement-park food. After, he took her to the shopping district. She was sorting through some jackets in a department store when she looked up to find him missing. She got an idea and went to a men's clothing store, where he eventually found her.

"What're you doing here?" he asked.

She held a shirt up to him and shook her head. "Just looking."

She picked out some shirts, pants, and other accessories, always comparing them to him, and took them to the cashier. Once they were in bags, she handed them to him to carry, smiling to herself. They stopped at a café and got some tea before going to a park. The fireworks started half an hour later and lasted for an hour. They sat on a bench the whole time, gazing at the huge fireworks display in companionable silence. When it finished, they made a quick getaway to the bus terminal, barely managing to catch the last shuttle bus to the palace.

"I gotta admit, you planned this well," he panted as they sat down.

She cracked smile. "I guess I should admit that you were a better replacement for Jae than I thought you were going to be."

Ha-Neul glared at her, but the glare disappeared at her next words.

"Thank you." Her smile became softer, more genuine. "My day wouldn't have been half as fun if you weren't here."

She rested her head against the glass and closed her eyes to hide the small amount of embarrassment she felt. Next thing she knew, something hard hit her shoulder. She startled awake to find Ha-Neul's head resting on it. A few moments passed as she just stared dumbly at him, her emotions a confused tangle. Then she leaned her head back against the glass and didn't wake up again until the bus stopped at the palace. She poked his head away to wake him, and he breathed in deeply through his nose as he woke. He got his bearings after a moment and quickly led the way off the bus. Once she stepped off, he held out the clothes bags he was carrying.

She waved them away. "Those are yours."

"What?" He blinked a little stupidly.

"They're yours for when you go out again."

"I don't—"

"I'm sure you'll make the time if you want to." Her expression made it clear she expected him to do so.

Ha-Neul scratched the back of his head. "Thanks."

"Have a good night. I'll see you in the morning . . . Wangseja-Mama."

She bowed and turned around, allowing a satisfied smile to form on her face as she walked away.

22

Ha-Neul sat at his desk the next day, staring at a report, his eyes unmoving. To his side, Lisa was typing on her tablet. He had given her another set of reports to look over, and she seemed busy typing her thoughts while he sat staring at the same report for almost twenty minutes. It didn't help that his chamsagwan was out sick with food poisoning. He slid the report away and turned to her.

"Tell me about your eomeoni," he said.

Lisa looked up, startled. She blinked a few times. "My eomeoni?"

He nodded.

She tapped something on her tablet before she turned it off. "Where should I start?"

"Hmm." He thought for a moment. "Was she like you? I heard she could be quite fiery."

Lisa laughed. "I wondered if Imo had been telling stories."

"She did when we were younger and she was still a nain." He smiled. "I remember her telling us that her eonni, your eomeoni, was so free-spirited she had the audacity to kick my harabeoji in the shin when she was ten."

Lisa laughed harder. "My halmeoni had her whipped ten times a day for a week. Eomeoni said it hurt to sit for a month."

"Irene said you have her temperament."

She smiled. "It is Imo's favorite complaint against me. Neither of us cared for the responsibilities of being a noble nor the decorum expected from us. Unlike Eomeoni, who learned to know when to at least act properly, I find myself getting into trouble."

"I think many other nain would have found themselves dishonorably discharged for everything you have said to us," he consented.

Lisa flushed. "I am well aware of it, Wangseja-Mama. Trust me when I say that I know one day my luck will run out and I will find myself unable to get out of trouble."

His smile changed as heat burst in his chest, and she studied him thoughtfully. "I hope it won't get to that point."

Someone knocked on the door. Lisa cleared her throat and turned on her tablet as he reluctantly called for the person to enter. After that, it seemed like there was a never-ending stream of visitors or new work to do for the rest of the day, but they would find themselves talking to each other when the atmosphere seemed too quiet.

The next day, Lisa and Ha-Neul ate lunch with Su and Ha-Na. Lisa remained relatively quiet as Su's nammae talked about the plans for the party to celebrate the changing of the seasons and how to handle some of the guests. Many nobles were coming to the party, and some of them wanted Ha-Na to spend time with their eligible adeul. Ha-Na was looking over their pictures and information to remind herself of who they were and whether she could tolerate them. Ha-Neul helped her while he looked at the information of the available women who would attend. Su just ate.

"How's Jae doing?" he asked through a mouthful of rice.

Lisa looked over at him with a small smile. "He's doing much better. He should be out of the hospital tomorrow."

"You two are still talking?" Ha-Neul looked at her in surprise.

Su buried his mischievous smile in his food.

"Yes, in fact, we video chatted last night before bed," she said.

Ha-Neul choked on some tea as Ha-Na smiled.

"Will you try to meet soon?" she asked.

"I'm not sure," Lisa answered.

"He'll probably be too busy with physical therapy for the next tournament," Ha-Neul interjected, looking a little too hopeful.

Lisa shook her head but didn't seem to notice Ha-Neul's behavior. "Actually, he has been ordered to not exert himself for a week."

"So will you try to meet soon?" Su asked.

"I'm sure we can arrange some time off if you want," Ha-Na said.

"Why should we do that?" Ha-Neul asked.

Ha-Na glared at him. "She hasn't had much time off anyway, Geum Ha-Neul. I think she should take a short break if she wants."

"Thank you," Lisa interrupted before Ha-Neul could reply, "I will give you my answer tomorrow, by evening at the latest."

"That will be fine," Ha-Na said.

Lisa excused herself soon afterward to attend to some duties Ha-Neul had given her earlier. Once the door closed behind her, Ha-Neul turned to Su. "Why did you bring Jae up?"

He gave his hyeong a wicked grin but said with all the innocence he could muster, "I was curious. Lisa still likes him."

Ha-Neul shot him a glare before reluctantly turning back to the women's information.

24

The party was held in one of the many gardens in the palace grounds. The garden chosen had an abundance of flowers that were still alive after summer's end and was full of autumnal flowers beginning to bloom. The menservants and gardeners had set up small pavilions to shade small tables placed around a grassy patio. Lisa oversaw the setup of a small section and the placement of the stacked food platters on each table.

Around a quarter past ten, the royal family entered the garden. Ha-Na quickly scanned the sections and the food, calling for some minor adjustments. The wang did his own inspection of the tables and pavilions, though he said nothing, ending at her section. He stood next to her and smiled politely as she bowed to him. She noticed that he wore a less formal version of his royal uniform, the same as his sons.

The wang glanced at her. "Stay by Ha-Neul's side today, Lisa. One of my own nain will take over your responsibilities for this section."

She bowed again with a calm face, though she was

curious as to why he would want her at Ha-Neul's side. "As you command, Wang-Mama."

He politely strode away from her, and she moved to stand behind Ha-Neul, who gave her a questioning glance.

"The wang commanded it, Wangseja-Mama," she whispered.

Ha-Neul nodded and moved with the rest of his family to greet the first arrivals. She followed him wherever he went, even if it was to speak to a Balhaen noblewoman who was considered an eligible match for him. He was quite charming to some, the ones who seemed more genuine, at least, but many of the women would glance at her as she remained silent behind him. Lisa kept her expression passive, though she was incredibly bored. Sometimes as they moved to another table, she caught a glimpse of the wang watching them, especially when the guests he was speaking with seemed to be discussing her, and she wondered what they were saying about her.

Occasionally she would hear Su causing a ruckus with some of the children in attendance. If they grew too loud, she would manage to catch Su's eye and give him a tiny shake of her head. Su would then rein in the other children and they would be quieter for a while.

Ha-Na seemed stuck entertaining two to four different men at once for much of the party. Lisa would see another female around Ha-Na's age among the group a few times, putting Ha-Na more at ease. A couple of times Ha-Na would catch her eye and give her a tired grin. Lisa always returned the gesture.

And on the rare occasion, once he was able to find an opening, Ha-Neul would lead her to a quieter part of the garden and steal a few words with her. This was the only time she would really speak and maybe get a small bite to eat before he forced himself back among the guests, seemingly more reluctant with each break. This lasted until about midafternoon, when many of the guests began to leave. When there were only a few left, all speaking amongst themselves or with the wang, the siblings met at a distant table—Ha-Neul pulled out a chair for Lisa to sit as well—and started playing a card game Su had brought, while eating the remaining food.

"Are you two chingu now?" Su asked her and Ha-Neul.

Ha-Na looked at Su, then at Lisa and Ha-Neul. Ha-Neul looked to her as well.

"Uh . . . um, well . . ." She glanced at Ha-Neul, feeling pressured to say something decent. "I guess we don't hate each other anymore."

Su gave an exasperated sigh. "So stubborn."

They finished their game and made their way back into the palace.

"Su, you have a lesson," Ha-Na said. "I'll take you."

He took his sister's hand and they left.

"'I guess we don't hate each other anymore.'" Ha-Neul mimicked her.

She groaned in annoyance. "Well, I guess I do not hate you anymore."

Ha-Neul let out a short laugh to show his disbelief.

"What about you, Wangseja-Mama?"

He shook his head. "I don't hate you. There's no guessing about it."

She turned her head away, feeling embarrassed and strangely warm. "I do not hate you either."

He glanced at her. "Does that make us chingu?"

"I gue—" She stopped when he looked at her questioningly, daringly. "Perhaps it does."

"Good." He tried to conceal the smile that revealed he was happy they were now friends.

They were silent for a while as they made their way to his office.

"When I visit Jeoncheon-do in two days, I will need to take two or three nain with me, and you would be a helpful addition. We'd only be gone for three days."

"Wangseja-Mama, whatever you order me to do as your nain, I must obey."

"I'm not ordering you as the wangseja," he said. "I'm asking you as your chingu."

She hesitated before answering, thinking about her plans with Jae. "I have never been to Jeoncheon-do."

"It's a great time to go," a smile played at the edges of Ha-Neul's mouth and reached his eyes.

"Yes, it would be," she admitted, feeling her chest warm a little.

"So, will you go?"

She hesitated for a moment. "I will."

Ha-Neul smiled, and she felt her chest grow ever warmer.

The dial tone never lasted long whenever she video called Jae, and tonight was no different. His finely crafted face and hazel-flecked brown eyes filled most of the screen. He was wearing a bathrobe, and his hair was tousled as if he had just come out of the shower. He gave her the smile she liked best—the one he had promised would only be hers when she was twelve. She smiled back.

"Hey, Lisa." Her name passed across his lips like he savored it.

"Hi, Jae. How's your knee doing?"

"So much better. My doctor says I can start therapy early."

"That's great news!"

"It is, but I'm afraid it'll stop you from visiting."

She blushed. "About that—I have to postpone it anyway."

"Why? What's going on?"

"Wangseja wants me to go to Jeoncheon-do with him. We'll have to leave Sunday night, and we'd be back at the palace Thursday morning."

Jae looked disappointed. "Oh, well, I guess you have to go, then."

She ran her fingers along her desktop. "Yeah, I guess so."

He watched her for a few moments. "Is everything okay on your end? You seem a bit preoccupied . . . Actually, you've seemed a bit preoccupied the past few times we've talked."

"Really? I'm sorry, Jae."

"It's okay. It just has me wondering if there's someone else you're thinking about."

She straightened. "What?"

Jae shrugged. "Honestly, I wouldn't be too surprised. You're a great woman, Lisa, one any man would be lucky to have. I just wish I hadn't waited so long to find you again."

"Jae . . ."

He smiled that smile. "I've seen that look on your face before. Usually I saw it when you were looking at me, but now . . . well, you're not. Of course, I shouldn't be too surprised if you did happen to meet someone else."

She put her face in her hands. "I'm not sure what's going on."

His smile became sadder. "Which means you're not as sure about starting us."

She put her hands down. "I wish you could have been there for my birthday."

"Me too. That's when I started to notice the change." He sighed. "Maybe the trip to Jeoncheon-do will be good for you—help you figure out what you want. You can tell me after."

"I can skip it if you want me to." Her tone sounded a little hopeful even to her, as well as a little unsure. "If I skip it, I can come visit you and be with you for a few days."

He just smiled and shook his head. "I want you to go. You'll like it there. It's so beautiful around this time." His smile slipped when he saw her lost expression. "You can tell me your decision after you get back. Okay?"

"Okay," she nodded.

"Hey, Lisa." He was smiling again. "No matter what, you'll be my first love."

She blushed as she remembered how he had rejected her four years ago because she had been too young. "You'll be mine as well, Jae."

He waved goodbye until she hung up.

25

Lisa double-checked the luggage in a side room off the main entrance hallway. She counted each trunk and suitcase, quickly scanning its contents before checking it off a list. A sang-goong entered the room, and Lisa reported that the luggage was in order. The sang-goong took the list and scanned it, then nodded and left, ordering a few men to take the luggage to the cars. Lisa supervised them, directing them to one of four cars for each personal piece of luggage. The rest went into a van. As the menservants closed the trunks, Ha-Neul, his adviser, and two other nain came out.

"Is it all ready?" he asked as she bowed.

"Yes, Wangseja-Mama. We can leave any time."

Ha-Neul nodded. "Then let's get to the train station."

The menservants opened the car doors. Ha-Neul and his adviser got in the first car, she and the other nain got in the second, and six menservants got in the other two. The two nain sat in the back chatting quietly while she picked up her tablet from the dashboard and checked her schedule for the trip.

"Nain-Nim," one of the others said, addressing her in Haoche, "you and the wangseja seem to be on better terms."

"We are," she addressed her in the same form without looking up from the tablet.

"Min-A here has just been saying that you seem to be a favorite with Gongju and Eorin Wangja, and now it seems you're becoming a favorite of Wangseja as well."

"What are you trying to say?" Her tone held a touch of sharpness.

"Are you trying to become the next wangsejabin?" Min-A asked.

"I have no intention of marrying Wangseja."

"I told you she would say that, eonni," the other nain said in a near whisper.

"Doesn't mean it's true," Min-A said.

"Apparently you're using your overactive imagination." Irritation surged through Lisa. "You've certainly heard the rumors that I hate Wangseja, and if you think that was a ploy to get attention, you are grossly underestimating just how much trouble that could have caused me—how much trouble it did cause me."

"But now—"

"Trust me. There isn't a reason for me to marry him. I have no desire to join the wangsil."

Her tone was such that the other nain couldn't say anything. Forty minutes later, they were at the train station. Lisa oversaw the transfer of the luggage to the royal family's train while Ha-Neul and the other nain went to their own train cars. With the luggage safely stored, she went to her own compartment on the nain car. The train smoothly pulled out of the station and began its journey to the northern province of Jeoncheon.

Lisa sat in the common room of the car early the next morning watching the mountain scenery pass by the window, making the large valley grow closer with every second. Wildflowers grew outside the sprawling towns and cities they passed. The sky overhead was expansive and clear. She pressed the side of her head to the glass.

"It's beautiful, isn't it?"

She turned to look at Ha-Neul. "Yes, Wangseja-Mama, it is."

"Jeoncheon-do is one of my favorite places to visit." He moved closer to her. "I was wondering if you received your updated schedule."

"I did," she said. "I noticed I have half of Wednesday off."

"Yes, I'm giving each of you most of a day to yourselves, and you will be last with the shortest day since you're the most junior."

"Of course. I would not expect anything else, Wangseja-Mama."

"There's one more thing I want to say." He seemed reluctant.

"What is it?"

His lips thinned. "I hope you won't mind what the other nain said last night. I did hear about it. Those two have set their sights on the title. I don't particularly care for them, but they do work hard—which is why I brought them—even though it's only to try to advance themselves."

Lisa kept her emotions in check before she answered. "You do not owe me an explanation, Wangseja-Mama, and I will not take their words seriously since what they said is ridiculous."

Ha-Neul tried to smile as he said, "Of course it is."

He didn't stay with her much longer as she made sure to keep any conversations he started short. The train pulled into Jeoncheon City a couple of hours later, and she hurried to make sure the menservants and station workers took proper care of the personal luggage. As she made her way out of the station, a wave of noise hit her, and she froze when she saw protesters gathered at the barriers. Hundreds had banners and shouted against the unfair treatment of witches and their lack of freedom to protest. They called for the release of the protesters who supported witches. She came to her senses and quickly checked how the luggage was stored before she turned to wait for Ha-Neul to be escorted out.

He looked at the protesters—and in the distance came the distant wails of police sirens, which incensed the crowd even more—before he turned to speak with a government official. The official frowned and nodded, then placed a finger against an earpiece in his left ear and began speaking. As they got in the cars, the sirens stopped wailing.

"I wonder what's gotten into the wangseja," Min-A said.

"What do you mean?" Lisa asked.

"He ordered off the arrests of the protesters. There could be witches with those people, but he still ordered the stand-down."

Lisa looked at the car in front of them, but she couldn't see anything through the tinted glass. She cracked her window open just a little so that more noise could come through, but as they drove, she heard nothing to indicate a mass emergency.

There were protesters at the hotel they were staying at as well, but Ha-Neul ignored them. She hurried the transporting of luggage to their rooms with a gleam of satisfaction.

Ha-Neul had appointments that started an hour after he arrived. Lisa and the other nain were with him for the day, while Min-A was free to explore. Min-A's friend kept shooting angry glances at Lisa whenever no one was looking because Ha-Neul tended to send her out on more errands while Lisa stayed by his side.

The next day was much the same, except Min-A never looked at her if she could help it. The other nain returned midafternoon so she could get ready for the banquet and ball that night. Even though they were nain, the governor had expressed his wish for the women to join the party so there would be more ladies for dance partners. Ha-Neul agreed and rented dresses for the three of them.

Laying it out on her bed, she studied the dress she had chosen. It was made of a light material and dyed a pale violet. It had a simple, open sleeve for her right shoulder that fed into a Sabrina-style neckline and went to a strap that hung diagonally on her left shoulder. At the waist was a band of sturdier material that dipped into a shallow V. The skirt had two layers, the top made of chiffon, which would hang loosely from her hips.

Resigned about having to go to the banquet, she sighed and removed her jeogori, chima, and undergarments then put on a shower cap to wash. She put on a strapless bra before slipping into the dress then sat in front of the mirror to reapply her makeup, making it barely noticeable that she was wearing it. Then she let her hair fall into natural waves that hung just past her shoulder blades. Her raven's eye hung on her neck.

When she left her room, she saw the other nain waiting for her. Min-A wore a tight, more revealing short black dress while her friend wore a blue dress that was slightly more modest. Both wore plenty of makeup to give them a sharper, more seductive appearance. They stared at her as she approached them.

"That's what you chose?" Min-A asked, looking at her dress with scorn.

"I am a nain. I am only here to serve," she replied coolly.

"Let's just go, eonni." The other nain lightly tugged on Min-A's arm to get her to move.

Min-A harrumphed before she led them to Ha-Neul's suite and rang the bell. A manservant opened the door and looked slightly flustered when he saw the first two nain.

"Wangseja has already left for the banquet."

Min-A smiled. "Thank you."

When the door closed, Min-A began to grumble until her friend suggested their entrance at the banquet might leave a better impression. Min-A quickly agreed and began talking about how they could enter the banquet hall. Lisa followed them in ill-humored silence.

Most of the guests were government officials and their spouses, if they were married, or their dates, if they could get one. Min-A and the other nain entered the hall as if they were models on a runway, causing many to stare, just as they had hoped. Lisa entered the hall a good distance behind them like the woman of noble blood that she was— with dignified grace, drawing more welcoming gazes. A waiter showed them to a table stationed near Ha-Neul's that was occupied by the governor, other top officials, and a man

—much younger than the officials but a few years older than Ha-Neul—who wore the insignia of a general.

The governor opened the banquet several minutes later with a gracious speech for Ha-Neul before proclaiming the room should eat. He bowed to Ha-Neul amongst enthusiastically polite applause before retaking his seat. The waiters brought in the food. Min-A and her friend ate just enough to look like they had an appetite, while Lisa ate most of her food as she made polite conversation with those who sat at the table. A few times, she felt eyes on her from the head table, but whenever she glanced that way, they were all busy with their own conversations.

Then it was time for the dancing to start. The party moved to the adjoining ballroom, where Ha-Neul was to open it. Min-A and her friend twittered away excitedly, hoping he would choose one of them as his partner. Lisa, doing her absolute best to tune out her coworkers, carried on a conversation with a couple she had taken a liking to until they stopped it to direct her attention behind her. Ha-Neul stood there, dressed in his royal uniform, and held a hand out to her.

"Will you honor me with the first dance?"

She hesitated, feeling another jolt of electricity shoot down her spine, and then curtsied. "The honor is mine, Wangseja-Mama."

She gave him her hand, and he led her onto the dance floor. When he put a hand on the middle of her back, a small shiver ran through her, and heat bloomed in her chest. She glanced up to see a polite smile on his lips, but there was something deeper in his eyes. She focused on his chin instead. The music started, and he led her into the dance. Other couples quickly joined them.

"Why did you pick me?" she asked.

"Should I not be able to dance with my chingu?" he asked in return. "Especially when she looks as beautiful as you do?"

A light blush colored her cheeks. "Please be serious."

He sighed, sounding slightly frustrated. "You are the only woman here closest to my age who doesn't look like she's on the prowl for seduction. Does that satisfy you?"

"It does." She felt the heat within her spread to her stomach.

He looked annoyed. "Do you hate getting such compliments from me?"

"I will admit that it is a bit strange."

"Why?" His tone betrayed some hurt, which startled her.

She looked him in the eye again. "It is just that until recently we were the master and servant who hated each other."

Some nervousness entered his features. "Lisa, I've—"

The music ended, and he quickly composed himself before they bowed to each other. Another man quickly asked her for the next dance after apologizing to Ha-Neul. She agreed, and Ha-Neul chose the governor's wife for his next partner. As the night carried on, she often found herself tracing Ha-Neul's movements, sometimes catching him watching her as well. Close to the end, the young general approached her.

"Woo Su-Han Daejang." He introduced himself and bowed. "I command the Northern Balhaen Army."

"Lisa, Illegitimate Princess of Slovka, nain." She curtsied.

"May I request the next dance with such a beautiful young woman?"

Something about him made her feel a little disoriented, but she hesitantly accepted.

"I'll come back for you soon." He bowed again and left, leaving her feeling uncomfortable with the way he'd addressed her.

She studied the general to try to glean any insight into his personality. He was tall—half a foot taller than she was, putting him over six feet—and he was strong. Nothing could hide the strength that naturally emanated from him. He sported the military haircut, which gave more severity to the sharp lines of his face. His bone structure was prominent in a very appealing way for a Balhaen; however, there was something closed about him. When she was near him, she felt no special warmth from his chocolate-cream skin, and when she looked into his dark-brown eyes, she realized they were almost devoid of any real emotion. When he finally led her to the dance floor, his large, finely crafted hand elicited no response as she slipped her much smaller one into it. No emotions sparked in her until he rested his other hand on her back. Then a cold shiver ran through her.

"You seem young for a daejang," she said to calm herself. "May I ask how old you are?"

"I'm thirty." His voice was smooth—eerily so.

"S-so young!" She silently chided herself to be more composed. "How did you rise so quickly?"

"I had some terrific sponsors who saw my potential, and they put me into the best schools," he smiled, apparently pleased with her interest. "I proved talented as an officer, and the army gave me opportunities to show my true potential, which astounded them."

"That is so wonderful for you. I am sure your significant other feels honored—"

"I haven't been able to seize her heart yet," his smile turned pointed.

She shivered again. Suddenly he felt too close, even though he held her just as any polite stranger would while dancing, and what she saw in his eyes frightened her. She saw a hunger there that would not be pleasant to satisfy—if it ever could be. The missing warmth from his body was actually a subtle coldness, one that snaked in little by little to get its coils around its victim's heart—her heart—without any struggle. She found it hard to breathe.

"Please excuse me. I do not feel well all of a sudden."

"Of course, Sitting Princess."

She recoiled from him before she gathered up the hem of her dress and left as fast as possible without appearing rude. She made her way to the banquet hall, where some guests sat refreshing themselves. Leaving the hall, she turned a quick corner through a doorway and entered a side lobby. She sat in a chair and started taking deep, calming breaths to get her heart under control.

"Oh, Woo Daejang-Nim," she heard, "where are you going?"

"I am going to check on my dance partner."

Sickness roiled through her, and her heart raced. At the far end of the lobby, away from the hallway, she spotted a men's bathroom with a lock and rushed toward it—only to find it locked. Muffled footsteps came closer. Desperate to escape, she put her hand over the lock to cover her magic and heard a soft click. When the door closed, she slowly clicked the lock back into place.

"—y won't you touch me like before? We used to have so much fun when we had private moments in the past." A woman spoke, addressing the other person in Haeyoche.

An exasperated response came from behind another door leading into the bathroom.

"Then just kiss me like usual. You don't have to do any more pleasuring than that if you don't want to—or do you want me to pleasure you?"

Another incoherent response, but it sounded angrier.

"Why? You once told me there could be a chance! I don't care that you played with Ye-Ji as well because I know you prefer me." There were a few moments of silence. "We've done this before." Her voice came smoother, more seductive. "This is all for you. Just take it already."

"Enough!"

The second door opened, and Ha-Neul stopped short when he saw Lisa. Behind him, Min-A was quickly pulling her dress up over her naked breasts.

"Lisa—" He reached out to her.

"You do not need to explain, Wangseja-Mama," her back hit the door as she hurried to put distance between them, her heart pounding. "I am nothing but a nain."

She pulled the door open, having unlocked it with magic again, and slipped out, shutting it behind her as Ha-Neul moved toward her. She hurried to the elevators and returned to her room to change and take some aspirin. Three hours later, they were back on the train going to their second and last destination. She locked herself in her compartment and immediately went to sleep.

The train arrived at the station in the early morning hours. She managed the transfer of the needed trunk to the hotel suite Ha-Neul would use for the day. Then she changed into normal clothes and made her way into the small city, instantly relaxing as she lost herself in the morning crowd. Many small cafés and bakeries were just opening their doors, so she slipped into a café to enjoy a leisurely breakfast. After, she walked around for a while looking at the small custom shops and then made her way to the middle of the city where a large park took up half of the city's acreage.

She entered a wooded section on the south end and took a few minutes to wind her way through it, coming out at a massive stretch of gardens full of blooming autumnal flowers. Vendors dotted the pathways, sitting pensively next to their wares or having conversations with those who stopped to browse. She went through a border of trees and walked around the large pond near the middle of the park. The sky above was a clear blue, letting the sun caress her skin with its warm northern rays. Out in the middle of the pond, a previously hidden fountain came to life, putting on an elegant show. She watched it for its entire duration before she made her way to the free zoo that held the animals found throughout Jeoncheon-do. When she exited the zoo, she found Ha-Neul waiting for her, dressed in some of the clothes she had bought for him.

"What are you doing here?" she asked, her tone a little cold despite trying to be civil.

"There's something here I want you to see, so will you come with me?" he asked her in Haeyoche.

"Don't you have appointments?" She switched to Haeyoche as well.

"They're canceled. Please, Lisa, come with me," he held a hand out to her.

"Just—" She took a deep breath to calm herself. "Okay."

She walked past him, and he turned and kept pace with her.

"We need to get a taxi," he said. He glanced at her. "Thank you for coming."

He only got a nod in response. They took the fastest route out of the park, and he waved down a taxi. She looked out the window as he gave the directions, refusing to look toward him for the whole ride, even when the taxi took them out of the city limits and stopped at the side of the highway. Ha-Neul paid the driver and took his business card. They got out, and she looked around at the grassland and hills.

"What are we doing here?" She let suspicion creep into her voice.

"Just trust me." His tone was reassuring.

He crossed the highway and found a faint path through the tall grass and wildflowers; she followed him at a distance. After five minutes, the path made its way up a fairly large hill that ran for several miles, and at its peak, they stopped. She took in a long breath, and her eyes widened. Ha-Neul smiled at her expression. They were at the edge of a long, low cliff, and below them was a gigantic marsh full of migratory water birds and marsh flowers.

"It's so beautiful," she said. "All of those birds . . ."

Ha-Neul sat on the edge of the cliff and lightly tugged at the knee of her pant leg. She absently sat beside him, not taking her eyes off the scene.

"I always come here when I pass through this city. I wanted to share it with you."

"Why?" She finally turned to him but scooched away a few inches when she realized how close he was.

"Because you're special," he said matter-of-factly, ignoring what she'd just done.

She felt uncomfortable, so she started to get up, but he gently took her wrist in his hand and stopped her.

"Please let go," she said softly in Hasoseoche.

"There's nothing between me and the other nain. I haven't pursued them in months, and even then—"

"You do not need to explain, Wangs—"

"Yes, I do," he insisted.

She sank back to the ground, and he let go of her wrist.

He calmed himself before he continued. "If I participate in any sexual activity with women I am not married to, I am at risk of losing the crown, though I have pushed the boundaries in the past. Just like the Slovkans, the Balhaens have done what they think is best to prevent power struggles."

"This does not concern me." She still would not look at him as her anger rose.

"Yes, it does—because I want to court you."

Her heart stuttered when she caught his eye and saw he was serious. "Wangseja—"

"Trust me, please," he pleaded with her. "I never hated you. I hated myself for liking someone who so obviously hated me and who had views I totally disagreed with. But you . . . you . . . you are not just the views I've disagreed with, and you are not just your hate as well." He laughed, releasing some of his nervousness. "You are the woman who stands up for what she believes in and who my gajok fought to keep. If anything could convince me to take another look at you, it was that they kept you with us, and every day I am more grateful they did. You are special, Lisa, and you are even more special to me."

"You"—she shook her head and then switched back to Haeyoche—"you are so sappy."

He laughed. "I expected that response as soon as the words were out." His hand went to hers. "It's still true, even if it's the sappiest thing you've ever heard."

She turned her head away from him and ran her free hand through the grass as she focused on the sensations his hand on hers sent through her.

"I'm not sure what I feel for you," she said. "I only know that I don't hate you—that sometimes I am happy to see the person you are, and you do affect me sometimes."

He waited.

"I don't know, Wangseja-Mama."

His hand squeezed hers a little tighter. "Please, Lisa, try to find out."

She sighed and shook her head, remembering Jae.

He removed his hand from hers, looking disappointed, and turned back to the marsh. More emotions crashed through her, and she struggled to understand what they were, but all she could really focus on was how empty her hand now felt. She looked up at him and saw that he seemed to be feeling a similar turmoil—that he seemed to want to run away from it all. Pain shot through her chest, and tears welled in her eyes. She put her hand back in his, twining her fingers through his, and her emotions settled. She felt liberated. He turned back to her, clearly trying to contain an enormous amount of hope.

"Let's try it . . . just . . . just for a little while," she said. "Is that okay . . . Ha-Neul?"

He closed his fingers around hers and smiled. "Yes, that's fine."

They watched the birds for a little while before he turned, wrapped her in a hug, and landed a quick kiss on her cheek. He turned back to the birds with an even bigger, goofier smile on his face. She turned away from him, her cheeks blazing and a smile creeping up to her eyes as her body filled with an incredible warmth.

26

Su burst with elated laughter, jumping and clapping, as soon as he saw Ha-Neul and Lisa together when they returned before lunch. Ha-Na looked at him, bewildered, then looked at them. Before she could ask anything, Su opened his mouth.

"They're courting!" he nearly shouted.

Lisa flushed as Ha-Neul pulled him into a headlock.

"Geum Su! That's not something to joke about," Ha-Na said as Ha-Neul hissed in his ear, "Shut your mouth if you don't want to get hurt."

Ha-Na looked in shock at Ha-Neul then turned to Lisa. Her mouth worked, but no sound came out. Irene entered the room, scanned the situation, and sent away the nain who'd accompanied her.

When the door was shut, she looked at Ha-Neul. "What is going on?"

"They're—" Su started to speak.

Ha-Neul put a hand over his mouth. "We're just playing."

Irene glared at Ha-Neul, and after checking to see if

Ha-Na was still dumbfounded, she looked at Lisa. "Speak, Lisa."

"It's really no—"

"Never mind," Irene waved away Lisa's answer. She looked at Ha-Neul again. "You know the protocol: no sexual activity, even if you are courting."

Lisa was mortified, and Ha-Na tried to cover Su's ears, but he was already giggling like crazy.

"Please, Bomo Sang-Goong-Nim," Ha-Na breathed, "we don't even know if—"

"Excuse me, Gongju-Mama, but Wangja is giggling like a schoolgirl, Lisa is mortified, and Wangseja can barely keep a smile off his face. They are courting."

Lisa's face was a deep red by this point.

"I came to tell you that the dates for the military review have finally been set," Irene said. Instantly the atmosphere became somber, though Ha-Neul still held Su in a head-lock. "Woo Daejang contacted the palace last night and opened up his schedule. The review will begin on Geuret third and will end on the sixteenth."

"That gives us six weeks," Ha-Na said. "Most of the preparations are already finished, though. Why is it so late this year?"

"It is because of the extra training they must carry out," Irene said. "Woo Daejang's forces are the first line of defense should the northern territories revolt."

They became uncomfortably silent, and Su glanced at Lisa to see her staring at the floor.

"Well, hopefully events will never lead to that," Ha-Na said.

"Even if it does come to that, the soldiers can't be hurt using the war machines," Su said lightly. "The fighting would be bloodless, just like the Expansion."

"That was only bloodless for the Balhaen armies, Eorin Wangja-Mama," Lisa said in a mild tone.

His expression fell. "Oh, that's right."

"Let us not dwell on it, shall we, Mama?" Irene said.

Su and his nammae nodded.

"Good." Irene looked between Lisa and Ha-Neul. "Nothing against protocol," she pointed to Ha-Neul. "Do not even push the boundaries. Do you understand?"

Ha-Neul nodded, looking properly scared. "Perfectly."

She looked at the couple again and sighed. "Gods, please be with them."

Irene left the room. Ha-Na looked at Ha-Neul, who was grinning at Lisa.

"She gave her permission," his hyeong said.

Lisa's mouth twitched. "Very reluctantly, though."

"It's still permission." Ha-Neul's grin turned into a smile.

"Stop," Ha-Na ordered. She pointed at Ha-Neul. "Let go of Su, Geum Ha-Neul." His hyeong did, and Su started bouncing and giggling again. "Explain how this happened."

Lisa blushed again as Ha-Neul grinned. "She can't resist my charm."

"Oh, gods," Lisa and Ha-Na groaned.

"Ouch!" Ha-Neul looked at Lisa, clutching his heart.

"Second thoughts?" Ha-Na asked.

"Yes," Lisa answered, though her eyes never left Ha-Neul's face.

Su giggled louder. "Liar."

Ha-Neul grinned and gave him a high five.

27

Ha-Neul had sneaking out of the palace down to a science. Since only his gajok, Lisa, and Irene Bomo Sang-Goong were aware of his piercings, he changed into his civilian attire and pulled back his hair, used his gajok's personal elevator, and snuck to the kitchen using the least-used hallways. It was easier since it was still very early in the morning and very few servants were about. He hurried toward the back entrance to the servant lodge where the shuttle bus idled—a clear indication that it was ready to leave—and he bolted for the door, making it just before the driver closed it.

"Sorry," he muttered to the driver as she cast him an irritated glance.

The driver waved for him to sit down, closed the door, and pulled out onto the access road. He found Lisa sitting in the middle of the bus and sat next to her, grinning.

"You cut it a little close." She seemed a little grouchy.

"Do you really think I'd miss a chance to go into the city with you?" he asked playfully, trying to lighten her mood.

She just shrugged.

A laugh of disbelief escaped him. "We haven't really been alone in two weeks. I'm not going to pass up this sudden day off."

Somehow that made her mood sour. "I bet Min-A and Ye-Ji wouldn't have minded spending the day with you."

Hurt and annoyance curdled his stomach. "I really hope you don't mean what you're implying."

She shook her head. "I apologize. I didn't mean it like that."

"Have they said anything to you?"

"Even if they have, I can take care of myself," she said calmly and distantly.

His irritation grew. "I know you can, but I want you to tell me these things."

"If I can take care of myself, why should I tell you?" Her tone was a little colder.

"I don't know. Maybe so we can talk about it together or —I don't know. We could do something!" he said.

"Why would we need to talk about it?" She looked incredulous. "I just said I could handle it."

"I guess so we can clear the air—clear up any misunderstandings."

"Would there happen to be any misunderstandings?" she asked.

"How would we know if we don't talk about it?" he shot back.

"You don't think that could imply I don't trust you?"

He pulled away from her as her words stung him, and he became defensive. "Would that imply you don't trust me?"

"I don't know, would it?" She narrowed her eyes.

"You're the one who said it."

She laughed, unamused. "That's just great. I was only asking to find out."

"Find out what? Find out if I think you don't trust me to be faithful?"

"That's not what I'm saying," she said a little bitterly.

"What are you trying to say?"

She shook her head. "Let's just stop. We're too angry to finish this conversation rationally."

He took his turn to laugh. "So we're both being irrational?"

"I'm trying not to be," she said.

"So now I'm the irrational one." He let out a derisive laugh and moved to a different seat.

They didn't say a word for the rest of the ride. She sat staring out the window while he stared, fuming, at the back of her head from a few rows back. She never once turned around to see what he was doing. As the bus neared the terminal, she gathered her bag and jacket. She turned to face him when the bus pulled in, but he only continued to stare at her.

"I only meant that I didn't want you to think I didn't trust you," she said. "I'm sorry I brought them up. They were just being especially infuriating this past week."

He felt his moodiness rise despite knowing it would only cause regret. "Maybe I should spend time with them to find out how you really feel."

Lisa's expression hardened, showing him no emotion, and he knew his mistake was bigger than he'd thought. She turned away and hurried off the bus. The moment she was gone, he groaned—leaning back in his seat—and rubbed his face.

"Ya!" the bus driver yelled. "Are you getting off?"

"Sorry!"

He rushed off the bus, through the terminal to the main entrance and to the sidewalk. He looked around for Lisa but only saw the heads of Balhaens.

"Come on, Lisa, where did you go?" he murmured.

He patted his pockets but only came up with his wallet. He rolled his head, sighed in annoyance at his own forgetfulness, and started walking to the left. After walking for a few minutes, he headed down into the metro and looked at all the stops the line would make. He stared at the stop's name for the performing arts district and debated within himself whether to take it or not. He grew more decisive as the train drew closer, and he bought a day pass. He rode the train for several more minutes before a woman's voice announced the name of the station. He got off and headed down the stairs to the street level.

Shops and studios lined the streets. He passed several entertainment agencies—both large and small—and some restaurants that served the people there. After a five-minute walk, he saw a nice-looking café that was quite busy. As he drew close, he noticed a couple of guys standing near one of the outdoor tables. Their posture looked aggressive and impatient—the people at the surrounding tables looked concerned or annoyed.

He looked up at the café's sign and walked faster. He entered the café's gate and saw a flash of light-brown hair at the table the two men were standing near.

"Well? Move!" one man yelled in Haeche.

As he approached, Ha-Neul saw Lisa look up at the man as if he were a petulant child. He brushed pass the men and pulled back the chair across from her—yanking it out from Lisa's feet, which had secured it. He saw her bag on the ground and picked it up.

"I'm sorry I'm late," he handed her the bag.

"Who's this jerk?" the other man asked.

"Ha-Neul, her namchin," he said without looking at them.

Lisa gazed up at them with a pleasant smile. "See? I wasn't lying."

The men stalked off amid the other patrons' grumblings at their rude behavior.

Ha-Neul looked at Lisa to find her gazing expectantly back at him. "I'm really sorry I'm late."

She gave him a genuine smile. "I could have waited a little longer." She took his hand that rested on the table and helped him open it. He hadn't realized how tightly it was clenched. "It's okay. We're both okay, right?"

He clasped her hand. "Yeah, we are, and I promise you can trust me."

She nodded. "I will. I promise."

He felt all of his emotions melt into a puddle of blissful goo.

After they ate a filling breakfast, they ordered a picnic from the café and walked to a large park. There, they played on the playground like the children. Eventually they were playing with the children as well. He usually played the monster or bad guy since he was the scary-looking one of the two, but sometimes Lisa would join him in chasing the children when they least expected it. When they or the children got tired, they left the playground to sit on a bench and share a water bottle from their picnic basket.

They ate lunch a little after one. Both were flushed and tired from playing so much. They laid out the blanket that came with the basket and began eating cold-cut sandwiches, fruit, salad, and brownies. At one point, Lisa pulled out her cell phone and held it up to take his picture.

"What're you doing?" He smiled.

"Capturing a memory," she said and took the picture.

He laughed. "Why capturing?"

She smiled, but something in her smile caused him to become concerned. She seemed to notice and unexpectedly sat in his lap, her legs on either side of his so her knees brushed his hips. Her hands went to his shoulders, near his neck, and she stared into his eyes. His heart raced, and he felt his insides shift with the want of having her so close and to pull her closer still. Involuntarily, his breath drew in a little more ragged, and he had to fight down his excitement.

"Capture," she said with quiet sincerity, "so these memories never fade, so we can always find them."

His eyes went to her lips as his hands slid to her hips and tugged her closer. She leaned in as a hint of a smile played at her lips, then she kissed his forehead, causing his hands to clutch her tighter as he let out a sigh of pleasure. She looked down into his eyes and smiled when she saw the effect she had on him.

"You see?" she whispered. "I've already captured you."

28

Ha-Na carefully examined the baduk board before she placed her white stone, capturing and removing several of Lisa's black stones. Lisa quickly put another black piece on the board, drawing her attention to the danger there, and she moved to block it. A smile appeared on Lisa's lips as she placed another black stone, capturing and removing a large number of her pieces.

"You've gotten better," Ha-Na praised.

"I learned from a great teacher," Lisa replied.

She chuckled. "I'm beginning to understand how you caught your abeoji by surprise. You've probably been watching baduk matches in your spare time."

"I'll admit I've watched a couple."

She breathed out a laugh. "I guess you've been preoccupied with Ha-Neul."

Lisa blushed. "He doesn't like being apart when we don't have to be."

"Are you all right with that? Since your trip to the city two weeks ago, he's practically been inseparable from you."

"It doesn't bother me most of the time," Lisa said with a smile.

Ha-Na's hand hovered over the board as she looked up at Lisa. After a couple of moments, Lisa glanced up as well.

"What is it?"

She was all seriousness when she spoke. "I thought you only agreed to court to make sure you weren't interested in him. Are you falling in love?"

Lisa didn't answer immediately, taking Ha-Na by surprise. Instead, she straightened and looked away. Ha-Na studied her chingu carefully, withdrawing her hand from the board. She watched the emotions warring in Lisa's left eye—the only eye she could see.

"Lisa," she said, getting her to turn back around, "what is going on between you?"

"I'm not exactly sure." Lisa stopped and shook her head. She took in a breath. "I'm not sure how deep my feelings for him are."

"Maybe you are too afraid to admit how much you do feel for him," she replied.

They sat in silence for a while—Lisa lost in her thoughts and Ha-Na continuing to watch the emotions play on her chingu's face. When she believed Lisa was thinking too much, she placed her stone on the table next to the board with a loud tap, snapping Lisa out of her thoughts.

"Before your feelings get any deeper, you should tell him your real name," she said. "I'd hate to see you end up like Rosalina, or worse."

Lisa nodded. "It is best to tell him."

"Tell who what?" Ha-Neul asked as he came into her room.

Both of them jumped at his interruption, but Lisa looked more startled.

"I was announced." He looked at Lisa and noticed her expression. "Lisa?"

She glanced over at Ha-Na.

"Tell you about my future plans," Lisa said. "About when I might enter university."

Ha-Neul's expression relaxed a little. "Oh, I didn't know you still wanted to go."

"It's why she came to the palace in the first place," Ha-Na said, a little disappointed that Lisa would not tell the truth while she was around to support her.

"That's right," he frowned a little. "I remember now."

"I have six months before I need to have my schedule in for the year if I want to go," Lisa said. "A lot can happen in that time to help me make that decision."

Ha-Na shot Lisa a quick glance, wondering if she was going to tell him now.

"I suppose you're right." Ha-Neul had a sly smile on his face.

Ha-Na placed her stone on the board. "Your move, Lisa."

29

L isa stood at the mare's stall, watching the horse sleep. The sky through the glass ceiling was dark and full of stars. The horse snorted irritably, as though something unpleasant had entered its dreams. Lisa smiled ruefully.

"Can't sleep?" Ha-Neul's voice asked.

She turned and shook her head. "You?"

He shook his head.

"Why not?"

"I'm worried," he said. He nudged his foot at some straw. "I'm worried about us."

She didn't say anything, though she twined her fingers in his when he took her hand.

"You seem distant recently—ever since I walked in on you and Ha-Na talking about what you want to do in the future." He looked expectantly at her for a few moments. "I thought you were starting to like me more."

Adrenaline rushed through her. "It's not that I don't like you, Ha-Neul."

"Then what is it?"

"Things are—slightly complicated."

"What's complicated?"

"When will I stop being a nain? Will I go to university next year? Will—" she stopped as she realized what her next words would be. She whispered, "Will you still want me?"

Ha-Neul pulled her into a hug, a huge smile on his face. "Why are you worried about that? I like you far more than you like me."

She smacked the back of his shoulder but felt his words begin to crush her.

"Honestly, by the way you're acting, people will think you're falling in love with me."

"Oh, gods," she groaned, trying to suppress her emotions, "this man's ego."

He planted a kiss on her forehead. "Don't worry," he said in a soft, sad tone, "I know you're not."

He squeezed her a little closer before he let her go and turned to leave, trying to hide his expression.

"Ha-Neul." He stopped and turned back because of the ache in her tone. Her lip quivered. "I am."

She could see he wasn't breathing. "You are what?"

A short tremble shook her body. "I am falling in love with you."

He cupped her jaw in his hands and leaned in. She froze. He grinned and kissed her cheek, right next to her mouth.

"These past five weeks of courting haven't been for nothing, then."

He held her for a few more minutes before he backed off. She still clutched some of the material at the back of his shirt. He smiled again and kissed her forehead.

"I'm glad I saw you again tonight," he said.

"Me too."

"We should go to bed," he nudged her.

She gave him a small smile. "You can go first. I want to stay a bit longer."

Ha-Neul looked into her eyes a little longer. "Please don't freak out and run away." He clutched her arms a little tighter. "Not now, when you finally seem to be opening up to me."

She stroked his cheek once, and he leaned in to the touch without thinking. "I won't."

"I'll take that as a promise."

She kissed his cheek and leaned in to whisper in his ear. "Go to bed, namchin."

Ha-Neul hugged her tighter, kissed her cheek yet again, and left with a huge smile on his face and a much lighter step—making it obvious how happy he was that she'd called him boyfriend.

She giggled as he walked away and turned her attention back to the mare, who was resting more peacefully, mirroring her state. She stayed for a few more minutes before she left the stable. As she headed back to the servants' lodge, she found Irene waiting for her. She quickened her pace and soon reached her aunt.

"What is it?" she asked in Common, noticing how grave Irene looked.

"Follow me. The wang wishes to speak with you."

She nodded, and they walked as fast as they could without appearing to rush. Neither of them spoke as they entered the palace and made their way to the wang's suite, adrenaline sweeping through Lisa. When the elevator opened, Evan greeted them. He bowed to them and led the way to the door. He knocked twice and waited for an answer before opening it.

"Please go in, my lady," he whispered in Common.

She went in and found the wang standing in front of her with a pleasant smile.

"Please sit, Princess," he said in Common as well, indicating an armchair in the middle of the room while blatantly ignoring the astonishment on her face. They both sat, and he took a few moments to study her. "Do you love him?"

"Wh-what?"

"My oldest son, Geum Ha-Neul. Do you love him?"

"I apologize, Wang-Mama, I—"

"Don't apologize—you shouldn't apologize," he said. "I should be apologizing."

She looked at him with her mouth slightly agape as he genuinely seemed remorseful.

"I know who you are, Vasilisa Aleksandrsdöttir. I've known you your whole life."

She sucked in a deep breath. He knew, yet he had still allowed her in the palace even though he had banished Rosalina. Lisa remembered her father saying he and the wang had attended school together as teenagers and interacted, but with his words, she now wondered if they had been friends.

"I've been hoping you could help change Ha-Neul's mind about spellcasters," the use of the correct term for witches surprised her for a moment, then she realized that his family situation would have allowed him to know the correct classifications for magic users, "which is why I personally placed you near my children from the very beginning of your employment and allowed you to become their nain. Then, when I learned about Ha-Neul's feelings for you, I took full advantage."

All of her interactions with the wang began to make sense. "That's why you told me to tell him what I know about Vires, why you had me stay with him during the party."

He nodded. "I, Geum Dong, Wang of Balhae, have done many things I am not proud of," he paused, his eyes blinking rapidly, "especially toward my own people—your people—and I fired Rosalina when Ha-Neul found out about her situation." He took in a ragged breath and slowly let it out. "It was all to appease my tortured son."

"I assume you mean the incident that killed your wife?" she asked.

The wang nodded and wiped tears from his eyes for a few moments. When he seemed calm, he continued. "Ha-Neul needs to heal, and I believe you are the person to help him."

"But—"

"No." He lifted a hand. "No, please listen." He leaned toward her, touching his fingertips together, pointing them at her. "I know your feelings no matter how hard you try to hide them. You know who sees past all the façade, don't you? You know who is a clairvoyant."

She nodded, not daring to speak the secret out loud.

"I want you to love him, and I want him to love you; however," he became grave, "you must tell him who you really are, and soon." His whole demeanor became kinder and more empathetic. "You know that, don't you?"

"Yes," she breathed out, tears forming. "Ha-Na and I talked about it last week."

"Our families have kept your secret from him long enough. It's time he knows the truth." He watched her carefully until she nodded. "I know it will be hard for both of you, and I know you know that as well. It will be worse the longer you wait."

"I know," she breathed out.

He held out his hand and waited. She placed her hand in his, and he covered it with his other hand.

"No matter what happens, I want you to know that I am grateful for everything you have done for my family, Vasilisa," he said. He patted her hand and withdrew his. "It is late. You have a long day ahead of you tomorrow, so you should go to bed."

They both stood, and she bowed to him, and he bowed to her in return.

"Sleep well, Wang-Mama."

She left the room to find Irene waiting, and all of the emotions she had held in check finally overwhelmed her. She collapsed into the outstretched arms of her aunt, who held her tightly and whispered comfort into her ear as her body trembled with silent sobs.

The generals and top commanding officers beneath them arrived at the palace the weekend before the military review of Old Balhae's forces was to begin. Lisa was by Ha-Neul's side as he greeted each one of the five generals. As General Woo greeted Ha-Neul, his gaze fell upon her, and the cold tendrils that had been cast around her heart the night of the banquet tightened their grip on her for the briefest moment. She couldn't help but shiver just a little bit. Then he moved on to give his greetings to Ha-Na. The wang had excused Su from receiving the guests.

Monday was the opening ceremony of the review, which was held on the palace's largest training ground surrounded by television crews streaming the event live. Each general gave a short speech to the royal family about the might of his army, all to the rousing applause of his army's best squads, who were allowed to be in attendance. Each general from the Central (led by the wanghoo's cousin), Eastern, Southern, and Western Armies spoke vigorously and proudly, except for General Woo of the Northern Army.

"Wang-Mama, you have entrusted me with the training and command of your Northern Army, which, as of late, has been put on alert. We are the first defense between you and those who may rise up against you." His tone was grave, his presence extinguishing any lighthearted atmosphere. "In the games of the review, we—the ones you trust most to keep your nation safe—shall prove that your faith in us is not in vain. We shall prove that we are indeed the best, that we are indeed the army that stands above all others." He paused, looking at the royal family. "We. Shall. Not. Fail."

His soldiers erupted in thunderous applause, and he bowed to the royals, who clapped politely. Lisa froze as her eyes moved chaotically around the training grounds, a strange fog having descended over them, then they stilled as General Woo's eyes caught hers. Something primal held her, and she couldn't breathe. Fear raced through her as the hunger in his eyes threatened to swallow her whole. Her body felt numb as her blood ran cold. The wang stood to give his speech, but she neither saw him nor heard him. She began to shiver violently.

Ha-Neul glanced at her, and the polite smile he wore fell. He touched her hand, and fear replaced his worry. He signaled to Irene, who glanced at Lisa and quickly signaled a few menservants, who rushed to her side just as she collapsed. When she woke, Ha-Neul was by her side, holding her freezing hand while asleep.

She squeezed his fingers and managed to whisper his name.

He sighed and slowly began to wake up. When he saw her looking at him, he straightened, moved closer to her, and held her hand tighter. "Hey, how are you feeling?"

"Like I've been caught in a blizzard," she whispered.

"You don't feel so cold anymore," he said. "It scared me how frozen you were."

"Ha-Neul." She remembered the fog and the strange vision she had seen in it.

"Yes?"

"Has the palace ever been att—?" She stopped, deciding the fog had been an effect of whatever General Woo had done to her.

"What? What is it?"

She shook her head. "Never mind. It must have been a dream."

"But you do feel better?"

She looked at their clasped hands and nodded, feeling warmer.

"Rest for today and return to work tomorrow." He kissed her hand, then her forehead. "Please don't scare me like that again. I was so afraid something was terribly wrong."

She stroked his cheek as he kissed her forehead again. "Go. I'm sure you're needed."

He nodded, squeezed her hand, and left. The cold around her heart began to tighten again, and she fell into a fitful sleep. She left the medical center early in the morning, having washed and eaten there. As she walked through the palace hallways, she kept pinching the corners of her eyes and blinking to clear the strange fog that had returned. Once successful, she noticed someone following her. She glanced back to see General Woo, and the cold tendrils started uncoiling.

"My lady," he said in Common.

She stopped and hesitated before turning to face him. "Woo Daejang-Nim." She bowed.

He stopped a couple of feet away from her. "I hope you are doing better? I saw you faint yesterday and was concerned."

"I-I thank you." She looked down so she didn't have to see the dark void in his eyes. "I am doing better."

He took her hand, bowing, and kissed it just below her knuckles. "I am glad to hear so, Sitting Princess." He whispered her title.

He caught her frightened look and smiled, making her freeze. His smile turned into a hungry smirk. He straightened and drew her closer to him.

"I hope you won't mind my saying that I wish to finish our dance," he said softly into her ear. "Perhaps you will wear a white gown and I a suit of your choosing."

She teetered, feeling faint, and he wrapped one arm around her waist and one around her shoulders. As he looked down at her, she was powerless to move.

"Are you sure you're well enough to be walking about?" he asked in a whisper. The hunger in his eyes was now mingled with pleasure. "Shall I carry you to the medical center, or would you care to go to my private chambers?"

"N—"

He swung her into his arms and easily carried her away. Her body felt frozen. When they turned the corner that led to the medical center, she was ready to drown herself into oblivion.

"Lisa!" Ha-Neul took her from General Woo's arms, and she felt her body start to warm. "You're freezing again." He looked to the general. "Do you know what happened?"

"No, Wangseja-Mama, we were just passing each other, and she collapsed."

"Lisa . . . Lisa! Say something, Lisa!" He looked back to General Woo. "Thank you. I'll take care of her."

General Woo bowed as Ha-Neul carried her into the medical center.

"Doctor! Get out here! She's freezing again!"

A few minutes later, the doctor had wrapped Lisa in warm blankets but left her hands out so Ha-Neul could hold them.

"I told you not to scare me again." He couldn't hide his worry.

"Ha-Neul," she whispered.

"What is it?"

"He . . . he . . . he—" She started sobbing.

He cupped her face in his hands and kissed her forehead, her cheeks, her nose, and her eyelids. Still she cried, her breaths coming in terrified splutters.

"Please, please calm down."

She couldn't, and then, out of desperation, he kissed her lips. She quieted, warmth returning to her lips, and he pulled back, mild shock on his face. They looked at each other and held the gaze a few moments. Her skin warmed considerably underneath his hands. Slowly, she wrapped her hands around the back of his head—her eyes on his lips —and pulled him to her. They kissed again, taking it a little slower, testing each other, and she felt her hunger rise. She deepened the kiss, he matching her, for just a moment before pulling away.

"Don't leave me alone," she said. "Woo Daejang—he terrifies me."

Ha-Neul shook his head. "I won't. I'll have Ha-Na ask to have your things moved to her room. We won't leave you alone. I'll be with you all day, and she'll be with you at night."

Relief and warmth swept through her. "Thank you."

He kissed her again, lingering just a little bit longer. "Let me make the call to Ha-Na."

A cot was set up in Ha-Na's suite, and Lisa's belongings were moved within half an hour. Ha-Neul made as many excuses as he could to keep Lisa by his side, and if it wasn't possible, he saw her safely to Ha-Na. Sometimes Woo Daejang hung at the edges of their vision, looking on with mild curiosity, but Ha-Neul and Ha-Na never left Lisa alone.

They watched the reviews at each of the sparing fields outside several nearby cities with fascination as soldiers remotely controlled agile war machines—humanoid robots —from war stations, shooting dummy bullets at each other, which sent messages of fake damage until the robots were "dead." Lisa always sat in a chair behind his gajok, between Ha-Neul and Ha-Na. Occasionally he would catch his abeoji glancing at her as he turned to talk to either him, Ha-Na, or Evan, who sat to his abeoji's side.

A week after the review began, on a day off from the matches, he and Lisa were walking in the gardens hand in hand. They didn't speak. They just enjoyed each other's company. After a few minutes, they sat on a bench, and he turned to her.

"Do you love me?" he said in a way that let her know he expected nothing less than the truth.

She nodded.

Hope filled his chest. "Will you say it?"

Lisa took a deep breath and let it out slowly. "I love you, Ha-Neul."

He couldn't help but smile. "I knew it."

"What about you, Wangseja-Mama? Do you love me?"

He nodded eagerly.

"Will you say it?"

His smile grew as his emotions for her started to overwhelm him. "I love you, Lisa."

He moved in to kiss her.

"I have something else to tell you," she said quickly.

He paused, a seed of fear cracking open. "What is it?"

"It's . . . actually something to show you."

She held out a seed, and his fear started to take root.

"A seed?" he laughed, trying to weed out the emotion.

She put the seed in her palm and raised it to her mouth. Gently, she began to breathe on it. The seed broke open and grew into a purple lily. Lisa held the flower by its stem. He stared at the flower, the atmosphere around him thick with his embattled emotions.

"Ha-Neul, I'm a—"

"Don't," he pleaded with her, not wanting to understand.

"Ha-Neul—"

"That was quite a—quite a trick. I don't know how you did it, but it was great. Are you cold? It's a bit chilly. I think we should go in." He stood to leave, pulling on her hand.

"I'm a witch, Ha-Neul," she said it quickly, forcefully, carefully.

He stopped, feeling as if he were suddenly dead.

"I'm a witch—from Vires."

Anger burned within him as he turned back to her. "No, you're not."

"Yes, I a—"

"Stop it!" He threw down her hand as his anger boiled into rage. "Stop it. Don't sabotage what we have. You promised not to run away."

"Our relationship would be a lie if I didn't tell you."

"You are not a witch! You can't be. You are Lisa, Illegitim—"

"I am Vasilisa Aleksandrsdóttir," she stood, talking over him, "Sitting Princess of Vires."

Her hanbok lit up and flickered as though it were being consumed by fire and transformed as she spoke, changing into a warm, ivory-colored gown decorated with pearls and a veil trailing from her hair. The transformation lasted less than ten seconds, but it was long enough for him to feel the blood drain from his face. She discarded the withered flower.

"Ha—"

"Shut up." An eerie calm settled over him. "You are stripped of your title as nain—"

"Ha-Neul, please—" Her face contorted in anguish, and she reached out to him.

"—and you are to leave the palace immediately." He backed away and looked her in the eye. All he could feel was hatred. "You are never to set foot within the borders of Old Balhae ever again. Do you understand, witch?"

Her emotions disappeared from her face, though her tears remained, and she perfected her posture. Then she performed a flawless bow. "I understand, Wangseja-Mama."

"Get out of my sight."

She straightened, turned, and walked away from him with such a dignified grace that it crushed him. She turned a corner around a hedge and was out of sight, and he collapsed onto the bench and wept.

"Revolutions are neither inherently good nor evil. They are necessary."

— THE OBSERVANT

32

Ha-Neul entered Ha-Na's suite, and the first thing he noticed was that Lisa's belongings were gone, which made his insides squirm. Ha-Na was comforting Su as she looked up to see who had entered. She stood, shaking with anger.

"What did you do?" she said slowly.

"She lied to us."

"About what?"

"She's a witch, Ha-Na."

"We know. We've known almost since she first came."

He looked at her like she was insane, and her anger intensified.

"Do you know what it took for her to tell you? Do you know that she could barely walk as she left, that Irene had her arm out around her just in case she could no longer support herself?" Her voice grew in volume as Ha-Neul's emotions went into a new turmoil.

"Do you realize how much you hurt her?" Su asked through his tears.

"What about me?" he screamed, unable to maintain control. "What about me!"

The door slid open, and Irene walked in alone. She bowed to them. "Wangseja-Mama, the wang wishes to speak to you."

He and his nammae continued to glare at each other.

"I have *never* been so ashamed of you," Ha-Na said. "You are wrong this time."

Devastation and rage warred for control inside of him.

"Wangseja-Mama, please, your abeoji is waiting."

Ha-Neul left the room seething, and Irene followed him. When they were alone in the elevator, he asked, "Why did you bring her here?"

"She needed money for university." Her tone was flat.

"You never should have allowed her in. It is against the law, and there will be repercussions."

The elevator door opened, and Irene led him to the suite door, opening it for him without announcing their presence. She closed the door behind him, leaving him alone with his abeoji. The wang sat in his usual chair, looking rather grim in his contemplation.

"Abeoji." He tried to look calm.

The wang looked up at him. "Please sit down, Ha-Neul."

Ha-Neul sat without being able to look up as his abeoji studied him. He was afraid what his abeoji might think, knowing he had fallen in love with a witch.

"I'm sorry, Adeul." His abeoji's tone held a lot of pain.

Ha-Neul looked up at him in surprise. His abeoji had tears in his eyes, and his shoulders sagged under some burden. "Wh-why?"

"I'm sorry for letting you get to this point." He wiped his eyes with a handkerchief, making Ha-Neul feel even more astonished. "Your eomeoni's death was nobody's fault. It was simply a tragic accident."

Ha-Neul stared in disbelief. Nobody in his gajok shared his feelings about witches. "Abeoji—"

"Don't live your life in fear of magic. It will only destroy you, Ha-Neul. It will destroy you and everything you love." He took a breath to calm himself. "Your fear has nearly destroyed a relationship you will never find a replacement for, and it may destroy the relationship between you and your nammae. After it has destroyed those relationships, it will surely destroy you. So please think carefully about what is truly important to you."

Ha-Neul felt numb. "I don't understand, Abeoji."

Someone knocked on the door. His abeoji looked up.

"Excuse me Wang-Mama, it is Evan."

His abeoji swallowed his worry and dried his eyes. "Enter."

Evan entered looking concerned. His abeoji nodded, his expression all business now, and turned back to him. "Ha-Neul, please take my advice or at least consider it. I don't want you to regret what happened today."

Ha-Neul nodded, barely aware that he did, and left the room feeling more confused than ever.

33

Geum Dong looked up at Evan, his brilliant teenage chamsagwan.

"Vasilisa has made it safely to the train, Wang-Mama," Evan said. "I drove her myself and bought her a direct ticket to Vires City, just like you requested. Aleksandr and Ivan will pick her up at the station."

He was relieved, but his old chingu's thoughts still concerned him. "What did Aleksandr have to say?"

"He did not say much, but he will wait to see what Wangseja will do." Evan seemed to hesitate for the briefest moment. "I believe he is afraid our efforts have failed, Wang-Mama."

"Why do you think so?" His curiosity was piqued.

"The assuredness he voiced when he told me how his plans were definitely on hold to see if Wangseja will overcome his fear of magic for Vasilisa seemed forced. I think something may be wrong."

Geum Dong took a deep breath to steady his nerves, but his eyes wandered around the room until they settled back on Evan's face. "Whatever it is, there is nothing we can do.

Alek is a master strategist. If he cannot control his plans while we have no idea what they are, then we have no hope of succeeding in preventing them. Let's wait and hope for the best." He paused as despair crept into him. "You are prepared for the worst, aren't you?"

Evan looked solemn. "Always, Wang-Mama."

He felt reassured.

34

Both Ha-Na and Su refused to speak to Ha-Neul. He carried out his business and watched the review as though nothing had happened. At one point, he turned to a nain, calling her Lisa, and his nammae looked over at him. Ha-Na quickly turned away, but Su watched him for a while. Over the next couple of days, Ha-Neul became increasingly despondent. He missed Lisa more and more.

The night before the closing ceremony for the review, he lay tossing and turning in his bed, unable to get her out of his mind. He slipped his hand under one of his pillows, and it snagged on a chain. He sat up and lifted the pillow. Tears slid down his cheeks as he picked up Lisa's raven's-eye necklace and finally accepted that he needed her. He fell asleep clutching it.

The next day, he sat on his abeoji's left, with Ha-Na and Su to Ha-Neul's left, Lisa's necklace hanging from around the high collar of his royal uniform for all to see—including the television crews. His abeoji glanced over at him before looking back at the Northern Army's victory procession.

"There are all kinds of magic in this world, Ha-Neul," his abeoji said.

"I know," he said, wondering where the conversation was headed.

"Witches, druids, readers, and dream walkers. We Balhaens even have Samjogo, the deity that lives in the Northern Mountains beyond the territories—"

"I know, Abeoji," he said a little impatiently.

His abeoji sighed. "This gajok has magic in its blood."

Ha-Neul looked at his abeoji in disbelief. "What do you mean?"

His abeoji held up a hand, indicating he could not respond straightaway, as his attention was focused on the procession. Ha-Neul looked down at the grounds as well— at Woo Daejang, who was now staring at the wangsil. Woo Daejang stood in front of his war machines, his hand out, palm toward them. In the center of his palm, the daejang had drawn a bright-blue circle. The tall war machines lifted their guns above his head, and in the instant his palm flashed, a bright light filled the stadium and the war machines opened fire. A force knocked Ha-Neul onto his back as the dummy bullets ripped into the box, clouds of red mist filling his vision and screams of agony deafening his ears.

Evan crouched in front of him and shouted, "Get up and move!"

The chamsagwan helped Ha-Na and Su to their feet and pushed them toward the barracks, away from the shredded bodies in the box, as the palace troops moved in to defend them.

"Go!" Evan shouted again over the screaming and gunfire.

They ran down the steps of the box as more bullets ripped into it. Evan followed them until they entered the barracks.

"What was that?" Ha-Neul yelled, his ears ringing.

"Apparently Woo Daejang is a witch," Evan said.

The silence hung heavy around them.

"Where's Abeoji?" Su said, fear in his voice.

Evan didn't look at them. "He didn't make it."

"How?" Ha-Na asked, becoming hysterical. "How? Those bullets—they shouldn't be real."

"The spell on Woo's palm made them real," Evan answered.

A bloodied palace soldier entered the barracks. "Move."

Evan led the way as they ran through the barracks, taking them to the commanding officer's room, where he shoved the desk aside.

"Shelter B route, prime," Evan shouted.

The floor slid away to reveal an old elevator shaft. Evan helped them jump in before getting in himself. The opening in the floor above them slid closed as they dropped several yards down the dark shaft, then zoomed into a tunnel. After a couple of minutes, they came to a stop, and a light flickered on.

"Keep moving," Evan said.

The tunnel around them rumbled, and dirt filled the air.

"What was that?" Su asked, coughing in the dust.

"The vertical tunnel has been filled in. This one will collapse as well in ten minutes."

They picked up their pace to a jog and soon came to a door with a handprint scanner. Evan put his hand on it, and the door popped open. When Evan had shut the door, it sealed itself, and the chamber rumbled. A light that was warm like the sun suddenly illuminated what appeared to be a common living area.

"What's going on?" Ha-Neul asked.

"I don't know," Evan answered.

"You seem to know a whole lot more than we do!"

"I have been tasked with keeping you safe, and that is what I will do."

"How?" Ha-Na asked. Tears were streaming down her dirtied face.

"I am not sure yet. I need information before I decide what is best." Evan walked over to a desk with two tablets on top of it. "This shelter can keep us safe for a little while. There are five bedrooms with some extra clothes. You should shower and change."

Ha-Neul looked at his nammae more carefully—they were covered in blood. He looked at his clothes and hands to find that he was drenched in it as well.

"Our—our abeoji." Ha-Na turned back to Evan, her tears coming faster.

Evan paused and looked at them with empathy. "You have plenty of time to grieve." He rubbed his hair, making it stand on end, which gave him an even younger appearance. "We have the time."

Woo Daejang Leads "Revolution" for Witches
Geum Dong Wang among Confirmed Dead
Woo Daejang Occupies Palace—Calls for Cease-Fire
Northern Army Defeats Southern. Eastern Surrenders
Central Army Joins Northern, Represses Western: Has the
war become a family affair?

Public Transportation Reports Battle Damages—Costs in the Trillions
Prince Aleksandr Dmitrisson Keeps His Silence

Ha-Neul sat at the desk with a tablet, reading the news headlines and viewing the short clips underneath them. Ha-Na stood behind him, reading over his shoulder.

"It's only been four days," she whispered. "How can he win so fast?"

"He's the top daejang," he said bitterly, "and a witch. We practically handed him the kingdom. It also doesn't help that Gwon Daejang betrayed us."

"I can't believe Eomeoni's sachon would betray us," Ha-Na said. "She treated him so well, even when no one else in their gajok did, and he was always one of our favorite relatives."

Evan entered the living area from a heavily secured door to their right.

"What did you learn?" Ha-Neul asked.

"Irene is working with Woo Daejang and seems to have been doing so for a while."

Ha-Neul clasped the raven's eye, his fear spiking.

"Do you think Lisa—?" Ha-Na started.

"No, noona." The words burst out of him with confidence.

Evan and Ha-Na looked at him with sympathy, but Su came out of his room looking angry.

"Lisa's not a traitor!" he shouted. "She wouldn't do that to us!"

"Su," Ha-Na said.

"I agree with you, Mama," Evan said to Ha-Neul and Su.

"Can we make it out of the palace without Irene?" Ha-Neul asked.

"It will be difficult. I do not know of a way to leave without going above ground."

"Ask Irene to help," Su told him.

"Wangja-Mama, it is not that simple," Evan said.

"Ask her to help!" Su screamed.

"She's helping the traitor!" Ha-Neul shouted as his emotions rose up like bile.

"No! No, she's not!" Su fell to the ground and started crying.

Ha-Na covered her face, and Ha-Neul knew she was crying as well. He looked at Evan for guidance, but the teenage boy just studied him.

"Is there no else we can trust?" he asked.

Evan shook his head.

Ha-Neul laid his head on the desk, burying his face in his arms as the crushing weight of his anguish and guilt became too much to bear.

35

Ha-Neul lay in bed, staring up at the metal-and-concrete ceiling and fingering the raven's-eye necklace under his shirt. Lisa consumed his thoughts, which shifted between anger, resentment, longing, and guilt. He never wanted to see her, but he still needed to hear her voice and feel her touch. With such emotions and desires cycling through him, driving him mad, he rolled out of bed and went into the common area to find Su and Ha-Na playing a card game. Evan had left an hour ago to search for an escape route again.

His nammae glanced up at him and studied him briefly before returning to their game. Their situation was still a little awkward, but the events of the closing ceremony had trumped most of their ill feelings toward each other. Ha-Neul sat by them, watching their game progress, and when an opening came, Su dealt Ha-Neul a hand so he could join. He gave his dongsaeng a grateful smile and played with them, though the awkwardness persisted.

Half an hour into their game, they heard the elevator. They glanced at the clock, then at each other, puzzled.

"It's too early for Evan to be back," Ha-Na said.

"Maybe something happened," Ha-Neul suggested.

The security door slid open, and Ha-Neul's heart began to race as his stomach dropped. Ha-Na gasped in surprise, and Su hid behind Ha-Neul as an angry Rosalina walked in. Ha-Na's former nain pulled out a disk and flung it at them, a hissing sound reaching Ha-Neul's ears and a sweet scent filling his nostrils. Within moments, he was lying on the floor, unable to speak.

Rosalina, a short, curvy woman with an imposing presence, dragged him across the floor before setting him on a dining chair and tying his hands and feet to it before propping his head up so he could look straight at her. Then she turned back and did the same to Ha-Na and Su. Once everyone was bound, she sprayed a mist into their faces that gave them back the use of their tongues, leaving Ha-Neul for last.

"What are you doing here, Rosalina?" Ha-Na asked, a trace of fear in her voice.

"How did you find us?" Ha-Neul added.

"Woo Daejang invited me to offer me a military position," Rosalina said. "I happened to notice the wang's new chamsagwan coming out of the kitchen one day, so I kept watch."

"What do you want?" Ha-Neul asked, fear clenching his stomach as Rosalina's hatred-filled eyes burned into him.

"Justice," she said, pulling a knife from behind her back. "I want justice, maldito culebra!"

"Rosalina! Please don't!" Ha-Na barely wriggled in her chair. "Hasn't he been punished enough?"

"No, Gongju-Mama, he hasn't," Rosalina spat. "He made it impossible for me to find a new job because I donated half of my wage to Vires welfare charities."

"It was against the law," Ha-Neul said. "No government employee is allowed to provide for a witch citizen."

"Yet your gajok did," Rosalina taunted him. "In fact, you even courted her."

Ha-Neul couldn't speak. His emotions welled up inside of him at Rosalina's reminder of Lisa.

"I don't know what Vasilisa saw in you to make her want to date you, but you never deserved her. You should join your abeoji to pay for your crimes."

Rosalina stood, drawing closer to Ha-Neul with her knife ready as Su cried and Ha-Na protested. As she raised the knife, Ha-Neul closed his eyes, tears running down his cheeks, and he could only think of how he would never be able to apologize to Lisa. A dam burst within him, and he sobbed.

"Callate! Deja de estar chillando!" Rosalina spat. "Why are you crying so much? Do you finally realize you deserve this?"

Though his vision was blurry, he looked into her eyes. "Can you tell Lisa I'm sorry?"

Her face darkened. "Sleep with demons, you puta madre."

As she moved to stab him, Ha-Na screamed and Su wailed.

"Rosalina Maria Anita Sigüenza!" a woman's voice cried out. "Stop!"

"Amparo." Rosalina looked shocked, then guilty. "Mija, mira lo que haces?"

A younger-looking version of Rosalina came into view and snatched her knife away. "This is *not* the best path." She spoke in Haeyoche.

"Says who? La Observante?"

"Si."

Anger filled Rosalina. "I do not believe that."

A bird's sudden croak shocked everyone in the room before Ha-Neul felt the animal settle on his shoulder, its black feathers tickling his cheek as it ruffled them. Rosalina stared at the bird in awe before turning her rage filled eyes on Ha-Neul.

"Porque chingados estas protengiendo a este carbon que es tan malo?" she spat at the bird.

The bird croaked back at her.

The woman called Amparo moved Rosalina to the side and pulled on Ha-Neul's necklace, bringing it out of his shirt. Rosalina gasped as Amparo pulled out her own raven's-eye necklace.

"Vasilisa gave this to you, did she not?" Amparo asked.

"She did," he answered. "Why does it matter?"

"It was your eomeoni's," Amparo told him. "Now it is yours. Protect it; keep it with you, Wangseja-Mama." She turned to Rosalina. "Déjalo en paz. El es de la Observante."

"How do you know all this?" Ha-Neul asked, desperate.

Amparo looked back down at him and smiled before glancing at Ha-Na and Su, whom she stared at a moment longer before she made eye contact with Ha-Neul again. "I am a clairvoyant, or a reader, as you would say. Now, let me tell you one more thing, Wangseja-Mama: your path will be the most difficult of anyone's in this world."

She bowed to him and left after handing Rosalina the knife, the raven following her out. Rosalina tightened her grip on the weapon before using it to cut them free.

"Después de todo lo que a hecho!" she murmured before catching Ha-Neul's eye. "Prove my yeo-dangsaeng's trust in you right, Wangseja-Mama."

"Wait!" Ha-Na called after her as she made to leave. "Can you help us?"

Rosalina turned to her. "I can't, but I know who can. Once you're free of this place, then maybe I can, but only if he"—she glared at Ha-Neul—"proves himself worthy."

She stormed away.

No one spoke for a long time. Ha-Neul couldn't because he was trying to process the whole situation, but one thing kept entering his mind: he needed and wanted to see Lisa to at least apologize.

"Hyeong," Su said.

"Yeah?"

"A magic user just helped you," he said.

Ha-Neul's thoughts turned to Amparo, and he was surprised to find a sense of gratitude blossoming within him. "Yeah, she did."

"Evan's going to freak out," Su added.

Despite everything, Ha-Neul laughed, then cried again.

36

Evan walked through the halls of the palace with his eyes cast down but not unaware, careful not to miss anyone again who might have taken notice of him. He observed the guards' positions and movements, and the servants and officials who could possibly identify him. He stayed away from the more restricted sections of the palace where there were less people but he was better known.

After a couple of hours in the palace, he went out to the grounds, entered a shed to change his clothes to the winter uniform of a gardener, and slowly made his way from the servants' road to the main entrance and back. When he reentered the shed, he stopped short. Irene sat on a stool.

"Hello, Evan." Her voice was calm as she addressed him in Common, but she looked haggard and cold in the early winter weather.

"Irene." He mimicked her tone.

"I hope you have been doing all right over these past couple of months."

"Yes, thank you. How about you?"

She shook her head. "Things have been much better."

He studied her, remaining silent to make her talk.

"I spoke with Rosalina and Amparo. Are they still safe?" she asked quietly. "Did you keep them safe?"

After a moment of determining if she was sincere, he nodded. She broke down into tears as a huge weight seemed to lift off her countenance. He let her cry until she could regain her composure and dry her eyes.

"So they know what's happening out there?"

"Yes." He still watched her closely and surveyed the shed. "I thought you worked for Woo Su-Han."

"It wasn't supposed to be this way," she whispered. "He was only supposed to free us."

"I have to get them to safety."

"Why haven't you used any of the tunnels out?"

"I don't know where they are."

"Didn't the wang tell you?"

"He only knew the general locations." Evan finally relaxed. "Can you help us?"

She nodded. "Which shelter are you in?"

"Shelter B."

Irene looked relieved and smiled. "That's perfect. The best escape-route entrance is fairly close to that shelter."

"We'll need to disguise them. General Woo has declared them dead and has even given evidence. If they're seen so quickly—"

"I know." Irene's eyes wandered. "Luckily Wangseja has practice blending in, but Gongju and Wangja—especially Wangja—haven't been out as much."

"They'll be fine. Wangseja has been working with them to speak Haeyoche and Haeche comfortably, especially with Gongju."

"Then let's get them out." Irene stood and moved to the

door. She stopped and looked at him with curiosity. "By the way, Evan, how did you manage to get the wang's trust?"

He gave her a cryptic smile. "I proved to him how valuable I can be."

She sighed. "Everyone has secrets, don't they?"

He nodded.

"I'll make contact when I get clothes for them," she said. "You can't have much food left."

"About a week's worth. They're anxious to move."

"Being confined for so long will do that to anyone." She opened the door. "I'll see you soon."

Evan changed his clothes and made his way back into the palace. He walked with purpose as he made a random path throughout the hallways. A few times, he made his way into storage closets when he saw high officials or nain who might recognize him. He made his way toward the kitchen and went into the canned-food pantry. He slipped in between the far wall and a shelf, his hand brushing the wall as he went. A door opened and he fell in, an elevator taking him to the shelter.

He entered the common area to find Ha-Na making a simple meal, Ha-Neul reading the news, and Su building an intricate card castle. They looked up when the door opened, and they noticeably relaxed.

"I'm only a few minutes late," he said in Haeyoche.

"Twenty," Ha-Na scolded him.

"I ran into Irene." He went to help her as he spoke. "Apparently she was the one Rosalina told you about."

Su looked up at him, hopeful. "Is she going to help us?"

"Yes."

"But you said she's working for Woo Daejang," Ha-Na said.

"She didn't know he would attack your gajok. She

wants you safe."

"How can you be sure?" Ha-Neul asked, his eyes narrowed in suspicion.

Evan looked from him to Ha-Na to Su, who seemed to be wondering the same thing.

"I know when people can be trusted—most of the time."

"Most of the time?" Ha-Neul asked.

He nodded. "I couldn't tell with Woo Daejang."

"But you can with Irene?" Ha-Na asked.

He nodded again.

"Are you going out again tomorrow?" Ha-Neul asked.

"No, I'll stay here just in case. Irene should come soon." He started setting the table. "She may be able to give us better information than what we can gather from the tablet."

"Will she help us retake the palace?" Ha-Neul asked.

"When the time comes, and if she is still in the palace, I believe she will."

They were silent as they sat down to eat and all through the meal.

"Where will we go?" Ha-Neul asked as he and Evan washed the dishes.

"I'm not sure," he said. "Anywhere that's safe. Can you think of any places in Balhae? We can't risk crossing the border since Woo has closed it down and it is constantly patrolled."

Ha-Neul didn't speak again until they were almost done with the cleaning. "We'll go to Vires. Woo Daejang won't expect us to go there, especially me."

He looked up at Ha-Neul and noticed Ha-Na and Su were listening. "Are you sure? Vires could be the worst place for you."

"For me, perhaps, but not for them."

"Are you sure going to Lisa is best?"

Ha-Neul nodded.

"We can try it. Your abeoji had me study every route throughout Balhae. We can make it safely, but it will take time."

"Apparently we've got plenty," Ha-Neul reminded him.

Su came up to them. "Are we going to go see Lisa?"

Ha-Na was listening openly now.

"We're going to try," Ha-Neul said.

"Assa!" Su cheered.

Starting that night and for the next three days, they mapped out possible routes to Vires and gathered the hidden money in the shelter to plan for expenses as best as possible. Evan and Ha-Neul were debating which mountain pass into Vires would be safest should it be snowing when they heard the lock on the door click. The siblings bolted for a room, and Evan pulled a gun from beneath his shirt. He aimed it at the door as it swung open and Irene stepped in. She froze when she saw the gun. He grinned and put it away.

"You seem very familiar with that weapon," Irene said in Common. "Almost like a soldier, but there's nothing about that in your file."

"The wang kept a lot out of my file." Evan looked toward the rooms. In a louder voice and in Haeyoche, he said, "It's Irene."

Su burst out of the room first and flung his arms around her. Irene stroked his hair and began to weep. She looked up at Ha-Neul and Ha-Na, relief sweeping through her. Ha-Na went to Irene next and hugged her, and she cried even harder.

"I am so sorry," she whispered in Hasoseoche. "I am so, so sorry."

They sat around the dining table, Irene dabbing at her eyes with a handkerchief.

"I was a messenger to Prince Aleksandr," the bomo sang-goong told them. "As his sister-in-law, I have private lines of communication with him. I gave information on all of you, and based on that, he made his decisions. The revolution was never supposed to overthrow the wangsil, and it was never supposed to take place when it did. The revolution was only supposed to free the northern territories."

"Then why are you staying with Woo Daejang?" Ha-Neul asked.

"I knew if you were alive you would need help from within the palace," Irene said. "I was going to wait until today, the end of the month, before—rethinking what I should do."

"To see if we were alive?" Ha-Na asked.

Irene nodded. They were quiet for a few minutes.

"You should go to Vires." The bomo sang-goong looked at the table as she spoke.

They stared at her.

"Why do you say that?" Ha-Neul asked.

"Your abeoji . . . and the prince . . ." Irene took a deep breath. "They were chingu many years ago." The bomo sang-goong gave Ha-Neul an apologetic look.

"They were . . ." Ha-Na shook her head, her head reeling in confusion. "But he never spoke of . . . Oh, gods, Ha-Neul," she looked at him as realization hit her, "his chingu Alex."

"His school chingu Alex?" he asked.

"Yes," Irene said, "the same. After your eomeoni's death, he talked about him as if he were two different people. So all you knew was that your abeoji and his chingu went to the same school as Aleksandr Dmitrisson."

Ha-Neul looked extremely uncomfortable.

"We were going there anyway," Su said.

Irene looked around the table and settled on Ha-Neul last. "Why?"

"He wants Lisa back," Su said happily.

Ha-Na hid her grin behind her hand, but Irene's expression remained unchanged.

"That—that may be . . . difficult," the bomo sang-goong said.

"I know," Ha-Neul said, "but I've got to try."

Irene looked away and wiped her eyes again. "I would let him know that you're going to him, but I'm not sure if Woo Su-Han has tapped into my lines of communication with him."

"Are they—" Ha-Na started.

"Aleksandr has privately shown displeasure at the daejang's deviation to the plan, but nothing more," Irene answered. Her volume dropped as she said, "He probably feels he can't.

"Anyway, we should hurry." Irene was all business now. "I went to two other shelters and gathered the merits from them. I have backpacks waiting for you in the escape tunnel. I have clothes and some dried provisions for you in the backpacks as well as the palace's top-of-the-line tablets, without the tracking devices, of course. While you are going through the palace, you will need different clothes. I brought musuri clothes for you, Gongju-Mama, and manservant uniforms for the rest of you. Wangja-Mama, you'll have to pretend you're slightly older than you are."

Su began to fidget excitedly.

From beneath her jeogori and chima, Irene pulled a cloth packet. "First, we need to cut your hair."

Each of them took a turn. Ha-Na's long hair became a fashionable bob, while Su's hair became a buzz cut. Irene took longer with Ha-Neul, giving him a shorter hairstyle that showed off his many piercings. When she was done with their hair, Irene gave them their clothes—Ha-Na a wig done up in a musuri's bun, and flesh colored plugs for Ha-Neul's piercings—looking them over once they finished changing.

"Good. You look good. Gongju-Mama, you will need to follow me as though I am leading you to do a chore. You have seen musuri in the halls; I hope you know how to act. Wangseja-Mama and Wangja-Mama, follow Evan. We will leave twenty minutes apart and go to the third cleaning closet," Irene said to Evan, "so it's not too far away."

He nodded. "How do we get into the tunnel?"

"Omega route open," the bomo sang-goong said. "It'll open quickly and closes after twenty seconds."

"How did you find it?" Evan asked.

"I found the hard copies of the blueprints a few years ago," Irene said. "I also had to decode the activation words."

"Okay," Evan looked around at them. "Are we ready to go, or do you want to eat first?"

They shook their heads.

"Let's just go," Ha-Na said.

"Then let's hurry, Gongju-Mama." Irene motioned for her to follow, and they went into the elevator. "We will have to squeeze between the shelf and wall, so be careful that you do not make any noise."

"Okay."

The door opened, and Irene grabbed Ha-Na and pushed her against the shelf. The door quickly closed behind them. The bomo sang-goong let her go and moved to the left. When Irene reached the edge, she peeked out.

"Won't they notice? The kitchen staff?" Ha-Na whispered as Irene waved for her to follow.

"No, it's hard to see who walks into this pantry for this very reason."

They left the pantry, and Ha-Na lowered her head and eyes but kept Irene's chima in view. The bomo sang-goong led her at a quick pace but one that wouldn't raise much notice. Even then, her heart beat wildly. Some of the kitchen staff tried to catch Irene's attention, but she offered a quick apology and kept moving. Ha-Na breathed a little easier once they were out.

They made their way quickly through the hallways. Ha-Na stiffened every time a palace guard, all of whom now wore the markings of the Northern Army, passed them. Irene stopped in front of a portrait and ran a finger along the left side of its frame. A door opened. She grabbed Ha-Na and pushed her in before quickly turning to disarm a guard of his blade and pinning his arm behind his back. She put a hand over his mouth and forced him into the closet.

"Close the door," Irene hissed to Ha-Na. As she did so,

Irene said the code words, and the back wall slid away to reveal another elevator. "Hurry in."

Ha-Na entered the elevator, and the doors snapped shut behind her. When the doors opened again, she stepped out into a semi-lit tunnel and waited for several minutes before the doors opened again and her nam-dongsaeng stepped out.

"Where are Evan and Irene?" she asked.

"Dealing with a couple of guards," Ha-Neul said.

Two minutes later, Evan and Irene joined them.

"Hurry," they both said.

Irene bent down, reached into a shadowed corner, and tossed each of them a backpack and thick coat. "Change at the end of the tunnel and get out of Balhae City as quickly as possible. Woo will soon figure out you are escaping the palace."

When they had slung on the backpacks, they moved to hug her again.

"No, just go, please. I will be fine."

"Thank you, Irene," Ha-Neul said. Then he grabbed Ha-Na's and Su's hands and led them away from Irene.

I rene stopped Evan before he joined the others.

"I don't know who you are," she said low enough so the siblings wouldn't hear her or the fear and awe in her voice, "but I trust you with them. I know you'll keep them safe. Head to Jucheon in Jeoncheon Province. General Moon Seong will help you there."

He squeezed her hand affectionately. "Stay safe yourself."

She lightly shoved him toward the tunnel and watched

as he ran to catch up to the siblings. She continued to watch them as they all started to jog. Then she turned back to the elevator and spoke the code words, traveling back up to the closet where blood soaked the floor. She clung to the shelves above it to avoid walking through it and exited the closet, going back to her normal routine as though nothing had happened.

The tunnel ended below a basement noraebang. They knew this instantly from the stripped-down melodies and either drunken or terrible singing coming from the room above the exit hatch. Unfortunately, they must have arrived there at the beginning of the group's hour or right in the middle of a two-hour run. They waited quietly until they were sure there was no more sound coming from above before they opened the hatch and peeked out at the room from beneath a couch. Everything was quiet. Evan and Ha-Neul moved the couch before jumping out to help Ha-Na and Su out of the opening. More terrible music drifted in from other rooms.

"We're going to surprise the employee when we walk out," Ha-Na said as Evan and Ha-Neul replaced the couch.

"Hopefully he'll be slightly drunk and we can get away by paying for a couple of hours," Ha-Neul said. He looked to Evan. "Can we spare that much?"

"I don't know. I've never been to one of these things."

"I want to go," Su said.

Evan nodded. "Ha-Neul, you pay."

He pulled some bills from his backpack and chose a couple of them. They left the room and walked toward the cashier's desk. A man about his and Ha-Na's age sat watching a small television set and looked up at them in surprise. Ha-Neul grinned and set down the money before following the others out of the aptly named "Wang's Escape Noraebang." They went up the narrow stairway to the busy street. People went in and out of bars, nightclubs, and other entertainment rooms or just walked the street.

"We're in the downtown area," he said. "The train station should be a ten-minute walk from here," he pointed down the street to their right. "We should get a train to the next city and take it slow from there—away from security cameras."

"Let's go," Evan said.

They weaved their way through the city, the crowds thinning significantly once they crossed a large intersection outside of downtown. Su let go of the hem of Ha-Na's shirt but still jittered excitedly. When they reached the train station, Evan led them to the lockers.

"What are we doing here?" Ha-Na asked.

"Surround me to give me some more cover," Evan said.

They did as he told them, and he thumbed open locker 621.

"I have several lockers rented under my name in every city that has public lockers"—Evan pulled out a pair of suspenders filled with ammunition clips, unzipped his coat, and lifted his shirt, revealing a well-muscled body for how slight he was —"that are filled with supplies. They are all locker 621—"

"Why 621?" Su asked.

Evan hesitated before saying in a soft voice, "It was the day my world changed." He shut the locker and locked it again as it was still filled with other items. "The pass code is 0617 if you ever need to get in a locker."

"Without you?" Ha-Na asked.

"It's a possibility," Evan said. "Let's go."

He took them to the ticket counter and bought each of them a ticket for the next train north. They made their way down to the platform and boarded the waiting train. Evan and Ha-Na sat behind him and Su. Ha-Na and Su started falling asleep before the train started moving almost ten minutes later. Ha-Neul had just started to nod off when Evan shook all of them awake as the train started to slow an hour later, making Ha-Na lean forward.

"Someone may have recognized you," Evan said. "Stick close to me and do as I say."

All nodded and grabbed their backpacks. Once the train stopped, Evan pointed them away from a man who was casually dressed but seemed to take a little too much interest in them. Ha-Neul helped Evan rush the other two off the train—he in the lead and Evan following behind. Evan muttered instructions to them as he scanned the platform and station. They went up to the main level of the station, staying on the outskirts of the crowd but walking with it. Soon they noticed four men monitoring their movements.

Evan instructed them to head outside and away from the building, taking them away from the busy street and down less crowded ones.

"What—" Ha-Na began.

"Trust me," Evan hissed, leading them down an alley and quickly finding three different spots for them to hide.

Evan hid out of their sight. Several footsteps came from opposite ends of the alley. Ha-Neul shrank back farther into his hiding spot behind a Dumpster that gave him a limited view of the alleyway entrance.

"They're in here," a man said.

He held his breath as they began to search the area. He heard a faint pop and then muffled gunshots. Men started shouting and firing.

"Where?"

"Two o'clock!"

"No! Six o'clock!"

They kept shouting until one man was breathing heavily somewhere in the alley. Then everything was silent.

"Where—?"

There was a pop and two gunshots. Someone moved around randomly out in the alley. There was a hushed murmuring, like into a com-device, and then more silence.

"It's safe to come out now," Evan said.

They came out to find ten bodies strewn throughout the alley. They looked at Evan to find him unscathed.

"How did you do that?" Su looked awed.

Evan looked them over and relaxed. "You're all fine. It doesn't matter how; we just need to get out fast. Anybody else will be off our trail for a little while. I made sure of that," he finished, leading them out the other side of the alley.

"The buses would have stopped by now," Ha-Neul said.

"We're not getting a ride. We're walking. They know we're here, so we can't risk getting trapped in a vehicle right now."

"But the next town—" Ha-Na started to say.

"We'll need to walk all night," Evan said. "We can reach it by afternoon and find a place to rest."

"Are we going to travel mostly at night?" Su asked.

Evan shook his head. "We'll move as much as possible, but like now, we'll be walking quite a bit."

They stopped talking and kept walking, sticking to crowds on busy streets or to the shadows in residential areas. At one point, Evan sent Ha-Neul and Ha-Na into a corner convenience store to buy bottled water and some food before they left the city. Evan led them silently, staying far enough away from the highway so observant drivers wouldn't spot them. Their pace was fast despite the fact they were walking across the snow-dusted, forested slopes of mountains. Three hours after leaving the city, Evan stopped them and had them eat some of the food before making them walk the rest of the night.

By morning, they were out of the mountains and headed toward a small town's skyline, reaching its outskirts by midmorning. Evan led them to a cheap hotel. They each took a brief turn using the bathroom before stuffing their dirty clothes into a laundry chute and resting on their individual floor mattresses. Evan seemed to stay awake the whole time as their clean laundry was already packed into their backpacks when he woke them up five hours later. They gathered their belongings after using the bathroom again and left the hotel. Su spotted a street-food stall, and they ate a good meal as a middle-aged woman moaned about the lack of business because of the revolution. They ate quickly, paid, and wished her better business.

"The railroad for this town is still under reconstruction," Evan said. "We can get a bus to the next town and walk from there."

They nodded and followed his lead.

39

Three miles outside the third town, the nammae stopped in their tracks and surveyed the ruined landscape in front of them. The rice fields and grasslands were deeply gouged and cratered, and scrap metal or chunks of human-shaped war machines were strewn across the land or stuck up, half buried, from wicked-looking graves. Even aircraft lay in ruin across the cold battleground.

"There'll be dozens more across Old Balhae," Evan said. "It'll be easier to clean up after winter is over."

Ha-Na shook her head, her expression one of utter disbelief.

"Fall was too difficult to clean up?" Ha-Neul felt himself shaking with anger. "No, he left this on purpose. He wants Old Balhae to suffer. This should have been cleared and prepared for spring."

Evan put a hand on his shoulder. "We have to go, but be prepared for worse. The fighting was more intense toward the north."

The battlefield stretched for miles, and the sight worsened the farther they went. Where there were once groves of trees, there were now burnt matchsticks and splinters. The metal graves grew in number.

"Who knew a bloodless war could cause so much destruction," Ha-Na said.

"I wonder how many soldiers actually died," Evan said.

Ha-Neul shot him a scathing look.

"Wh-what do you mean?" she asked, looking between them. "None controlling the war machines should have died."

Evan looked uncomfortable.

"How could soldiers die?" Su asked.

"Let's take a quick break," Evan said.

They found a patch of ground blocked from view by near-whole war machines. Ha-Na and Su looked to Ha-Neul for an explanation.

"You know that soldiers remotely pilot these war machines—everyone does," he said, "but in times of war, it's not through hand controls."

Ha-Na leaned away from him, looking apprehensive. "How, then?"

"A helmet mentally links the soldiers to the war machines," he said. "It increases reaction time and creates smoother movement for the machines. However, the soldiers must go into a lucid, dreamlike state to control their machines. The helmets assess the damage the machines take, or will soon receive, and are programmed to wake the soldiers before the machine receives a fatal blow, but if the damage is a surprise . . ."

"Oh, gods." Ha-Na looked sick and ready to faint, and Su was ready to break down into hysterical sobbing.

Ha-Neul shot another scathing glance at Evan, who looked extremely uncomfortable at this point. Ha-Na went to her hands and knees, coughing and hacking nearly to the point of vomiting. Evan went to her side and started rubbing her back while Ha-Neul went to Su to calm his dongsaeng down. After several minutes, Ha-Na stopped being sick, slowly got to her feet, and started walking, looking dazed and numb.

The farther they traveled, the more war-torn the landscape became. Even the smaller towns they went through showed obvious signs of battle damage. The siblings stared at the broken buildings, damaged roads and railroad tracks, and the scars left on civilians who had been too close to shrapnel or flying debris. Their countenances fell lower with each scene of destruction that showed no signs of receiving aid, but Evan hid how much the scenes hurt him. He needed to stay strong and alert for them.

As they went farther, their progress was slowed. Winter had fully set in, snow building up and hiding some of the dangers left over from the war debris. Also, military aircraft began patrolling the skies. They had been wary of the possibility before, but with each passing day, the patrols seemed to increase. He led them to more heavily forested areas to keep them out of sight.

They came across many small, abandoned villages as they traveled. The landscape—and many of the buildings—was ravaged by the revolution. He would occasionally have them take shelter in an untouched, or mostly untouched, building or home and search it and any other buildings for nonperishable foods. The royals gathered close to a small fire to sleep while he stuck to the twenty-minute nap schedule he had been keeping since they stayed in the hotel.

He even patrolled the area during the times he was awake since the military patrols also included ground units by the time they reached Jeoncheon-do.

They were in a small village that overlooked the war-torn valley. He was patrolling the surrounding area when he saw flickers of movement too quick to be a passing animal and too large to be owls or bats.

Using the small ledges of a building, he climbed to the rooftop—crouching low, his gun at the ready. He spied another flicker of movement—a shadow moving from one building to another—before seeing a small group, all at different buildings, follow. From his jacket pocket, he pulled out his silencer and attached it to his gun, then took aim at the soldier at the back of the group. He squeezed the trigger, and the man fell to the ground. He quickly took aim again, and another man fell. After a fourth went down, the rest of the patrol took notice. Gunshots peppered the building he was on, but they couldn't reach him.

"Find the wangsil!" someone shouted.

He stood and shot two more men before going back into hiding. Two soldiers searched for him while two left to find the siblings. One noticed the faint flicker of fire in the building where the siblings slept, and he shouted at the others. Evan shot the soldier and then his partner as the other two soldiers turned the corner. He killed them with two more shots. A radio cackled from one of the men, a voice asking for confirmation on their precise location. He turned toward the royals' shelter to see Su staring at him.

"Get your hyeong and noona."

Su nodded and left.

Evan scaled a different building and scanned the area. When he noticed the royals all standing in the doorway of their shelter, he climbed back down, took his backpack from Ha-Neul, and led them away without saying a word.

"How'd they find us, and where are we going?" Ha-Neul asked.

"One of the patrols probably spotted us. We'll head west, staying in the mountains for more cover," he said, "then turn north when the mountains do."

"But" —Ha-Na was already struggling with her breathing—"food."

"We can go into a bigger town in a day," he said. "Right now, we move."

They heard a helicopter, and he urged them to run for the tree line. A spotlight fell on the village and started weaving its way among the buildings. They made it into the forest before the light came close to them, but they kept running for a few more minutes. Then two more helicopters appeared overhead.

"If only there wasn't any snow," he muttered.

The helicopters made their way west and started sweeping the forest with their searchlights. Evan made them run again to try to keep them ahead of the helicopters' careful search. Having had little rest, they all stumbled repeatedly. By morning, he spotted a little cave the royals could rest in while he turned back to sweep away their tracks. The helicopters were still close, so he knew they wouldn't be able to do much. When he got back to them, they were already huddled together and fast asleep as far back in the cave as they could go. He sat in the middle of the cave, looking out the opening, waiting and listening. The helicopters drew closer and passed overhead; he didn't dare move or sleep. When more than two hours passed, he finally turned to look at the royals behind him.

Any body fat they'd had during their life of luxury was

now gone. Weeks of eating only what was necessary and the near-constant walking had taken its toll on them. They were mostly skin, a bit of sinewy muscle, and bone now. Their neat appearances were haggard—giving them a more aged look, and he knew he must look the same. He pulled out his tablet and turned it on, touching the map icon. He studied it for a while to see where Jucheon was before turning the tablet off and returning to watch the cave entrance.

E van woke the royals when he heard the helicopters grow more distant. They put on their backpacks and started heading down the mountain, Ha-Na and Ha-Neul obscuring their tracks every few yards as best they could with the pine-tree branches he had given them. The helicopters seemed to be circling a wide area.

"Why are they doing that?" Su asked in a soft voice.

"There are probably more ground troops," Evan said. "We need to get to an occupied town and try to blend in."

He led them down the mountain as fast as they could go without making too much noise. Occasionally he would stop them to listen and scan the trees and any nearby bushes. The sky was beginning to darken when they approached the foothills of the mountain—Jucheon throwing off some light in the distance. A bullet clipped Ha-Neul's left ear, making him cry out in shock. Evan whirled, firing his own gun into a clump of bushes, and a heavy thud reached his ears.

"Run," he commanded.

They sprinted for the town, and a short time later, bullets started whizzing toward them. The helicopters drew closer, the searchlights gaining on them. Evan paused to locate all of the shooters he possibly could, then turned in place, returning fire. The enemy gunfire paused for a minute as he started running again, and then the helicopters started shooting at them. He tucked his gun away and scaled a tree, going as high as the branches would allow, and pulled out his gun again. With four quick shots, he put a neat hole in one helicopter's windshield and killed its pilot. The helicopter went down as he jumped out of the tree, and the other two helicopters fired at him.

He bolted toward the royals, adrenaline surging through his body. As he got closer, he heard the sounds of three different car engines and reached up into his shirt to pull out three small silver-disk grenades. The cars came from behind him, and he turned to throw one grenade at each car. The grenades magnetically propelled themselves toward the cars, latched on, and detonated. The helicopters had backed off a bit but were still concentrating their gunfire on him as he ran toward the royals.

In front of them at the town's edge, soldiers gathered. Evan pulled out a flash grenade, this one slightly larger than the others, and threw it like a Frisbee. The grenade landed near the soldiers and blinded them, along with the royals. He took Ha-Neul's and Ha-Na's hands, while Ha-Na's other hand tightly grasped Su's, then led them away from the soldiers and entered the town. After going in a ways, he stopped them in an alley and checked Ha-Neul's wound.

He sighed with relief. "It's just a nick."

"What are we going to do?" Ha-Neul asked.

"We have to find a place to hide," Ha-Na said.

"They'll tear the town apart to find us," Ha-Neul shot back. "We have to leave."

"I'm so tired," Su said with tears in his eyes.

"Let's keep moving," Evan said.

The royals stood and turned to find their way blocked by an old, northern Balhaen man. The old man studied them from underneath his fedora, his eyes mere slits. Sirens, shouts, and helicopters framed his whole suspicion toward them.

"I doubt you had papers to pass the inspection line, right?" the old man asked in gruff Haeyoche.

"Yes, sir," Evan said in Hapsyoche.

The old man tsked and shook his head. "I'll take you to my home. Hurry." He turned and started shuffling away.

The royals looked to Evan, and he nodded, knowing they could trust the old man, recognizing him from the wang's files as General Moon Seong, predecessor of General Woo who'd retired shortly after Geum Dong became wang. They left the alley and followed the old Balhaen around the corner and into an antique store. Mr. Moon led them upstairs to an apartment, pausing to remove his shoes and hang his hat, revealing his neatly trimmed white hair. The old man turned to them as they removed their shoes and held out his hand.

"I'll take your coats and bags. Take a seat around the table."

Evan handed his things over first.

"Thank you, sir," they each muttered.

"Bweh. Just sit."

Mr. Moon went into a side room and a short while later came out empty-handed. Then he went into the kitchen and started warming up food from the refrigerator.

"My ddal prepares meals for me for several days," Mr. Moon said over the sound of the warming food. "You can eat as much as you want. She has no sense of portions, so the food often goes to waste." He set out dinnerware and started brewing tea.

Once everything was out, Mr. Moon grumpily told them to eat and grinned as they jumped to obey.

"You look as if you haven't had a decent meal in weeks." The old man hovered over them. "I guess escaping from the palace on foot does that to you."

Ha-Neul and Ha-Na gaped at Mr. Moon as Su kept eating. Evan watched the situation, interested to see how much the former Northern

Army general would reveal.

"What're you doing? Eat!" Mr. Moon snapped.

Evan started eating again, as did Ha-Na and Ha-Neul.

"That's

better."

Someone pounded on the door below and shouted for the old man to open it.

"Keep eating," Mr. Moon started to shuffle off. "No matter what, keep eating."

Evan heard him go downstairs, grumbling the whole time, to open the door. Mr. Moon sounded grumpy as he spoke in a younger, more authoritative voice. The sound of voices got louder as the old man led the visitors through the shop.

"You kids better still be eating!" Mr. Moon called from the stairs.

He entered the apartment, followed by three soldiers.

"Let's see their papers, old man."

Mr. Moon held up a hand and nodded, a sour look on his face. Then he turned to the table and motioned for them to keep eating. They did so as he went back to the room where he had put their things and came back with their coats, searching the pockets. Mr. Moon pulled out four packets of paper from the coats' pockets and held them out to the soldiers. The royals looked stunned. Evan watched the scene intently, but all quickly went back to eating when Mr. Moon cleared his throat. The soldiers checked the packets and handed them back before leaving.

Mr. Moon chuckled as the downstairs door slammed. "Poor fools." He turned to them and scowled when he saw them staring at him. "What are you looking at? Eat!"

They didn't.

"Who are you?" Ha-Na asked.

"A very unsatisfied Balhaen witch!" Mr. Moon harrumphed. Evan saw Ha-Neul's mouth fall open, and the old man chuckled again as he took in the siblings' surprised faces. "Not expecting that?"

The royals shook their heads, and Mr. Moon did his best to hide a smile.

"After you've finished eating, you should take baths," he said, wrinkling his nose. "You smell fierce. I'll take care of your dirty clothes tonight if you give them to me."

"Why are you helping us?" Ha-Neul asked.

"The michinnom daejang in power is far worse than you." Mr. Moon's whole demeanor changed, showing both anger and kindness, determination and defeat, and it was clear to Evan that Ha-Neul was the recipient of Mr. Moon's better emotions. "You're heading north, aren't you?"

Ha-Neul nodded again.

"Good. You need to find Prince Aleksandr."

"You're not the first to say that."

"Nor will I be the last if you run into other *friendly* witches, of which you won't find many," Mr. Moon said. "Many blame you for the current situation, which you can't really blame them for." Ha-Neul reluctantly nodded his agreement. "So it's a good thing most believe you're dead."

"Most?" Ha-Na asked.

"Woo Su-Han may be a witch, but he's colder than

ice." Mr. Moon looked worried. "Some believe he's fully capable of lying, especially with the 'evidence' he presented for your deaths, and now there's the business of providing papers when you travel, and all the patrols. There are quite a few people who can put those clues together and realize you're still alive." He waved his hand to dismiss the subject. "Finish eating, bathe, and rest. We can talk more later."

They did as Mr. Moon instructed then cleared the food and washed the dishes before they each took a turn in the bathroom. Mr. Moon went back downstairs to lock the store's door before locking the door to the apartment. The royals had already gone to bed, but Evan sat at the table waiting for the old man to return.

"I know who you are, Moon Seong Daejang-Nim," he said.

"I am not surprised considering you were a cham-sagwan to Geum Dong," the old man answered. "Tell me, how old are you?"

"Does it matter?"

Mr. Moon smiled. "I have seen people of all ages and countries here on Dunia. I know you are a foreigner, though I cannot place from where, and I know that you have to be at least sixteen, and yet you carry yourself as someone twice your age."

"You are truly perceptive, just like your file says."

"You are no different, but you will probably be much better practiced than I by the time you are my age."

"People from where I am from do not tend to live very long," Evan said as his memories of home began to over-whelm him. "We live violent lives."

Mr. Moon frowned slightly. "For some reason, I believe you all too well."

"That is because I speak the truth," he looked back into the old man's eyes to refocus.

"Look at us; we are both speaking Hapsyoche to each other." Mr. Moon cocked his head to the side a little. "Perhaps that's why I find you more honest."

He smiled as respect for the old man filled him. "Balhae lost a great man when you retired."

"Bah! They were tired of me, especially since I revealed myself as a witch after Geum Dong passed the first Stake Law to appease Ha-Neul," Mr. Moon said in Haeyoche.

"The wang regretted that he worked with you for such a short time. I see why."

Mr. Moon dismissed the words with a wave. "It doesn't matter now. What matters is that we keep those kids safe." He shook his head. "But you're more of a child in age than the two oldest. I wonder who you are for Geum Dong to trust you so completely with his heirs."

Evan couldn't help but frown a little. "I am only a person who tries to do what is best."

Mr. Moon nodded. "Very well, go get some rest. You look closer to death than the wangsil do. They'll be safe in this house, I promise you that."

Evan bowed and went into the bathroom.

H a-Neul woke early, his stomach feeling the pain of hunger again after eating only one good meal in several days, but he didn't open his eyes just yet. A soft, warm light tickled his eyelids, rousing him from sleep to the point where he heard muffled whispering. He couldn't make out the words, but Evan's voice was recognizable. A large, slightly staggered breath woke him even more and he opened his eyes to see Evan pulling down the window shade. Evan turned to him and gave him an apologetic look.

"I'm sorry if the light woke you," he whispered in a slightly louder voice.

"Who were you talking to a moment ago?"

Evan looked a little flustered and shook his head. "No one."

"You should sleep longer," he said. "You still look as if you haven't yet."

"I will."

Evan lay down on his floor mattress as Ha-Neul stood and quietly left the room. The old witch looked up at him from the table and greeted him with a low rumble from his throat before pouring a cup of tea for him. Ha-Neul thanked him and began sipping it.

"I thought you'd be asleep longer." The witch's voice was gravelly.

"The morning light woke me up."

The witch gave him an odd look. "It's 5:30 during the winter. Not much light will be coming through a north-facing window, if any."

Ha-Neul blinked as confusion spread across his mind. He looked around the room to get his bearings straight, and his confusion turned into mystification. "I could have sworn . . . Even Evan was . . ."

"Did you get enough sleep?" the witch asked, too impatient to carry on the topic.

He nodded.

"Well, I won't let you starve until the others wake up," the witch groaned as he got to his feet. "I'll make everyone's breakfast while I'm at it. They can just reheat it if they need to."

"Do you need any help?"

"Not with the food, but you'll have to help with the shop while you're here. It's part of your cover and your way to repay me."

Ha-Neul nodded and watched the witch grab several containers from the refrigerator and pots and pans to cook the food. After a few minutes of being lost in thought, he looked back up at the witch.

"What's your name? I just realized we never asked and you never said."

The witch chuckled. "You can either call me Moon-Nim or Harabeoji—it doesn't matter." He started setting the food and utensils on the table, ignoring Ha-Neul's surprise at being allowed to use a familiar term to address him. "You may start eating."

"Why are you helping us, especially me?" he asked without lifting a utensil.

Moon-Nim paused his work to look Ha-Neul in the eye. "Does anybody really need a reason to be a decent person?"

There was a short pause as Ha-Neul struggled with his own—though private—impoliteness toward the man and realized he was supposed to answer. "No, they don't."

Moon-Nim grumbled again and finished setting everything out. They sat in silence, partly because Ha-Neul was too busy eating, and too embarrassed, to say anything. Moon-Nim waited to speak until Ha-Neul slowed down.

"You and your guardian will help me in the antique store—mostly taking inventory and moving the heavy furniture. Your noona and dongsaeng will be working with my ddal in her shops."

"How are we supposed to move around without getting caught?" Ha-Neul asked.

"I have protection spells set up between my place and

my ddal's. As long you stay on the path and in our homes, you'll be fine. It's a good thing witches can't sense each other's magic in this case." Moon-Nim leaned back in his chair. "Anyway, after a few days, you'll be free to leave and take my car."

"What!" Ha-Neul looked up at him.

"Those 'papers' will only last a month," Moon-Nim said. "I have more protection spells in the car to hide your identities, and the papers will get you through the checkpoints on the way to Vires City. Once you get there, you'll need to find Prince Aleksandr quickly. You'll be more noticeable up there."

Gratitude stunned Ha-Neul for a moment before he could express it.

Moon-Nim grumbled again. "Just pay me back by working hard."

He nodded and continued to eat, unable to say anything as his emotions were at war again in trying to decide how to feel about Moon-Nim. By the time he finished, Ha-Na and Su were awake and eating. Moon-Nim's ddal entered the apartment and introduced herself before taking out a comb and hair clippers to start cutting Ha-Neul's hair. When she was finished, he went downstairs to join Moon-Nim in the shop.

40

M r. Moon set a key in front of Evan before joining them and his daughter at the table.

"What is this for, Harabeoji?" he asked, picking it up and examining it.

"It's a car key." Mr. Moon said.

All looked at him in shock, except for Ha-Neul.

"Abeoji," his daughter said in a soft tone.

"It's time they go," Mr. Moon rapped his knuckles on the table and sniffed. "They look clean and healthy now, and with the papers I gave them, they shouldn't draw too much attention." He looked at them all. "You need to find the prince. Don't make me say it again."

"Yes, Harabeoji," they answered, even Ha-Neul.

"I've got your packs and the car filled with food and supplies," Mr. Moon went on. "Eat the food in the car first. Do you understand me?"

They nodded.

Mr. Moon let out a short grumble. "Good."

"We'll leave here tomorrow morning," Ha-Neul said.

"A very good idea. Now, let's eat."

Mr. Moon and his daughter kept the conversation light, like they had for the past two weeks, without letting the others know of his true identity. When they finished the meal, Mr. Moon's daughter served them a small plate of fruit for dessert. They watched some television programs for a couple of hours before preparing for bed. Evan, Ha-Neul, and Su set out the bedding while Ha-Na showered, and then they each took a turn in the bathroom.

"Harabeoji will be okay, right?" Su asked when they were all in the room.

"Of course," Ha-Na said. "He's too smart and stubborn to get in trouble."

Su grinned as he closed his eyes. Eventually only Evan and Ha-Neul were awake.

"How much do you know about my gajok?" Ha-Neul whispered.

The turn in conversation piqued Evan's curiosity, and he turned to look at Ha-Neul. "Only what I need to know."

Ha-Neul stared at the ceiling and swallowed. "Did you know there was magic in it?"

Evan felt pity for him. "Your abeoji informed me of the situation."

"Do you know who it is?"

He weighed his choices for a few moments. "If I do know, do you think you are ready to know?"

Ha-Neul turned away from him. "No, I'm not."

Evan looked up at the ceiling, letting out a soft sigh, then closed his eyes.

The next morning, they quietly folded their bedding and put it in the corner of the room. They had breakfast with Mr. Moon before quickly finishing their preparations to leave. Mr. Moon led them to the car and gave each of them a handshake. He saved Ha-Neul for last and looked him straight in the eye.

"Do everything you can to bring *justice* for Woo Su-Han's crimes, Wangseja-Mama," he said in Hasoseoche.

Ha-Neul nodded. "I will, Harabeoji."

Mr. Moon grumbled and scolded them into the car, drawing a slight grin from Ha-Neul. Evan turned the ignition and pulled away as Mr. Moon watched over them.

I t took them a day to leave Jeoncheon-do, as well as Old Balhae, and to enter the northern territories. Burgos was covered in forests of coniferous trees mixed with deciduous. They stopped in every large town they came across to fill the tank, so they would be prepared for anything, and finally left Burgos after two days. Ha-Na and Su gasped as they made their way out of the mountain pass and into western Slovka. The landscape was filled with gnarled trees that grew at least ten feet away from each other, and even though it was winter, golden-silver blossoms graced their branches. Small birds with shimmering plumage no bigger than large dragonflies flitted among the blossoms. Snow-white rabbits were occasionally seen munching on tall, dried bunches of grass that poked out and hung limply over the drifts of snow and sparsely strewn crags of rock that jutted up from the ground.

"Phoenix blossom trees and fairies," Su said with awe. "They're found only here in Slovka."

"How much longer until we get to the border?" Ha-Na sounded reluctant to ask.

"A day," Evan said, "if everything keeps going smoothly."

"The soldiers may take longer to let us through since we're Balhaen," Su said.

Evan nodded. "The northern territories haven't been touched by the fighting, and Woo Daejang has loosened some of the restrictions on them."

"How are we going to find the prince?" Ha-Na asked. "He's kept his exact residence hidden from the palace and governor."

"We'll find it." Evan's tone was firm, reassuring. He glanced over at Ha-Neul. "Did Lisa ever mention any clues about where they might live?"

Ha-Neul thought for a couple of minutes before he shook his head. "She always spoke like she was an outsider, only knowing as much as the general public—or the general public of the northern territories."

"Lisa tried to hide her upper-class upbringing," Su said, "and she was good at it. So her gajok probably lives a middle-class lifestyle despite their wealth."

Ha-Neul turned to look at his dongsaeng in shock and confusion and found Ha-Na also staring at Su, but Su faced his window, engrossed with the trees.

"You know, I wouldn't be surprised if that's true." Evan's tone was thoughtful. "Aleksandr has been using his own wealth to keep the witch population from going into debt and bankruptcy. It would make sense if he lived moderately to allow him to do more for the witches."

"We know he lives in Vires City," Ha-Neul said.

"So perhaps he's on the outskirts of the city proper and not in the urban ring," Ha-Na put in. "That would allow him to live modestly but not have a long commute to his offices in the city's center."

"That leaves one neighborhood for him to reside in," Evan said.

"Only one?" Ha-Neul was skeptical.

"Before your 'Stake Laws,' as they're so affectionately called in the northern territories, Aleksandr funded a program to develop a middle-class-suites apartment-complex neighborhood just outside the city's center and business district. It's situated so residents can go to work quickly but close enough to cheaper markets. It was a very popular program aimed to revitalize a dying section of the city. Aleksandr could have easily purchased his own suite or received one as repayment for his funding."

"That sounds logical enough," he said. "How did you know that?"

Evan shrugged. "I've done some research."

Snow began to swirl around the car and throughout the landscape, though the clouds weren't heavy in the sky. Ha-Neul took to gazing out his window, watching the fairies flit playfully among the trees and in the falling snow. His eyelids grew heavy with sleep after a while, and he rested his head against the window. His breathing became deeper and more rhythmic as Lisa's face floated in his mind.

She sat on a stone bench in an unfamiliar though beautiful garden fingering a lily, and he felt that they were both at least a couple of years older. She was dressed in the royal garb of the sitting princess, a faded veil covering her face. He stood a short distance away from her, watching her gently stroke the bottom of one of the flower's petals, and he slowly grew to realize just how much he missed her. He tried to move toward her, to sit by her, but he couldn't. He struggled to reach her, to touch her, but he couldn't move. Exhausted by his efforts, he had just given up when Lisa's head lifted, looking toward him.

Sadness and loneliness washed over him as the flower in her hand wilted and browned. Then she started to fade away. He tried to reach out and call to her, but still he couldn't move or make a sound. She disappeared, and the garden went up in flames—the heat blackening his skin and making it peel away from his bones.

He woke up panting and trying to catch his breath as the sensations of the flames and the emotions faded away. The sky was dark, the snow no longer falling, and everyone else was asleep. They were at an old rest stop, one that looked rarely used, a few miles from the mountains that formed the border between Slovka and Vires. Feeling suffocated and restless, he unbuckled his seat belt and got out of the car. The freezing-cold wind hit him, cooling him and waking him. He bounced a little to warm himself and to clear the sleep from his brain.

Stars filled the sky. Looking up, he soon spotted the crane, tree, and candle-flame constellations. With some searching, he found the Guiding Star in the god's-finger constellation and moved his eyes directly below the star to find the only female in the sky, the bride. Behind him, a car door opened and closed. Soft footsteps moved around the car, and Su came to stand beside him.

"Hyeong." Some concern colored his tone.

"What is it, Su?"

"Everything keeps changing so fast."

He looked at his dongsaeng and saw that he was close to tears.

"It'll be okay, Su," he put a hand on the back of his dongsaeng's head to comfort him. "If not soon, it will be eventually."

"What if you no longer love me?"

Hurt and confusion filled Ha-Neul. "That will never happen. You are my dongsaeng, so I will always love you no matter what. Do you understand me?"

Su nodded. "Yes."

Ha-Neul ruffled Su's hair and kissed the top of his head.

"Can you show me the winter constellations?" Su asked.

"Of course."

He positioned Su in front of him and began pointing out all that he had found.

Coniferous trees laden with snow covered the mountains leading into Vires. Evan drove carefully through the narrow pass, slowing for each turn whether it was a sharp one or not. After two hours in the pass, they came to a checkpoint patrolled by ten Viresians. Evan handed over the papers Moon Harabeoji had given them, and the guard took his time studying each paper and each face. The guard handed the papers to a superior, who also took his time studying all of them. The officer stamped them, handed the papers back to Evan, and waved them through. All four of them breathed a sigh of relief, and Ha-Neul's nammae noticeably relaxed.

"It looked like they wanted to stop us," Ha-Na said.

"They wanted to, but they couldn't find anything wrong with the papers," Evan replied.

"What's on those papers anyway?" Ha-Neul asked.

"Nothing except for the stamps the border guards put on them."

"How much longer until we see Lisa?" Su asked.

"Vires City is a two-day drive from here," Evan answered. "We've got two more days, hopefully."

Vires wasn't covered in mountains like Old Balhae and many of the other territories, but it was covered in coniferous trees with large deciduous trees towering slightly over them from time to time. Every so often the forests would disappear, replaced by small towns or a small city surrounded by a large section of river or a lake. The farther they traveled north, the rarer the deciduous trees grew.

"This place . . ." Ha-Na drifted off into her own thoughts.

"What is it?" Ha-Neul asked. "What about it?"

"It feels . . ." She seemed to be searching for what to say. "It feels more alive."

No one spoke, but they all seemed to be more alert, more open to their surroundings. It became apparent when they all grasped what Ha-Na had said. Ha-Neul was the last to do so.

"Lisa told me that nature and magic coexisted, that they couldn't survive without each other," he said. "With most of the witches living here, nature and magic both flourish. I guess she was being completely honest."

A deep, staggering breath shook him as fresh pain over-whelmed him, and he covered his eyes. He couldn't speak for a long time, and the others left him to his feelings.

41

V ires City rose out of the forest like a majestic, glittering crystal ringed by smaller but no-less beautiful precious stones that were the suburban rings. In sheer size, it wasn't even half the size of Balhae City, but it far surpassed the capital city in beauty, with the forest surrounding most of it and the clear-glass lake to its northeast border. With the sun setting, the city gave off a soft glow that complemented the oranges and pinks in the sky while still allowing it to shine.

Traffic moved smoothly on wide, leveled highways. Ha-Neul and Ha-Na did their best to ignore the occupants of the other cars as they were sure to catch their attention, but Su looked at everything in awe and pointed out interesting objects to them. Evan had a tablet out and was using its map to find the way to the neighborhood Aleksandr had funded. The closer they got, the more nervous Ha-Neul became.

It only took them an hour from leaving the forest to reach the city proper, and from there another ten minutes to pull into the neatly landscaped street that led to the apartment complexes that twinkled just as softly as the stars.

Evan pulled into an empty guest parking space beside the neighborhood's park and turned off the car.

Su bounded out of the car and into the park while they were still unbuckling their seat belts. They stepped out, taking in their surroundings.

"So, how do we plan on finding him?" Ha-Na asked.

There were at least thirteen buildings. Each one was fifty stories tall and put together like crystalline blocks that jutted out randomly from an egg-shaped center, making the task seem impossible.

"I'm not sure about that," Evan said.

Ha-Neul and Ha-Na looked at him in disbelief.

"What?" he said.

"Well, mostly I've been concerned with getting you here safely." Evan looked around. "By the way, where did Su go?"

They started looking around in panic, but Su came running back, waving at them.

"Hyeong! Noona! I got lost, but this guy helped me find you again!" Su pointed back toward a young man with light-brown hair and eyes, dressed neatly in slim slacks and a button-up shirt.

Ha-Neul stopped in his tracks and grasped Lisa's necklace. "It's Ivan." Evan and Ha-Na looked at him. "Ivan Aleksandrsson."

Ivan stopped when he was close enough to see what they looked like but stared angrily at Ha-Neul, who removed his hand from the necklace. Ivan glanced down at it, and his face drained of all color. Ivan moved toward Ha-Neul, his eyes locked on the raven's eye, and stopped an arm's reach away.

"Where did you get that?" Ivan had a deep tenor voice, but it was hard to hear for how softly he spoke. "Where did you get that!" Spit flew into Ha-Neul's face as Ivan's familiar eyes looked at him in rage.

"Lisa left it for me," he answered softly.

Ivan took hold of him and pushed him back onto the hood of the car, then lifted him and slammed him back down again to the sound of Ha-Na's shrieks.

"Tell me the truth!" Ivan slammed him back down. "Where did you get it?" Ivan kept slamming him against the car, even when Evan pulled out his gun. "Where? *Where*! WHERE!" Ivan slammed him with increasing intensity.

"Enough, Vanya," a voice said in Common.

Ivan quickly backed away, looking ashamed. Ha-Neul briefly caught a glimpse of Ha-Na holding a sobbing Su as tears streamed down her face, before he slid off the car and onto the snow-covered grass. A handsome gentleman with slicked-back brown hair and wearing a well-tailored suit kneeled down beside him. The man's dark-brown eyes looked at him with concern as his quick and skillful hands examined his battered upper body. When the man was done, their eyes met.

"You are more shocked than injured, Wangseja-Mama." The man's voice was a smooth bass, comforting yet authoritative. "You should be able to stand if you are willing to try. Would you like me to assist you?"

The man didn't wait for him to answer before firmly taking ahold of him and gently helping him to stand.

"I apologize for Vanya's behavior. He has yet to learn how to put his hatred toward you aside, and seeing Vasilisa's raven's eye with you has greatly upset him, even if it was originally your eomeoni's." The man turned to Ivan, who looked slightly shocked and confused, and spoke in Common instead of Hasoseoche. "Vanya, after we remove their belongings, get rid of the car. It would be best if it's never found by Su-Han."

Ivan bowed his head. "Yes, Father."

Ha-Na's and Su's eyes widened as they looked at Aleksandr, and Ha-Neul was sure they felt exactly what he did —complete awe at how gentle yet authoritative the prince was.

"Please get your packs and follow me," Aleksandr said in Hasoseoche. "We have much to discuss, I am sure, and I believe you will have a few questions."

They nodded and grabbed their backpacks. Evan gave Ivan the key to the car, and Ivan drove off before they had even turned their backs to follow Aleksandr through the park toward the closest apartment complex. The prince walked smoothly, his back straight and squared and his head held high, just like Lisa carried herself.

"You must be exhausted from your long journey." Aleksandr spoke affectionately. "I fear you have been through much hardship to get here. Irene managed to send a brief missive to expect visitors, and I prepared as best I could so suspicion was not raised. Fortunately, you met Moon-Nim along your way, which insured your safe arrival."

Aleksandr stopped talking as they entered the building and passed a guard who seemed on the verge of waking up from an unexpected nap. The prince sighed regretfully toward the guard once they had entered the elevator and pressed the button for the twelfth floor.

"Each apartment is the size of a normal, two-story house"—Aleksandr's head bounced from side to side a couple of times—"sort of. They are probably slightly bigger considering there are greenhouses attached to each one."

The elevator opened, and Aleksandr led them to a door marked 1223. He pressed his hand to a scanner, and the door unlocked. As they entered, soft lights faded into existence, creating a homey feel to the space.

"Have you had dinner?" Aleksandr asked. "The kitchen is stocked with some Balhaen food if you wish to eat something you are more familiar with. It can be prepared in a few moments if you just say the word."

"Dinner would be great," Ha-Neul finally managed to say. "Anything is fine."

"Very well. If you set your packs on the table here," Aleksandr put a hand on a side table in the entranceway, "Vanya will take them to your rooms when he returns."

They put their backpacks on the table and followed him into a larger lobby that had an open staircase and balcony that branched off in two separate directions. Aleksandr led them under the balcony and into a sitting room conjoined by a small step that ran the width of the room to a dining room that could be closed off by decorative, sliding partitions.

"Please sit," Aleksandr motioned to the nice furniture, "while I put in an order to the electronic chef. Once you have eaten, we can talk if you wish to do so, or we can save it for tomorrow."

"I think tonight will be best," Ha-Neul said, feeling more up to the task of speaking with him.

Aleksandr gave him a respectful nod. "I agree." He motioned again to the furniture before turning to go through another door off the dining room.

"Is he really Aleksandr Dmitrisson?" Ha-Na asked. "I thought he would be different, more like Lisa."

"He is like Lisa," Su said, already sitting in a chair, "but older."

Ha-Na looked to Ha-Neul as he studied the house. "I wonder where Lisa is."

The room was filled with a heavy silence as Ha-Neul began to wonder the same thing.

"I'm sure we'll soon find out." Evan kept his tone light, unaffected by the atmosphere.

Aleksandr came back into the room. "If you want to wash up or use the restroom before dinner, we passed a water closet. It will be to your right. It is sectioned off into private stalls for multiple people to use at the same time, so do not feel uncomfortable about using it all at once. Dinner will be ready in ten minutes."

Ha-Na left first, and the others followed when she returned. As Aleksandr directed them to the dining room, a dark glass lid rose to reveal a table set for their meal. The prince encouraged them to eat but spent most of the meal politely studying Ha-Neul. When Aleksandr's eyes rested on the raven's eye, the air surrounding the man changed, seemingly contracting around him.

The door from the entranceway opened then slammed closed as angry footsteps entered, paused, and then went up the stairs. Aleksandr gave them an apologetic smile, saying Ivan's name, and encouraged them to keep eating, though the others all looked at Ha-Neul, making him even more nervous to face Ivan again. A couple of minutes later, Ivan entered the room and sat at the opposite end from his abeoji, pointedly not looking at them as they ate. When they finished, Aleksandr led them back to the sitting room as the glass lid once again descended upon the table.

"I'm sure you have a lot of questions, especially about my involvement with Su-Han, so allow me to start." They nodded as he made himself more comfortable in his chair. "A little over a decade ago, it became apparent that the relation-ship between the palace and Vires would no longer be amicable, so I started taking measures to ensure that a witch would be able to enter the military without detection. During that time, some aides found Su-Han, and seeing his potential, convinced me to sponsor him through a Balhaen charity. I had never met him in person nor had direct communication with him; instead, I let an aide take charge of his care. After a few years, it became clear that Su-Han was exhibiting sociopathic tendencies, but we did not have the time to look for a replacement due to our economic circumstances."

"So he strayed from your plan," Ha-Na said.

"Yes, we wanted to keep the fighting to a minimum, and we never wanted the deaths of the wangsil—that would cause too much chaos, and your abeoji was a dear chingu. We wanted to convince you to give us our freedom by showing you we could overcome the one fault of the war machines and exchange it for autonomy."

"What do you mean you overcome the one fault?" Ha-Neul asked, unease filling him.

Aleksandr looked uncomfortable. "Vasilisa is extremely talented in creating spells. Before she worked in the palace, she finished a spell that would prevent the soldiers' dying from a surprise hit." The prince's words upset Ha-Neul as he began to fear Lisa had betrayed him. "I assure you she had no idea what it was for."

"Was she sent to the palace on purpose?" Anger rose in Ha-Neul.

"We tried to convince her not to go," Ivan said scornfully, "but she wanted the wage."

The prince gazed at Ha-Neul with sympathy. "When we realized what your feelings were for each other, your abeoji and I hatched a new plan. He knew we were planning something and that it might be violent, so he wanted to avoid it at all costs, but he knew that he could not repeal the Stake Laws without angering you."

"Are you saying you worked together to have Lisa and Ha-Neul fall in love?" Ha-Na couldn't contain her shock at the notion, while Ha-Neul couldn't speak due to his own astonishment.

"We could only stand back and watch, or in my case, wait and listen," Aleksandr said. "There was someone else doing all the work for us."

"Who?" Ha-Na and Ha-Neul asked, Ha-Neul starting to feel apprehensive.

"A very talented reader."

Ha-Neul felt the color drain from his face when he realized there was another person with magic in the palace. He looked over at Ha-Na, who looked much the same as he felt. Su seemed a little anxious, but Evan looked unsurprised.

"Irene?" Ha-Na guessed.

"Goodness, no, she did not have the necessary relationship to do anything. Besides, she has no magical blood."

"Then who—"

"It's me."

The tone was mature for his age—not the breathy, childish voice Ha-Neul was so used to hearing—causing him to jump, and they all looked at Su. Ha-Neul and Ha-Na were speechless. Su looked at Ha-Neul and saw how dumbstruck he felt. His dongsaeng's expression turned remorseful but no longer hid just how intelligent and mature he really was. Ha-Neul remembered Su's concern from a couple of nights before, and fresh pain hit him.

"Abeoji told you the day of the review, hyeong, there was magic in our gajok. I'm a reader, just like Eomeoni was. After Eomeoni died, Abeoji never mentioned it to you or anyone else that she was a reader because you would automatically know that I am one as well."

"Su." Ha-Na had tears in her eyes.

"Abeoji told me several years ago to act challenged to hide my ability. I understood why he did, so I listened to him." Su's remorse deepened as he spoke to Ha-Neul. "I'm sorry for lying, hyeong."

"So the bursts of clear observation—" Ha-Neul began after he found his voice again.

"Were all planned and precisely executed," Su said. "It was the hardest and most rewarding task I happily undertook, influencing you and Lisa to court."

"Su . . ." Ha-Neul felt weak.

"Unfortunately, you broke off the relationship during the review," Aleksandr said, looking reluctant to break his contemplation. "Su-Han was already getting impatient and took matters into his own hands."

"What do you mean?" Ha-Na asked when it was apparent Ha-Neul couldn't speak.

"I had decided to wait and see if Wangseja would attempt to repair the relationship."

Ivan let out an angry breath. "But that doesn't matter anymore."

"Vanya," Aleksandr's tone contained a sharp, clear warning.

Dread filled Ha-Neul, and he cautiously asked, "Where is Lisa?"

"She is no longer in this house," Aleksandr answered after a moment and sounded unwilling to admit it.

"What do you mean—"

"Precisely what he said," Ivan snapped.

"Enough, Ivan." The prince's countenance was cold. Ivan bowed his head again and wouldn't look up. Aleksandr turned to them with a fatherly demeanor. "You have a lot to process. May I suggest that you rest for the night? Talk amongst yourselves," he looked at Ha-Neul and Su, "and any other pressing concerns will be addressed tomorrow."

The others nodded, but Ha-Neul had one more question. "How did Lisa get my eomeoni's necklace?"

Aleksandr studied him for a moment. "She gave it to me at your birthday party to give to Lisa on her eighth birthday."

"Why?" he asked.

"I don't know. If that is all, I suggest you rest now."

They nodded.

"Very good." Aleksandr looked over at Ivan. "Vanya, show them to their rooms, please."

Ivan stood and started to leave the room. The others thanked Aleksandr and wished him a good night before following Ivan. The young man didn't speak to them as he led them into the lobby and up the stairs, turning left toward a circular common area that had five doors.

"Straight ahead is the bathroom." Ivan pointed to the first door on the left. "Evan's room, Wangseja's room," he continued to point, "Gongju's room, and Eorin Wangja's room."

Then he left them standing there.

"Let's get cleaned up and meet back here," Ha-Neul said softly. "We do have a lot to talk about." He glanced over at Su, who looked guilty, his posture one of contrition.

They nodded and separated.

Vanya went back to the sitting room and found his father standing by the large fireplace, staring into it. He waited for his father to make the first move.

"You must control your anger, Vanya," he said after a few minutes. "From now on, Vasilisa must be less of a concern. While the royals are here, our safety is our top priority."

"I know, Father."

"Do you, Vanya?" His father turned to him, leveling a steady, hard-to-read gaze at him. "Your actions have shown otherwise."

"I'm sorry, Father. The fact he has the raven's eye when she clearly wore it the day before—"

"I know, Vanya. I know. It is a curious thing, but evidently he knows nothing." His voice held some desperation.

Vanya didn't speak and couldn't look at him.

"The wangseja is at a delicate stage right now. He has learned hard truths tonight, and he has more to learn tomorrow. You cannot make things more difficult right now, so keep quiet about Vasilisa until I deem it right to tell him. Do you understand, Vanya?"

"Yes, Father."

"I hope so. We cannot have this discussion again." Aleksandr's eyes grew kinder. "Now, have you found a pupil to teach?"

"Not yet."

He nodded thoughtfully. "Don't worry about it for now. A student will present itself to us soon. You'll be able to pass your master's qualification by the end of the year."

S u woke early and crept silently out of his room and down the hall to the other circular lobby where there were only three doors. He looked at each door carefully before making his way to the one on the right—the one that felt lonely. He tested the doorknob and found it wasn't locked. Opening it a crack, he peeked in and found it empty. He slipped in and shut the door soundlessly.

Lisa had tastefully decorated the room, neither overly feminine nor sparsely neutral. It showed that she kept fond memories at the forefront of her thoughts, but the room was lonely, stale. Life had left the room. He stepped farther into the room, taking in every detail. A picture on her vanity called out to him, and he moved closer. An image of Ha-Neul stared back at him from a small frame. The picture showed his hyeong from his chest up, and parts of the background were visible. He was dressed in a sleeveless shirt, his hair pulled back to show off his piercings, and he was smiling like he was seeing the most beautiful sight he had ever seen. Behind him was a park.

Su barely touched the edge of the frame and felt a longing emanate from it. Unbidden, a tear sprang to his eye.

B reakfast was a quiet affair after their brief morning greetings. Aleksandr and Ivan ate with them, but one was politely silent while a heavy, anxious air hung over the other. Once everyone was finished, Aleksandr ushered them to the greenhouse and a smallish circular patio filled with cushioned metal patio chairs. Aleksandr sat next to a small table with an empty flowerpot. Evan and Ivan sat on either side of the prince, while Ha-Na and Su sat next to Ha-Neul.

"Is there anything I can clarify for you?" Aleksandr asked.

Ha-Neul exchanged glances with the others before most eyes settled on him.

"The spell for the war machines, the one Lisa made to prevent the soldiers' death from surprise hits, can it be broken?" he asked in Common.

"All spells can be broken if one has the knowledge and ability."

"So we can end Su-Han's protection on the war machines."

Aleksandr hesitated before answering. "No."

"Why not?" Evan asked.

"Vasilisa has not told anyone the weakness of the spell."

"So Lisa can break it," Su said.

The glance Ivan shot at his abeoji was not undetected by Su.

"There's something you're not telling us." Su spoke

bluntly but not in an accusatory way.

"Vasilisa is indisposed at the moment," Aleksandr said.

"By indisposed, do you mean—" Ha-Na started.

"He means indisposed," Ivan said.

"Now is not the time to discuss what Vasilisa is doing," Aleksandr cut in. "There is one pressing matter that must be addressed."

"What's that?" Ha-Neul asked, his impatience coming through in his tone.

"The reason behind your mother's death."

Ha-Neul went from shocked to angry in a matter of moments. "What are you trying to say, that your brother didn't kill her?"

Aleksandr only nodded once, with great care.

A derisive laugh escaped Ha-Neul. The others remained deathly silent. "So who did?"

"A young witch not yet in control of his magic."

He made no attempt at controlling his anger now. "What young witch? The only witches there were you and your brother."

Ivan shook from anger but remained silent.

"No, Wangseja, there was a third, and he unknowingly caused a tragic accident."

Ha-Neul slapped his hand against the arm of his chair and stood up. "Lies! The only ones in that room were my family and yours! It was your brother who cast the spell between his hand and mine, and I was bitten by that viper!"

"That is correct. The spell was cast between his hand and yours," Aleksandr said calmly. "Your hand was also there as the spell was cast."

Ha-Neul spluttered once and grew silent as the implication sunk in. He collapsed in his chair as confusion and disbelief contorted his face.

"A rare occurrence has been presenting itself more frequently over the past seventy years." Aleksandr spoke as if he were teaching a class. "Magic has been manifesting itself in families with absolutely no history of magic in their lineage, and in cases of established magical families, changing the form it manifests in." From the empty flowerpot beside him, Aleksandr pulled out a small silver sphere. "This has caused many problems, especially for families who have suddenly produced a witch. Accidents have occurred, sometimes with tragic consequences. So we devised a test to detect magic in people, and the form it comes in."

Ha-Na gasped. "Is that a Witch Hunter?"

Ivan cleared his throat in irritation and shot her an angry look. Aleksandr merely grimaced. "That is what it has been most popularly called by the vast majority, but among magic users—its creators—it is known as MaNA: magical nature ascertainer." He held it up and pressed its top. "It orbits around the head for normal people."

Aleksandr tossed it at Ha-Na, and it circled around her head. He took out another and turned it on. "It hovers in front of the forehead for readers." He tossed the second one at Su, and it hovered near his forehead. "Behind the head for dream walkers, to the left for druids, and to the right for witches." He tossed a third sphere up in the air, and it hovered at the right side of his own face. He pulled out a fourth sphere and turned it on as he looked at Ha-Neul, making him feel nauseated. "If I am wrong, I offer my deepest apologies for my error, which in effect places myself and my family in your service until you release us."

Ha-Neul swallowed the bile rising in his throat. "What happens if you're right?"

Aleksandr's eyes were indescribably kind as he

answered, "Your pain will be great. I guarantee that. There is nothing I can do to ease it. I want you to know, though, that you are not the first to experience what you have and that it is not impossible to be forgiven, even by yourself—especially by yourself—because *it was not your fault*."

Everyone looked to him, waiting. Ha-Na and Su removed their MaNAs and watched him with the greatest concern.

He took a deep breath. "Toss it."

The MaNA flew at his face, but before it hit him, it veered to his right and hovered there.

Ivan gasped, Evan looked away, and Ha-Na and Su grasped his hands and began to cry as Ha-Neul sat in wide-eyed shock. Aleksandr stood, his MaNA now gone, and walked over to Ha-Neul to kneel in front of him.

"Please listen to me, Ha-Neul," Aleksandr whispered, getting him to focus on him. "I will help you in any way that I can if you allow me to. Allow me to be the master of your education so I can teach you to avoid greater tragedy in the near future." His voice grew softer so only Ha-Neul could hear him say, "You know you don't have much time left if you don't use your magic, and you must learn because you are needed. Your country needs you, your family needs you—and Vasilisa needs you."

The words pierced through the fog in his brain, and he realized that there were tears in Aleksandr's eyes.

"I'm a witch." The words felt heavy on his tongue.

Aleksandr nodded. "If you don't use magic—"

"I will die soon." He looked at Ha-Na and Su, who were watching the silent exchange with distress, and knew they had heard the last bit of the conversation. His revulsion for magic and the knowledge of what he was warred within him. He turned back to Aleksandr and really looked at him, and he saw sincerity in the prince's eyes and the desire to help him through anything that came his way. It reminded him so much of Lisa whenever he felt conflicted. He felt himself change in that instant. "Teach me."

"Truth does not change just because it is inconvenient, unbearable, or because the vast majority wants it to."

— THE OBSERVANT

43

Su knocked on Ha-Na's door and waited for her to answer before he entered her room. She sat at a loom Aleksandr had purchased for her so she would have something to do in her downtime other than observe Ha-Neul's magic lessons, which mostly focused on Ha-Neul reconnecting with his magic.

"What have you been doing?" Ha-Na asked, taking a quick glance at him.

"I just finished my online class," he said. "I've got a half hour before my next one starts."

"So you came to visit me?"

He nodded. "What are you working on?"

"Abeoji's portrait." She leaned closer to the loom. "I want to make it while his face is still fresh in my mind."

"I'm sure he appreciates it."

"I hope so," she muttered. She looked over at Su and gave him a half smile. "There's something else on your mind, isn't there?"

He nodded again.

"What is it?"

"Hyeong."

She waited for him to continue.

"Do you think he secretly knew?"

Ha-Na set aside her work with a sigh and turned to face him. "Ha-Neul was eight when it happened. Before that, he loved magic—wanted to do magic. When Eomeoni died, that all changed. Perhaps he did know, or maybe he suspected it. Maybe he felt it but didn't realize it. Whatever the case, he shut himself off from it. I knew he blamed himself for Eomeoni's death, along with Aleksandr's hyeong."

"Did you think he had magic?"

Her hands shook. "Occasionally, strange things did happen around him. Eomeoni knew this too and would tell Abeoji, but when she died, it all stopped, so I thought nothing more of it."

"He locked up his magic tight."

"Yes, yes, he did." She wiped her eyes. "You should get going to your lesson."

"All right, noona, I'll see you at dinner."

She grabbed his hand and squeezed it affectionately before he left.

"I think that's enough meditation for today," Aleksandr said. He lifted a bowl of fruit from the table he sat at in the white practice room. "Come grab a quick bite to eat."

Ha-Neul stood from a cushion and made his way to the table.

"Thank you." He grabbed an apple and bit into it hungrily.

"It's time for you to know magic's roots, at least as far as we know for certain." Aleksandr settled comfortably in his chair. "First, I need you to eliminate the labels you have for those with magic—namely witch, druid, and so on. Those names are inaccurate and carry bias that has arisen over hundreds of years of misunderstanding, and there is often misclassification as well."

"So you have your own labels, then?" he said in surprise.

"*We*, the magical community and those who seek to understand us, use a different classification system." The prince flicked a piece of dust off his pants. "To start, we are called spellcasters. What you call druids are spellweavers, readers are clairvoyants, and dream walkers are astral projectors."

"Wait, what's the difference between spellcasters and spellweavers?"

Aleksandr smiled. "I'm getting to that, so please be patient." He popped a grape into his mouth and quickly ate it. "Each type of magic is inherently different, though we believe it comes from the same source, which possibly explains why occasionally a spellcaster may come from a clairvoyant lineage," he motioned to Ha-Neul, "but the closest two lines are spellcasters and spellweavers. We both channel magic through spells, but where casters are powerful individually, weavers are stronger communally."

"So in a one-on-one fight, a caster will win."

"Yes, easily, maybe even a one-on-three fight, depending on the strength of the caster. However, weavers usually work in groups of four."

"What's the difference between strength?"

"Casters and weavers can use simple spells quickly and efficiently, but the strength differs in favor of the caster when it comes to individuals. The greatest disparity shows itself with complex spells. It takes longer for a caster to use more complex spells because we can only use our own magic, but weavers use their magic together, drastically cutting down on production time and pouring more magic into the spell."

"So their spells can do more given the same amount of time as a caster."

"Precisely. I could cast a wind spell in thirty seconds, whereas they could cast a storm spell in the same amount of time."

Ha-Neul began to absently spin the empty bowl with a finger as he thought everything over. "What about clairvoyants and astral projectors?"

"Clairvoyants use magic to see the truths of the world that are on or just below the surface. Astral projectors can send a part of their consciousness to invisibly observe the world or enter the sleeping mind of a person to read their memories and thoughts like a book—or perhaps view it like a movie in the case of memories. That's a basic summation, especially for clairvoyants. Only they truly understand what they can do and how it works. Clairvoyants are the only magic users who don't need teachers to learn how to use and control their magic. It's instinctive."

"Lucky Su." He removed his hand from the bowl.

Aleksandr laughed. "Clairvoyance is the simplest form of magic, though its magic is not to be underestimated." He looked down at the table and smiled. "I think you're nearly ready to start your real training."

Ha-Neul looked down and was amazed to see the bowl spinning by itself.

Everyone sat at the breakfast table, silently eating. Ivan still wouldn't look at any of them, especially Ha-Neul, even though they had been there for three weeks. Aleksandr, however, seemed to study the two closely, and when the meal was half done, he cleared his throat. They all immediately looked up at him.

"Ha-Neul has reconnected with his magic well enough to start training," the prince announced.

Ivan snorted with contempt and went back to his meal.

"I will remain the master of his education, but Vanya will be his teacher."

"What!" Ivan and Ha-Neul exclaimed, both horrified by the idea. Su kept his amusement to himself.

"You heard me well enough." Aleksandr picked up his fork as if to start eating again. "Ha-Neul needs to learn to control his magic, and Vanya needs a pupil so he can pass his master's qualification. It's quite convenient."

Su looked from Aleksandr to Ha-Neul to Ivan, who caught sight of his glances.

"You had this planned from the beginning," Ivan accused his abeoji.

"I thought it a likely possibility." Aleksandr's tone was calm and light as he forked a piece of sausage. "Observing both of you, I think it's the best course." He slid the sausage into his mouth, looking his adeul in the eye—almost daring him to object to his decision.

Ivan bowed his head. "I'll do as you say, Master."

Aleksandr turned to Ha-Neul as he swallowed. "From now on, you will call Vanya Seonsaeng-Nim."

Ha-Neul bowed his head. "Yes, sir."

"May I ask what you mean by a master's qualification?" Ha-Na asked.

Aleksandr smiled. "Of course you may. Masters are spellcasters who have completed extensive training of magical use and have demonstrated that they have a thorough enough knowledge of magic to be able to teach the next generation. To be a master is one of the requirements to be able to compete for the title of prince."

"So Ivan will be able to compete if he teaches Ha-Neul successfully."

"Yes, he'd be one of the youngest ever able to do so if Ha-Neul is able to learn the basics and acquire the intermediate magical knowledge level by the end of the year."

Ha-Na looked at Ivan in wonder, which made him slightly blush.

"How old is, or was, the youngest?" Su asked.

"Lisa told me they have to be twenty to compete," Ha-Neul said.

"That rule was made shortly before the last competition because only one spellcaster managed to gain the title of master at a young age," Aleksandr said.

Ha-Na was intrigued. "How old was he? Or she."

"She was thirteen when she became a master," Ivan said with envy.

Su cracked a smile and pronounced. "It was Lisa."

Aleksandr caught Su's eye, then Ha-Neul's, before he dipped his chin. Ha-Neul's hand shook as he reached for his glass. Ha-Na looked even more amazed than before.

"She was so talented, but she didn't want the title," she muttered.

"That's correct," Aleksandr responded. "She didn't want or envy the responsibilities that came with being a noble. She wanted to forget it all."

"Where is Lisa?" Ha-Neul asked. He looked up at Aleksandr, dying to know.

"It—" Ivan began angrily.

"I'm asking Master, Seonsaeng-Nim," Ha-Neul snapped, not letting his gaze stray from Aleksandr, "and this time I want a straight answer."

"May I assume, Eorin Wangja, that if I don't tell him, you will?" Aleksandr didn't let his gaze stray from Ha-Neul as he spoke.

Su felt a terrible weight pressing on his shoulders as he saw the pain and worry boiling in Aleksandr's countenance, confirming his suspicion. "I didn't know the truth until now."

Ha-Na looked scared, and Ha-Neul could barely hold in his fear. Aleksandr's composure slipped then fell under the same crushing weight Su felt.

"She disappeared one night after going to bed." A tear slid down the prince's cheek. "She was gone when we went to wake her."

The air was thick with grief and defeat. Ivan's show of collectedness shattered, and he broke down in tears. Ha-Neul sat in disbelief while Ha-Na began suggesting methods of searching for their missing chingu.

"What about magic? Can't you track her with magic?" she finally offered.

Aleksandr shook his head. "Even magic has failed us. There is no log in the security system of her departure— voluntary or otherwise."

Ha-Na hid her face in her hands as the second loss of Lisa overcame her, and Ha-Neul's mouth worked like a fish's trying to comprehend all the thoughts and emotions within him. Su turned away from them as he desperately tried to blink back his own tears and saw that Evan looked extremely uncomfortable.

"W-when?" Ha-Neul finally asked.

Aleksandr wiped his tears away with a thumb. "The night before the revolution."

Ha-Neul was barely holding himself together as he asked, "Did . . . did Irene . . . did she know this before . . . before we left?"

Aleksandr nodded.

The air escaped Ha-Neul as his hope of seeing Lisa was extinguished and the weight of everything that had happened left him feeling devastated once again. With his elbows on the table and his hands clasped, Ha-Neul's head fell between his arms. His breathing turned into sobs as he raised his hand to hold the necklace we wore and began to topple out of his chair.

Su shot around the table to steady Ha-Neul as the sobs wracked his hyeong's body. Ha-Na wrapped her arms around him as well, resting her head against Ha-Neul's back, crying as well. Evan looked at them with pity, Aleksandr with empathy, and Ivan in shock. As for the first two, it was evident that they grieved for more than just Lisa's disappearance.

After some time, Ha-Neul slowly straightened, gently dislodged Ha-Na, and turned to Aleksandr. "She sent it to me before she disappeared, didn't she?"

Aleksandr nodded.

There was a fierce determination in Ha-Neul's eyes and demeanor. "So I need to find her. I need to find her and get my kingdom back."

Aleksandr rocked back at the force of Ha-Neul's words.

"What?" Ivan gasped.

"There's that legend about the Northern Mountains, the ones protected by the spellweaver nation," Ha-Neul said with growing conviction. "We call it Samjogo, the three-legged raven deity, but many northern territories call it the Raven's Eye."

Aleksandr was impressed but mostly frightened. "You want to go north?"

"That's suicide," Ivan said. "No one steps foot into the deep Northern Mountains and comes back. Your family's armies were forced to retreat mere hours after starting to move into the first range of mountains."

"But if, as the legends say, Samjogo exists and is omniscient, we could learn of Lisa's location, and I could find the best way to take back the kingdom," Ha-Neul said.

Aleksandr shook his head. "You wouldn't be able to get past the spellweavers' defenses, let alone find your way to Samjogo, the Raven's Eye."

"But—"

"You don't have a chance, especially as you are now," Aleksandr cut in.

Ha-Neul paused in his retort. "Wait, what are you saying?"

"With your skills now, you would be turned away or killed. That may happen no matter what, though. The spellweavers are extremely protective of their land—it's true of all spellweavers but especially the ones in the Northern Mountains."

"But you think this Samjogo exists?" Evan asked Aleksandr and Ivan.

The table fell quiet, but Su saw the truth stirring within them.

"Tell them, Father," Ivan said.

Aleksandr sighed and nodded. "Samjogo, the Raven's Eye, is acknowledged as the most powerful magic in existence—whether it be a person, deity, or not. We believe the gods created the Raven's Eye first, and from it, all magic was given form."

"There's a *but* in there, isn't there," Ha-Na said. It wasn't a question.

"No one outside those mountains has ever been able to absolutely prove it exists," Aleksandr said, "but for those with magic, the more we learn about magic and see how it's grown in others, we believe in it more."

"You can't really explain it well beyond that, can you?" Su asked.

Aleksandr shook his head, then looked at him incredulously. "Do you sense something?"

"It's tiny, but it's everywhere, and it has a similar. . .taste," he drew out the word a little, "as human magic, but it comes from something that doesn't feel entirely human."

"You can sense magic?" Ivan asked in disbelief. "If you can, how did you not know about your own brother?"

"I sense it when someone uses it," Su told him. "Hyeong didn't use his."

"I don't believe it. You would have known Vasilisa was a spellcaster as soon as you met her," Ivan said.

"I did, and she knew I was a clairvoyant, though she acted otherwise."

Aleksandr chuckled when Ivan became flabbergasted. "You see the heir of a powerful line of clairvoyants, Vanya, and he is strong, even for them. Only the strongest clairvoyants can sense magic," he said to Su's nammae and to Evan.

Ha-Na and Ha-Neul looked at Su with renewed respect, which made him slightly uncomfortable. Evan studied him a little more closely, but the secrets Evan kept remained hidden.

"Anyway, it is nice to have further evidence of the existence of the Raven's Eye," Aleksandr continued. "However, the spellweavers guard it most ferociously. It will be next to impossible to travel their lands without their consent."

"So what do I do?" Ha-Neul asked.

"You train," Aleksandr stated. "You train to make your abilities the best they can possibly be, and then we'll talk more about your retaking the kingdom."

"What about Lisa?" Ha-Neul demanded.

Ivan and Aleksandr felt crestfallen.

"You, Wangseja, are the priority," the prince said. "Trust me, even though it's hard, it will be better for the kingdom, and the world, for us to help you."

"But it could take years for me to be fully prepared."

Aleksandr's heart seemed to break. "I know."

The silence that hung over them nearly drowned them.

As Ha-Neul stood, Su could sense the unquenchable drive within his hyeong. "Seonsaeng-Nim."

Ivan looked Ha-Neul in the eye. "What?"

"We should get started."

Ivan nodded after a few moments of confusion, stood as well, and led Ha-Neul away.

44

H a-Neul stared at the thick, cracked-leather tome Ivan had just placed in front of him on the wooden table in the white practice room, then gingerly opened it in the middle. Cramped drawings, diagrams, and handwriting filled the pages, making his head swirl. Ivan sighed impatiently and flipped the pages to the beginning, where there was only a circle drawn.

"Spellcasters need to visualize what they are about to create," Ivan said. "To help us do that, we either physically or mentally draw a circle around the object or area to be affected." The circle in the book turned green, throwing off a faint glow. "Within that circle, we either create the necessary symbols for the spell by hand or visualize them and will them into existence." Four symbols appeared in the circle at the cardinal points. "Then we release our magic to activate it." The circle flashed, and suddenly a pebble lay on the book. "That is the basics of spell casting. Now, repeat it back to me."

He did so as Ivan removed the pebble.

"Good." Ivan sat in the chair across from him. "Today

we'll start with basic, one-symbol spells. First, you will hand draw the symbols and practice releasing your magic into them." He turned the page to reveal a large chart full of tiny symbols. "We'll start with the first symbol."

Ha-Neul took a piece of paper from a stack beside him, as well as a pencil, and began to draw.

Aleksandr sat in his room reading when Vanya entered, surprising him.

"Finished already for today?"

"He's determined to learn, and he's learning remarkably fast," Vanya said. "We got through half of the first chart already."

Aleksandr's breath hitched a little. "So soon? Did you test him like you should? Did he remember all of them?"

Vanya glowered a little and nodded.

Aleksandr set his book down and tapped a finger against the arm of his chair while he thought. "Teach him at his pace but with caution."

"Father . . ." Vanya looked down, but not before he caught the uncertainty in his son's expression.

"Ask."

"Tell me about the day the wanghoo died and about Uncle Nikolai's death."

Aleksandr tapped his finger a few times before he nodded, realizing his son deserved to know the truth. "Nikolai was casting a transformation spell on a flower blossom in between his and Wangseja's hands. He told me later that he was going to change it into a raven's-eye necklace and give it to him as a present, but he felt another's magic—uncontrolled and quite strong—hijack the spell at the last moment. The viper came out as a result and attacked."

"He hijacked a master's spell?" Vanya couldn't hide his amazement.

Aleksandr was grim as he nodded. "Remember what I said about love and magic."

"The stronger the love, the stronger the magic produced," Vanya repeated immediately.

"The wang and wanghoo loved each other deeply. I knew they would produce a strong clairvoyant, but they also produced a spellcaster, one capable of hijacking a master's spell even without control of his magic."

Dread filled his son. "He could be a terrifying wang."

"And he would have a clairvoyant wangja by his side."

Vanya shuddered. "And yet he must be trained."

"Yes," he agreed solemnly, "but he is training with the knowledge of how terrible magic can be. He will use it with care."

"What about Uncle Nikolai?" Vanya reminded him. "Why was he left to die in prison?"

Deep sadness filled Aleksandr as he thought of his brother. "Wangseja refused to allow me near him, and so I could not use the MaNA to test him. Geum Dong was in no place to persuade him either, so Nikolai remained the only suspect capable of the wanghoo's death. Nikolai had been traveling the world before that day and contracted a tropical disease that had no cure at the time. By the time anyone knew about it, Nikolai had died, and there was no more evidence that Wangseja was a spellcaster."

Vanya took a while to digest the information before he nodded. "All right, I'll teach Wangseja at his speed . . . and try to get to know him better, for Vasilisa's sake."

Aleksandr smiled in relief. "I'm glad to hear you say that."

Ha-Neul stood in front of a mirror in the practice room as royal purple circles appeared on his clothes and forehead, the symbols filling the space inside in a spiral. The spells flashed, and a completely different man stood in front of the mirror. He had the appearance of a southern Balhaen man: darker skin and eyes, a wider face, slightly lighter hair, and a shorter, stouter frame. He also appeared to be wearing the uniform of the Southern Army. Satisfied with what he saw, he turned and walked out of the practice chamber, down a short hallway, and into the lobby of the suite. From there, he went into the dining room where everyone sat.

Su and Ha-Na gasped when they saw him. Evan turned around and started to reach for his gun, sending a shot of fear down Ha-Neul's spine and causing him to lose his focus on his spells for a moment.

"That's Ha-Neul," Aleksandr said. "He's practicing self-concealment spells."

"He needs to work on his concentration while doing other tasks," Vanya added.

Ha-Neul sat down between Ha-Na and Aleksandr. "Today's task is eating lunch and talking to people."

"However, your image already flickered when Evan went for his gun," Aleksandr stated. "The flicker was bad enough that your cover was blown."

Disappointment and irritation stirred his stomach. "I'll try harder next time, Master."

"Just proceed as planned," Vanya said.

He bowed his head. "Yes, Saem."

They started to eat.

"Are we going to do anything for hyeong's birthday?" Su asked.

Aleksandr and Vanya glanced at each other then at Ha-Neul, but he kept his eyes down.

"If I remember correctly, it's Jua fourth," Aleksandr said.

"Yes, that's right," he answered.

"That's a week away," Vanya said.

"It's also the last day of winter," Aleksandr mused. "It's definitely a time to celebrate."

"So we'll do something?" Ha-Na asked, looking hopeful.

"I think we can manage something." Aleksandr grinned. "Since you've spent most of your time inside for the past nine and a half weeks, I think you more than deserve a breather."

"Assa!" Su beamed.

Out of nowhere, Woo Daejang appeared behind Su, who sat in front of Ha-Neul. Before Ha-Neul realized what was happening, Evan had fired a bullet through the daejang's head, making Ha-Neul jump and lose focus on his concealment spell. The daejang disappeared, and Aleksandr looked displeased when he turned and saw the bullet hole in his wall. Ha-Na uncovered her ears.

"You've failed your assignment, Ha-Neul," Vanya said. "We'll try again tomorrow."

Aleksandr looked at Evan. "I thought you had blanks."

"That was a blank," he replied sheepishly.

"The hole in my wall says otherwise." Aleksandr turned away from Evan. "Anyway, we will go out for Ha-Neul's birthday. Vanya and I will start preparing today." The prince turned to Ha-Neul. "By the way, you must always assume there will be surprises or something to create high stress. You cannot let yourself slip because of that."

"I understand, Master." He bowed his head.

Aleksandr motioned for them to continue eating, took one more glance at the hole in the wall, and sighed in exasperation.

Vanya and Aleksandr scrutinized their four guests. Ha-Neul and his nammae were disguised with concealment spells while Evan let his long hair hang loose around his face to obscure his features. Not one of them had had a proper haircut since leaving Mr. Moon's home.

"Everything is hidden except for hair length," Aleksandr stated. "Perhaps we should stop by the barber. They are looking rather unkempt."

"That may be more unreasonable for me," Evan said. He looked uncomfortable as he kept glancing at his hair, obviously hating how long it was though it made him appear his actual age. "You and Vanya already have your spells cast on them and can't spare the concentration for me."

"We'll have to take him under disguise later," Vanya agreed.

Aleksandr nodded. "Very well, then if we are all ready, we can head out."

The prince led them out of the suite and to the elevator, which took them to the underground parking garage. Ha-Neul and Su entered Aleksandr's car while Ha-Na and Evan went with Vanya. Their first stop was a small hair salon the two men seemed to frequent as the stylists greeted them with warm familiarity. They introduced the wangsil and Evan as distant cousins they were showing the city, explaining they all needed a haircut—all except Evan, who refused. The stylists guided Ha-Neul and his nammae into their own chairs and quickly went to work. Within an hour, he paid for their haircuts and they got back in the cars.

They then went to an art museum Ha-Na had expressed interest in. The exhibit they went to had hundreds of woven portrait and landscape tapestries hanging from the walls and ceiling. Many of them were well-known pieces from different countries and celebrated weavers. Some of the works were thousands of years old. One tapestry made Aleksandr gasp in surprise. It was a detailed piece that depicted an ancient cavern with a raven's eye hanging over a stone bird.

"This is a Northern Mountains tapestry," the prince said.

Ha-Neul and Ha-Na examined it more carefully.

"How can you tell?" she asked.

"Look at the thread very closely." They did. "What do you see?"

"I don't—" Ha-Na started, then leaned in so close her breath fogged the thin protective glass. "The real threads are tiny, nearly indistinguishable from each other, woven so tightly they look like larger thread! The weaving is so tight and the thread so fine it's no wonder such detail is in the piece. It's every professional weaver's dream to produce such handiwork. How did I not notice this at first?"

"Spellweavers weave more than magic," Aleksandr said. "The fine craftsmanship and the subject matter would lend itself to make me believe that this is a Northern Mountains piece."

"But how is it here if they don't let anyone into their lands, or let them leave if they get too far?" Ha-Neul asked. "They don't even come out of their lands."

Aleksandr shook his head. "I don't know."

They moved on from the museum to the largest indoor botanical garden in Vires. Su immediately ran off, dragging Aleksandr and Evan along to look at the insect specimens, leaving the other three to walk at their own leisure.

"How far can I move off without straining your spells too much?" Ha-Na asked Vanya.

"Ten yards. Just stay where we can see you."

Ha-Na nodded and set off on a path that ran close to theirs.

"Vasilisa loved this place," Vanya said once Ha-Na was out of earshot. "Su wouldn't shut up about visiting it to my father once it was suggested that we go out today. Apparently, she'd told your brother all about it, knowing how much he likes to study bugs."

Ha-Neul grinned, thinking about Su's enthusiasm. "I'm glad that's one thing that wasn't fake." He stopped to admire a flowering tree. "I can only imagine how much she liked this place."

"She worked here briefly before going to the palace." Vanya laughed. "Sometimes I can still smell flowers, dirt, and fertilizer lingering in the lobby from when she would come home." He turned to face Ha-Neul. "Would you like to see her patch of the garden?"

He nodded eagerly and followed Vanya, keeping an eye on Ha-Na to make sure she stayed in sight. His attention was seized as they crossed a small bridge over a pond full of water lilies, then headed toward a stone bench surrounded by bushes blooming with lilies. One lone lily grew proud and strong in its own patch of ground in the middle of the stone patio that held the stone bench. In his mind's eye, he saw that proud lily wilt in Lisa's hands as the garden behind her started to burn as she faded away.

His throat constricted and he stopped breathing as the emotions and pain of the dream rushed back. He faintly heard Vanya say his name, then felt him shake his shoulders and try to catch him as he fell. His vision began to swim from lack of air, and tears clouded his sight. Someone pressed what felt like a small picture frame into his hands, then smallish hands forced him to look at his own face smiling back at him.

"She's alive, hyeong," Su's voice said softly in his ear. "She's alive. I can feel her life because of this picture, and I can tell you she's waiting for you."

He began to breathe. "I saw her . . . in a dream . . . here." He closed his eyes and shook his head. "She disappeared just as this garden went up in flames, burning me with it."

He opened his eyes and saw everyone looking a little unsettled, except for Su.

"She may be gone, but she's alive," his dongsaeng said, the conviction in his voice driving each word into him. "You just have to find her."

Ha-Neul nodded.

"If you don't mind me interrupting," Aleksandr said, "you need to set up your concealment spells right now."

Ha-Neul took in a deep breath and began to focus. The spells reappeared on his forehead and clothes, flashed, and concealed his true appearance just as several paramedics reached them. Aleksandr turned to them with an apologetic smile and started rambling about low blood sugar and a small bout of asthma—the asthma attack was over and they were just about to get lunch. Su took the picture from Ha-Neul's hands as Vanya and Aleksandr helped him stand before leading them to the botanical garden's restaurant.

After eating, they all decided to stop for the day and go home. As he and Su rode in Aleksandr's car, Su handed the picture frame back to him, and he realized it was the one Lisa had taken to capture the memory of him. Aleksandr glanced quickly at the picture in his hand.

"Vasilisa never kept many pictures," her abeoji said. "She once told me she only kept keepsakes or pictures to remind herself of something important."

Ha-Neul took in a deep breath as his emotions for her resurfaced. "We had an unexpected day off, so we went into the city. The time before this last one we went was on her birthday." He stopped, his chest heaving as he tried to calm himself. "We had an argument—it was just something stupid—and once we got there, we separated." He turned the picture over and set it in his lap. "About an hour later, I found her fighting with a couple of guys outside a café she wanted to visit. I think they wanted her table. So I sat down and apologized for being late."

He closed his eyes as the memory of that day took over. "She told me she could have waited a little longer." He gave a small laugh through his tears and turned to look at Aleksandr. "She was always waiting for me to come around."

Aleksandr's hand shook as he wiped away the tears from his own eyes.

They didn't speak for the rest of the drive, but they seemed to have reached an understanding. Once they parked in the garage, Su quickly got out, but Aleksandr held Ha-Neul back.

"What your brother said—"

"Please don't tell me to prioritize my kingdom over your daughter," he cut in, "because I can't do that. I lost them both on the same day, and I plan to get them both back as soon as possible." He looked Aleksandr in the eye. "I'll need your help to finish my training before summer."

Aleksandr gaped at him. "You can't be—"

"I can go faster, but I'll need two teachers to switch off, and I don't plan on qualifying to be a master."

"Ha-Neul—"

"I can do it. I will do it."

Aleksandr looked through the windshield to see the others waiting for them. "If you can't pass your concealment-spell test tomorrow, you have no deal."

Something in Aleksandr's tone made him hesitate. "What's the test?"

"You will be serving dinner to my guest, General Woo Su-Han."

"Wh—What?"

"The trick in passing this test is to think of it as a reconnaissance mission." Ha-Neul had never seen a more serious expression on the man's face. "Do you understand what I'm saying?"

"If I fail, we all die."

Aleksandr nodded.

"At least I lived to see my birthday today."

45

"Woo Su-Han has become extremely cautious. He believes you're alive and out there somewhere plotting your revenge, so he has increased his security and, I assume, magical protection. Trying to kill him tonight will not be possible or practical. He is a man who has surrounded himself with like-minded allies who can and will fill his place.

"What we need tonight is information, and he is more likely to give it because I have starved him of my support both publicly and privately, and I will require information to give that support. You will be in the room under concealment and acting deaf. If he is not convinced of either, he will kill you."

Ha-Neul fiddled with and straightened his waiter's uniform as he stood in front of a mirror, his mind endlessly running through Aleksandr's instructions and warnings. He stood in an opulent dining hall set for a party of two. Aleksandr had brought him early to let him get accustomed to his surroundings and the ornate counter that would deliver the food he would serve to the two men.

His watch alarm went off, and he quickly silenced it, turning it to vibrate. He stopped fidgeting and focused on his image in the mirror. A concealment spell appeared on his forehead, flashed, and turned him into a plain Viresian male. He then turned and stood at attention as the door opened and another, truly deaf servant ushered Aleksandr in, followed by Woo Su-Han Daejang. The men sat, and he stepped forward to pour water into their glasses.

"He's deaf as well?" Woo Daejang asked in Common, eyeing him.

"Of course." Aleksandr sounded a little bored.

Ha-Neul stepped back, turned, and picked up their salads—spinach leaves with cashews, thin strips of onion, a hint of carrot and cucumber, a sprinkle of fine Viresian cheese, all lightly topped with a vinegar-based dressing— just as the manager of the restaurant had instructed him.

"You probably assume I will ask why you haven't given me your full support."

"I thought it highly likely you would." Aleksandr sprinkled a little more dressing onto his salad. "As you well know, there was a plan to see if Wangseja would change his views about spellcasters, but, unfortunately, before we could see anything definitive, you took action."

"I was led to believe you viewed it as a failure." Woo Daejang spoke around his mouthful of salad.

"I believe my wording would not lead to such misunderstanding."

"Either way, I still took action," Woo Daejang waved off the comment with his fork, and Ha-Neul did his best to keep his features from changing with his anger.

"Yes, you did, and you took more action than originally planned."

"Do you really think the wang and wangseja would have caved to such pressure?"

Aleksandr set his fork down. "With our combined forces surrounding the palace and the rest of his subdued, yes, I believe they would have caved."

"And then the hidden royalty of the northern kingdoms would have taken their rightful thrones and lived happily ever after," Woo Daejang jested lightly.

"The first part of that statement would be true." Aleksandr cast the daejang an irritated glance.

"I think your plans were naïve," Woo Daejang sat back to look at Aleksandr better.

Aleksandr mirrored the daejang's pose but looked a little displeased with him. "At least they wouldn't have cost half the lives your actions did had either one succeeded."

"I did what I believed was best in light of the circumstances at the time."

Ha-Neul's watch vibrated, so he cleared the salad and set a light soup in front of them after discreetly stopping his watch.

"I feel what you did was to appease your pride," Aleksandr continued, ignoring him.

"I did it for our community." Woo Daejang leaned forward, his demeanor imposing. "We are now prospering once again!"

"And what of the normal Balhaens?"

Woo Daejang just smirked. "They'll recover eventually."

Ha-Neul placed his hands behind his back to hide how they shook from anger, but he continued to stare blankly forward.

"And when will that be? When you are declared of

royal blood and become wang? You need two-thirds of the nobles to verify your status."

"Yes, well," Woo Daejang sat back again, flicking his hand as though a fly were irritating him, "I am working on that."

"Really? I heard rumors that the nobility . . . are currently indisposed."

"It's true they fled, but I am searching for them." Woo Daejang sounded a little bored, but his right index finger tapped a quick beat against the arm of his chair.

"What if you can't find them by the three-year deadline to declare you royalty? What will you do then?"

"I will show the world I am the capable ruler this country needs." Woo Daejang's tone was like steel, and it left Aleksandr staring at him quietly. "I have shown my might as a military leader, and I will show my iron will as king."

"You will forsake the title of wang if you cannot have it and become a conquering king."

"It has always been that way with kingdoms, especially throughout the history of Old Balhae and its parent kingdoms."

Ha-Neul's watch vibrated again, and he cleared the untouched soup and set out a fish with lemon juice squeezed over it.

"I, of course, wish to avoid more bloodshed along my path to secure my government, which is why I need help finding the nobles." Woo Daejang picked up his next fork and separated some of the meat.

"How do you expect to find them?" Aleksandr appeared intrigued as he began to cut into his fish.

"I need the help of the spellcaster you employed to

create the protection spell for the war machines," Woo Daejang told him as he took a bite of the fish.

Aleksandr paused and looked up at his guest. "Why?"

"Why else but to create more powerful tracking spells? Of course, I would also have to personally oversee the spells' production."

Aleksandr stopped eating. "This isn't about the nobility, is it?"

Woo Daejang put his knife and fork down to stare coldly at Aleksandr. "If you are unhappy with other implications, then don't think about them."

Aleksandr smirked. "Follow you blindly?"

"No, not blindly. You just need to look the other way after giving me the aid I need. We will all be better off for it."

"I can't do that, for I feel your course of action is not best."

"Now look here—" Woo Daejang pointed his fork at Aleksandr.

"Do not patronize me." Aleksandr spoke coolly, a warning in his eyes. "I do not doubt you want stronger tracking spells, but I do doubt that is all you want with the spellcaster. You want power. You want to expand that—" He stopped as he gazed at Woo Daejang's dangerously closed expression.

Ha-Neul's watch vibrated, and he removed the fish and set down a dish of lamb.

"So you'll kill the wangsil, set yourself as wang or king, and expand through war."

Woo Daejang took a bite of lamb, chewed leisurely, and then swallowed. "Where are the nobles, Aleksandr? With how well they disappeared, I assumed some spellcasters hid them, but I remain hopeful you are not among them."

Spells activated around Aleksandr, washing the room in a dark-blue light, and immediately, several white spells blazed into existence.

"Did you honestly think I would not be prepared for hostilities?" Aleksandr sounded amused. "You are indeed a strong spellcaster, but you are neither a master nor the prince of Vires."

Ha-Neul looked uneasily at all the spells surrounding them. Woo Daejang seemed to be emitting an icy atmosphere that started to freeze the water in their glasses.

"You may be the prince of Vires, but I am the head daejang of Balhae's forces, which have only improved over the last one hundred years."

"I understand your meaning quite clearly."

"Then I believe we are finished with our meal."

"I believe so as well."

Woo Daejang stood. "Then I will count on you to take care." He left the room.

Only when the blue spells had completely faded did Aleksandr turn to Ha-Neul. "You *will* need to finish your training by summer."

"You think he has more planned, don't you?"

"He wants power"—Aleksandr shook as he said the words— "pure power. Not just magic or control over a country, but power."

"I don't understand, sir."

"Magic is a product of pure power," Aleksandr said, "and the only power that exists in this world is the Raven's Eye. He will try to conquer the Northern Mountains."

"Our gajok tried to conquer the Northern Mountains years ago but were turned back within hours," Ha-Na said. Ha-Neul, his nammae, and Evan were strewn about in his room. "Why does Woo Daejang think he has a chance?"

"The protection spell for the war machines," Su said.

Ha-Neul nodded. "The invasion was a disaster because of the sudden attacks. Every person controlling one of those destroyed war machines died. That's no longer a problem."

"But the cost will be astronomical even if war-machine production is so efficient and cheap," she countered.

"They'll go to war for more resources," Evan said. "Old Balhae will need them since Woo Daejang has done nothing to repair the battle damages, so food will start to be scarce in the next year or two. He'll use the money he should have used to rebuild and put it toward the war effort instead."

"So he just has to wait for our food reserves to be nearly empty," she said.

"No, he also needs complete, unopposed authority." Evan sighed. "Many think you're all dead, but what if that is suddenly proven wrong?"

"There'd be civil war," Su said.

"That is the most probable outcome." Evan looked to Ha-Neul. "We just need to find a way to tip the odds in our favor for a surer victory."

"For that, we need information from the palace we can't get here or from our locked palace tablets, but we don't know who to turn to for help either," Ha-Na said. "Aleksandr has even said that he wouldn't be of too much help and neither will Irene since it's too difficult for her to contact us."

"We need a someone who knows and who will freely give that knowledge," Evan agreed.

Su grinned. "So we go to the Raven's Eye." They all looked at him. "If it's really as the legends say, it will know we come peacefully and only for information."

"But will the spellweavers know that?" Evan asked.

"We can hope so," Ha-Neul said, "but be prepared for the worst just in case."

Someone knocked on the door.

"Yes?" he answered.

Aleksandr opened the door and glanced around the room before settling his gaze on Ha-Neul. "We should start your new training regimen right away. If you are ready, come to the practice room."

He nodded. "I'll come soon."

The prince nodded and closed the door. He waited a few moments before he spoke.

"Once my training is done, I'll go to the Northern Mountains."

Ha-Na laughed. "We're all going. There's no room for argument on that."

"But—"

"Evan's been training us," Su interrupted him. "We'll be able to handle ourselves."

He looked to Evan. "When I have time—"

"I'll train you as well."

He nodded and left the room.

46

Vanya opened the door to his father's room, stepped inside, and then quietly closed the door behind him. It was late at night, but his father was still dressed in his suit. He sat in his chair with a single lamp turned on, a silver picture frame in his hand. Vanya knew that frame well and couldn't help but sag with grief knowing his father was hurting. He moved closer to the opposite chair, and his father looked up as Vanya sat down and smiled at him in apology.

"Is it finished?"

He nodded. "When will you do the test?"

His father sighed and rubbed his eyes with his free hand. "Soon. It will have to be soon." He sighed again. "He certainly did as promised."

"He's been training with Evan as well. He's learned to shoot and do hand-to-hand combat, though it's like nothing I've ever seen."

"Evan's techniques and weapons certainly are on the unique side." His father's thoughts seemed to be in turmoil. "They'll do well against most fighting styles, I think."

His father looked at him a little closer. Vanya felt anxious, jittery, and wary, knowing his father wouldn't like what he was about to say. His father turned his eyes back to the picture.

Vanya finally worked up his courage. "They've been talking about going to find the Raven's Eye—making plans for months."

"Yes, I know. I've caught them at it as well."

"I'd like to go with them."

His father's head jerked up, and fear shone in his eyes. "Why?"

"To find Vasilisa for you."

"Vanya—"

"We've lost two family members already, Father." His conviction rose with his voice. "I won't let us lose another, not if she is still alive like Su is adamant about her being."

He watched as his father traced what he knew was Vasilisa's outline.

"I always wondered if she would leave."

"We can get her back," he asserted.

His father shook his head a little. "We can try. The path you have chosen is extremely dangerous. The spellweavers of the Northern Mountains are far different than the spellweavers we have met."

"Father—"

"If Ha-Neul passes his exam, you will be a master and I will have no more hold over you, Vanya. You will be free to do as you please, and I—I will support you with my whole heart."

Relief swept through him. "Thank you, Father."

His father had a sad but proud smile on his face. "You have grown well. Your mother and sister would be proud of you, just as Vasilisa was proud of you."

Vanya let out a breath as he smiled. "She was proud to call you her father."

"It was my honor." His father's breath caught, and tears sprang to his eyes as he traced Vasilisa's outline again. "Bring her home if you can. I have so many things to say to her and apologize for."

Vanya squeezed his father's free hand before he stood and left the room.

Sweat dripped off Ha-Neul's face as he stood shakily on his feet. Aleksandr and Vanya sat in chairs, looking deeply impressed. Only Vasilisa had performed better on the test. Aleksandr tapped a finger against his arm and nodded solemnly. He looked to his son, who couldn't say anything.

"Very well, your testing is done, Ha-Neul," he said. "You have shown impressive and remarkable skill and knowledge of spellcasting. I almost fear what you could have been like had you studied magic earlier. I believe, like Vasilisa, that you would have been a master by now."

"Are you saying I passed?" Ha-Neul barely had enough breath to speak.

He turned to his son. "You are now a master, your pupil having passed his test."

Ha-Neul smiled, and Vanya grinned.

"You certainly are a force not to be underestimated," Vanya told Ha-Neul.

Aleksandr couldn't help but be satisfied with how his son's and Ha-Neul's relationship had improved. "Now that you have finished your training, what is your plan? I suppose you will still search for the Raven's Eye."

The smile on Ha-Neul's face faded.

"Don't worry, I won't stop you. I couldn't if I wanted to." Aleksandr turned to Vanya for a second before he turned back to Ha-Neul. "I just hope you will accept Vanya's request."

"What request?" Ha-Neul asked, turning to Vanya.

"I want to go with you to help search for Vasilisa," Vanya said.

Ha-Neul's mouth worked a little, but he said nothing.

"She's my sister," Vanya continued, some anger coming out in his tone and through his expression. "I have as mu—actually no, I have more right than you to search for her as I please."

"I don't deny that," Ha-Neul whispered.

"So you agree?" Aleksandr asked.

Ha-Neul nodded.

"Thank you." He was surprised by how relieved and grateful he felt. "Now, I imagine the others are waiting for your results so you can finalize your plans. You are both dismissed."

Ha-Neul bowed to him before he followed Vanya out of the practice room. Aleksandr stood and straightened his suit as the door slowly closed. He walked to the middle of the room, lifted his right arm, and slowly brought it down to fade the lights and lock the door. He cast five white spell circles in a half circle around him. The symbols grew increasingly complicated inside the circles, and after ten minutes of intense concentration, the spells activated.

"The current Prince of Vires, Aleksandr Dmitrisson, stands before the council."

"We take it the wangseja's test is over," Professor Tep said.

"How did he fair?" Astrid asked.

"He has passed with astounding marks, nearly matching Vasilisa's score."

"Nearly? In so short a time?" Señor Mijares's voice was disbelieving.

"Had he been given more time . . ." Kisasszony Vajda's voice trailed off.

"He may very well have surpassed Vasilisa," Madame De la Mare said.

"So what happens now, Prince Aleksandr?" Professor Tep asked.

He sighed, reluctant to tell them. "He plans to find the Raven's Eye for aid."

"What!" some said as others exclaimed, "Madness!"

"You don't plan to stop him?" Kisasszony Vajda asked.

"If he doesn't return, everything we have planned is ruined!" Señor Mijares shouted.

"Be quiet," Professor Tep commanded.

There was an awkward silence.

"Prince Aleksandr, do you believe—truly believe—he has a chance?"

"He is going with his siblings, his guardian, and my son." He spoke in a firm tone. "I believe they have the potential to find the Raven's Eye."

"Very well, then we shall continue to do what we can."

"At most, we can give them until next spring to return," Astrid said. "After that, we'll have to cut our losses and revise our plan."

"I am well aware of that fact," Aleksandr said.

"Risks must be taken," Professor Tep said, "and this could be a risk worth everything."

The others agreed.

"We will continue to follow your lead, Prince Aleksandr," Professor Tep assured him. "We have taken up much of your energy already. Please end the spells."

"Until the next scheduled meeting," he said, then ended the spells.

He slowly collapsed to his knees, breathing heavily after using so much magic. After some time, something in his peripheral vision caught his attention, and he looked up at the still-dark lights, confused. A shiver passed through him, and he suddenly became transfixed on a spot a ways above his head and in front of him. A large raven's eye took shape and stared down at him.

A shock jolted through him, and he gasped for breath. He felt his heart pound wildly in his chest—his shirt, vest, and jacket moving slightly to its rhythm. The eye still stared down at him—unblinking, unmoving—and he could not help but stare back. Then it was gone.

He woke on a couch, everyone surrounding him and looking greatly concerned.

"Sir, are you okay?" Evan asked.

He nodded slowly, and then gasped in surprise.

"What is it, Dad?" Vanya was startled by his gasp.

"You should leave quickly," he said. Excitement rushed over him. "You need to leave tomorrow. Everything can be ready by then."

He moved to stand, but they stopped him.

"What are you saying?" Ha-Neul asked.

"You must go tomorrow," his voice shook, but he was indescribably happy. "I can't exactly explain why I feel this way, but I feel hope—utter and complete hope that if you leave tomorrow, you will be safe."

Vanya contemplated his father's expression before he looked at the others. "We should listen to him."

"I agree," Su said.

Evan nodded. "So do I."

Ha-Neul looked reluctant but said, "Then we'll leave tomorrow."

Aleksandr stood and made himself busy with the vigor of a much younger man.

The ferry smoothly sliced its way across the lake toward Otium, the small town on the other side. Ha-Neul looked out on the crystal blue lake and the forest beyond, his pack lying on the deck between him and the ferry's railing. Ha-Na and Evan stood on either side of him. Su and Vanya had gone off to buy a snack for everyone. The sun climbed a little higher, hitting the lake just right for a few minutes so that the water became like glass, revealing its contents for all to see.

"Pictures don't do this place justice," Ha-Na muttered, her eyes following the tiny schools of fish below them.

"All because of the strong interchange between life and magic here."

Ha-Na glanced at him for a moment and smiled.

"I don't care what you've been taught," Evan said, "I just think life is magic."

Ha-Neul let out a short, amused laugh. "Says the boy who is probably the most dangerous of all of us."

Evan's eyes grew heavy, his shoulders slumping forward a tiny bit. "It's not something I take pride in but have found necessary."

His feelings sobered. "I know. I didn't mean to imply—"

"It's okay, Wangseja-Mama." Evan whispered his title. "I did choose this path, though."

Ha-Na lightly bit her lower lip as she stared at Evan. "Where are you from, Evan?"

A wistful smile appeared on Evan's face. "A place you wouldn't have heard of."

"They didn't have any danpatbbang." Su came up behind them, talking to Ha-Neul. "I got you a muffin instead."

He took the muffin. "Thanks, Su." He looked up at Vanya. "Are we still going straight to the mountains after this?"

Vanya nodded. "My friends here have left their mountain bikes at the ferry station. We can take them anytime and use them as long as we need."

"There really are no trails in the Northern Mountains?" Ha-Na asked.

"No one goes in far enough to find out," Vanya said. "Once they realize they've crossed the border, they quickly cross back over."

They looked toward the front of the ferry where a range of short mountains ran toward a much larger, cloud-topped range that looked peaceful from this distance.

"This is going to be a lot harder than it looks." Su put a hand over the right side of his face. "Those mountains are thickly wrapped in magic."

"The spellweavers have their defenses all over that place," Vanya muttered. "It's why your armies didn't last once they crossed the border. Stories say the mountains came alive and fought the invaders off by themselves, but the spellweavers probably just worked from a distance."

"If we're found, it'll probably be the same," Evan said. "If they work best from a distance, they'll work against us like that."

"Hopefully we'll meet some nice spellweavers." Ha-

Na's tone was light, though her expression was anything but.

Vanya nodded. "Hopefully."

Ha-Na smiled at him, and Ha-Neul suppressed an eye roll. He knew Vanya well enough to know that the Viresian didn't underestimate difficult situations. He caught Su's eye, the twinkle within it confirming Ha-Neul's suspicions.

The ferry docked an hour later, and Vanya led them to a bike rack near the entrance of the ferry station. There were five mountain bikes locked to the rack, along with four street bikes. Vanya approached a rusty-red mountain bike, fiddled around underneath its seat for a few seconds, and the chains locking the bikes popped off. Everyone grabbed a chain, stored it in their own pack before they took a bike, and hopped on, following Vanya through the town to its western borders.

Vanya set a good pace toward the short range that met the Northern Mountains, and within twenty minutes of leaving the town, they were biking northeast on the trails. Occasionally they would pass a hiker or two, sometimes another cyclist or a small group, but as they drew closer to the border, they ignored any passersby who tried to get their attention. One cyclist seemed resolute about making them stop, but with a carefully planned spell from Vanya, he was forced to stop to check the chain of his bike while they kept going.

They rested briefly to eat a small lunch, taking only twenty minutes, before they picked up their bikes again. When it was midafternoon, Su shot out from between Ha-Neul and Vanya to bypass Vanya and block the path. Vanya stopped their progress and looked at Su curiously.

"What's up?" Ha-Neul panted for breath.

"There's strong magic ahead," Su said. "I don't think its spellcaster magic."

Vanya nodded. "It could be the warning magic of the border."

"We're that close already?" Ha-Na's breathing was a little harder than the others'.

"Maybe another mile or two," Vanya said. He unzipped his jacket halfway. "I know we can't be too far away." He looked back at Su. "So you can tell the difference between magics?"

Su seemed to consider the question for a moment. "It seems to both . . . feel and look . . ." He shook his head. "I'm not sure how to put it in words, but taste is in there as well. Anyway, it's different from what I've sensed from spell-casters and that ever-present magic I think is Samjogo, the Raven's Eye."

"Uh, okay." Vanya looked up to the canopy, thinking things over. "I wonder . . . maybe you'll be able to sense when the defenses activate." He paused, then shook his head to clear it. "Anyway, thanks for the heads-up. If you sense anything else, shout out next time. I don't want you riding past us again and possibly setting off a trap."

"Okay."

"Good. Let's keep riding until six, then stop for the night." Vanya looked back to see the others agree before he pushed off to pass Su.

Almost an hour later, Ha-Neul felt a chill run down his spine and a sense of dread fill the air. He knew Su and Vanya felt the same when he saw them shiver. But Vanya called back to them to ignore it, saying it was the border warning and that they had finally passed into the Northern Mountains.

47

R iding in the Northern Mountains wasn't difficult. They stayed relatively low where the ground wasn't too rocky or covered in flora. The silence, however, did seem to press in on them. The animals —even the birds and insects—didn't make a sound. It was like they traveled in a bubble of silence, the only real noise coming from their bikes, breathing, and occasional comments, but even those sounds seemed muted.

They traveled in a semi-loose pack, with Vanya in the lead and Evan at the back. Each one of them took in their surroundings, searching for some sign of life or road, but they traveled for three days without finding anything, and they saw that they could soon turn into the mountains through a pass.

"There have never been any reports of human life on this side of the range," Ha-Neul said that night by the fire. "Even when the army invaded, there was nothing."

"Vires and Slovka have never seen anything either," Vanya said.

"So we'll turn inward tomorrow morning." Evan threw some wood on their fire.

Ha-Na wrapped her arms around her legs to warm up faster. "We'll probably run into defenses, won't we?" She looked up at them. "The farther we go in, the more there'll be."

Vanya nodded.

"Do you think they already know we're here?" she asked.

"It would probably be best assume they do," Su answered. "The silence isn't natural."

"You don't sense anything?" Vanya asked.

"The magic is too thick here," Su said.

"They probably have defenses against clairvoyants as well," Ha-Neul muttered. Then he spoke in a louder voice. "We should start having two people on watch tonight. Vanya and Ha-Na can take the first shift, then Su and I, and finally Evan and Vanya."

Everyone nodded and went to their places. When everyone was asleep, Vanya moved closer to Ha-Na, and her heart beat faster.

"Are you scared?" he whispered.

She shuffled her feet a bit as she sat with her back to the fire. "A little. So much has changed in the past year that it's not so bad anymore."

Vanya took her hand and kissed it. "Vasilisa always admired your strength. So do I."

She stifled her laughter, but she couldn't stop the heat rising in her cheeks. "I'm probably the most useless person here. Actually, I am."

"I feel better that you're here. I didn't want to, but I do."

She leaned into him, taking comfort from him as well.

"I'm glad you're here as well."

He let go of her hand and put his arm around her, pulling her close to his side.

The mountain pass was six yards wide at most in some places and three yards wide in others. The silence hung heavier as they moved farther in, nearly becoming a tangible weight after a couple of hours. Ha-Neul noticed Su become more alert and slowed, calling out to Vanya.

"Su?" he asked.

His dongsaeng stopped, and so did everyone else. Su held up a hand as he stood over his bike and studied the surrounding area. After a couple of minutes, his body relaxed and then suddenly tensed as he looked up.

"There!" Su pointed.

They looked up to see a flock of sparrows diving down at them.

"Vanya, do a compression spell ten yards up," Ha-Neul said in Common.

"Wh—"

"Do it! And don't activate it until I say go."

Vanya did so as Ha-Neul cast a different spell. Vanya's eyes widened when he saw Ha-Neul's spell activate.

"Go!"

Vanya's spell activated, reacting to his spell, and an explosion ripped through the flock of birds—sending body parts up before they rained down around them.

"The trees!" Su shouted.

Their branches elongated and twisted toward them. Everyone abandoned their bike and pulled out a machete from beneath their jackets, hacking at any branch that came close, but the branches seemed to stretch limitlessly.

"Run for it!" Vanya yelled and ran deeper into the pass.

As the branches increased in speed, the ground rumbled and roots shot out. More birds started to dive at them. Evan stopped in his tracks and pulled out a long, thin gun from his backpack. He pumped the gun once, took aim at the birds and branches, and released a stream of yellow fire. Then he aimed the stream at the roots starting to crawl up his legs.

Farther in the pass, Ha-Na threw the disk-like grenades Evan provided her into the trees, the blasts blowing apart the surrounding foliage. She crouched for cover, which allowed the roots to swallow her whole.

Su kept shouting warnings as Ha-Neul and Vanya quickly cast offensive spells, sometimes activating them at the same time for more devastating results. A rock came hurtling out of the trees and smacked Su in the stomach. When Su doubled over, another rock hit him in the head, and the branches dragged his limp body away.

Ha-Neul activated a spell on his machete, and it glowed hot, slicing through the plants easily. A falcon's talons scraped his head, and then hit Vanya in the back of the head. It began screeching and clawing at him. Vanya struggled with the bird as another swooped down near him, and he knocked it to the side.

"Go!" Vanya screamed. "Find safety!"

Ha-Neul glanced back, saw the others were still missing, and ran as the roots overwhelmed Vanya. He cast a quick succession of spells, piling them on top of each other, and activated them rapidly, one after the other. The combination blasted a hole through a wall of branches he jumped through before it could close. In front of him stood a line of four men—one, a much older-looking man with long gray hair and a matching beard, stared at him as though he were scum. Partial spell circles that glimmered brown, red, dark green, and teal in front of each man merged and activated, sending a torrent of branches and roots he could not escape. As he tried to fight them off, the neckline of his shirt split open halfway down his chest and his raven's-eye necklace swung out.

"Stop!" a voice cried out in Common, the accent thick and unfamiliar.

The branches crumbled as the youngest of the men, a forty-something-year-old with black hair and green eyes, ran toward him. The man reached out and grabbed the raven's eye.

"It's him! Hurry! Release the others!"

The older man strolled calmly toward them. "Are ya sure?" His accent was even thicker.

The younger man pulled the necklace off despite Ha-Neul's protests and showed it to the leader. The old man looked at it, at him, and sighed.

"Do it," the leader muttered.

Four partial spell circles appeared near each other, quickly combined, and grew more complicated before there was a flash. The ground rumbled and opened to push Evan, Ha-Na, Su, and Vanya out. Another spell circle flashed, and their wounds started healing as they gasped and coughed, finally able to breathe. The leader sized him up.

"Ya showed great talent. I've never seen a spellcaster think and act like ya did. Did ya draw inspiration from us?"

"From the theory," he spat in anger now that his emotions were finally catching up to him. "Will you please let me go?" He struggled against the branches and roots that held him.

The old man smirked, his ice-blue eyes lighting up. "Not just yet. Ya need to calm yourself."

"Why—" Su coughed. "Why did you let us go?" His voice was raspy.

The younger man, who still held the necklace, gazed at Su like the answer was the most apparent thing in the world. "We've been expecting you. We were told to find the Balhaen young man with the raven's eye and to bring in him and his companions."

"Told by the Raven's Eye?" Ha-Na asked.

The old man scoffed. "The Raven's Eye? Please."

"McKennon," the younger man warned.

Ha-Neul barely paid attention to the exchange. "If you were looking for my necklace, can I please have it back now that you've seen it?"

The younger man jolted, apologized, and put it around his neck.

"Dunway, ya go ahead of us. Get things ready," McKennon ordered.

"Yes, sir," the younger man said before disappearing into the trees.

"O'Donnell, Gibney, help me bind and blind them." McKennon looked at Ha-Neul fiercely as spell circles flashed. The roots and branches disappeared, but ropes bound Ha-Neul's hands and feet as his eyes darkened. "We don't want our secrets or captives getting out, now do we?"

Something that felt like a hook yanked on the ropes that bound his hands so that his arms couldn't move. He heard the others awkwardly get to their feet, then the only sound that came from them was their breathing. Someone in front of him moved, not McKennon, and went behind the others.

"We'll be walking for a ways, but it'll be easy going if ya don't struggle," McKennon told them in a mocking tone.

Something pulled on Ha-Neul, leading him well in his blindness.

"Where are you taking us?" he asked.

"You'll see when we arrive." McKennon's voice sounded bored. "No more questions or I'll have ya go mute."

They walked on in silence, but it was no longer oppressive. Birdcalls filled the forest now, and there were the sounds of their softly placed footfalls on old leaves. It all seemed normal, not part of a country that guarded its secrets with thick spells and merciless spellweavers. After walking for some time, something stopped Ha-Neul, and he stood still, trying to sense everything he possibly could. He felt the air stir unnaturally, tickling his skin, until it whipped his whole body, making his skin feel raw. He heard his companions' gasps of pain join his.

"Was that really necessary, McKennon?" a voice asked in the same accent as the others'. It sounded old, so old it was hard to discern whether it was male or female.

"My job is to guard our secrets."

"Yes, however, you need not use such unnecessary force with guests."

"They are not guests."

"We have been told otherwise."

"I do not take orders from ya'll."

The person let out a breathy laugh. "Am I not the gate-keeper? Am I not an elder?" The old voice darkened, sending chills through the air.

McKennon's voice sounded resentful but chastened. "Forgive me."

Suddenly Ha-Neul could see, and his feet and hands were free. When he looked around, he saw they were in a chamber with a rounded ceiling that displayed a mosaic of precious stones forming a map of the world and its two massive continents. He also saw four ancient-looking people sitting in high thrones placed at the four cardinal directions. Each one was robed and hooded with a cowl made of rough looking, purplish-black cloth. They looked at him with amusement as he looked at them with unease.

"Welcome, guests," they said, their voices blending into one. "As gatekeeper and an elder, I welcome you to Our Fair City. Should you experience any difficulties with your guides, you may report your grievances to any elder at your pleasure. Action will be taken."

"I get it!" McKennon snapped, and Ha-Neul quickly stopped his mouth from twitching up in a smirk. "Where's Dunway?"

"He is speaking with his wife and eldest," the gatekeepers said.

"Fine, I'll see ya'll sometime later." McKennon stormed out the door between the north and west elders.

"Continue to observe him, O'Donnell and Gibney," the gatekeepers said.

The two men put their hands over their hearts and bowed deeply.

"Come with us, please," O'Donnell said.

"Please enjoy Our Fair City," the gatekeepers said as O'Donnell led them to the north wall, where a small door now stood open.

The spellweavers led them out into the sunlight. Giant glass spires rose and twisted like extremely lazy swirls of soft ice cream to dot the mountainsides, bridge a canyon river, wrap around the many-fingered lake, and even rose out of the water at the far end. The spires had vines growing up their sides, some of them sporting giant blossoms as round as the sun at high noon. Rough obsidian paved the outdoor pathway where they stood, glistening whenever the sunlight reached it through the thick leafy canopy. A sleek, grayish-black serpentine train in the far distance exited one spire, floating in the air as track plates moved it along, the farthest plate zooming to the front to continue the train's movement. The train wound its way through the other spires. Soon, several more trains filled the air.

Everyone stared at the sight, the wonder in their expressions matching what Ha-Neul felt. O'Donnell and Gibney had gotten a few yards downhill before they realized their guests weren't following. Ha-Neul turned to look at the spired building they had just left and saw it was more ornate than the other spires. It was plated in silver with swirls and strange symbols etched all over it, vines following many of the swirls.

"Millennia of isolation have allowed us to advance in both technology and magic in ways not seen by the outside world," Dunway said.

Ha-Neul turned back to see Dunway standing nearby with a pretty woman about the same age who had red hair and green eyes, as well as young boy. Something about the trio put him and the others at ease.

"How do you hide this from satellites?"

"A mix of magic and technology," Dunway's wife answered. "Allow me to make introductions. My name is Anne Dunway. This is my husband, Sean, and this is our son, Stephen. We'll be your neighbors during your stay in Our Fair City."

"Are you really a spellcaster?" Stephen asked Ha-Neul, eyeing him in disbelief.

"Stephen." Anne put her hand over her son's mouth. She looked up at Ha-Neul with an embarrassed smile. "I'm sorry, it's just we don't see many spellcasters, especially from the outside and of Balhaen descent."

"It's okay," he said, though he now felt uneasy.

"Great." Dunway clapped his hands and rubbed them. "Well, lass and lads, let's get going or we'll miss our train since McKennon is an impatient fellow."

"We're going on one of those?" Evan seemed awed.

"Yup, we're going to She Who Rests Peacefully," Dunway pointed at some obscure spire. "You're going to love it there. Great food, the best entertainment, and even better people. Except McKennon—he's a sour one, that man. Luckily he's rarely there."

"Sean!" Anne looked scandalized.

"What? I can't help but say the truth. Most would say so as well."

Anne rolled her eyes and took Stephen's hand. "We'd best catch the train." She looked at them. "Follow along, please."

Anne turned and began leading Stephen down the mountain path. Dunway beckoned them to follow, and they did, glancing at each other with amusement at the couple's interactions. They walked down the winding path, occasionally spotted with a few steps, until they reached a short train waiting in a clearing. The other three men were already inside. Once they had taken their seats, the doors slid shut and the train rose smoothly into the air above the trees, then began its winding path over the mountains and forest, and—rather quickly—through the spires.

From what Ha-Neul could tell through the glass, each spire housed its own community. He could barely make out the outlines of buildings in many of them. Other than that, details weren't clear as they floated gracefully through the air.

"Trains leave every fifteen to twenty minutes," Dunway

said, "much like your subway systems, but they run every twenty to thirty minutes from midnight to five."

"Best part is it's free," Anne added. "The trains are all automated, and the energy they use is renewable, and there's enough of life going on at night that the trains need to run."

Another train arced gracefully over them, and they dipped below a third.

"Our lives are basically like yours," Dunway continued, "with some details differing."

"We'll take your word for it," Vanya said, looking out his window in amazement.

Dunway chuckled.

"So, what's your job?" Su asked.

Dunway gave him a winner's smile. "I'm basically military. Anne here was in research and city planning. In fact, she helped plan She Who Rests Peacefully."

Anne blushed. "I didn't have a major role in the planning. I just helped design traffic and the commons."

"She designed the commons by herself." Dunway's voice was full of praise. "It was so well done she got an award for her work, but she won't mention that herself."

"I honestly don't find it a big deal," she said. "I only made it as simple and efficient as possible."

Ha-Neul's companions smiled awkwardly, probably feeling a little lost, like Ha-Neul did.

"Sorry, it's just . . . we don't quite understand what you're talking about," Ha-Na said.

The Dunways laughed.

"Don't worry," Dunway said. "All in good time."

"Will ya please pipe down?" McKennon growled. "Some of us are trying to rest."

"You won't rest until you're dead, you old fart,"

Dunway shot back, "and don't start pretending like you care about other people's well-being."

Anne elbowed her husband in the ribs, eliciting a yelp from him, and he rubbed his side, hissing as he drew in a breath.

"We'll do our best to keep our voices down, McKennon." Anne's tone was reassuring, but McKennon harrumphed as he closed his eyes and crossed his arms, earning him a secret scowl from her. "Seriously, I hope you get partnered with someone else soon," she whispered to her husband.

"How long have the spellweavers been settled here?" Su asked.

"Always," Stephen said. "Most of the magic users left a long time ago."

Anne nodded. "Aye, though we don't resent them for that. We know that the others being out there helps the world thrive."

"It's just that they are more likely to fall to evil being out there," Dunway said. "We respect why your ancestors left, but they knew it would have consequences for their children."

"Total lockout?" Evan asked.

Anne and Sean nodded.

"Except for you five, of course," Anne added.

"Because you were ordered to let us in?" Vanya asked.

"Well, yes," Dunway said.

"By the elders?" Ha-Neul prompted.

"The elders only relayed the message," Dunway answered. "You'll find out the rest when you need to."

"Until then we'll be staying at She Who Rests Peacefully, which is the name of one of the spires that makes up the whole city?" Su asked.

Dunway laughed. "You make it sound like a prison sentence when it's not. You'll be free to visit the other holdings in the city as much as you like until the midsummer festival."

"What happens at the midsummer festival?" Evan asked.

Dunway and Anne smiled.

"The temple opens," Dunway said.

"That's enough for now. We're arriving," Anne said.

They approached a spire on the southern banks of the lake. Countless vines thicker than human bodies gracefully scaled its sides, smaller tendrils holding clusters of poppies, their colors mixing wherever the vines crossed. A door slid open in the side of the upper part of the spire to let them enter, and the train turned in the wide space above the community. Before the train settled on the side of the spire, Ha-Neul caught a glimpse of a large park with a small replica of the lake outside, surrounded by four rings of buildings.

"Ah, it's so good to finally be home." Dunway stretched his arms. "We'd been waiting for you to show for a couple of weeks."

"Let's just get them to their house," Anne said. "Then we can get a bit of lunch."

"We have a house?" Ha-Na looked shocked.

"Of course, since we've known you were coming for quite a while now," Dunway said.

"How long is a while?" Evan asked hesitantly.

"About thirty years," Anne said as if it were common knowledge.

"Thirty years?" Ha-Na's voice was almost shrill.

"Don't worry." Anne waved off her astonishment as though it were no big deal. "We'll answer your questions as best we can once you're all settled."

The Dunways led them down a shallow but lengthy ramp that followed the curve of the spire. As they walked, people heading toward the train whispered excitedly when they saw Ha-Neul and his nammae. Some even looked at them in awe. They reached a large lift with seats and harnesses. The Dunways sat and pulled their harness down, locking it into place. Ha-Neul and the others followed the Dunways' example, and within five minutes a voice warned them of departure before the doors slid shut and the lift sped down the wall of the spire a half minute after that. Just as he began to feel sick, the lift stopped neatly, the harnesses popped up, and the doors opened again.

They stepped out onto a platform that overlooked She Who Rests Peacefully. The houses were built on a giant, shallow slope split into shallower levels before the slope completely leveled out in the center of the spire. The homes were loosely spaced in groups of six that shared a large grassy space in the back. There were one or two wide trees on their front lawns, with about three in the shared space. Every so often, a small park dotted the landscape, usually surrounded by six clusters of houses on every side. The roads gave plenty of room for people to stroll along them or ride bicycles while scooped-out, egg-shaped floating trams ran smoothly along their middles, picking up and dropping off passengers at their homes. The seats were set on both sides of an eight-sectioned tram. Many of the trams ran back down the slope to the center, where the four rings Ha-Neul noticed from above were made up of business-lined streets. He could see tiny figures eating out on balconies or patios in the rings or picnicking beside the lake or on floating plat-forms on the water, occasionally jumping in to swim for a bit.

Anne touched his shoulder to get his attention. "Come along now. You can explore as much as you'll like soon enough."

He nodded and followed her to a tram, where he sat between Stephen and Su. The tram lifted and zoomed off, winding its way through the curvy streets as it kindly warned pedestrians of its approach with ever-changing music. After a few minutes, the tram stopped halfway down the slope, a quarter of the way around the spire to the left, in front of a couple of two-story homes made of tinted glass and woodlike tempered steel. It looked elegant in its near normalcy.

"You can look through all the outside walls, but no one can look in until you place your window specifications." Anne looked pleased with the houses. "All the public rooms have transparent walls while all the private rooms are darkly tinted to act like real walls from the outside. Of course, that can be changed too—by parents or the room's occupant."

The door to the house on the left opened and three smaller children ran out to hug Dunway. He scooped each child, another boy and two girls, into his arms to give them tight hugs and big kisses on their cheeks.

"Little runts," Dunway growled to their delight. He lifted his chin toward the others as he held a small girl in his arms. "Greet the guests, kids, and be polite about it, like I taught you."

The two middle children did a Balhaen bow while saying, "Annyeonghaseyo."

"I hope they did well." Dunway suddenly looked nervous.

Ha-Na smiled. "It was fine." She smiled bigger at the three younger children and waved as she said, "Annyeong!"

The kids looked embarrassed and became shy.

"Anyway, let's show them the house." Anne had a laugh in her voice.

As they entered the house on the right, they found themselves in a large sitting room decorated and furnished more for ease and relaxation than for formal visits. The stairs leading up were tucked neatly into the far-right corner to be as out of the way as possible. The room behind the sitting room was a kitchen-and-dining-room combination large enough to fit a party of twenty if they wanted. Off to the right, running along the dining room and sitting room, was an even larger living room furnished with the same theme of ease and relaxation as the sitting room. The stairs to the second floor led to a large open area where four doors were set in each wall. Three doors led to bedrooms—two of them with two beds—and the last led to a large bathroom for guests, though each bedroom had its own bathroom. The house also had a basement. The stairs to the basement were under the stairs to the second floor, accessible by a door in the kitchen. The basement was one wide-open room.

"Basements are generally used for magic practice," Dunway explained. "The materials in this room can absorb anything you throw at them. This one was made for your particular use," he said to Ha-Neul. "After seeing how you used your spellcasting, I understand why this basement was more particularly reinforced than others."

"This whole house was planned for us from the beginning?" Su asked.

"Aye, that it was."

"Interesting," his dongsaeng mumbled.

"Well, now that you've toured the house, why don't you clean up while I get some lunch ready?" Anne said as they walked up the stairs. "Just come over to our house and walk right in when you're done. Make yourselves at home, okay?"

"See you in a bit," Dunway said. "Afterward, we'll get you a few groceries."

The Dunways left with smiles on their faces, leaving them all to nearly collapse with the overwhelming experience.

"What is going on?" Ha-Neul sat in a cushy chair once the door was shut.

"I can't believe they started preparing for us thirty years ago." Ha-Na looked lost and dazed, trying to sort all the information they had just received.

Evan fingered his belt. "How could they know about us that long ago?"

"Perhaps it's Samjogo, the Raven's Eye," Su said.

"Did you see how McKennon reacted when it was mentioned?" Vanya asked. "He mocked the idea—mocked the very fact that we brought it up."

"I think he was just trying to make us leave, or at least make us doubt ourselves about whether it exists," Su said.

"I hope it does," Ha-Na muttered.

Su grew serious. "It does. This place is covered in that weird magic. The spellweavers brought us to the Raven's Eye location."

"The temple," Ha-Neul whispered as he remembered that piece of information. "We can't get to Samjogo until the temple opens."

"Which won't be until midsummer," Vanya reminded him.

"So we've got plenty of time to wait until it does," he said. "We should find out as much as we can about this place and how the Raven's Eye is connected to it. And maybe why Aleksandr thought it was a good idea for us to get here so early."

"I think the Dunways will tell us more about this place and why they were expecting us now if we ask," Su suggested.

"They don't seem too keen to talk about the Raven's Eye, though," Evan said. "But if this place is tied to it, they won't be able to avoid the subject forever."

Ha-Neul nodded. "Then let's get cleaned up and get some lunch."

48

The Dunways refused to answer any questions about the history of the city, saying there would be plenty of time before midsummer to talk and that their guests should get settled over the next couple of days. Once they had agreed after trying to change the couple's minds, Anne served thick sandwiches on hardy bread that more than satisfied their empty stomachs. As they ate, Anne told them she would show them how to call a tram and choose their destination, as well as show them where the closest grocery market was. She did as she promised once they finished eating, leading them to the front door, where she pressed a blue light that called up a screen. She showed them how to call a tram, tell it when to come, where to go, and for how many people.

"This allows traffic control to plan the most efficient routes for all the trams," she explained. "The more time you choose to wait for the tram, the better the efficiency. Many of our watches," she held up her wrist to show a clear glass band, "allow for on-the-go calls. If you want, we can get you some while we're out. Otherwise, I'll just point out the tram call stations so you know what to look for if you're out and about."

"I think the call stations will do fine enough," Ha-Neul said.

"Very well." She looked outside as a small chime tinkled from the wall. "Our tram's coming. Let's go out now."

"I'll stay here with the kids," Dunway called from the kitchen, already wrestling all four of them.

"Just take it somewhere safer!" Anne looked exasperated. She added in a softer voice, "I swear, they always pick the worst places to have their wrestling matches."

With amused expressions, they followed her outside just as the tram pulled up. A few people got off the tram, stopping in their tracks when they saw Ha-Neul, his nammae, and Vanya with their epicanthic eyes and the wangsil's overall appearance, marking them out as foreigners. Anne greeted a couple of people as they took their seats on the tram, and then they zoomed away, lively music coming from the tram as it made its way through the streets. After a couple of minutes, it stopped at a group of buildings partially open to the air. They were filled with stalls of food, small appliances, and other, random wares. Anne led them to a display tree and chose four canvas bags, giving one to each male, before they started to make their way through the crowd—many of whom stopped to stare at them—to choose the foods they wanted.

"Your kitchen is stocked with every utensil and appliance we thought you'd want, and we have some ingredients for your traditional foods," Anne told them. "So feel free to get whatever you want. There is a fund for your use."

They stopped.

"You even have a fund for us?" Ha-Na asked.

Anne turned around and nodded. "Of course, we knew

you'd need money for food and clothes, as well as some entertainment expenses."

They continued to make their way through the market, and at one point, they seemed to pass a more medicinal section. A woman let out an excited cry and hugged a root to her breast, tears streaming down her cheeks.

"Oh, thank the Observant! It's finally here!" she said and kissed the root.

"Well, do you have enough for now?" Anne asked.

Ha-Na and Su nodded.

"Good—"

"Anne?" Ha-Neul motioned to her.

"What is it, dear?"

"What's the Observant?"

Anne smiled. "Why, it's exactly as it sounds. Don't worry about it for now. We'll tell you more once you're settled. How about we go pay for the lot, okay? You all look exhausted and likely need some rest. Goodness knows what McKennon put you through before Sean recognized you." Then she looked surprised, as if she'd just remembered something. "Oh, I almost forgot to show you the calling stations for the tram! Silly me!" She laughed.

They paid for their groceries once they had placed their bags on a large pad and a list of their contents was displayed on a screen. Anne had Ha-Na scan her eye with a small camera set next to the screen, and the transaction was made automatically. They left the market at a different entrance so Anne could show them a small hovering half egg with a pleasantly lit screen, then helped Su call for a tram.

Once they were at the house, Anne helped them put the groceries away and showed them the house controls. She then left after encouraging them to rest for the remainder of the day. Ha-Neul turned to Su, who was drinking a glass of water in the kitchen.

"Will they ever actually tell us what's going on?"

Su set his glass down on an island countertop. "They seem serious so far, but I think we'll get the information only in bits and pieces until midsummer."

"Why?" Vanya asked.

"Perhaps they think it'll be hard for us to handle if we get all of that information at once."

"So they'll be adamant about spoon-feeding us the information," Ha-Neul said, a little exasperated.

Ha-Na sighed. "That'll get old fast."

"Not if it's what we need," Evan said thoughtfully.

"What do you mean?" Vanya asked.

"They've known we would come for thirty years," Evan reiterated. "Someone had to tell them, which means someone knows us well."

"That's almost like a god," Ha-Na said.

"Or Samjogo," Ha-Neul added.

"The Raven's Eye?" Vanya looked incredulous, then caught himself. "Maybe."

"There seems to be something about this Observant as well," Su said. "It almost sounds like an incredibly strong clairvoyant."

"One of the many answers to eventually learn," Ha-Neul muttered.

Evan laughed. "We have plenty of time before midsummer. We can look for the answers ourselves."

He grinned. "You're right, and we have been told to explore as much as we want."

"So let's do some exploring," Ha-Na said, excitement blossoming in her eyes.

It didn't take long to get used to the trams and trains, and within three days they were getting used to the other spires' modes of transportation as well. They soon learned that most spires were community holdings—all designed very differently from each other—and that some spires were more laid out like a metropolis and its suburb, the metropolis hanging high above the suburb. Other spires were mostly for agricultural or industrial purposes, with very limited space for inhabitants. One spire was purely for entertainment. The bottom of that spire was designed for water recreation, whereas amusement parks, theaters, and other facilities rose high into the spire. They were soon able to distinguish what a spire might contain by its name.

Occasionally, Dunway would act as guide, having an uncanny knack for appearing when they were to visit the busier spires. Sometimes on their excursions, they would meet a robed and cowled elder who would take interest in their activities.

"Have you noticed there aren't any churches?" Vanya asked.

Dunway seemed to hear Vanya as he spoke quietly with an elder.

"We don't gather in large congregations," the elder replied. They all looked to her. "We worship in small groups, with close family or friends. The only time we have large gatherings are for celebrations. The only religious structure we have is the temple."

"Where is the temple?" Su asked.

The elder smiled kindly. "Not in any of the holdings." She turned to Dunway, nodded, and left.

"Well," Dunway said, "how about we go eat lunch with

Anne and the kids? Afterward, while the kids go play, Anne and I will answer some of the questions you have."

They nodded and followed him to the train. When they arrived at Dunway's home, Anne was serving slices of meat pie to the children and had a few more plates set out for them. As they ate, the children asked them questions about their country, making them look at each other a little uncomfortably, but they still answered their questions, editing out some information. Occasionally Anne or Dunway would ask a question as well—their own curiosity getting the better of them.

Once they had finished eating, Anne shooed the children to the backyard, where a few other kids waited with their faces pressed to the glass of the back door. With the door soundly closed behind the children, the atmosphere became more serious.

"What would you like to know?" Dunway asked.

"Is the Raven's Eye here?" Ha-Neul said.

Amused smiles lit their faces.

"We don't use the name Raven's Eye for a person," Dunway explained. "The raven is only a symbol—"

"I know the mythology behind the raven," Ha-Neul cut in. "It was explained to me last year."

Anne pointed to the others. "Do they know?"

They all nodded.

"Good, that makes this a little easier." Dunway looked a little relieved. "I assume you've believed the Raven's Eye is a thing you can make requests to, but that's not true."

"So what is it?" Su asked.

"It's a power," Anne answered. "However, that's all we're allowed to say on the subject except, since you know the mythology of the raven, you won't be too far from the truth. It will be more fully explained to you on midsummer's day."

"Next question," Dunway said.

"Who told you we were coming?" Ha-Na asked.

Dunway looked even more amused. "I suppose you will also want to know how it was known you would be coming for thirty years."

"Yes," Vanya agreed, "and why we are here so early if we have to wait until midsummer to get answers."

"For your second question, all we know is that it was for your safety. Had you waited any longer, it would have been far more difficult for you to come. For the first question, you will meet that person midsummer," Dunway said.

"Is the Observant the one with the Raven's Eye power?" Su asked.

Anne smiled. "A clairvoyant is a difficult person to hide information from." She sighed. "You will find out more midsummer."

"Why midsummer? Why not now?" Evan asked. He looked a little irritated, along with Ha-Neul and the others.

"It's when the temple opens to the public, and so is the only time when you can get better answers than the ones we can give you," Dunway said. "Trust me, I'd tell you everything I could, but it's been determined that it's better for you to wait to get the full truth from the source."

"That's four weeks away," Ha-Neul said, unable to hide his bitterness.

Su looked from Dunway to Anne and back several times. "So the Observant is in the temple and has known we were coming for thirty years." They gave Su a steady gaze, not revealing anything. "We'll have to wait, then." He looked at the others. "We won't get any more information that may concern either the Observant or the Raven's Eye."

"Then who are the elders?" Ha-Na asked.

"They are older, stronger spellweavers who are also well-educated and knowledgeable in our theology," Anne explained. "Elders come in twos most of the time—as husband and wife. They help make sure we don't forget or change the history of our people and doctrine of the gospel. They also serve as judges and juries if necessary."

"What about the gatekeepers?" Vanya asked. "What's the gate, anyway?"

"The gate is where the gatekeepers sit," Dunway said. "It allows us to teleport to specific points all over the Northern Mountains. The gatekeepers are the elders who manage the gates—they determine who can use or access them. We can't enter any city unless the gatekeepers allow it."

"So they're incredibly strong, even for elders," Evan stated.

"Individually, yes, but together, it would be stupid or deadly to underestimate them," Anne said. "Spellweavers' magic is more powerful the better we act as one. The gatekeepers have to act nearly perfectly as one or terrible accidents occur."

"So that's why they spoke as if they were the same person," Ha-Neul said.

"They still remember their own individuality," Dunway said, "but they understand better than most of us the benefits of acting as a group."

"Any more questions?" Anne asked.

Ha-Neul looked at the others and saw the answer in their eyes before they all shook their heads.

"Well, if you do think of something, please feel free to ask," Anne assured them. "I know you're not satisfied with all of our responses, but you will get your answers soon."

"The elders have granted you access to our spellcasters' libraries," Dunway told Ha-Neul and Vanya. "You may find something new in their books." He looked to Su. "We also have libraries for clairvoyants, which you are free to access as well. There are also weavers who are willing to pass along what they can to you," he said to Ha-Na.

"And you can look forward to all the festivities," Anne said with a smile. "The three weeks leading up to midsummer are the best."

A child knocked on the back door. Anne stood and opened it, crouching down when the child, looking incredibly nervous, beckoned to her so he could whisper in her ear.

Anne stood and turned to them. "He wants all of you to play with them."

"Sure," Su said, bouncing up.

Ha-Na stood. "That'll be fun."

Ha-Neul and the other two agreed and followed the boy outside.

49

All of the holdings were busy preparing for the festival for the next two weeks. Whenever they went out, the streets, trams, and trains were packed full of people getting ready. Booths and stalls began popping up in parks and squares, their signs teasing would-be festival-goers of wares and delicacies to come over the thirteen-day celebration. Dunway was with them at all times whenever they went out, or if they separated, O'Donnell and Gibney would show up as well—sometimes even a very put-out McKennon, though he never joined Ha-Neul's group.

They spent most of their time in their house, reading, practicing magic, or doing other activities, sometimes even playing with the neighbor kids. The children started to teach them some of the games that were played at the festival. Sometimes they took delight in explaining wrong directions only to watch the foreigners look ridiculous or lose the game before breaking down in hysterical fits of laughter and then teaching them the correct way to play.

However, as the festival drew closer, the atmosphere of

all the holdings began to change. They became brighter but more solemn, excited yet more reserved, and full of anticipation. The whispers that followed the foreigners wherever they went fed the atmosphere, but they could never quite catch what it was about themselves that caused such energy.

The first night of the Festival of the Creators celebrated the "Redeemer," the Creator responsible for the exaltation of all the others and one of two the festival would end with. Children ran between game booths, food stalls, and small storytelling stages where men and women enthusiastically retold small portions of the Redeemer's story—or the first half of the Creator's story the day was celebrating—and stories of minor Creators. Teenagers and adults took part in their own games, music performances, or dancing.

As the night sky grew darker and the stars made an appearance, the lights in the holdings slowly dimmed, and the residents moved toward the center of the holding. Finally, the only lights were the stars, and everyone quieted. A low, slow drumbeat sent a wave through the crowd lining the large street separating the park from the businesses. The drumbeat built in intensity as the first float of the parade appeared. It was a simple stage with a man dressed in a white robe singing a cappella of tragedy, heartache, love, and sacrifice in a clear voice. The song was emotional, and for some people, Ha-Neul could see, cathartic. Most people shed at least one tear, while others had tears streaming down their cheeks.

The man's song finished, calling for the masses to celebrate, and the drumbeat quickened its pace, becoming the sound of multiple drums. Large floats made their way through the crowd, depicting tales of the battles the Redeemer—a male or female performer dressed in white— fought before the Creator's brilliant transformation into a higher form before making the ultimate sacrifice. Cheers spread throughout the crowd.

As the final float passed, the crowd began to chant. "Saoraidh fhèin iobradh air ar son. Saoraidh fhèin iobradh air ar son. Saoraidh fhèin iobradh air ar son."

When it seemed the entire holding was chanting, a series of quick drumbeats shook the crowd. The holding went silent. The people pulled candles from their pockets and lit them. They stood there for several minutes with their eyes closed, letting a feeling of peace and assurance settle over everything.

"Tha sinn a 'toirt taing dhut airson do ìobairt," they whispered as one.

They blew out their candles and went home.

The festivities for many of the other Creators were similar, though the ends of the parades were not as somber and created a greater sense of hope and excitement. The days passed quickly, and soon it was the third to last day of the festival, the day the city celebrated the Warrior. Ha-Neul, his nammae, Evan, and Vanya wandered the streets, watching various sword dances, many of which featured two blades. As they watched one performance, Anne and Dunway came up to them.

"Do you like it?" Anne asked.

They all answered that they did.

"I can't wait to see the Sunderer tomorrow," Ha-Na said.

Dunway laughed. "That is a mighty-fine performance."

"But the best is probably the Redeemer and Advocate's performance," Evan said.

"It should be, since it's the last performance," Ha-Neul nudged him.

"It is." Anne looked a little disappointed.

Su turned to face her as soon as she'd spoken. "We won't be able to see it."

"No, you won't," Dunway shook his head. "You'll need to be at the temple before it opens, so you won't be able to see the performance and make it there in time."

"Why do we need to be there when it opens?" Vanya asked.

"So there will be enough time for you to do what needs to be done," Dunway answered.

"But we'll get our answers?" Ha-Neul pressed.

"That you will," Dunway assured him.

On the last day of the festival, they met Dunway and Gibney at a large gate that opened onto a mountain trail. It was midafternoon and the sky was partially cloudy, making the weather nice enough to hike comfortably. When they all seemed ready, the two men led them out of the gate to walk the path.

They didn't speak much as they hiked the tall mountain, its path winding lazily, switching between natural ground and boardwalks that made the hike easier. Every hour and a half, they took a short break before continuing up the mountain. One break was longer, so they could eat a little dinner. Just as the stars were starting to make their appearance, they reached a cavern entrance. Dunway and Gibney led them inside, and as they moved deeper into the cavern, several lights faded into existence on the walls and ceiling, revealing a smoothly worn rock face leading to a stone desk in front of a pair of oak doors set in a granite wall. Behind the desk sat two elders.

"Welcome to the temple, honored guests." The elders spoke as one. "You are permitted to enter and wait until the appointed time for your audience. Misters Dunway and Gibney shall continue to be your guides inside the temple."

Two more elders held the double oak doors open. They walked around the desk and entered an all-white room, the only colors—though they were mellowed—came from the furniture and gold-encased wall borders. To their left and right were corridors leading to other rooms while in front of them was a stone door that looked as though it opened for an elevator. However, what stood out to Ha-Neul was the atmosphere of the place: it was peaceful, comforting, sacred. Never before had he felt such a tangible feeling from just walking over a threshold.

Dunway and Gibney took a seat in one of the many lightly cushioned chairs and motioned for them to sit as well. They did so, and Ha-Neul found that the furniture was more comfortable than it appeared.

"How long do we have to wait?" he said in a near whisper, not wanting to disturb the feeling of the place.

"It will be a couple of more hours," an elder replied in the same tone. "Please feel free to nap while you wait. You have a long day ahead of you tomorrow."

The elder's words were almost like a spell, making his eyelids droop with exhaustion before they finally closed and sleep overcame him. Then something woke him. It was a sensation so light, yet it demanded his attention. As he sat up, he saw Dunway and Gibney dressed in new clothes that were clearly military but designed to be loose, allowing for freer movement, and the same black color as all the elders' robes.

"It's almost time," Dunway said, motioning to the stone door.

They all stood and faced the door, a sense of expectation buzzing in the air.

Somewhere, perhaps deep within the mountain itself, a deep bell tolled throughout the temple, and the stone door started to slide open. As the twelfth and final toll faded away, the door was completely opened, revealing a staircase that led farther up into the mountain.

"Follow us," Gibney ordered, "and stay behind us until we say otherwise."

The staircase easily had two hundred steps before it leveled out and led down a long hallway that gradually grew darker. At the end were two large natural-rock doors. On the face of the doors were three circular disks in a triangular formation that looked as if they rotated. The disk at the top had a clean line through it. Dunway and Gibney each placed their right hands on either side of the line, and the door began to swing in, letting out slightly warmer air on a soft breeze.

"You will enter first," Dunway told them.

They stepped into a huge, naturally carved cavern, and they could see two flickering points of light at the other end, beckoning them forward. Ha-Neul felt as though anticipation and longing filled the cavern, growing more pronounced the farther they went in. As they moved forward, the two points of light slowly grew to form two flames atop two stone basins carved from the same stone of the cavern, and McKennon and O'Donnell—both dressed in the same clothes as Dunway and Gibney, though they held bladed staves—stood in between and next to a large, imposing statue of a raven ready to strike out, its wings nearly reaching the opposite sides of the cavern and its head nearly touching the lower ceiling.

It wasn't a statue.

It was a throne.

The inner claws of its outstretched legs were armrests.

A figure that sat on the throne several feet above them slowly became more discernible as they approached. Fine black cloth completely enshrouded the person before it bound him or her to the throne. The cloth then spread out behind the throne. They stopped several yards away, unable to come any closer due to the raw power that surrounded it.

"Show your respect and bow!" McKennon ordered.

"That is enough, McKennon." A female voice full of warmth, sympathy, empathy, and authority filled the cavern, and the atmosphere around them changed to match her tone. "They are my guests and deserve your respect."

McKennon turned to the statue and bowed deeply. "Please forgive me, My Lady. I did not mean to cause thee offense."

"I know, McKennon. It is all right." The atmosphere changed, a sense of longing, fatigue, appreciation, and resolution gently washing over Ha-Neul. "I must speak to them alone."

"M-m-my Lady, we cannot do that," McKennon said. "We are tasked to guard thee."

"I shall be safe. They will not harm me."

McKennon still looked uneasy, making Ha-Neul even

more irritated with the man.

"I must order it, McKennon," the voice said, sounding more authoritative.

McKennon looked defeated as he bowed and gave them a withering glare, especially Ha-Neul, then led the other spellweavers away. The doors to the cavern closed a few minutes later, leaving them to stare at the woman on the throne in awe.

"Who are you?" Su asked, clearly enthralled. "Are you Samjogo?"

The air around them grew warmer as amused laughter filled the silence. "I am the Observant, the Creators' Chosen to hold all power so that I may guide this domain."

"You have the Raven's Eye," Ha-Na commented.

"That is correct," the Observant said. "The Raven's Eye is my greatest power."

"Which is what, exactly?" Evan asked a little anxiously.

"The Raven's Eye is the power to see all paths. I see the past, present, and every possible future." Evan's unease grew as Ha-Neul's own emotions began to boil thinking of what her words implied. "I not only see the grand scope, but each and every person's path."

"How can one person possibly see all that?" Ha-Neul's tone was incredulous.

"Did you not come in search of the Raven's Eye because you believed it would know how to help you in retaking your kingdom and finding your lost loved one?"

He didn't answer, but his anger boiled.

"You, along with any magic user, know that many impossible things become possible because of magic. Imagine what a person could accomplish with raw power. I can merely make almost all impossibilities possible."

"Wh-why were you chosen for this?" Vanya asked.

"I am one of the first children the Creators brought to this world. I have been here since the beginning. Because of me, magic was born."

"You're immortal?" Ha-Neul, Vanya, and Evan exclaimed.

"Not in the true sense. I can and will one day die."

"So you've simply been watching everything for millennia?" Ha-Na looked shocked.

"Of course not. My task is not merely to watch. Among other duties, where it is needed and possible for me to do so, I shape, guide, and do my best to help my domain take the best path possible."

"You meddle." Ha-Neul's tone was eerily calm as he spoke in Haeche, but the fire of understanding and anger burned within him. "You play with people's lives. You made me and others like me a spellcaster and caused my eomeoni to die. Just how much have you played with our lives to help your domain 'take the best path possible'?"

The cavern became slightly oppressive as the Observant's voice filled with indignation. "I do not play with lives."

"No, you *guide*, you *shape*, and you have them *killed*," he spat.

"Ha-Neul," Ha-Na whispered.

"You *guided* us here," he accused. "You've been *playing* with us. Why?"

The atmosphere chilled, but then warmed to a more comfortable temperature. "I do what I do to get the best possible outcome."

"The world's a mess! My kingdom is a mess because of your tampering!"

"You must trust that it is all for the best; otherwise darkness will swallow this world."

"It's already been swallowed whole, no thanks to your meddling!"

He turned and started to walk away. As he neared the center of the cavern, a small pedestal holding a single black feather appeared in front of him.

"What is this?" he asked in exasperation.

"It's a Memory Object," said the Observant. "Aleksandr Dmitrisson taught you about them. You can test it to see if it is a true Memory Object if you so choose."

He cast a spell on the feather, but nothing happened, the sign that it was real.

"What's the memory?" he asked as his curiosity matched his anger.

"Your life," she paused, then spoke with careful, deliberate clarity, "the one you would most likely have lived had I not chosen to be the Observant."

Intrigued, he stared at the feather, debating whether he should pick it up. Behind him, he heard the others approach, and before they could say anything, he took the feather, and a tidal wave of memories smashed into him.

He rode in a rickety car with his bumo and a much younger Ha-Na. Outside the windows he could see rundown buildings that were not nearly as well constructed as the buildings he knew. The economic wealth of his country seemed to be barely efficient, from what he saw. He also noticed that the city seemed to be half as populous as it should have been, and the people he did see—including his gajok—did not seem to be as well rested or as healthy as in his own memories.

"The plague is coming back," his abeoji muttered to his eomeoni.

"Oh, gods, yeobo! What are we going to do?"

His abeoji shook his head. "The only thing we

can do."

The memories raced to his fateful birthday. There was Aleksandr and his hyeong, though the man seemed different in a way Ha-Neul could not place. He watched through his own eyes again as a viper came out of their hands and attacked him and his eomeoni. He relived his eomeoni's funeral and was shocked to see how his abeoji had aged ten years in three days.

As Ha-Neul grew and took up his responsibilities, reports of plague, famine, war, and small population growth slowly crossed his eyes on printed papers held in small binders. He also saw harsher laws passed against magic users in his kingdom, all under his own direction because his abeoji's health was failing.

Lisa never came to the palace.

The revolution came, and he watched as armed soldiers assassinated his abeoji and wounded Su. He and his nammae managed to escape, even though Evan was not there to help, and they vowed to fight back. A war started under his direction, with Ha-Na and Su by his side, but once he learned Su was a clairvoyant, he had his dongsaeng executed for treason. He watched Ha-Na leave then Woo Su-Han's forces eventually captured her. Woo Su-Han personally staked her head on the palace wall. As the years of war raged on, he saw himself grow weaker—both politically and physically.

On his twenty-ninth birthday, his unused magic literally exploded out of his body, wiping out all plant life within a fifty-mile radius.

His vision cleared as he gasped for air because of the faint, lingering sensation of his magic ripping itself out.

"There are many factors I cannot change." He realized he was back in front of the Observant, lying on the ground, his chingu and nammae hovering above him. "You were always going to be wangseja, you were always going to have Su and Ha-Na as your siblings, you were always going to be a spellcaster and Su a clairvoyant, and you were always going to be accidentally responsible for your mother's death. However, you have seen that the world would be vastly different if I did not become the Observant."

"Why did you choose this?" he asked in Common, standing along with the others.

"I am the one who set the domain off the best path," the Observant told him, her voice and the surrounding atmosphere heavy with penitence. "I committed a horrible crime, and the moment I did, I knew I had a choice: repent of it or relish in it. I chose to repent, and in doing so, the gods asked me to set the domain right after introducing such evil. They showed me the path your worst life would have been on, and such power running through me, an unchanged mortal, shortened my life to mere minutes. So I chose to become the Observant, to be bound by this cloth that extends my life far beyond its capacity, and guide the domain out of darkness as my atonement."

"But there's still evil in this world," he countered, "so much corruption."

"The path to a perfect world for its whole history was one of an infinite number of others; darkness would find its way in."

"Why?" Ha-Na asked. "Couldn't you have ensured it or put it back on track?"

"It is not my place to force." The Observant's voice had a sharp note to it, and the atmosphere grew uncomfortably warm. Then it all softened. "Every life is precious, and so is that life's freedom to choose. I can make the best paths available to everyone, but I will not—cannot—force the choices they make."

"You always present us with the best path?" Vanya asked.

"I do."

"But we choose whether to take it or not," Su muttered, "which can also affect other people's best paths."

"That is correct. The choice is theirs." The atmosphere grew a little heavy, a little depressed, and a little disappointed. "Sometimes, however, a soul prefers the darkness."

"So why are we here?" he asked.

"The best possible path showed that I needed to personally involve myself in your life. You are here so that we may benefit from one another, though I will not need your direct help for some time."

"So you'll help us find Vasilisa and win his kingdom back?" Vanya asked.

Everything in the cavern seemed to focus on Ha-Neul.

"Until you are finished with war, Vasilisa will not return."

It was as if the Observant had knocked the wind out of him. He fought for breath as tears forced their way out. No one else seemed capable of speaking.

"Vasilisa is alive," the Observant said, and the air seemed to flow of its own accord into Ha-Neul's lungs and warm him. "You will see her face again—if you succeed in winning the war."

"I *will* win it." He felt ablaze with renewed determination. "What do I need to do?"

The cavern grew brighter and the air warmer. "You are the wangseja *and* a spellcaster. What do you think is your first step?"

He only thought for only a moment. "I need to win over

as many magic users as possible. I need to formally renounce my old ways. But I also need soldiers—more importantly, seasoned officers who can help me lead those soldiers." He looked up at the Observant again. "I need the retired generals, the ones loyal to my father, especially General Moon Seong, the former commanding officer of the Northern Army."

"We've already met him," Evan said.

"What!" Ha-Neul and his nammae said.

The Observant chuckled. "You called him Harabeoji while you stayed with him."

"Moon Harabeoji is Moon Seong Daejang?" Su asked in shock. "No wonder he didn't want me snooping around his place or his ddal's home. He didn't want me to find out."

"He did not want you to know until you were ready," the Observant said.

"But you knew, Evan," Ha-Neul said.

Evan nodded. "General Moon made me swear not to tell you until you were ready."

Ha-Neul sighed and turned back to the Observant. "What about the others? Can you lead us to the other officers?"

"I do not need to so long as you remember to ask and use the people you know you can trust to help. Now, what else do you need?"

"Weapons," he said simply, knowing through his experience with the Dunways that he wouldn't get any more out of the Observant. "We'll need our own war machines and a way to make the protection spell obsolete."

"Those two problems have the same solution, which will make itself known as you keep my advice in mind," the Observant said.

"And I need outside allies—reinforcements."

"Now is not the time for the Northern Mountains' spellweavers to go to war. I promise they will fight by your side when needed. However, once you have proven yourself ready and worthy, old allies will quickly come to your aid."

"Then I don't think there's anything else for us to discuss." He looked at the others to see if they wanted to say anything.

"No, there is nothing more. However, I do have a gift to bestow."

His raven's-eye necklace flashed brightly. Afterward, it seemed to have a faint glow. "Your necklace will now grant you access to Our Fair City no matter where you are, but there is one condition you must remember. It will take you back to the last location you traveled from before coming to Our Fair City upon using the spell again, so choose your locations wisely if you use it."

He felt astounded. "Why?"

"It is a condition of the spell. I must also add that you can bring along any or all of your current companions at will when you travel, even if they are not with you, though the same condition applies—they will return to the last location they were in."

"Thank you," he said sincerely.

"No, Wangseja, do not thank me just yet."

"Will we be able to come see you again?" Ha-Na asked.

The cavern grew brighter and warmer. "If you so choose. My cavern opens to the public at the start and midpoint of every season, but you will not need me for quite some time."

"That's probably meant to be a good thing," Evan said.

The Observant laughed, the sound filling Ha-Neul with the warmth and nostalgia of better times. "Yes, it is. Now go. You have much to do."

They bowed and walked away.

McKennon approached the Observant, determined to convince her to take another path.

He bowed. "My Lady."

"We have had this conversation already. I am doing what is best to win the coming war."

"There are other—" The air around him froze, stealing the air in his lungs and his ability to argue back.

"The risk of failure is too high, and you know the consequences of failure. Do you really wish to take that risk? I do not." The air warmed and McKennon started coughing. Once his breathing was normal, the Observant continued. "I know you care greatly for my safety, but you do not accept that no matter what path is taken, I, like every other living being, will one day die."

Tears fell down McKennon's face as he could no longer contain his grief. "Is there no other way?"

"You already know the answer."

"Only in times of conflict do we learn a person's true character."

— THE OBSERVANT

50

D unway stopped outside of the gate to the city and turned to face them.

"I will go no farther than this," he said. "I . . . I want you to take care."

"We will," Ha-Neul said.

Dunway nodded. "You are all very capable. As long as you're together—"

"Oh, gods, Dunway. Please don't get cheesy on us now," Ha-Na said.

"Right you are, lass." Dunway motioned them to the door to the gate. "You should get going. The gatekeepers are waiting for you."

They each took turns shaking Dunway's hand before entering the gate. The gatekeepers sat in their lofty chairs looking down on them.

"We bid you farewell, honored guests, and shall await your return," they said. "Please keep in mind that you are welcome to return at any time. Now, if you will stand in the center of the room, we will send you on your way."

Once they were in the center of the room, the light

around them flashed brightly, and Ha-Neul felt a slight stinging sensation on his skin. They stood at the end of the pass, where they had entered and found their mountain bikes beside them. After adjusting their packs, they took the bikes and set off.

O tium, the village across the lake from Vires City, seemed more subdued than it had been before they left. There also seemed to be more police about. Vanya guided them to the ferry as fast as what didn't seem conspicuous, and they locked the bikes outside the station.

"I'm going to give Father a call and let my friends know their bikes are back," Vanya said. "Wait for me inside the station."

Vanya separated from them as they moved toward the station. They took their place in a long line for ferry tickets and were almost at the counter when Vanya returned, grabbing Ha-Neul's elbow. Silently, Vanya shook his head and looked pointedly toward the station's doors, so Ha-Neul quietly got the others' attention and led them away.

"What's going on?" Evan asked once they were outside.

"We all need identification to use any form of public transportation," Vanya said, "identification none of you has."

"You do?" Su asked.

"My father got it for me after we left and has been sending it here every day for the past few weeks. I'll explain later."

"So what are we going to do?" Ha-Na asked.

"Father has a private boat," Vanya explained. "He drove it here and left it for 'repairs' with my friend's dad when the engine wouldn't start. Fortunately, Father hasn't been able to come get it and my friend's dad is too busy to return it."

"Will your father meet us at the docks?" Evan asked.

Vanya nodded.

It didn't take them long to find the repair shop. A worker helped Vanya put the boat into the water before everyone boarded it. Vanya backed it away from the dock, turned the boat toward Vires City, and sped off.

"Don't you think we're going too fast?!" Ha-Na shouted over the wind.

"No!" Vanya shouted back. "You've got to get back before the lake patrol catches up. I can handle things from there once you leave with Father. Whatever you do, don't turn around, and look like you're having fun!"

Vanya flipped a switch, and loud music started to play. It took them a moment to find the beat before they awkwardly started to do a half bounce, half dance as they clung onto the boat's railing with one hand. When they were halfway across the lake, Ha-Neul turned to glance behind them and saw two police boats chasing them, their sirens obviously drowned out by the music. He didn't take another glance back after that and let Vanya drive the boat as fast as he wanted until the city's docks came into view. Vanya pointed the boat at more private-looking docks and barely slowed down enough to enter them safely.

Aleksandr stood at an empty stall looking anxious, and when Vanya pulled in, he quickly ushered them off. Aleksandr looked to Vanya, who only nodded, then stayed with the boat as the police sirens drew closer. Aleksandr then ushered the others quickly to a pair of black cars with tinted windows.

"Hurry in," Aleksandr said. "We have to get you out of sight, and we have much to discuss."

They separated into the cars, a stranger behind the wheel of each, and once the doors were closed, the drivers quickly pulled out into the traffic. Ha-Neul didn't speak as they traveled deeper into the heart of the city. The drivers turned into an underground garage, driving to a more private sector a few floors into the ground where there were very few cars. Aleksandr and the drivers opened the doors to the cars once they had parked and led the travelers to a private elevator, accessible only by eye scanner. The drivers left them at the elevator. Aleksandr inserted a key at the top of the panel and turned it, and the elevator doors closed and they started to ascend.

"What's going on, Aleksandr?" Ha-Neul asked.

"General Woo has tightened security throughout Balhae and the territories," the prince said. "There are cameras in every public place, and the military has infiltrated the regular police force. It has become a felony to travel without identification—the new identification cards he has distributed. They are satellite tracked, and by now, everyone should have one."

"But we don't," Su said.

The elevator door opened to a penthouse suite.

"And it's impossible to get a proper one, isn't it?" Evan asked.

Aleksandr motioned to a sitting area in the wide-open suite. "We had to register for one with the military a day after you left," he said as they sat down. "I had to get Vanya's identification."

"But you said it's satellite tracked," Ha-Na said.

"Yes, it is. I set it in a remote-controlled helicopter and had it programmed to move like a human while staying away from too-populated areas because I also had to cast a spell so his image would appear on camera."

"You can't have people walking through Vanya on camera," Evan stated.

"Precisely, so Vanya has been visiting friends across the lake often and for days at a time. Luckily, it was still over there and inside a friend's house when you arrived. Hopefully no one will notice the different Vanyas who appeared today."

"Because he came in from two different locations, the real Vanya traveling with us," Ha-Neul said.

"Yes, so you see the danger lies with your movements. It always has been, but it has become more dangerous for you to move around outside."

"So how will we?" he asked. "We need to travel. We need to make contact with General Moon and the other retired officers."

"Contacting General Moon will be fairly easy," Aleksandr assured them, "but the other officers will be more difficult. General Moon knows their locations, but he can't help you beyond that—General Woo is monitoring them closely. He knows they can be a liability if you're alive."

"I also need to gain the support of the other northern territories and, if possible, the Western Territory as well," he said. "Will you be able to help me contact the old kingdoms' nobles?"

Aleksandr grinned. "Of course, they all know General Woo needs to be removed." He studied them all a little closer. "You seem ready for war."

"We're ready to start preparing for war," Ha-Na said.

Aleksandr looked to Ha-Neul. "What about Vasilisa?"

He glanced away, unable to watch Aleksandr's reaction. "We'll see her when the war is over. We've been assured of that."

"She's alive. That's enough for now."

"Yes, so let's get busy so we can see her again." He looked at the others. "The first thing we need to do is convince the northern territories to stop supporting General Woo."

"That can begin almost immediately," Aleksandr said.

"We also need to find a way for Ha-Na and I to move separately."

"What do you mean?"

"We can work faster if we separate," Ha-Neul explained. "She has better relationships with many of the retired officers than I do since she took over many of Eome-oni's responsibilities after her death, so Ha-Na will travel with Evan and Vanya while I go with Su."

"Why only the two of you?" Aleksandr looked concerned. "You should have a third person as well, especially since both wangja will be traveling together. I—"

"I need you here to coordinate everything. Besides, if you start to move out of your normal zone, General Woo will most likely move against us faster. You'll need to stay, especially if he becomes even more suspicious of your involvement. We'll also need you here to cover for Vanya."

"Very well."

"Will Vanya get into any trouble for his actions today?" Evan asked.

Aleksandr frowned. "If he does, I hope it won't be soon."

A flash of frustration flickered within Ha-Neul. "It was unavoidable, but it could have been worse if you weren't here to help him. We'll have to move quickly. I need him to travel with Ha-Na to show our unity."

"And you will show your change by revealing that you are a spellcaster," Aleksandr stated.

Ha-Neul merely nodded.

"What about the war machines?" Aleksandr asked.

"Retired officers are not without trusted contacts or useful information."

Aleksandr had a faint smile on his lips. "Welcome back, Wangseja. Tonight, we will contact the council and discuss plans with them."

"What council?" he asked.

"The council are those who are the rightful heirs to the northern kingdoms and the Western Empire." Ha-Neul felt both shell-shocked and hopeful at Aleksandr's revelation, and then he remembered the prince's conversation with General Woo about the original plan Woo Su-Han had ruined, with the general mocking the idea that the rightful heirs would retake their place and live happily ever after.

"They're still alive?" Ha-Na asked. "I thought Jeungjobu killed all the rightful heirs during the Expansion."

"Of course, General Woo mentioned it during my concealment test," Ha-Neul said before Aleksandr could answer her. "The northern territories hid them as well as Old Balhae's nobles."

"We did," Aleksandr grinned, "so you see, you have more support than you realized."

He relaxed the slightest bit. "Thank you."

"Get some rest." Aleksandr stood. "The council meeting is tonight at ten, and I will need your help to contact them."

He agreed, and they all separated to find a room to sleep in.

V anya arrived at the penthouse twenty minutes before ten. Aleksandr gave instructions to his son and Ha-Neul on how to construct a couple of spell circles. He then told them when to activate the spells and to keep channeling their magic into them for the duration of the meeting. When he gave the signal, they activated their spells.

"The current Prince of Vires, Aleksandr Dmitrisson; Sitting Prince of Vires, Ivan Aleksandrsson; Geum Ha-Neul, Wangseja of Balhae; Geum Ha-Na, Gongju of Balhae; Geum Su, Wangja of Balhae; and Evan, former Chief Chamsagwan to the Wang, stand before the council," he announced.

"We welcome you back to your country, Mama," Señor Mijares said.

"It is a relief that you have returned safely from the Northern Mountains," Astrid said. "Most of us feared you would not."

"Fortunately we were honored guests, Grand Illegitimate Princess," Ha-Neul replied. There was a collective silence. "Come now, if we are to work together, such secrecy is not needed. I am sure you are very well aware of the education I have undergone during the time my family and I were forced out of the palace."

Aleksandr looked over at Ha-Neul.

"Whether we work together depends on you," Professor Tep said.

"That voice belongs to Professor Tep," Ha-Na commented.

Su started laughing. "I get it. Obscurity in prominence. The grand illegitimate princess is actually the crown princess. The leading scholar on Western Empire politics is the crown prince. Which means the other heirs are symbols for what their country was most notable for before the Expansion. It's clever."

"It seems we cannot hide from a clairvoyant even if we only reveal our voices," Madame De la Mare said.

Ha-Neul smiled. "It seems so. Between the three of us, we'll be able to discover who you are without you telling us, Madame De la Mare. I believe the first gentleman was Señor Mijares."

"Which could mean the final heir is the president of the Pannonian Cultural Museum, Kisasszony Vajda," Su said.

"That would be correct," she said.

Aleksandr cut in. "Now that we are all introduced, we can get to the more important issues."

"I need to know where I stand with your specific populace," Ha-Neul said. "How many actually believe we're dead, and how many think we may be alive?"

"Any forums or articles that speculate you are alive are quickly removed," Madame De la Mare answered. "However, this has greatly but quietly fueled the rumors that you are still alive. Many Balhaens still support your return to power, while the territories are largely mixed on the prospect."

"What has been done by the nobility to fuel the rumors?"

"We must be very careful of what we say," Professor Tep said. "General Woo can only guess who we really are at this point, and we plan to keep it that way for our protection."

"You think he would have you killed?" Ha-Na asked.

"His goal is power," Señor Mijares responded, "and his power won't be complete until he has removed all legitimate potential heirs."

356 | ADAM GOWANS

"I believe you will ask for autonomy if we succeed in deposing him," Su stated.

The council was silent.

"Don't worry, I understand your point," Ha-Neul answered them. "We will discuss that at a later time, and I will work out the particulars with you when the time comes."

An unrealized tension in the air relaxed.

"First, I need military leaders to prove that these are not crazy rumors," Ha-Neul said. "Who do I need to help persuade your people?"

"Get your father's former generals and advisers, the ones who left as the Stake Laws were being passed, on your side first," Astrid told Ha-Neul. "Once you do, we will start leaking proof that not only are you alive but that you are a spellcaster. When the people have seen you are a spellcaster and have embraced what you are, many will believe the prohibitions placed against magic users and their supporters will disappear."

"Our own military leaders are prepared to follow you upon our word," Kisasszony Vajda said. "Those soldiers who will desert us will do so when the time comes."

"Hopefully that number will be small," Aleksandr said.

"Next issue," Ha-Neul continued. "I need a way for the five of us to move around the country safely."

"First, before we plan for Vanya, we will need to see if any questions arise about his movements today," Aleksandr said. "If the authorities take interest, he may be . . . delayed."

"We'll deal with that when we need to," Ha-Neul responded. "If it becomes a problem, Evan will travel with Su and me. Ha-Na . . . will have to stay."

"Señor Mijares and I will be able to help you," Madame De la Mare said. "When our countries were one before the Slovkan Empire, many tunnels were constructed to access other countries without their knowledge. We still have a few leading into Old Balhae that have not been discovered. Once you reach Jeoncheon-do through Burgos, Mr. Moon's daughter will be able to pick you up and take you to him."

"She will have to take her time on the back roads once she has you so you won't run into as many checkpoints," Professor Tep added. "General Woo has vastly increased those as well. That will be another problem for your travels."

"We hope Mr. Moon will have a solution ready by the time you arrive," Señor Mijares said. "He still has trustworthy contacts in the military."

"So how will we travel through the northern territories?" Su asked.

"I assume you know my nephew, Yi Jae-Woo?" Astrid asked.

Ha-Neul's face darkened, and Su and Ha-Na couldn't hide their amusement.

"We do," Ha-Neul said.

"He has a match in Vires City in two weeks. His team will be able to bring you from Vires to Slovka where I will handle your transportation into Burgos."

"His team is willing to do this?" Ha-Neul asked.

"They are against General Woo, and Jae-Woo won't let past feelings affect their only hope for a better future."

"Ha-Neul will tread carefully while with them," Su said. He looked over at his brother, sending him a clear message.

"Of course. I don't need any more enemies."

"Señor Mijares and I will start making the arrangements," Astrid continued. "I assume you will contact Mr. Moon, Aleksandr?"

"Of course," he said.

"Just keep them safe for now," Señor Mijares said.

A red light on the ceiling flashed momentarily. Aleksandr glanced up and felt his adrenaline spike at the warning. "I will." He kept his tone calm. "If that is all, we shall end the meeting and reconvene a week from today."

They all agreed.

He motioned to Vanya and Ha-Neul to stop their magic.

"Father?" Vanya asked, glancing at the light.

"Let's move quickly."

The urgency in his voice had the royal family and Evan on edge. He led them from the sitting room to a back closet down a hallway. He opened the door, activated a deconcealment spell, and the shelves disappeared to reveal another elevator.

"This will take you to a bunker," he told them. "We'll come for you when we can."

They heard the main elevator ding.

"Go!" Vanya whispered.

They entered the second elevator and watched Aleksandr close the closet door before the elevator doors shut.

"Ivan Aleksandrsson! Show yourself, hands in the air, in one minute!" a voice shouted.

Vanya looked to him and nodded before raising his hands and returning to the sitting area where five soldiers waited, guns aimed at him. Aleksandr followed slowly, his hands out to show his compliance. The leading soldier motioned to another, who pulled Vanya away from Aleksandr and started handcuffing his son.

"Ivan Aleksandrsson," the leading soldier said, "you are

under arrest for traveling without your identification, passing it off to another individual, and for traveling with unidentified individuals. Your trial will be next week. Aleksandr Dmitrisson," she said, slightly turning to him, "do not leave the city. We are still investigating your possible involvement as well."

"I will stay," he said.

"You are allowed to visit your son once before the trial, unless you are arrested as well," she continued. "You have three days to visit, starting tomorrow."

"Thank you for your generosity." He regally bowed his head.

"Let's take him out," she ordered the others.

He watched them leave without any emotion on his face, but a plan began to form in his mind.

51

The soldiers cuffed Vanya to a chair in an empty room and left. He felt needle-like pricks in the cuffs and studied the chair. It was embedded in the floor, cement encasing the legs so it could not be moved. The needles pierced the veins in his wrists and injected a fluid into his bloodstream. Time passed, and he felt his head grow a little groggy.

"Good evening, Mr. Aleksandrsson." A soothing male voice filled the room. "I hope you are not too uncomfortable. I just have a few questions to ask you before we take you to your cell. So please remember, the more you cooperate, the less stressful this will be. Do you understand?"

He nodded as he grew groggier. "I understand."

"That is wonderful to hear." There was a slight shuffling of paper. "Now, for the first question: Will you please state your full name and birth date?"

"My name is Ivan Aleksandrsson. I was born on Vleseska 18, 2187," he mumbled without much thought, which made him realize he had been injected with some sort of truth serum.

"What are your parents' names?"

"Aleksandr Dmitrisson and Sonya, Former Second Grand Illegitimate Princess of Slovka."

"And your sister's?"

He blinked in confusion. "My sister's?"

"What is your sister's name?" the voice repeated, still soothing.

He gave a groggy chuckle, wondering if they really knew the truth. "Lisa, Illegitimate Princess of Slovka, or Vasilisa Aleksandrsdöttir. There are two names."

"Where is your sister?"

"Gone." He put the full weight of emotion he truly felt into the word.

"Very well. What were you doing in Otium for the past few days?"

"Talking to friends."

"And who are your friends?"

He listed their names and their parents at the interrogator's request. Never once did the voice's tone change.

"Who were the people you were with on the boat today?"

He fought the fog in his mind. "Balhaens and a foreigner."

"A foreigner?" A hint of curiosity laced the voice. "Where is he from?"

He tried to shrug. "Don't know," he slurred out the truth.

"How did you meet them?"

"They asked for help."

"So you freely gave it without knowing who they were or asking for identification?"

He nodded his head bouncily.

"Please speak your answer."

"Yeesss." The serum was really thick in his mind now.

"How kind of you."

"Thangssss."

"Where did they go?"

He shook his head lazily. "Don't know."

"Very well. Who did you pass your identification card to?"

"No one."

The voice didn't say anything more, and some time later, just as Vanya was about to fall asleep, two soldiers came and took him out. They led him to a cell and pushed him in. He stumbled and hit a cot, falling onto it. He rubbed his face into the small pillow to hide his smile.

Vanya noticed Aleksandr carefully studying his face through the glass wall. He knew his father would notice the makeup covering the areas that showed signs of drugging and dehydration. The soldiers had warned him not to say anything about his treatment, but such simple means could not easily deceive his father. In fact, nobody but Vanya would be able to see his father's displeasure as the prince took in his son's appearance.

"You look well," Aleksandr said.

"It's been pretty decent here. Will you be at the trial on Wednesday?"

"Of course. I must go to show my support."

"Will anybody else be attending?"

"No, all of your friends are too busy, but they asked me to pass along their well-wishes."

He nodded, knowing his father was up to something.

Aleksandr studied him a little longer. "Do you think the punishment will be harsh if they find you guilty?"

"We both know that answer."

His father nodded. "Okay, then, I will see you in five days at the trial." He stood and walked to the door, then paused. "No matter what happens at the trial, it'll be all right. You have nothing to fear."

He smiled just a little bit. "Thank you, Father."

Aleksandr knocked on the door, and a soldier opened it. Another soldier came in from a door behind Vanya and helped him stand. Each allowed their respective guards to lead them away.

There were only a few witnesses at the trial, but there were plenty of news crews broadcasting it around the country. The prosecution presented its evidence, along with Vanya's taped interrogation sessions. Once they were done with their presentation, the judge turned to where he sat alone at a small table and asked if he wanted to add anything to the presentation just given. He shook his head.

"Very well," the judge said. "Based on the evidence given and the interrogation sessions, I am ready to give my verdict. Ivan Aleksandrsson, I find you guilty of all charges, and based on the presentation, I sentence you to five years of parole during which you will be constantly monitored. You will be injected with a tracking device immediately after this trial and then released to your father's care. Your parole officer will contact you once you are home. This trial is closed."

A young Balhaen soldier helped Vanya to his feet. He

caught sight of his father still sitting in the crowd, staring at him with a blank expression and deaf to the spectators' mutterings. Aleksandr barely nodded before Vanya lost sight of him. The Balhaen soldier led Vanya down a long, empty hallway occasionally broken up by a doorway. The soldier stopped him at one door and opened it for him. Inside was a man who looked exactly like Vanya. The guard pushed him in and quickly took off his hand and ankle cuffs.

"Hurry and change clothes," the guard said. "You have two minutes before the injection team gets here."

Vanya looked at his double as they exchanged clothes. "Thank you."

The double shook his head. "Just make that bastard pay."

"Cloak yourself," the guard ordered, pointing to the room's left corner before slapping the cuffs on the double.

Vanya had barely activated his spell when the door opened and a group of three entered. One set up a massage table with holes for a person's arms. The double was ordered onto the table, and two people plus the guard helped cuff and strap him to it so he couldn't move. Meanwhile, the third person was carefully measuring out fluids from a large case, mixing them in a tube, and inserting the tube into a gun-like syringe. She turned to the massage table.

"Is he ready?"

They nodded, so she approached the table as one of her team rubbed the double's neck with a sterilizing pad. The woman shot the solution into his neck. Within a minute, the double was convulsing as the solution spread throughout his body. The other three held the table steady when it began to shake violently. This went on for a couple of minutes before it suddenly stopped, Vanya's double breathing hard.

"The tracking device is settled in his brain," the woman said. "You can let him go in five minutes. He'll be adequately recovered by then."

The guard nodded his understanding, and the woman left. The other two men whispered to each other until the double's breathing returned to normal. They unbound him from the table, and the guard removed his cuffs. The double slowly got to his feet and swayed a little as he stood. The table was folded up, and the men left. The guard pulled out a picture from his pocket and held it in Vanya's general direction. He uncovered himself and took it.

"Disguise yourself as this man and come out in about an hour," the guard said. "You're less likely to be caught if you do so. Follow the emergency-exit signs. The alarms will be off. You'll have a twenty-minute window."

"Thank you," Vanya said sincerely.

"Only he is doing this for you," the guard said. "I'm loyal to the wangsil."

He nodded. "Still, thank you."

The guard led the double out as soon as Vanya had concealed himself again. After fifty minutes had gone by, he disguised himself as the man in the picture and left the room. He walked with purpose, as though he was meant to be there, just in case he ran into anyone. The closest emergency exit was only a couple of minutes' walk through the building, and he was soon on the street. A taxi stopped next to him and honked to get his attention. The passenger's side window rolled down.

"Hail, Sitting Prince," she said. "Your father asked me to pick you up."

He opened the door and climbed in.

Ha-Na and Evan sat at a desk looking at identical maps on two large screens. Both had one of the tablets Irene had given them before they'd left the palace in front of them as well and were muttering together, drawing lines on the screens that showed up on the tablets. A half hour earlier, Aleksandr had come into the bunker he'd sent them to when Vanya was arrested and occasionally made a comment on their work, sparking a renewed frenzy that cleared some lines away, and he would pace unless he saw or heard another problem with their travel plans.

An hour and a half after Aleksandr came down, they heard the elevator ding as someone else entered the bunker. She and Evan followed Aleksandr out of the sparse room to see Vanya coming toward them.

"You're all right!" Relief swept through Ha-Na.

"Yes, I'm fine." He looked to his abeoji. "My double?"

"Resting, but he's prepared to take your place for as long as possible."

"Where are Ha-Neul and Su?" he asked.

She glanced at Evan to have him explain. "They're gone. They're already at General Moon's place."

Vanya was stunned. "How?"

"The soldier who helped you was Ha-Neul's middle-school friend," he continued. "The day after you were arrested, Ha-Neul accessed the palace's military database on our tablets. He saw his friend was here in Vires, and he made contact. Apparently this friend has a lot of connections, both reputable and disreputable, who were able to find them safe passage to Jeoncheon-do."

"Our connections are better than we originally thought," Aleksandr said. "This soldier's paternal uncle is a construction magnate, CEO of the company that built the military facilities for the war machines, and his wife is the daughter of a notorious illegal arms dealer—though she has publicly renounced her father."

"She can now help us if that connection is renewed," Vanya said.

"Or was never broken in the first place," Ha-Na added. "We Balhaens do like to put on a show for the public, you know."

There was a beep from Aleksandr's jacket, and he pulled out a thin, mostly screen, cell phone. It lit up momentarily before he slipped it back in. "The rumors are spreading."

She and Evan relaxed yet tensed as well.

"What rumors?" Vanya asked.

"That the wangseja was seen alive and well in southern Old Balhae—performing a small feat of espionage," Aleksandr answered.

Vanya looked shocked. "But—"

"In two days, he'll be seen in the northern part of the Western Territory stealing weapons from a small shop as well," she said, making him look confused.

"It's all been carefully planned," Evan assured him. "His friends will be behind all the rumors, through trusted connections, to make it seem like he could be alive or that there are people impersonating him. General Woo will be forced to investigate each sighting, which will occur every two to four days."

"Meanwhile, word is quickly spreading that my brothers may be more than they seem," she added. "It's quite contained right now, waiting for the perfect moment to break loose."

"So it's started," Vanya said, turning more toward her,

"and what about you two?"

"We're planning our negotiations tour," she said, feeling a little warm inside. "We leave in a couple of days to meet the first general who took up residence in Pannonia. We'll briefly meet Su and Ha-Neul in Our Fair City every two weeks to trade information before moving on to the next general, high-ranking officer, or former adviser."

"We'll also check in with the council once a week," Evan said, "to better coordinate our movements. We should be back here in Vires in about six months."

"You've planned all this in a week?" Vanya asked.

She gave him a wry smile. "Your arrest was quite beneficial."

52

A little over four weeks after Vanya's release, Ha-Neul sat in the trunk of a moving SUV, strapped to the wall of a metal box made livable by an air tank. As the vehicle moved, he read reports, news articles, messages from officers and chamsagwan he had won over, and occasionally responded to one of those messages on his tablet. Every once in a while he would call up GPS to check their progress and to make sure they were truly on track, and when he was satisfied, he returned to the reports. He knew Su would be doing the same thing in the container next to his.

They had about an hour left of travel time when they came to an unexpected stop. He paused his reading and let his work fade to the background as muffled sounds found their way into the container. From what he could hear, one seemed urgent while another seemed calm. An instant message popped up on his screen: *Slight delay ten minutes out of Silla-si. Unexpected guard post.*

He sighed and watched the commanding officer

respond to the message. He waited for a few minutes, during which time his container was carefully jostled but never opened, before he felt the SUV start up again. The soldier messaged his commanding officer the all clear, and he returned to his work, reviewing the amount of funds available to him so far.

A little over an hour later, the SUV stopped again. After a few moments, he felt his container being slid out of the SUV, and he shut down his tablet. The latches to the container released, and he breathed in a lungful of fresh air.

"Are you all right, Wangseja-Mama?" a soldier asked.

"Yes, just help me stand," he said as he unstrapped himself.

Two soldiers helped him stand as Su's container, marked as highly explosive, opened. Su was rubbing sleep out of his eyes but woke up faster when a soldier started taking off his straps.

"I can do that myself."

"Apologies, Wangja-Mama, but we are pressed for time," the soldier said.

"How long have you been asleep?" Ha-Neul asked.

Su awkwardly checked his watch as the two soldiers helped him stand. He gave an embarrassed laugh. "About two hours."

"Let's move," Ha-Neul said to the soldiers. Then he turned back to Su, who looked apprehensively at him. "We had a ten-minute delay."

"I see." Su winced as he took a step and looked down at his legs. "I hate those containers."

Ha-Neul winced too as the blood started flowing more freely back into his legs. They entered an elevator from the loading garage they were in, and a soldier pressed the button for the thirty-fourth floor, the top floor, and then hit the close-doors button. To help the blood flow, Ha-Neul and Su rocked back and forth on their feet as the elevator made its ascent. The elevator opened, and they were taken to a waiting room where Ha-Na, Vanya, and Evan sat.

Ha-Na stood and gave a small smile. "You're finally here."

"Everything going okay?" he asked.

"Ryu Chamsagwan is still being overly cautious, and it's starting to get on my nerves." Her expression slightly changed to annoyance as she spoke of Evan's predecessor.

"There's probably a reason, then," Su said. "I'll have to meet him, hyeong."

"We can manage that this week," he agreed. "Anything else?"

"President Hwang's meeting is running a little long, so we may have to wait a few more minutes," Evan said about their current appointment with the company that supplied Balhae's war stations. "Hopefully it isn't anything too serious. He's meeting with the board of directors right now."

Ha-Neul looked at Vanya. "How are you doing?"

"I don't feel as awkward now," Vanya said, "but I still feel out of place."

"But you have been needed," he said. "I heard about last week's raid on your hotel."

Ha-Na colored and looked ashamed.

"It wasn't your fault, noona," he assured her, remembering that she had been spotted driving into the parking garage.

"But it's the reason we have to ride in containers now," she said.

Ha-Neul shrugged. "If everything goes well here, that won't be an issue for long."

A secretary entered the waiting room and got their

attention. "President Hwang apologizes for the delay, Mama. He will do his best to ensure the meeting ends in ten minutes."

"Thank you," Ha-Na said.

The secretary bowed and left the room. No one took any of the seats. Ha-Neul and Su paced the room, Su catching up on the information he'd missed because of his nap. Evan caught Ha-Neu's attention to discuss the plans for his and Su's transportation to meet Ryu Chamsagwan and rearrange their schedule as needed. In fifteen minutes, the secretary was back to escort them to a conference room. When they entered, a neatly dressed, fifty-something-year-old man stood waiting and bowed deeply when he saw them.

"It is so good to see you alive, Mama," the man said in Hasoseoche. Out of the corner of his eye, Ha-Neul saw Su relax. "I will do everything I can to help you reclaim your throne."

"It's our pleasure to finally meet you, President Hwang," he said. "You have done so much for us already, and we know the great risks you are taking for us."

"I assure you it is nothing, Wangseja-Mama," President Hwang said. "When my joka Ui-Dong told me you had contacted him to help the prince's adeul," he bowed his head to Vanya, "I knew things would be better than before everything happened. It was always my hope to see you turn things around once I heard you became Ui-Dong's chingu."

"He's proven himself and all my other old chingu better than I imagined."

President Hwang smiled. "Please, take a seat."

Once they all sat down, Ha-Neul went straight to business. "I hope you will be able to help us build war stations. We will need our own machines for the coming war."

"Yes, I knew you would ask that; however, I do not have access to the plans. Once rumors started that you were popping up every few days, Woo Daejang used the military's right to act in the wangsil's stead if incapacitated to send his own men to seize the blueprints and any copies we had. We have nothing, not even a layout for the station's restrooms."

"Is there a way we can obtain one?" Ha-Na asked.

"None that I know of. The military knows about every blueprint copy and where they are," President Hwang said. "I suppose . . . you can obtain a copy if you take over a war station, but even then each station is one of eight different stations, and you will need all eight."

"Why would we need to take over eight different stations?" Su asked.

"Each station has a copy of its blueprint—that is standard for any building for repairs and maintenance—but each station is also a factory that makes a variant of the war machine. That is why you will need eight different stations. However, you will face a major problem if you take over any stations."

"I suppose you are referring to the Scatter," Ha-Neul said.

"Precisely."

"What's the Scatter?" Vanya asked.

"The Scatter is the nickname for the power plant that services every war station in Old Balhae," Ha-Neul explained. "Power substations are divvied up in sections so they are literally scattered. One power substation can fuel a war station in Goryeo-do and another war station six hundred miles away in Silla-do. The system was designed so that if a substation was destroyed during war, a region wouldn't be left defenseless. However, if an enemy were to take over the war stations, they'd have the ability to cut power from the substation or the main plant if one section was lost."

"So if we take over war stations, they would need to be from different sections?" Evan asked.

Ha-Neul sighed. "We would need two different stations from each Scatter section, or a war station and the substation, so not only are we shut down but Woo Daejang's war stations as well."

"Shut down the whole system and start over?" Ha-Na asked.

"If you want war stations and machines, yes," President Hwang said. "Otherwise, I do not know how else you can get them."

"Do you know which stations belong to each section?" Ha-Neul asked.

"Unfortunately, I do not, but I know who does," President Hwang said. "Ryu Chamsagwan."

Ha-Neul sighed again. "I'll meet with him soon."

"The sooner the better," President Hwang urged. "Meanwhile, the steel used for war machines is officially experiencing a major delay in production, and thus, delivery. The military does have backup stores, as you well know, but they will not be receiving any new material for the next two months."

"That's a lot of steel," Ha-Neul grinned.

"And a large monetary loss to our company since we are the largest provider."

"Hopefully your problems will be resolved within two months."

"Yes, that would be best for all of us."

Ha-Neul stood, as did everyone else. "Thank you."

The small car made its way through the building-crowded residential neighborhood at a crawling pace, turning constantly through the labyrinthine streets of a southern Balhaen city. Ha-Neul sat in the back, wearing aviator glasses and a baseball cap with some punk-rock clothes, feeling all too much like a celebrity "trying" to hide from the public while knowing full well it didn't work all the time. Meanwhile, Su sat in the front playing an old handheld console. He was dressed in most of a middle-school winter uniform—a neat button-up, long-sleeved shirt with a vest over it, and somewhat loose-fitting slacks. The name patch on his vest read "Hong Min-Su."

The driver was silent except to update their progress every ten minutes, the last update being when they were five minutes from their destination. The updates got old after the first half hour, which was an hour and a half ago. The driver had been driving randomly, or seemingly randomly, without passing many busy streets where cameras were sure to be a constant presence.

The crawling pace finally slowed to a stop outside several small, two-story houses surrounded by concrete walls and accessible through a set of locked bars-over-metal-plate gates. The driver turned to look at them both.

"You want the house with the green gate on the left."

He nodded to the driver. "Thanks."

Su opened the glove compartment and slipped the handheld inside. "That was fun, thanks."

Their doors opened just wide enough to let them out.

The car pulled away, and they walked to the closest green gate on the left. Su pressed a button on the intercom, and they heard a doorbell chime.

"Hong Min-Su?" said a strong, sturdy voice.

"Ne, Harabeoji," Su answered.

The gate buzzed, and Ha-Neul pushed it open. Inside, the small courtyard was neatly arranged with stepping shelves that held a wide variety of potted plants, all surrounding a bent tree barely taller than he was. The tree was young but dying, many of its branches bare, its leaves ready to tumble off at the slightest touch. Ryu Chamsagwan, tall and solid for an old man, stood at the front door. He looked at Su with a warm tenderness and barely gave Ha-Neul a glance.

"You're a little late visiting your harabeoji today, Min-Su," Ryu Chamsagwan said in a strong, sturdy voice.

"Sorry, Harabeoji, the driver took the long route."

"It's quite all right. Come in and have some snacks."

Ryu Chamsagwan entered the house first and held the door open for them. They saw he had shoes on, so they didn't take theirs off. Ryu Chamsagwan closed the door behind them and led them to a small dining room. Ha-Neul noticed a small backpack in a corner of the room. The chamsagwan motioned to the table where fruit tea and snacks waited for them.

"You forgot your backpack last time, Min-Su." Ryu Chamsagwan moved to the only window in the room and pulled the string to lower the shade. "You should take it home today." He closed the door as Su nodded and sat across from them. "The charade is now over, Mama. Please, hand over the identifications you have."

"It's good to see you again, Ryu Chamsagwan-Nim," Ha-Neul said as he handed over their ID cards.

"You have both grown well," the man said. "Your bumo would be pleased."

"Why the charade?" Su asked.

"Many think I am paranoid, I know this all too well, but I assure you I am not."

"Sir—"

Ryu Chamsagwan silenced Ha-Neul with a steady gaze. Su didn't dare to speak either.

"I would have helped your noona had I not had a personal message to deliver to you, Wangseja-Mama." Ha-Neul felt himself straighten under Ryu Chamsagwan's gaze, his senses sharpening. From Su's change in position, he could tell something was coming, but Ryu Chamsagwan didn't speak.

"A message from whom?" Ha-Neul's voice was soft.

Something glimmered in the man's eyes. "Your eomeoni." The glimmer was pity.

"Eom—Eomeoni?" Ha-Neul whispered, his confusion weighing heavily on him.

"During her pregnancies and for the year after your births, I was assigned to help her carry out her duties," Ryu Chamsagwan said. "I was in contact with her quite often besides that, but especially after she gave birth. Because of my position, I was one of the few who knew she was a clairvoyant, so she sometimes confided in me. While she was pregnant with you, she often said she felt uneasy, but it was not because you were a difficult pregnancy, Wangseja-Mama. In fact, you were extraordinarily easy."

"Why did she feel uneasy?" he asked.

"After your birth, she held you often, even during our meetings," Ryu Chamsagwan continued, "and once, when we were alone, she started to cry."

R yu Myeong-Ki went rigid as the tears slid freely down the wanghoo's cheeks. Never had he seen her cry so freely. He couldn't bear to ask her why. She kissed the aegi's forehead before wiping her tears.

"Ryu Chamsagwan-Nim." Her voice was still melodic despite her tears, capturing his attention at once. "In the near future, this aegi—this dear, sweet, innocent aegi—will have a small birthday party, and on that day, he shall unwittingly cause my death."

"Wanghoo-Nim . . ."

"One day in the later future, when your garden tree is dying prematurely, he will come for your help—first through Ha-Na, which you must reject—and then in person, with my clairvoyant heir." Her voice was crisp and clear, power and authority strengthening her words. "On that day, you must tell him that I do not blame him—that I love him."

He left her office in a daze, and seven years and nine months later, her words rang through his ears as he bowed in front of her casket.

"H ow did she know so many details?" Su whispered five minutes after the tale, still holding Ha-Neul after he had broken down in tears.

Ryu Chamsagwan shook his head. "All she said was that the Observant had shown her." Ha-Neul and Su stilled. "Your eomeoni said you might understand."

"We do," Ha-Neul said.

"At least the name," Su added.

Ryu Chamsagwan checked the time on a wall clock and became uneasy.

"What is it?" Su asked.

"It is nearly time." Ryu Chamsagwan stood and retrieved the backpack. "This pack has all the information you came here for and what you will need."

"What?" They were both confused.

"Tablets I personally developed under your eomeoni's instruction. They have all the functions and information you will need, including the war stations' sectors."

"What's going on?" Ha-Neul asked, noticing how strangely calm the chamsagwan was.

"Simply, we are going to be killed today"—Ryu Chamsagwan pressed the wall, and the floor in the opposite corner next to the outside wall dropped away—"if you do not leave now."

"But you should—" Ha-Neul started.

"I have been implanted with a tracking device."

Out of the tunnel came two boys around their ages, the younger wearing a uniform identical to Su's and the other wearing clothing similar to Ha-Neul's.

"No." He nearly shouted, realizing what was about to happen.

"It is the price of war," Ryu Chamsagwan said. "One of many that must be paid."

"Please go," Min-Su said. "We are okay with dying so you can have more time, Mama."

"You have to live," the other man said.

Ryu Chamsagwan shoved the backpack into Ha-Neul's arms as he stared in shock and grief. "I accepted this fate a long time ago. Now go."

Su yanked Ha-Neul out of his chair and toward the

tunnel, tears in his own eyes, stopping only so they could both say "Thank you, and I'm sorry."

Ha-Neul put the pack on and jumped in, Su following him. The floor covered them and they began running as fast as they could. Five minutes later, an explosion echoed through the tunnel.

53

There was a video message waiting on the tablet with Ha-Neul's name on the case. He tapped the Play icon, and a plain Balhaen woman appeared on the screen. Her straight, wide eyebrows made her heavily lidded eyes appear slightly smaller than they actually were, giving them a sterner, more mature slant. Her face was of average southern Balhaen width, with no child-like roundness to it, and the bones in her face were slightly prominent. Her nose was wide and had very little bridge to it. Her head sat neatly on a longish neck, and her hair was braided in the jjokjin meori and curled around a gold yong-jam-binyeo, with a gilded yong cheopji resting on her head. In the video, she wore a rich-red hanbok Ha-Neul recognized all too well.

"Ryu Chamsagwan-Nim." His eomeoni's voice was melodic. "It is almost time for Ha-Neul's eighth birthday party. I know you are resting today, so I will be brief.

"The day Ha-Neul comes for you will be the day you die—and if you do not help—he and Su will die as well." A tear gleamed in her eye. "Please, not just for the sake of my eorini or the throne, but for the world, do the best you can to ensure their safety that day. I hope with all my heart that you will choose the best path."

The video stopped, and Ha-Neul turned off the clear, glass-like plastic tablet by sliding his trembling finger along an indentation on its edge. He put it back in the backpack after sliding it into the protective case and turned to Su. His dongsaeng only nodded, and they continued running down the tunnel. Every so often, they would come across a small fountain, and they always stopped to drink. Occasionally the fountains would have a small morsel of food for them to eat. The tunnel seemed never-ending.

Sometimes it connected to the storm drains that ran under the streets, but there was always a small chime from the backpack, and he would take out his new tablet, which would lead them to the next tunnel with a green arrow that flashed slowly on the screen for five seconds. After some time, he was sure they had left the city.

"Where do you think he's leading us?" Su asked.

He shook his head. "We just need to keep going to get out and contact noona."

At one point, they entered a circular chamber with a vent. Behind them, a door slid silently shut. A surge of panic settled in his stomach as he feared they were trapped.

"What's g—?" Su stopped himself as voices filtered through the vent.

"Get in and don't make a hassle," a woman's voice said. "We have to sort you."

A man sighed. "At least we've got them silenced now."

"Just hurry and bind them," the woman said.

Ha-Neul listened to heavy footsteps start, stop, start, and stop for a few minutes as he barely breathed to keep as quiet as possible. He heard a door close. Someone with lighter, more calculated steps walked around the room, pausing occasionally.

"Numbers five, thirteen, fourteen, twenty-nine, thirty-two through thirty-six, forty, and forty-eight," said a cool voice. "Strip them."

Several different footsteps came from above as well as the sound of ripping cloth, making Ha-Neul realize that prisoners filled the room above them. The footsteps went back to their starting point, and the sound of calculated steps came again. It was silent for several minutes.

"All stripped are good enough to be sold," the cool voice said, and Ha-Neul's blood churned with anger. "The strong, ugly ones go to the labor camps; the others go to the comfort homes. You know the drill—the best and youngest go to the ones often visited by the daejang and his officials."

A different door in the round chamber opened, and Ha-Neul went through it as fast as he could so he wouldn't do anything rash, breaking into a run once he thought he was far enough away not to be heard by the soldiers. Su kept pace with him but forced him to stop after twenty minutes.

"Ha-Neul!"

He turned and started pacing so that the sickness he felt wouldn't settle in deeper.

"What are you thinking?" Su asked.

He shook his head. "We can't leave them."

"Not during the war."

He nodded.

"It would take more time to free them quietly," Su pointed out.

"We can't leave them, Su."

"I know, but are you sure *you* want to do this? You'll have to wait longer to see Lisa."

"It's the best path, not for me but for all of us," he said automatically, knowing it to be true as the words came out.

The backpack chimed. He slid it off and took out the tablet. There was another video. He pressed Play and saw his eomeoni appear on the screen.

"Eorini," she said, and Su moved closer to get a better view of the screen, "I know you are well if you're watching this. Eomeoni needs to tell you something very important about my gajok.

"You know by now that I come from a long line of powerful clairvoyants. What you don't know is that we are also messengers for the Observant. To clarify, we help the Observant help others choose the best path. A clair-voyant's token of our duties is the raven's-eye necklace. I tell you this so you may recognize others with the same duty.

"I have always taught your noona and tried to teach you, Ha-Neul, to choose the paths that help others before your-self, that to do so is not only essential for the wangsil but for a human being as well.

"One day soon, now that my raven's eye has been returned to Ha-Neul, one of you will be chosen as my offi-cial replacement, but I hope that all three of you, though Ha-Na is not with you when you first view this, will live as though you were chosen. I love all three of you so very much."

The tablet switched off. Su looked up at him, and he saw that their expressions matched.

"How did the tablet know?" Ha-Neul asked. "How did Eomeoni and Ryu Chamsagwan know to do this?"

"The Observant must have a heavy hand in this," Su said, clearly thinking about it as he spoke. "We could go ask, though we would end up back here the next time we use the magic."

Ha-Neul shook his head. "No, it makes perfect sense that she guided them with this." He put the tablet away and looked at their path forward. "Let's keep going."

Ha-Neul and Su finally exited the tunnel a full day after meeting Ryu Chamsagwan. The tunnel ended behind a hotel reception desk, where a middle-aged woman looked unsurprised to see them climbing out of a hole in the floor. She subtly waved them back down as she finished helping customers through the small glass window that separated her from the impatient couple and kept him and Su from their view. Once the couple was gone, she turned to them.

"So Ryu Myeong-Ki Obba is dead then?" she asked.

Ha-Neul nodded from the floor.

The woman sighed. "Come on, follow me. I will show you where you can wait for someone to pick you up, Mama. I promise you will not be bothered."

She was off her stool and at the door waiting for them. They followed her out and down the hall, which was decorated with the occasional picture of various couples in different stages of passion with half to very little of their clothing on. He and Su seemed to decide to keep their focus on the woman in front of them. She stopped in front of a door marked as a cleaning supply closet and unlocked it. Inside was a room that would have been up to a nice hotel's standard.

"You have pretty good internet connection here, so the tablets obba gave you will work just fine," she said. "It will take a while for someone to come get you, but there is plenty of food in the fridge. Tell your escorts to tell me they are here for my clean guests and I will lead them to you. If you need anything, just pick up the phone. Take care, Mama."

The door closed behind her, and she relocked it, leaving them feeling winded.

"What an interesting woman," Su said.

Ha-Neul only nodded.

"Can I shower first while you send the message?"

"Go ahead. I have to check the GPS to find out where we are anyway."

Su opened the door to the bathroom. "She's even got clothes for us to change into." He closed the door.

Ha-Neul sat on one of the beds, slid the backpack off, and took out his tablet. Several apps were featured on the screen, many bearing a locked symbol. The only two apps that weren't locked were a messaging app and a map app. He pressed the map icon, and it quickly zoomed in to his location. A message appeared on the screen: *Share this location with friends?*

He tapped the Agree button and was taken to the messaging app, where Hwang Ui-Dong's private email address was readily available. After typing the necessary message, he tapped Ui-Dong's name and sent it to him. It only took a couple of minutes for his chingu's relieved and confirming message to come. He exited the two apps and nearly turned off the tablet until he realized more apps were unlocked and bore simple but detailed names:

Scatter Sect
Prsnr Trade
Stns Bluepr

Watched Mlty
Arms Dealers

He entered the Prsnr Trade app, and a simple menu popped up with options that would lead him to labor camps and comfort-home locations, and information on who was placed or sold where, officers in charge of the trade, and everything else he needed to know. He spent the next ten minutes looking at the lists of the hundreds of people in the trade. The lists were detailed—giving locations and slave status. He felt ill seeing how young some of the slaves were and the tasks they were forced to do. He left the app and entered the Watched Mlty app to find that it confirmed his suspicions—it tracked those deemed possible loyalists to the wangsil. The app constantly updated the whereabouts of those watched. He did a quick search for all his chingu in the military and found some of them marked high-risk while Woo Daejang considered two safe.

Su came out of the bathroom wearing new clothes, and Ha-Neul exited the app.

"Did you send the message?"

"Yeah, they'll be here tomorrow night. We'll see the others in three days."

Su studied him carefully. "Is everything okay?"

He hesitated. "The tablets have me a little freaked out. They're nothing like the palace ones, and Ryu Cham-sagwan designed those as well."

"He was a technological expert," Su muttered pensively. "Do you think he was holding back the best he developed for those tablets?"

He shook his head. "I don't know, but it has information Woo Daejang wouldn't want out to just anyone, especially us."

"I'll take a look at mine while you're in the shower." Su sounded a little excited.

Ha-Neul went into the bathroom and locked the door. He tossed his hat into a corner, the shades he had taken off at Ryu Chamsagwan's house, and quickly got out of the rest of his clothes. The only thing he left on was the raven's-eye necklace, which he never dared take off. He stepped into the tub, sliding its door closed, and turned on the shower, the water already running warm. He swept his hair back a few times to get it out of his face, and then his hand went to the necklace.

The raven's eye was comfortably warm in his hand, just like it always was against the skin of his chest. His hand naturally clutched the necklace tight, as though holding Lisa tightly so she couldn't disappear. With water pouring over his face and drowning out any sounds, he let his emotions and the accompanying tears he'd held back flow freely.

"We have to wait, Lisa," he whispered. "I'm sorry, but we have to wait longer. Will you still love me by the time this war ends?"

The sound of the shower faded away, though the water still gushed out of the showerhead. Though he knew no one was in the bathroom with him, he felt her arms wrap around him and hold him close. Her cheek seemed to press into his back. The phantom embrace was enwrapped in a peace and assurance that seemed to last a lifetime.

54

Ha-Neul sat in the private penthouse's sitting room President Hwang had provided for him, his nammae, Evan, and Vanya the previous day. Evan had been studying the wangsil's new tablets for some time, comparing them with the palace tablets Irene had provided them. Su filled Ha-Na and Vanya in on what happened at Ryu Chamsagwan's house five days before, whereas Ha-Neul remained silent. He only took notice when Evan suddenly took in a sharp breath and went back and forth between various points of the opened tablets.

"What is it?" he asked.

Evan pointed to a central component in his new tablet and secondary components in each palace tablet that were all placed in the same location.

"Okay, what are we looking at?" Ha-Neul asked.

Evan sighed and motioned to the palace tablets. "Ryu Chamsagwan's team designed those chips. Though they're seemingly innocuous, they're quite handy at improving every aspect of a computer, especially communication between every connected device. It's almost like a secondary processing unit and an intranet put together."

"So this is the technology responsible for the palace's connectivity? Why files are transferred so easily among us and the other officials?" Ha-Na asked.

"Yes."

"Keep going," she said.

"Well, like she said, this is in every government official's technology, and it's in every major corporation's and news-related business, as well as many other businesses," Evan said. "So there's no accidental communication among each entity, the chips are tailored to connect with other—twin-tailored chips. However, they all share this."

Evan used a high-powered microscope attached to the table to zoom in on one of the chips in a palace tablet and broadcasted the image onto the table's screen. They saw what looked like a clear V embedded into the chip, and as the microscope zoomed in, they saw little lines of copper running through it.

"What are those?" Vanya asked.

"They look like the lines in the plug for USB ports," Su said.

"That's exactly what they are," Evan said. The microscope zoomed in even closer to the sides of the chips to show a faint line between the logo and the chip. "The logo is detachable, and it's the same for every single logo in each tablet. Even the logos of the casings of the central processing units are detachable, so I assume every other logo in every device is as well."

"So what does that mean?" Ha-Neul asked.

"The casings became standardized in every electronic device the same time the chips became standardized in every government-affiliated device, which would have been around the same time Ryu Chamsagwan made these remarkable tablets."

"Okay," he prompted.

"So the CPU casing is the same for your new tablets, but the CPU is a much more advanced version of the chips," Evan said. "They're so far ahead of the chips it's possible it's able to communicate to any device that shares the logo—the logo being a hidden transmitter."

"That's—" Ha-Na began.

"Big Brother," Vanya finished.

"I agree," Ha-Neul said.

Evan nodded. "However, looking at all the apps that are unlocked so far, it seems like these tablets were made for your war effort—for this war effort."

They were all silent for a while.

"And it was Eomeoni who commissioned these," Ha-Na said.

"Under the Observant's direction at that," Vanya pointed out.

Ha-Neul shook his head. "Su and I have been wondering about that over the past few days. The Observant only does enough to let a person be more likely to make a certain choice. Eomeoni probably knew or guessed enough to think to ask Ryu Chamsagwan for this."

"Ryu Chamsagwan didn't like Big Brother watching him anyway," Su said, "so I'm sure he wouldn't give us the ability to become one. The tablets seem to give us only what we need."

"That makes Ryu Myeong-Ki a genius instead of an expert," Evan said. He started putting the tablets back together. "Even if the tablets become more Big Brother-like, we should use them."

"Really?" Vanya asked.

"Ryu Chamsagwan was a brilliant man," Evan said. "I'm sure he devised a way to rid these tablets of their abilities when they're no longer needed, just as they gain more abilities when necessary. I see no reason why we shouldn't use them."

"I agree," Ha-Na said. "Besides, Eomeoni would have made sure we would never gain too much power over the people."

Ha-Neul and Su agreed, while Vanya just looked resigned.

"So what's next?" Su asked.

"We get ready to free the slaves," Ha-Neul said. "That will take some time if we want to end the trade and the camps in one blow. Meanwhile, President Hwang will get started on our war stations once some of our soldiers have secured locations to build them. When enough of them are nearly complete, we'll infiltrate enough of the Scatter to have it shut down without too much concern."

"So nothing too difficult." Ha-Na sighed.

He gave her a grim smile. "That's only the beginning, noona."

"You said the slaves have tracking devices implanted in them," Vanya said. "How are we going to deal with that?"

Evan gave Ha-Neul his new tablet, and he quickly turned it on and began tapping on it a few times before he put it on the table to pick up the image. They all looked at a formula.

"The trackers are inserted through the solution Vanya was almost given," he said. "Since the tracking device attaches to the brain, the experience would be more traumatic without the solution's effects. In fact, it causes death in most cases where the solution isn't present. The solution also changes brain matter to be a better battery for the device, ensuring it doesn't die."

"So what does this formula do?" Vanya asked.

"It returns the brain to its natural state and kills all mechanics present in the human body," Evan said. "Unfortunately, that includes pacemakers and other implants."

"How many slaves would that affect?" Su asked.

"About a thirty-sixth of them," Ha-Neul said. "Less than half of those will be in serious condition once they take the formula."

"Will you have plenty of medics on hand for these people?" Ha-Na asked.

"We're working on it," he said.

"To successfully complete this operation, we'll need to shut down the identification system at least temporarily," Evan said.

"We're working on that, too," he ruffled his hair, "but that may take a while. I don't think Ryu Chamsagwan anticipated that program, or they're not using his technology to run it."

"They may have stayed away from it since he developed it," Evan agreed, "which could mean it's easier to break into with older methods." He picked up his tablet. "I have some contacts who could help. They have experience hacking into older satellite-based programs."

"If they're trustworthy, do it," Ha-Na said. She turned back to Ha-Neul. "Is this strike going to be human combat only?"

"Hopefully no war machines will be involved."

"Then Su and I are coming with you," she said. "That's non-negotiable. We know you'll head it yourself, and you're not going in alone. Evan has trained us for this."

He looked to Evan, who glanced up at him from the tablet.

"They've progressed well. Ha-Na is quite capable, and Su is . . . well, his clairvoyance obviously helps a lot," Evan said as he typed on his tablet.

Ha-Neul nodded. "We'll get you trained with soldiers when we get to Slovka. I need to practice as well. Evan, will you teach me what you've taught them?"

Evan nodded.

"Good," Su said. "It's late. We should go to bed if we want to be ready to move tomorrow."

Evan stopped typing and turned off the tablet as they all went to their own bedrooms.

The training uniforms were Ha-Neul's least favorite part of the practice scrimmages. Even though the cloth of the black uniform was thin, its tightness and the stiff wire threads that ran through it made him think he knew the reason why snakes were more aggressive before shedding their skin. Over the one piece, he also wore soldier's mission gear. He stood a good distance apart from a Slovkan man a few years older and dressed the same. Both held what looked like a combat knife. The handle looked normal, but the blade was made of stiff-looking wire that gave off an almost imperceptible hum.

"Positions," a voice commanded in Common.

Both men crouched in a fighting stance.

"Begin," the voice said.

They judged each other's stance before they moved in to strike. Their movements became a flurry of punches, kicks, swipes, and stabs, along with blocks and dodges. If the wire knife made contact, the black suit simulated the blow, weakening its wearer appropriately without real injury. Both men fought using the same combat style, but once Ha-Neul's opponent seemed to be in the flow of the battle, Ha-Neul changed his attack style. His opponent, caught off guard, soon received a knife to the chest—the blade collapsing into the handle.

"Match," the voice said. "Good work, gentlemen."

The other man shook his head. "No matter how many times we spar, that new style takes me by surprise every time."

"So, are you going to let Evan teach it?" Ha-Neul asked.

"Of course, since you won the contest," the man said. "If it is effective against me and every other soldier you use it on, it will be effective on our enemies. I will send the message immediately, Wangseja."

He nodded. "Thanks for giving it a chance."

The man laughed. "I had to once you laid out my best fighter."

A chime came from the corner of the room.

"Please excuse me," Ha-Neul said.

The man bowed as Ha-Neul went to the far corner of the sparring hall, picked up his tablet, and pressed the screen to receive a message. A little earpiece popped out of the tablet, and he put it in before the screen changed to show Aleksandr. He turned his back to the corner.

"Good afternoon," he said.

"I assume you finished your contest since you answered?" Aleksandr asked.

"I did. They'll have Evan teach the instructors today."

"That is good to hear. Anyway, President Hwang has just broken ground on two sites for war stations. They are in the two dead zones we discussed, so there should not be any problems."

"Is he using the machines like we agreed?"

"Of course," Aleksandr looked a little irritated, "since we agreed to cover the costs of smuggling them there to avoid using human construction workers."

"I know you didn't want to use them because of wages, but it's better than risking a worker being tracked to the sites."

"There is no need to remind me of the reason, Wangse-ja." Aleksandr sighed. "There are also some troubling signs on the Western Territory's border."

"What kind of signs?"

"Military movement from our two neighbors down that way. It may be purely defensive considering Woo Daejang's behavior, but some of the equipment and troops being moved to the border indicate possible offensive action."

"Has Woo Daejang taken notice?" he asked.

"He has steadily been strengthening the borders since the revolution. It is not possible that he has not noticed anything. Professor Tep is keeping an eye on the situation as well, but he thinks we should be wary of a three-way war, especially if there are no war machines available."

Ha-Neul sighed in exasperation. "The alliance between those two has always been bothersome. I suggest we restructure our timeline to accommodate this latest development. We'll need at least three stations in full operation and a couple more producing at half operation before we infiltrate the Scatter."

Aleksandr nodded. "I will inform the council and the Balhaen resistance. At the latest, we can hold a conference shortly after the dinner hour."

"That would be best."

"I will contact everyone now."

Aleksandr's image disappeared and was replaced by the tablet's home page, which had three more apps unlocked since his stay at the "love" hotel three weeks before. He turned the tablet off after putting the earpiece back into it and went into an adjoining locker room to shower and change. As he walked through the halls of the training center, he came upon a Balhaen soldier who looked to be his age.

"Yeong-Chan," he said as soon as he recognized his school chingu.

The soldier smiled and clapped him on the back. "What's up, chingu?"

"Way too much. When did you get here?"

"A little before lunch," Yeong-Chan said. "I've been looking forward to seeing you again. Luckily the michinnom never seemed to find out we made amends after school ended, or I wouldn't be here."

"How many did you bring?" he asked.

"My whole troop and my girl's troop as well." Yeong-Chan nudged him. "That took some leveraging, but once he learned she was a spellcaster and we're planning on getting hitched, he couldn't refuse. Besides, we both look loyal to him."

"Thanks for bringing so many." He felt a little less burdened.

"Anything for you, and most of them have been negatively affected by his rise. The others are purely loyal." Yeong-Chan smiled at him. "I wouldn't have brought them if I wasn't 100 percent sure of their trustworthiness."

He smiled back. "I know." He checked his watch. "Listen, I've got to go, but I'll see you either tonight or tomorrow."

"No worries. Get going." Yeong-Chan clapped him on the back again before they parted.

S u stood in a large room with a glass floor, looking down into the mess hall below. He moved every so often to get a better look at different groups of people, but he never took much interest in any one group.

"Is everything still clear?" Evan asked.

Su didn't even glance up at his sudden appearance as he had sensed Evan coming. "Yes, even the two new squads are completely clear."

"Ha-Neul will be relieved to hear that."

He frowned the tiniest bit. "Ha-Neul has complete trust in his friends, though I admit that doesn't mean he or they can't be duped."

"I sense a 'but' there," Evan said.

"The Observant told him to use those he could trust," he finally glanced up for a brief moment, "so I'm just making sure that trust is well-placed."

"Clairvoyants really are something else." Evan seemed impressed.

"Then what are you?" He noticed Evan stiffen. "You're more than observant, and the night before we met Harabeoji—I've never heard or read of anything like what I saw you do."

Evan cocked his head as if to listen better, then gave a faint smile. "Does it really matter as long as you know you can trust me?"

Su studied Evan intently. "No, it doesn't really matter. However, it could be helpful to know everything you are capable of."

"Even your abeoji did not know that," Evan said.

"I've gathered as much, but you still entrusted him with certain information for him to trust you."

Evan nodded. "I did."

"You won't tell me that at the least?" He gave Evan a slight glare.

"What he knew, you already know," Evan countered, but Su could sense his abeoji still knew more and Evan wasn't going to divulge any more.

He returned his attention to the mess hall. "How fortunate for me. Why are you here?"

"There is a conference after the dinner hour."

"I understand." He spread out his hands, palms facing the floor, closed his eyes, and inhaled deeply. He opened his eyes, and a white sheen covered his vision. Back in Our Fair City, he had looked at himself in the mirror once while in this state, and he knew his irises and pupils were now covered in that white sheen and that it reflected so much more than any normal eye could actually see. "Be sure to tell your friends thank you for all the help they've provided us. Gratitude should always be spoken aloud to such people."

Evan looked at him in awe before he bowed and said with deep respect, "I will."

Ha-Neul sat at a desk in a tiny office, looking over reports of arms and ammunition, troop numbers, the progress of the three new war stations, the formula's development, and details of each strike plan for more than one hundred locations. The room was relatively dark, with the time well past midnight and only a desk lamp illuminating his work area. He tapped his tablet to check slave and laborer numbers again. Some people had disappeared while more were added—most of those who disappeared ended up on the dead list.

Someone tapped on the office door, and he called for whomever it was to enter. He was surprised to see Vanya.

"I thought you'd be Ha-Na," he said.

"She asked me to come and check on you since I made her go to bed." Vanya sat across from him as he returned to his work. "She's afraid you're working yourself to death."

He let out a breathy chuckle. "It's nothing I'm not used to doing. I had plenty of sleepless nights doing work at the palace. She just never knew."

"I think she was plenty aware of that fact. She just seems to think you're avoiding sleep as much as possible."

"Well, I'm not. Besides, there's enough change to these numbers that our plans need to be updated almost once a week."

"Is it possible for us to keep up?" Vanya's tone was worried.

Ha-Neul shook his head, sighing. "I can't be sure until I check everything over again."

"You do know that no matter how long we wait or how many soldiers we have, there will be casualties, right?"

"Of course I know!" he snapped. He held up his tablet with the updated slave-and-laborer dead list. "I am constantly reminded of that fact whenever I open this app! Do you know how most of these people die? They're killed!" he said when Vanya couldn't answer the question fast enough. "They're killed because they've disobeyed or are no longer of value!"

He set the tablet back down and took a deep breath. "The formula's finally been tested useable. It's been five weeks since they've started trying to make it, and we finally have it, so now we've just got to mass produce it, which will take more time."

"How much time?" Vanya asked.

"A few days," he sighed.

"So what's wrong?" Vanya asked. "What's really wrong? Why are you so angry?"

He leaned back in his chair and turned his head away. "Most of these people are where they are because they've supported me in one way or another. Their crimes are also logged here. When I see it—see the sacrifices they're making for me for whatever reason—I dream of Ryu Chamsagwan and his grandsons. Every night they keep telling me they're happy to sacrifice themselves for me, and I can't help but feel I'm not worth it. I know I'm not worth it after everything I've done in the past. I'm not worth anyone to sacrifice themselves for."

Vanya considered his words for several seconds before nodding. "You're right. You're not worth it. If it wasn't for your hatred of magic, it's possible none of this would have happened."

"So you agree?"

"Of course. Your hatred made it so my father found Woo Su-Han, a brilliant soldier and general with socio-pathic tendencies," Vanya said. "Your hatred made him power hungry, which made him disregard every plan that would result in the least amount of casualties. It's all your fault, so you're not worthy."

He stared at Vanya incredulously.

"That's the look I should be wearing."

"What are you saying?" Ha-Neul asked.

"I think you know what I'm saying." Vanya leaned in closer, his hands clasped on the table. "The Observant told you there are events that always occur no matter what and that she personally got involved in this matter. I think this war was always going to happen and you were always going to be at the center of it. You can almost call it fate, but I think you've been given a choice." Vanya pointed at the raven's-eye necklace. "If you want to, you can run from it."

He was shocked. "Then I'd have to leave Lisa behind. You're saying I'd have to try to forget her."

"You probably could if you chose to."

"I don't want to."

"Then why save the slaves first? You can see her faster if you don't."

"I can't leave thousands of people like that in order to see the woman I love when she's safe."

Vanya smiled. "That's why you're worth it. We know you're in this war for others and not yourself. Those people"—he pointed at the tablet—"they must have seen what you are capable of as well. They must have seen that deep down you are actually a decent person who went astray but are not a complete lost cause." Vanya leaned back and folded his arms. "Although I think you may be taking things too slow. There's no perfect plan—only the best plan. That's one thing I learned from the Observant. I hope you know when you have the best plan and when to use it."

Ha-Neul couldn't say anything for a few seconds. "You're right."

"I'm glad you think so."

He grinned at Vanya's sarcastic tone. "Seriously, though, you're right. I'm almost being too cautious to the point of waiting too long, and that can cost more lives."

"So what will you do now?" Vanya asked.

He looked over all the reports. "To be honest, I was hesitating about deciding the date for the operation, but I've known for several hours when it should be." He looked up at Vanya. "We've got to be ready on Geuret seventh and move on the eighth. We declare war on the tenth."

"The tenth?" Vanya looked surprised. "Really?"

He nodded. "Why?"

"You do remember what happened that day last year, right?"

He hesitated as the memory resurfaced. "It's the day I kicked Lisa out of the palace."

Vanya gave him a hard stare. "Are you sure that's the best plan and timing?"

"That's why I was hesitating," he said. "However, I honestly think we can be ready."

"Then go for it, Ha-Neul. Go for it without reservation or embarrassment." Vanya checked the time. "It's time for bed."

He nodded. "I'm going to send the message, so you go first."

Vanya nodded and stood as Ha-Neul began to type out the message on his tablet.

"By the way, Vanya," he said as Vanya reached the door. "I think it's best if you court my noona openly now. Su and I have no reservations against you doing so."

Vanya didn't turn around when he said an awkward, "Thanks . . . I'll let her know."

Ha-Neul grinned mischievously as Vanya left the office.

55

A persistent chiming woke Ha-Neul early the next morning. He groaned, rubbing the sleep out of his eyes as the chime kept going. He glanced at his tablet to see Moon Harabeoji was trying to contact him. After pulling on a shirt, he pressed the Accept button.

"Harabeoji," he said, "is something wrong?"

Moon Harabeoji grumbled, "We have received a message from Gwon Daejang of the Central Army."

He blinked. "A message? How?"

"One of the construction managers found a message written on one of the walls of site D," Moon Harabeoji said. "Apparently he wants to meet you there in about two hours."

"He betrayed us," he said. "He used Central Army—our own personal army—to help Woo Daejang conquer Balhae."

"I read the news as well, Wangseja-Mama," Moon Harabeoji growled. "However, he promises to meet with you by himself."

Ha-Neul didn't say anything as he thought it over.

After a couple of minutes, Moon Harabeoji spoke. "Wangseja-Mama, if I may give my opinion, I recommend you speak with him."

"Why?" He couldn't hide his curiosity.

"If he knows we are building war stations, he knows President Hwang is helping us. We do not know how much he knows; however, he reached out to us first and with conditions that are favorable for us. He has no way of knowing if you will come due to his method of contacting us, and once the message was found, we took precautions to ensure President Hwang's safety as well as the company's and all that it entails."

He considered Moon Harabeoji's words for a few seconds. "Can I get there safely in that time?"

"Yes."

"What about Su?"

"If you think it is best to take Wangja with you."

"Can we trace Gwon Daejang?" he asked.

"Evan has accessed the program," Moon Harabeoji said. "Apparently he is still at home, though he should have left for the site by now."

He nodded. "Postpone the meeting until just before lunch."

"Understood, Wangseja-Mama. I will have a transport ready for you in half an hour. I shall inform Wangja of the situation as well."

"Thank you, Harabeoji."

He ended the call and sprang out of bed, showering, brushing his teeth, and dressing quickly before going to the mess hall. Su was already there finishing breakfast when he entered. He sat in front of his dongsaeng and tore into his food.

"Are you sure this is a good idea?" Su asked.

"Harabeoji thinks it is."

"So you'll disguise me and have me make sure nothing is wrong?"

"That's the idea."

"Fine." A chime came from both their tablets, and Su checked his as Ha-Neul continued to eat. "The transport is ready."

He wiped his hands and face then took a drink of water. "Let's go."

They walked through the halls of the facility and came to a large hangar. A vehicle that was a cross between a small car and a low-flying jet waited for them, the pilot behind the controls. As soon as they were secure in their seats, the vehicle took off, leaving the underground facility at high speeds. They were in the air headed east toward Pannonia within three minutes. The vehicle was fast as it flew low and glided smoothly over any high terrain.

"You look tired, hyeong," Su said.

"I am, but I'll get more sleep starting tonight," he said.

"Your nightmares have stopped?" Su looked surprised.

He smiled. "I think so."

They didn't say anything else for most of the ride. Within an hour, the vehicle had flown almost halfway across Slovka before it finally crossed a mountain range into Pannonia, then headed toward a second range that also ran north and south. He placed a concealment spell on Su, making him appear as a middle-aged officer, as they drew closer to the mountains. Soon they circled over a small valley that had traces of ongoing construction before the pilot took them into a steep dive to land in a good-sized clearing.

"Your contact should be about twenty yards north of

this point," the pilot said. "Moon Daejang has given his assurance that you will not be alone, though you will appear to be."

"Thank you," he said as they got out.

He and Su walked into the forest just north of their transport and measured the distance carefully. It wasn't necessary as they soon saw Gwon Daejang, a tall figure in his fifties and of solid stock, waiting for them where he could be easily seen. He bowed to Ha-Neul as they approached.

"It is good to see you well, Wangseja-Mama," the daejang said.

"I wish I could say the same for you, Gwon Daejang." He didn't return the bow.

The man seemed unsurprised by his behavior. "I understand, Wangseja-Mama. I have done nothing in the public eye that would indicate any loyalty to you."

"So why are you here?" he asked.

"I knew that you would need war machines eventually," Gwon Daejang said, "so I made sure I had trustworthy people where they could be of use in finding you, and I made sure that Woo Daejang would have none among President Hwang's employees."

Ha-Neul glared at the man suspiciously. "Why?"

"To help you."

He couldn't help but show his disbelief. "Help me? You used Central to help Woo Su-Han take over Balhae! How is that helping me?!"

"It has given you more spies than you could hope for."

Ha-Neul leaned back in surprise. "What?"

"The Central Balhaen Army remains loyal to you, Wangseja-Mama," Gwon Daejang said. "At the very beginning, I knew Woo Daejang would gain control. His forces proved he would during the review, so I made a tactical decision to cut losses and ensure you would have loyal soldiers in play for when you made your move."

"And they all agreed to this?" he asked.

"They did. If you do not believe me, I am willing to go in front of Wangja and say the same thing."

"Why would you go to Su?"

Gwon Daejang gave him a pathetic smile. "Because he is like your eomeoni, a clairvoyant."

Ha-Neul didn't respond immediately. "How do you know?"

His tone seemed to comfort the daejang, and his posture relaxed a little. "Please, Wangseja-Mama, she was my favorite sachon, and she and her gajok were the only ones besides my bumo who were willing to accept me, an adoptee."

Su stepped forward. "He's telling the truth, hyeong."

Gwon Daejang looked at Su in shock. "Geum Su Wangja-Mama?"

Ha-Neul cut his flow of magic, and the concealment spell disappeared. Gwon Daejang looked from Su to Ha-Neul. "Are you—are you a spellcaster?"

"I am," he nodded.

"Oh, gods above," Gwon Daejang said. "What a thing to know."

"This is a secret until my hyeong deems it proper to reveal," Su said.

Gwon Daejang nodded. "Of course. I kept your eomeoni's secret all these years."

"You said you have people ready to help us with the war machines," Ha-Neul said. "What did you mean by that?"

"I have loyal soldiers in most of the war stations and

Scatter," Gwon Daejang said. "At the first sign of war, they are ready to secure what they can."

He shook his head. "We don't mean to secure the Scatter. We aim to destroy as much of it as possible. We can't risk Woo Daejang retaking them."

"So that is why you are building your own war stations," Gwon Daejang muttered.

"There is something you can do for us, though," Su said.

"What's that?" Ha-Neul asked.

"I am listening," Gwon Daejang prompted.

"We still don't have the full set of stations under construction," Su began. "In a few days, we can provide a great distraction so that your men can steal as many machines as possible for us and make sure the Scatter and many stations become permanently inoperable."

Ha-Neul smiled. "Su, you're brilliant." He turned to Gwon Daejang. "How many of your high-ranking officers and aides can we contact within the next hour?"

"They are all on standby, Wangseja-Mama. What is this about?"

"We're going to kill two birds at the same time," Su said as Ha-Neul tapped away at his tablet. "We can free the slaves and cripple Woo Daejang at the same time."

"You think we can do that?" Gwon Daejang asked.

"We have access to the identification program," Su said, "and plan to make many people disappear from it. It's the best we can do since we're not able to shut it down—unless you can?"

Gwon Daejang shook his head. "I cannot help you there."

"We'll make do," Su said and turned to Ha-Neul. "Are you finished, hyeong?"

He nodded and looked up at Gwon Daejang. "How long can you stay here?"

"Most of the day if I need to."

"Good, we have a planning meeting in an hour," he said, "and I need you and your officers in on that."

"I will contact them right away."

H a-Neul and Su returned to the facility late that afternoon. Soldiers filled the halls, getting ready for the operation. Those who were paying attention and saw them moved out of their way as they walked through the hallways. Ha-Neul opened a door to a conference room where the other three waited for them.

"You're back." Ha-Na's tone was full of relief.

"You took a huge risk going to meet General Gwon," Vanya said. "Even Irene had no clue he was still loyal to you."

"We got very lucky," Evan said.

Ha-Neul shook his head. "No, if he was as close to Eomeoni as he indicated, he was prepared. Whether he knew it or not, he was prepared for this."

"You're talking about the Observant," Ha-Na said.

"Eomeoni was her messenger," Su said, "so it makes sense that he was guided."

"What really matters is that he did take the best path," Ha-Neul said, "just as Eomeoni advised everyone to do."

"So what do we do next?" Vanya asked.

"We get everyone into position," Evan said. "We have already run many simulations of the operation. Now we get ready for the real thing. There is nothing else to do."

Ha-Neul nodded as excitement and anxiety mingled

within him. "We'll be leaving in four days, and we're sticking together. I wouldn't have you go anywhere else during this operation."

Ha-Na smiled and looked at him sympathetically. "We wouldn't let you go anywhere without us for this."

The others laughed at his reaction.

56

E veryone donned their uniforms in silence. For as much excitement as there was over the past week, the same amount of nervousness hung in the air now. Outside, the sun was still setting, but the last vestiges of natural light were losing their grasp on the sky. It was as if the light was taking one last giant breath before plunging into an ocean of darkness, not knowing if another breath would be taken again. Then those last few rays of precious daylight finally disappeared as though someone had snuffed them out of existence.

Ha-Neul's team seemed to take in a collective breath as the city's lights filled the night sky. On his mark, they set their watches and waited for half an hour before every light along the streets and in the buildings blinked off, the darkness nearly swallowing the city whole. The team stood as one and exited the back of their building into an alleyway maze, grim determination replacing their nervousness. They followed him as he led them with confidence, and after several minutes through the alleys, he paused at a corner to check the next alley to make sure it was clear. He signaled for two out of his group of fifteen to move.

Two soldiers moved into the alleyway with their guns ready to shoot. The earpiece in his ear beeped after five minutes, and he motioned for the rest of the team to move. They met the two soldiers at a door they had opened. Another two soldiers and Evan entered the large building. A voice from the inside started to speak loudly but was quickly muffled. A few seconds later, another beep sounded in Ha-Neul's ear, and he sent another group of three in with Vanya leading.

A third beep went off, and he sent Ha-Na and Su in with a soldier. More voices started making a commotion inside, and then they heard gunshots. He entered the building with the rest of the soldiers, providing support for their team as they fought enemy soldiers in various states of dress in a large entertainment room. The screams of fleeing slaves filled the air. As his team moved through the building, four soldiers secured the front and back exits while two more began to administer to the slaves still in the room and those eventually sent to them.

Ha-Neul thoroughly combed the building with another soldier to make sure there weren't any stragglers from the fighting. A few times, a random soldier popped out of a room or some other hiding spot, and they quickly took them out. An hour after the first group entered the building, his earpiece beeped again once the gunfight had been silent for several minutes.

"Everything seems to be clear," Evan said in Common, the language for the operation.

Ha-Neul pressed his earpiece twice.

"We're holding back the slaves up here," Evan said.

"We'll start our downward sweep," Ha-Na replied.

Twenty minutes and several gunshots later, he and his partner met up with Ha-Na's group.

"Come down, Evan," he said. "We have half an hour before we meet teams L and N."

"Copy, leader."

He and Ha-Na moved back downstairs with their group and met the other soldiers in the large entertainment room. As soon as they entered, the room quieted as all slaves' eyes moved to them. A woman who seemed to be in her thirties approached them, closely studying Ha-Na and Ha-Neul.

"It *is* you," she said in Hasoseoche.

Much to his astonishment, she went to her knees and performed a keunjeol.

"Thank you, thank you so much for coming for us, Mama," she said from the floor.

Many of the slaves went to their knees and performed a keunjeol as well.

"Please stand up," he said in Haeyoche. "If you want to thank us, then do so once we get to safety. We've got a long night and day ahead of us."

Most of the slaves who had bowed were able to stand by themselves while others needed help. He reached down and helped the woman to her feet.

"Wangseja-Mama . . ." she said through tears.

He gave her a small smile. "It'll be all right sooner or later."

She nodded and wiped her tears away. A couple of minutes later, the rest of the team and slaves entered.

"Everyone, please listen," a soldier said in a loud voice. "If you don't have any major medical implants—like pacemakers, cochlear implants, or any similar devices for major health conditions—please form eight lines to receive a formula that will deactivate your tracking devices. The rest of you will receive it when we can get you to a medical team."

Most of the slaves formed the necessary lines, and eight of the soldiers quickly injected them with the formula. Another twenty minutes passed before they were ready to go.

"Group one," Ha-Neul said, "you lead."

The group slipped out the front doors.

"Clear," said a voice in his earpiece.

"Groups two and three, lead the people out."

The mass exodus took five minutes to clear the building, with his and Su's teams following. The streets were deserted besides the soldiers and refugees. They walked another five minutes to a large park where two more teams of soldiers waited with more slaves. Two soldiers approached him.

"Backup is waiting outside the city limits," the team leader reported. "We are expected at the medic camp in two hours."

"Then let's go."

The team leaders relayed the instructions, and soon the soldiers were shepherding the freed slaves to the north while he saw other teams of soldiers scouting the city. When they reached the city's outskirts, they combined with all the teams and other groups of refugees before they met with the backup. The refugees were loaded onto buses and large trucks after walking passed disabled military check-points. As each vehicle was filled, they slowly made their way off with an escort of jeeps carrying heavily armed soldiers.

Ha-Neul's team stayed until the last of the refugees had boarded and were in the distance before his and four other teams escorted him as they drove northwest toward

Burgos. After driving for an hour, they came upon the medic camp. Most of the refugees received a quick scan, food if they were hungry, and clothes if they needed them, whereas a very few others by comparison waited for operations. He watched in confusion as another tent was set up.

"Camp leader," he said into his earpiece.

"Yes, leader?" Rosalina replied.

"What's the new tent for?"

"It's there to take new recruits, leader," she said. "Many have expressed a desire to join your army. I believe similar tents have been deemed necessary in every medic camp."

"Very well. I'm going dark for five minutes." He pulled out the earpiece, stuck it in a pocket, and pulled out a different earpiece from another pocket. "Status report, Aleksandr."

"Evan's contacts are fighting off all attempts to reestablish the program while deleting the necessary files and several thousand others," Aleksandr said, "but they may have less than an hour left before the program is back up."

"Understood, and what about the Scatter effort?"

"General Moon says it is going live in half an hour in response to the program effort."

"Very well. Let's start shipping out the refugees. Apparently we'll have recruits as well."

"I am well aware of the fact, and the possibility of new recruits was taken into consideration several days ago."

"Without my knowledge?" he asked in shock.

"Yes, it was done without your knowledge. Your siblings deemed it appropriate."

He looked over at his nammae, who weren't too far away and were trying to hide their amusement from him.

"Very well. I'll check back in after an hour."

He took out his earpiece and put the first back in. "Camp leader."

"Yes, leader?"

"Start the evacuation," he said.

"Copy, leader."

He turned to Ha-Na and Su.

"Before you say anything about the camp alterations," Ha-Na said, "we just want to tell you that Su was able to adjust the plans so well it shouldn't cause any problems."

Ha-Neul just shook his head. "Thank you."

His nammae smiled and together, with a few other soldiers, they oversaw the start of the evacuation. The medics performed the operations as fast as they could and sent the recovering patients along as soon as they were stable enough. He checked his watch to see it was approaching 0200. His earpiece beeped in a slightly different tone, so he switched pieces.

"Speak."

"You have hostiles approaching from the southeast," Moon Harabeoji said. "You have an hour at most before they arrive."

"Copy." He put the first earpiece back in. "Start emergency evac now. We need to be gone in half an hour."

"Copy, leader."

Two high-pitched chirps sounded throughout the camp, and the soldiers began to rush about. The medics and their patients cleared out first, followed by refugees who weren't recruited or didn't have any training. He and his nammae helped where they could and relayed orders when they needed to. Twenty minutes after the order to evacuate went out, he put the second earpiece in his other ear.

"Speak."

"Fifteen minutes," Moon Harabeoji said, and Ha-Neul's adrenaline spiked. "Get yourself out."

"Fifteen minutes," he relayed. "Let's go, teams. Camp leader, connect with Moon."

Ha-Neul, Ha-Na, and Su ran to a group of jeeps, converging on several other soldiers from varying territories, along with Vanya and Evan. They hopped into the backs of three different jeeps, and the drivers took off. As the lights of the camp grew smaller, he could make out the lights of several helicopters in the far distance. Within five minutes, explosions lit the night sky and illuminated a host of humanoid figures ripping through the remains of the camp.

He pressed the second earpiece. "What's the progress on the Scatter?"

"General Gwon was met with more resistance than thought possible. They're working on shutting down the war station closest to your location," Aleksandr said.

"We don't have time." He pressed the other earpiece. "Turn around. Casters, prepare."

The jeeps turned as one and went into a spread-out formation. They passed fleeing jeeps and buses full of refugees before they saw the first line of helicopters coming toward them.

"Air defense," he ordered.

A few soldiers, as well as Ha-Na, Evan, and Su, pulled out rocket launchers from the back compartments of their jeeps. Each one took aim and fired. Several helicopters exploded a split second later. The light of the fire illuminated the long rows of war machines.

"Casters, thirty seconds," he shouted. He, Vanya, and a few soldiers steadied themselves on the bar that hung between the back and front seats or the windshield. "Ten seconds!"

Various spell circles of different colors appeared—all overlapping the others. They were huge in size, and soon symbols appeared in them.

"Activate!"

The circles exploded, throwing back the first three rows of war machines as they split into pieces.

"Retreat! Casters, keep going, and air defense, do what you deem necessary!"

The spellcasters worked together to create spells that reacted violently together while the other soldiers targeted the approaching aircraft. But the rows of war machines were gaining on them, and enemy Humvees rushed out from behind them. The spellcasters continued to focus on the war machines while half of the air defense started to focus on the approaching Humvees, but it wasn't enough. He tapped Vanya, who stood next to him, and Vanya nodded.

A line of royal purple and green circles appeared on the two farthest jeeps and activated quickly. The jeeps exploded, catching the closest three jeeps in their demise. He and Vanya had already moved on to the next farthest jeeps to repeat the process. Their jeep hit a large bump, and the soldier in the front passenger seat grabbed them to steady them.

"Mountains, leader!" a voice said in his ear.

"Get to the defense line!"

He and Vanya sent out volleys of exploding spell circles in rapid succession.

"Brace!" a voice shouted.

Everyone standing grabbed hold of the middle bar just as they all hit a huge ditch.

"Better sit!" the same voice called out.

They all buckled in as they moved into the mountains.

The enemies behind them started firing. A line of missiles and rockets roared back at their enemies from higher up the mountains.

Ha-Neul pressed the second earpiece. "Aleksandr, the Scatter!"

"They've just hit the main station! Give them a few minutes!"

"We may not have a few—"

An explosion tipped the back of his jeep into the air before it crashed back down on its wheels. Ha-Neul's forehead hit the seat in front of him, and he fought to keep the darkness threatening to overwhelm him at bay.

"—Neul! Ha-Neul! Do you hear me?!" Aleksandr shouted into his ringing ears.

"Stop shouting," he slurred as his head spun. He slapped the earpiece. "Casualties?"

"None, leader."

He slapped the second earpiece. "Tell them to hurry."

"They're on it." Aleksandr sounded anxious.

Another line of missiles and rockets rained down the mountain behind them. He looked over at Vanya, who watched him with a pale face.

"What?" he asked.

Vanya swallowed. "You must have one powerful guardian angel."

"We're at the line!" a soldier shouted.

Ha-Neul looked up just in time to see the jeep pass through a blockade. Heavy gunfire ripped through the forest as the blockade fired on the war machines. More rockets, missiles, and even grenades soared through the air, the explosions ripping the mountain forest apart. Ha-Neul's group of jeeps continued to race up the mountain until it came to a pass and roared onto the road into Burgos.

An earpiece beeped. "What?"

"The Scatter is down," Aleksandr said in a subdued tone. "Central Army received heavy losses but managed to procure plenty of machines for us."

"Anything else?" he asked, anxiety and adrenaline making his hands shake.

Aleksandr seemed to hesitate. "General Gwon was captured an hour ago. His head is hanging from the palace gate."

Ha-Neul closed his eyes as he remembered the image of Ha-Na's head hanging on the gate. "His gajok?"

"He sent them away as soon as the power outages were reported. De la Mare's Massalian troops have them in safe-keeping at their facility."

"Thank the soldiers for me, and tell Madame De la Mare I'll send for them when I can."

"Understood," Aleksandr said. "And Wangseja . . ."

"Yes?" His voice broke as his exhaustion swept through him.

"Congratulations on your first successful mission."

It was weird for Ha-Neul to look at his reflection in the mirror. He now sported a huge bruise and goose egg on his forehead for all the world to see since his hair was cut short and styled slightly up. His many piercings were on full display, glinting proudly in the light. Yet this was not what made it weird for him to stare at his reflection. What made it weird was the Balhaen Royal Uniform of the wangseja. Every detail was as it should be, and it fit his soldier-trained body perfectly.

When he looked into the mirror, he expected to see the wangseja of the year before, but he was not there. This Ha-Neul was completely different from the one who last wore the uniform.

Ha-Na entered his spacious new room wearing a beautiful pink seuran-chima and floral-patterned, green dangui. Her hair was long again, thanks to unnoticeable hair extensions, and fashioned into a gwimit meori with a jebiburi-daeng-gi. Su followed her, his hair also trimmed neat, wearing the Balhaen Royal Uniform of the wangja. They stood behind him and on either side of him—Ha-Na on his right and Su, a head shorter, on his left. Both had bruises and cuts from the previous day's operation.

"This is rather strange, is it not?" Ha-Na said in Hasoseoche.

"It is," Ha-Neul replied, also in Hasoseoche.

Su followed their lead. "The wangsil are much different than what the world remembers."

"Not only that, but they will know that we are strong," Ha-Neul said. "They will know that we do not give up, do not surrender, and do not die easily."

Ha-Na gave them a pleased smile. "They will also know, my dear nam-dongsaeng, that we are a team not to be underestimated."

Vanya moved to stand behind Ha-Na, and Evan moved to stand behind Su. Both wore tailored suits.

"Nor are they alone," Evan said.

"Those who once stood against them now stand with them," Vanya said.

Ha-Neul burst out laughing. "I'm sorry, I can't help it," he said through his laughter. "I can't help but think that Lisa would say we're all so corny and cheesy."

The others started laughing as well.

"And she'd be right," Vanya said. "She was usually right."

Aleksandr knocked on the door before he entered. The prince studied all of them with a look of admiration. "It is time, Wangseja-Mama."

The others filed out, leaving Aleksandr and Ha-Neul alone.

"I have a question, Aleksandr." He scuffed the floor a little timidly.

"I am anxious to hear it, Wangseja-Mama."

"Why do you and Vanya only call Lisa Vasilisa?"

Aleksandr smiled. "We call her Vasilisa because that is her true name."

"But she's also Lisa," he countered.

"No, Wangseja-Mama," Aleksandr said. "Lisa and Vasilisa are two very different people. You just happened to meet Vasilisa under the name of Lisa and fell in love with her."

Confusion swirled within him. "I'm not sure I understand."

Aleksandr smiled. "Ask Vasilisa when you see her again. It is only right for her to explain." He checked his watch. "We must go, but before we do, there is one other matter."

A surge of panic rose within Ha-Neul. "What is it?"

"I want you to know how proud Vasilisa would be of you," Aleksandr said. "I know she would because I am proud of you as well. One day I hope to call you my son-in-law."

Ha-Neul bowed his head and blinked back the tears. "Thank you."

Ha-Neul stood behind the podium with the Balhaen Seal of a bonghwang and a yong intertwined together around a rising sun towering behind him. Off to either side of him stood Ha-Na and Su, with Vanya and Evan behind them. A camera in front of him had a lightbulb that suddenly turned on. He gripped the edges of the podium and took a deep breath.

"Good morning, citizens of Balhae. I am Geum Ha-Neul, Wangseja of Balhae. I stand before you this morning after a tremendous battle—a battle to free the slaves, laborers, and comfort-people who were abused by the greed and maliciousness of pretend rulers. This battle also saw the destruction of much of the war-machine dominance, though it is not completely gone. To bring this to pass, many good and great people have perished."

He paused briefly to regain his composure as he remembered his last meeting with Gwon Daejang.

"My fellow citizens, because that is what we are, I will do all I can to make our country great again, but I need your help—we need your help. If you share our dream to rid ourselves of the rot in our country, please do not hesitate to join our efforts. Together we can remove Woo Daejang and those like him."

Behind Ha-Neul and the others, Aleksandr, Astrid, Madame De la Mare, Kisasszony Vajda, Señor Mijares, and Professor Tep walked onto the stage wearing their countries' respective royal apparel.

"Our alliance is already strong, but we will be stronger with you. I hope with all my being that you will choose the best path. Though it may not be the easiest path or the safest path, I ask that you choose the best path."

He felt the raven's eye against his chest grow warm at that moment, and suddenly he stood in the gate holding of Our Fair City with his nammae, Vanya, and Evan.

"Please do not move," the gatekeepers said. "You have not yet finished traveling."

Before they could reply, they stood in front of the large stone doors leading to the Observant's cavern. Dunway, Gibney, O'Donnell, and McKennon stood in front of them.

"Dunway? What's going on?" Ha-Neul was full of indignation and confusion.

"What else but the Observant has summoned you all?" McKennon snapped.

"She couldn't choose a better time?" Ha-Na exclaimed.

"Do not doubt the Observant's timing." McKennon threatened her with his stave.

"Take it easy, McKennon," Dunway said. "Remember who they are."

McKennon was displeased with Dunway's words, and he left his group, brushing past them in a huff.

"Seriously, Dunway, what's going on?" Ha-Neul asked.

Dunway pulled out a tablet and showed it to them. Ha-Neul took it as he realized it was flipping through every country's news, which was all abuzz with the events in Balhae. One story was a video clip of the address he had just been taken from, and it showed a large raven's eye swallowing him and the others before the news feed cut off. He looked up at the Northern Mountains men, dumbfounded.

The doors opened, and the Geum family, Evan, and Ivan entered. The Observant watched the group walk through crowds they could not see or feel. From where she sat out of the time she presided over for the domain, she watched them and their present echoes approach as their near-innumerable future echoes moved about in the cavern and in scenes yet to be or to never be. Trillions upon trillions of more echoes moved through her vision and beyond. Her time was seemingly infinite but over all too quickly. She was the only mortal to know every possible fate, to bear the burden of sifting through so many paths and influencing them for the better.

Finally and always, they stood in front of her. The Observant could see them through the cloth, though they could not see her. Never in so many millennia did she wish as much as at that time to be free of her bindings.

"Welcome," she said with all the warmth she felt. She knew the cavern would reflect her emotions.

"Why did you summon us?" Ha-Neul asked. He was respectful but so full of doubt.

She smiled because, even though they could not see it, she knew they would feel it caress their skin. "You have put the world on the best path possible, and because of that, you have become worthy to be marked."

"Marked?" Su asked. His emotions were simple but powerful, just like all great clairvoyants.

"You have been marked as messengers," she said, then summoned raven's-eye necklaces to be place around Ha-Na's and Su's necks, "and as messengers the world shall know you."

"The magic community—especially the clairvoyants—they'll understand?" Ha-Neul asked, the Observant knowing that he was thinking of Amparo and her own necklace.

"They will indeed," she said, "and they will soon know just how truly special you are. The raven's-eye necklace is the token of messengers."

"Whose messengers? Yours?" Evan asked.

"I am merely your partner. Our purpose is to help put the world on the best path, which you have helped me do today."

"Then why did Ha-Neul's mother pass her necklace on to Vasilisa? Vasilisa certainly wasn't a messenger," Vanya said.

"Jin Bo Wanghoo did so because I instructed her to," the Observant told him. "I knew that if Vasilisa chose the best path, she would give it to Ha-Neul."

Ha-Neul said nothing, though she knew his emotions were swirling inside him.

"So what are we supposed to do?" Ha-Na asked.

"If you continue on the path you have set yourselves on, all will be well."

"This is all you brought us here for . . ." Ha-Neul said, incredulous.

"No, it is not." She became solemn. "Geum Ha-Neul"— she watched him shiver as the power and authority in her voice passed through him—"thou art hereby chosen to be a messenger and a proxy. Where I cannot stand, thou shalt go to deliver the message. Art thou willing to take this responsibility upon thyself?"

As she had seen in many of the few branches splitting from this present, he did not answer. She knew his hesitation well, and her sympathy went out to him.

"Please leave Ha-Neul and me alone."

The others bowed and walked away. Once they were gone, Ha-Neul spoke. "Why am I the one chosen? Why not Su?"

"Though Su does indeed have the more easily seen advantage, he has not shown the same resolve."

Ha-Neul swallowed the many emotions she saw played out in other paths. "Is this because of what Lisa has done to me? Because you guided her into my life?"

She watched as the comfort and reassurance she knew Ha-Neul needed, and wanted, from Vasilisa wrapped around him. She watched as his eyes filled with tears and his hand unconsciously clutched his raven's eye. "What you have done is of your own choosing, and what Vasilisa has done to help you was of her own choosing."

Ha-Neul's tears broke free, and he slid to his knees. Vasilisa's comfort and reassurance grew stronger, and he reached around himself as though he were trying to physically touch his lover as she embraced him.

"I feel her with me even now," he sobbed.

"That is because Vasilisa is always with you, no matter where you both may be."

"How is it possible?" he asked through his tears.

"Because you love each other," she told him with all the conviction she could muster.

It took Ha-Neul some time to calm down, and when he did, he got to his feet and seemingly looked her in the eye, though she knew he couldn't.

"What will my responsibilities be?"

The Observant smiled again, and the cavern warmed to let him know of her pleasure.

"I am bound to this role," she said. "Because of that, I cannot leave this throne until I am given permission or I am no longer needed. Until that day, I need you to be my messenger and proxy when my knowledge is needed."

"When will that be?"

"Not for some time, but soon."

"And you really didn't choose me?"

"I did not choose you," she assured him. "Your actions made you chosen. You simply became the person I needed." She sighed, and a wind caressed his skin. "Your war has just begun, but it will not be over until a much larger war is won."

Ha-Neul looked up in shock. "A larger war?"

"Yes, and for that war I will need to become an active player," she said, "and to do that, I need you. Your role will be simple. All you need to do is be willing and ready at any time to relay my message in my stead. Will you accept that responsibility?"

Ha-Neul thought about it for a long time, and she watched many paths vanish. "I will."

The Observant's pleasure swept through the cavern

once more. "Thank you, Ha-Neul. You don't know how much I appreciate this."

She reached out to his raven's eye with her power and touched it. Ha-Neul clutched it as it momentarily blazed with warmth.

"With your acceptance, you are granted access to this cavern so long as I can uphold the power. Feel free to come when you need to. I will only summon you here when I must."

"Really?"

"Yes, but it is only for you. Any others you bring will be taken to the gate of Our Fair City. In addition, you can travel freely between here and any safe haven. You will not be taken back to any dangerous area if you so choose, but it cannot be the same for any others. This is the extent that I can expend my power. I hope you understand."

Ha-Neul nodded. "I think I do."

"Then go, and fare well in your war. We shall see each other again."

He bowed to her, and she knew that he felt a little over-whelmed from the way he walked away from her. She felt sorry for him. Her showing the world he was chosen would make his war more difficult for him, but she knew it would help him as well. She could not tell him, though, and as he left her cavern, the Observant knew she would not see him despite all the questions he would have until she needed him.

DICTIONARY

Abba (아빠): Dad

Abeoji (아버지): Father

Adeul (아들): Son

Aegi (애기): Baby

Annyeong (안녕): "Hi"/"Bye." This is Haeche, or banmal.

Annyeonghaseyo (안녕하세요): "Hello"; used for elders, people of higher authority, or to be polite. This form is Haeyoche.

Assa (아싸): Korean exclamation of happiness

Baduk (바둑): An ancient Chinese strategy game called "Go" in English, usually played on a 19 x 19-space board

Bomo sang-goong (보모상궁): The woman in charge of taking care of the princes and princesses

Bonghwang (봉황): Or "fenghuang" in Chinese; often called the Chinese phoenix

Bumo (부모): Parents

Chamsagwan (참사관): Adviser, councilor

Cheopji (첩지): a Korean hair accessory for various

hairstyles of women when wearing ceremonial
dress. It is usually made of silver, and a frog
shape is its most common form.

Chima (치마): A type of skirt worn together with
the jeogori of women's hanbok

Chingu (친구): Friend

Daejang (대장): General

Dangui (당의): Ceremonial dress or jacket similar to
a jeogori. It is characterized by a shaped front
and back lower parts, like part of a circle with
pointed ends. The striking difference between
the dangui for royalty and that of the other
court attendees is that those of the royal family
have geumbak.

Daeng-gi (댕기): The generic term for all types of
ribbon worn in the hair; usually red.

Danpatbbang (단팥빵): A pastry filled with sweet
red-bean paste

Ddal (딸): Daughter

Ddeok (떡): A rice cake that looks like a short, thick
noodle

-Do (도): A province (Jeoncheon-do)

Dongsaeng (동생): Younger brother/sister. This is
for family or friends who are younger

Eomeo (어머): Similar to "Oh, dear" or "Oh, my"

Eomeoni (어머니): Mother

Eonni (언니): Older sister; used by females for
siblings or older friends

Eorin Wangja (어린 왕자): Little, or young, prince

Eorini (어린이): Children

Gajok (가족): Family

Geumbak (금박): Gold foil patterns on hanbok or
daeng-gi

Gongju (공주): Princess

Gwimit Meori (귀밑머리): A hairstyle worn by women before they marry. It is parted at the front before it is braided and is tied at the end with a daeng-gi.

Haeche (해체): The lowest and most informal level of Korean speech, also called banmal (반말); mostly used among people who are in each other's closest circles, friends or family, or those who are younger; otherwise it is very rude to use

Haeyoche (해요체): The second lowest level of Korean speech, though it is polite

Halmeoni (할머니): Grandmother

Hanbok (한복): Korean traditional clothes; refers to both male and female clothing

Haoche (하오체): The third highest level of Korean speech used mostly for those of the same rank or lower who still maintain a moderate degree of respect

Hapsyoche (합쇼체): A formal, or polite, level of speech in Korean just below Hasoseoche

Harabeoji (할아버지): Grandfather

Hasoseoche (하소서체): The highest level of politeness for addressing someone in Korean, usually reserved for nobility or other high officials and scriptures

Hyeong (형): Older brother; used by males for siblings or older friends

Imo (이모): Aunt on the mother's side

Jamae (자매): Sisters

Jam-binyeo (잠 비녀): A thick, long-bodied hairpin

Jang-gwan (장관): Ministers

Jebiburi-daeng-gi (제비부리댕기): A daeng-gi worn only by princesses and higher nobility

Jeogori (저고리): A basic upper garment of hanbok worn by both men and women. It covers the arms and upper part of the body.

Jeungjobu (증조부): Great-grandfather

Jeungjomo (증조모): Great-grandmother

Jinjja (진짜): Similar to "Really?," "Seriously?" or "Is it true?"

Jjokjin Meori (쪽진머리): Classic Korean hairstyle for married women, formed by first parting and holding down the front part of the hair and then tying the hair into a bun at the back of the neck, then held together with a binyeo—and other accessories if wanted

Joka (조카): Niece or nephew

Jokgu (족구): A game introduced in Korea in the 1960s, it is a cross between soccer and volleyball and is played on a tennis court.

Keunjeol (큰절): A respectful bow. The performer goes on their knees and touches their head to the ground. Their hands are usually flat on the floor just above their head

Mama (마마): Your Highness

Michinnom (미친놈): Psychopath, for men; also translated as "crazy bastard"

Musuri (무수리): A female servant who does odd/menial jobs around the palace

Nain (나인): There are two levels of nain: the trainees and the official nain. Trainees traditionally become official nain after fifteen years of service. Besides the two levels, there were also several stations of nain. Girls of the middle class, usually found through family/personal connections, personally served the king and queen.

Namchin (남친): Boyfriend. It is a short form of *namja chingu*.

Nam-dongsaeng (남동생): Younger brother(s)

Namja (남자): Male

Nammae (남매): Siblings, including brothers and sisters

Ne (네): Yes; an expression of agreement

Negadak (네가닥): Four parts in the hair; to have the hair parted in four places

-Nim (님): An honorific to denote respect for a person (seonsaeng-nim)

Noona (누나): Older sister; used by males for siblings or older female friends

Noraebang (노래방): Literally translates to singing/song room

Obba (오빠): Older brother for women; used for siblings, close friends, or significant others

Sachon (사촌): Cousin

Saem (샘): Teacher (sounds like "sem")

Saeng-meori (생머리): A hairstyle for the younger court ladies and nain. The hair is parted several times, then braided and folded. The number of parts depends on the departments in which the court ladies work

Samjogo (삼족오): Three-legged bird, either a raven or crow, depending on the country or legend

Sang-goong (상궁): A lady-in-waiting who was an official nain for more than fifteen years. She is given very specific responsibilities and is of high enough rank to have her own servants and living quarters.

Seonsaeng (선생): Teacher

Seuran-chima (스란치마): A chima with geumbak

-Si (시): City (Silla-si)

Wang (왕): King

Wanghoo (왕후): Literally, king's wife

Wangseja (왕세자): Crown prince

Wangsejabin (왕세자빈): Crown princess-consort

Wangsil (왕실): Royal family

Ya (야): "Hey"

Yak-honja (약혼자): Betrothed; fiancé/fiancée

Yeobo (여보): "Honey," used between married couples

Yeo-dongsaeng (여동생): Younger sister(s)

Yong (용): Dragon. Unlike Western dragons, yong are serpentine but with four legs and no wings.

Yongjam-binyeo (용잠 비녀): A jam-binyeo shaped like a yong's head on one end and is worn by a queen.

Grand Illegitimate Princess: The firstborn
  illegitimate princess or her succeeding firstborn
  heirs.

Illegitimate Princess: While these women are of
  noble blood, they wield no political power
  unless the queen appoints them a position.
  However, the queen often arranges their
  marriages to foreign nobles to strengthen
  alliances. This title also denotes any woman
  born to an illegitimate princess if their mother
  was not married to a foreign noble.

Prince of Vires: The victor of a competition
  comprised of a series of trials. Vires holds the
  competition every ten years unless the prince
  steps down or the people take the title away.
  The people of Vires consider the prince the
  protector of their interests and way of life. If a
  prince can hold the title for more than one term,
  his or her respectability and magical talent are
  deemed fairly considerable. A spellcaster must

be a master spellcaster and twenty years old to qualify.

Sitting Prince/Princess of Vires: The child of the prince, but they hold no real political power. Many spellcasters believe that the sitting prince or princess will have the potential to succeed the prince if the prince has held the title for more than one term or there has been a procession of a child succeeding the parent.

ACKNOWLEDGMENTS

Raven's Eye has a special place in my heart. After a few years of not knowing what to do with it, I finally knew what needed to be done and how to do it after two years of living in South Korea. Writing the first draft took me less than a year—the shortest timeframe for me so far—and was nearly everything I wanted it to be. This version of the original idea changed the characters and story drastically, but it was all for the better.

Thank you to my South Korean friends and coworkers who helped me with my language and cultural questions. Some of those people may never read this novel, but their help was valuable.

Brandon Dorman, thank you for the artwork. It was far better than I hoped for.

More thanks to Heidi Brockbank and Michele Preisendorf for their hard, and wonderful, work. Their input and suggestions helped Raven's Eye be better. I also thank everyone else who worked on Raven's Eye with me.

To my friends and family who read the earlier drafts of

Raven's Eye, thank you. Your encouragement helped me realize that Raven's Eye was worth everything it took.

Last, to my readers. Thank you for buying Raven's Eye. I hope you enjoyed it as much as I enjoyed creating its world and characters. I promise that we will return to Balhae soon.

ABOUT THE AUTHOR

Adam Gowans is the youngest of five Air Force brats, out of which his siblings have voted him the weirdest. He loves anything that deals with stories, including movies, novels, television dramas, music, video games, manga/manhwa, and webtoons.

In his mid-twenties he lived and taught English in South Korea for four years before returning to the States to live, like many LDS authors, in Utah.

www.ingramcontent.com/pod-product-compliance
Lightning Source LLC
Chambersburg PA
CBHW051538250626
47157CB00001B/92